*To my frien
fellow thesp, mm*

Book I

A Circling of Vultures
– Ed Lane –

with all good wishes

Ed Lane

All characters are fictitious

www.fast-print.net/store.php

A CIRCLING OF VULTURES
Copyright © Ed Lane 2010

ISBN 978-184426-896-2

First published 2010 by
FASTPRINT PUBLISHING
Peterborough, England.

An environmentally friendly book printed and bound in England
by www.printondemand-worldwide.com

Mixed Sources
Product group from well-managed
forests, and other controlled sources
www.fsc.org Cert no. TT-COC-002641
© 1996 Forest Stewardship Council

PEFC Certified
This product is
from sustainably
managed forests
and controlled
sources
www.pefc.org
PEFC/16-33-415

This book is made entirely of chain-of-custody materials

Acknowledgements

For the thin red line.

"Then it's Tommy this, an' Tommy that, an' Tommy, 'ow's yer soul?
But it's 'Thin red line of 'eroes' when the drums begin to roll"

'Tommy' by Rudyard Kipling.

With grateful thanks to:-

My editors, Veronica and David Stonehouse, who found and corrected my mistakes.

My wife, Barb, for her patience and understanding of what glued me to my computer for hours on end.

'Help for Heroes' for allowing me to stage this money-raising event on their behalf.

Soldiers talk a language of their own littered with initials, acronyms and frequent dives into the vernacular. I have used artistic licence to reduce these instances to a minimum whilst endeavouring to keep the dialogue authentic. However there may be instances where either initials or acronyms have been used without explanation and there is a glossary of terms at the end of this book.

"If you prick us do we not bleed?
If you tickle us do we not laugh?
If you poison us do we not die?

If you wrong us shall we not revenge?"

The Merchant of Venice Act III, Scene I
William Shakespeare

Dulce et Decorum est.

It is sweet and honourable (to die for one's country)

*I*t was one of the strangest stories I'd ever heard. There had been whisperings of course but no firm intelligence. Now that soldiers are required to sign an undertaking not to speak to the press hard news was hard to come by, especially from a regiment as secretive as the Special Air Service.

These notes are taken from my case files and are in the words of the men involved. Their own stories, unexpurgated and as gritty as only soldiers can make them. There are heroes here, people of courage and determination, but there are also fools, cowards, opportunists and downright villains. Such is ever the way of men...and of course, women.

Parts of the trial were held in Camera due to the secret nature of the operation to which it pertained. What records there are were buried deep in the archives of the Ministry of Defence, the Home Office and the Office of the Director of Public Prosecutions.

I left this manuscript in a sealed package in a locked vault at my Chambers in Lincolns Inn with instructions that it should only be opened in the event of my sudden or unexpected death or disappearance. Melodramatic? Maybe, but that you are reading this can only mean one thing. Someone wanted me silenced.

I am sure that the threat against my person is real. I am not brave but I do believe the power of justice should rise above all else; including my fear. Not only justice done but justice seen to be done.

The truth is sometimes a quality unrecognised as it comes in many guises but it does have a habit, irritatingly for some, of unmasking itself. Whether it is believed is another matter. You must make up your own mind.

Ann FitzPatrick. Barrister,
Lincolns Inn.

PART I
Action on

Chapter One

M ajor Ricky Keane winced as an American C5 Galaxy broke all legal decibel limits as it screamed out of Bagram air base. He spooned another mouthful of cold ham and pea soup from its tin and swallowed it without enjoyment. Bagram wasn't the cosiest place to billet and the old building in which he was squatting had seen a happier time. Someone who knew his regimental history had dubbed it The Haunted House. It was a title left over from the SAS's Borneo campaign back in the1960s. Then, regimental headquarters had occupied a house overlooking the Sultan's palace. It had been used by the grey-uniformed Kempi Tai, the Japanese equivalent of the Gestapo, throughout their occupation during the Second World War to interrogate prisoners and it was said that the spirit of a young European woman who had died under torture wandered the place.

Why this building should be termed the same eluded him. Maybe the ghosts of the many Afghans murdered by the Taliban filled the place with their wailing ululations; or maybe it was just the constant dust-laden wind on this barren part of the base. More likely it was the comings and goings of dust covered soldiers, looking like spectres as they slipped furtively in and out at all hours.

Ricky was glad to have the time to speculate. His boots had hardly touched the ground since his recall to the Regiment. He was in his early thirties with brown curly hair that tended to make him look younger, a pleasant face and muscular build. His career prospects were excellent, already he was listed for a place at the Staff College in Camberley.

He had seen action in Iraq and was under no illusions about the mythology of dying for his country. Battle was a terrifying, bloody, stinking, mind-numbing hell which ever way you looked at it but someone had to do it. He knew that some of the troopers actively loved the fray, lived off the adrenaline, but he had too much imagination to be like that. He would do it because he was capable and committed. It was a logical conclusion to his training; it was what soldiers did.

Something big was about to unload and he was waiting for some troopers to report in. In truth he did not have a clue what was expected of him. The recall had been sudden and mysterious with no explanations given. The Regiment was short of soldiers, he knew, but not short of officers. All the command posts were filled and no present incumbent would take kindly to being replaced, especially with action in the offing. So he was marking time, keeping his head down until the chain of command saw fit to brief him.

He licked his spoon clean and pulled out a letter to Gill, one of many begun but never finished. She had never said much about her tour with the Walts in Ulster but he knew that serving with 14 Intelligence Company was draining on the nerves, working in such close proximity to some of the most vicious killers in Ireland. Even with the Peace Process in full swing gangsterism and punishment killings were still rife on both sides of the sectarian divide with a brooding tendency to wait and see if the peace would stick. He thought of her now safely tucked up in the MoD, driving a desk. He knew she would hate it but she was out of harm's way and he was pleased. It amused him that she might think the same about him. She did not know of his re-secondment and he wasn't allowed to tell her. His `bluey', should it ever be posted, would be routed via his parent unit and Gill would be none the wiser.

There was a sharp tang of plastic in his mouth as he sucked the cap end of his biro and studied the blank paper in front of him. What could he say? The weather here is unseasonably dusty after two years of drought. The food was awful. His bed was made up of a sleeping bag resting on two packing cases. The sun rise on the peaks of the Hindu Kush reminded him of her smile, lighting up the day with its radiance. Now he was getting slushy. As true as it might be, he could not write it down. It gave too much away, both with the geography and more importantly how he really felt about her.

It had been one of life's missed opportunities and he regretted it more each day but there was no use crying over it. They were both professionals and both in it for the long haul; both army-barmy as the squaddies had it. It was not an ideal platform on which to base a relationship.

An American army truck squealed to a halt outside and he could hear the sounds of men debussing. Gratefully he folded the bluey into a breast pocket. It would keep until he had something to say.

The truck was grinding away into the dust and he sauntered out. "Special Projects?"

Stu Dalgleish turned. "I know that voice. Hello, boss, what are you doing here? Thought you'd bought a nice cosy billet somewhere?"

"Hi, Stu, you old bastard."

Dalgleish shook Keane's offered hand. "Yeah, we're part of Special Projects" Stu said. "Others are on their way. Cruncher broke an ankle yesterday which leaves us a man short. Aptly named is Cruncher, caught a packet in the arm on our last tour here, smashed up a Pinkie Land Rover and a trail bike and now his ankle. Our boss, Bill Cowley, is sorting out his ticket home and should be here shortly."

"Come inside," Keane said. "There's a brew on. After that there's an op in the offing so don't wander away from the area. There's some bashas set up in the dip with all the home comforts. You can gonk down there for now."

"What's the score, boss?" Stu asked.

Keane shrugged. "Lot's of high level comms flying around. Head Shed's at an 'O' Group right now. We'll know more when he gets back. Story is we're to stay near this building and keep a low profile."

"Gut feeling?"

"Could be the Yanks have finally pinned down bin Laden."

"That'll be nice," Stu said. His tone of voice said otherwise. He'd heard it all before too many times to get excited.

"Yeah, well it's all speculation up to now. Get your boys sorted with some brew."

"Who's that then?" Sponge Roberts asked and nodded at Keane's retreating back." Not like you to brown nose the Ruperts." Sponge was a Londoner in his late twenties with too much hair that grew low down on his forehead and stuck up at the back like the spines of an anti-personnel mine. He had a natural aversion to officers.

Stu gave him a hard nudge in the ribs. "Be nice, Sponge. His name's Keane. He was the Adjutant a year or so back and I was on ops with him. He's okay. Looks like a schoolboy but don't let that fool you."

"What's he doin' here?"

"A whole squadron is on the way, that's the rumour," Pete Cooke said. He was walking back with three mugs of steaming tea clasped in his fist having spent a few minutes boning up on the gossip from one of the Scaleys squashed into a back room with the comms kit. Scrounging was one of Pete's talents, that and picking up the scuttlebutt. He was an experienced ex-Para from Nottingham, a quiet man who had ears like a bat and eyes like a hawk. He rarely missed anything of note and could be relied on to find, beg, borrow or steal any item of equipment that was needed and unavailable through normal channels. He was a highly valued commodity to his mates.

"So maybe Keane is right then," Stu muttered. "Maybe the Yanks have tagged bin Laden."

"And they want us to do the dirty work as per," Sponge said.

Pete thrust a mug into his hand. "Got anything else to do?"

★ ★ ★

"Must be the best part of a whole squadron over there in that hangar," Sponge said. "All the comforts of home too and us here in this shit hole keepin' our profiles low."

"Must be something big brewing," Pete said.

"Don't you know?" Stu asked over the rim of his mug.

Pete grinned back at him. "Rumours, that's all. Scuttlebutt is that the Old Man is determined that we'll get bin Laden before the Berets and the Rangers get themselves sorted and on the move."

"That'll be a feather in the cap of the Regiment. Won't do the Old Man's promotion chances any harm either," Stu said.

"Whoops! Your slip's showin', mate," Pete said. "Not like you to be so cynical."

"True though, ennit," Sponge chipped in. "Top brass gets the praise and we get the shit end of the stick."

"Was it ever thus?" Stu murmured. He was a melancholic looking lanky soldier of English birth but Scottish parentage. He was on his fourth consecutive tour with the SAS. "Sorry, boys. I've just realised how long I've been at this game and still only a sergeant. Back in the Paras I'd be looking at WO1 or a Late Entry Commission. Life seems to have passed me by and it's times like this that you realise it."

"You'd be on your second wife with kids all over the shop. Jack rabbits all the Paras I've ever known," Sponge said, grinning.

"You jealous or something," Pete said. "That's the trouble with you crap hats, you can't keep up with the real thing."

"So how many kids do you have then?" Sponge asked, trying to look innocent.

"How's the wife?"

Pete gave Sponge a look between surprise and aggression; how did Sponge know? "She walked off with a woodentop from G Squadron. Hope the bastard gets his balls blown off," Pete said.

"Sorry to hear that." Stu pulled a sympathetic face. It was a too common occurrence in the Regiment.

"Ahhh. Water under the bridge, mate."

"Still…"

"Yeah, sure. Not that I saw much of her. We were just passing strangers in the last year or so. Too much to do, not enough time to do it. Usual thing. Poor cow's not going to fare any better with the new bloke is she?"

"What about you, Stu?" Sponge said, still game for a wind-up. "You're ex-Para too."

"Which blows your pet theory to bollocks, Sponge. I've never been married and I've got no kids..."

"That you know of," Sponge interrupted with the age old line.

Stu shrugged. It could be possible. He'd put it around a bit in his earlier years with the Regiment but it was unlikely. There was only one woman who could have tempted him to settle down and she had ended up under the wheels of a taxi after a night out in Hereford. Even now, after almost six years, the thought was too much to bear and he closed his mind to it before the pain could grow. He nodded into the darkness. "It looks like our little soirée is about to come to a premature end."

Pete looked over his shoulder. "Yep. 'O' Group imminent I'd say."

★ ★ ★

"Any idea why you're here?" Mike Quentin asked. Mike was the Intelligence Officer, or Green Slime as he was affectionately known. Here he was doubling up as Operations Officer and he liked the craic.

Ricky shrugged. "That's the tenth time I've been asked that today and the answer's still the same. I don't have a clue."

"That's just as well or you might not have come."

Ricky winced and grinned. "That good, huh?"

"It's a bastard, Ricky, but I reckon you're the best man for the job – given how thin we are on the ground."

It was said with a straight face but Ricky caught the amusement in the other man's eyes. Even Slime wasn't above the occasional wind-up which, in Ricky's mind, just went to prove how serious the situation was. "You'd better fill me in then."

"I'll get around to the operational details in a moment. First I want to give you some background." He tapped a large scale map which was pinned to a board leaning against a wall. "Afghanistan," he said unnecessarily, "The Stan as it's lovingly called, bordered on the north by Turkmenistan, Uzbekistan and Tajikistan, three of the old Soviet republics, with a little bit of China thrown in. To the east and south by Pakistan and to the west by Iran. Once ruled by the Taliban, which gave succour to al-Qaeda by providing shelter and training facilities for Mujahideen fighters and al-Qaeda terrorists who filtered through from Pakistan, Iran and a few from the north. As you know the Taliban were an oppressive regime and their overthrow by the Americans with help from the Northern Alliance was long overdue."

Ricky nodded. None of this was news but he waited patiently for Mike to continue.

"One of bin Laden's many business enterprises is a construction company. He used this and his family money to construct a whole series of bolt holes in the mountains along the Pakistan border. These are quite sophisticated, much more so than you might think, with built-in bomb shelters and communications systems. Many of the larger ones have been attacked and destroyed by American Special Forces but many more are still in existence and bin Laden uses these to carry on the war against the West. He moves around a lot, mostly at night when there's good cloud cover and can't be seen by satellite or Predator UAV, especially at this time of year with winter in the offing.

"Now we have good intel that he is a sick man and had laid up in a complex in the Sarlath Range, west of Quetta, with just a few of his men." He tapped the map again and Ricky paid more attention.

The Sarlath Range was south-east of the Rigestan region and rose up to a height of around 3,000 metres, that was if the poor map could be trusted. Not that high for a serious mountain range but high enough, where the temperature could drop as much as thirty degrees below that at sea level.

"Rugged country."

"Very, and it's on the wrong side of the Pakistan border but that's why we've brought over the Special Projects Team. To keep things on the QT."

"And you brought me over, why exactly?" Ricky asked.

"It needs a ranking officer."

"To let the Americans know we're serious?"

"Exactly," Mike grinned. "All falling into place?"

"I'm getting there."

"From this moment on everything is need to know only," Mike said. "This is a black op and it's top secret. You're going after bin Laden.

"It's not going to be easy. The Regiment has brought over a full squadron for an attack on an al-Qaeda drug distribution centre in Helmand Province which is meant as a diversionary tactic. Once Op Witham goes in bin Laden's comms will light up like the Eiffel Tower on Bastille Day and should give you the element of surprise and a window of opportunity while his attention is focused elsewhere. Drugs are important to him, he raises most of his war chest that way and it'll shake him up a little and may take his eye off the ball right when we need it. I should warn you surprise has been sadly lacking of late. Several times we and the Yanks have been within smelling distance of Osama's deodorant but each time he's managed to slip the net.

"Somehow he's getting an occasional heads-up on ops. Most of The Stan leaks like the proverbial. I reckon there's a dicker under every sodding rock. We've planned this so only you and the boys from Special Projects will be in the loop.

Bill Cowley has been around longer than instant coffee and knows which end is up. And you already know Stu Dalgleish's capabilities.

"There's pressure from on-high to get a result and the Old Man's stuck his neck out to get first dibs, so don't cock it up...all right?"

Chapter Two

The inside of the Hercules C130 was hot and stank of aviation fuel. The seventeen men concealed under tarpaulins in a container at the front of the aircraft's hold were in no position to make themselves any more comfortable. The only people who knew they were aboard were the crew who had flown in from Oman, ostensibly to drop the eight-man troop from G squadron who were at the rear of the aircraft preparing for a Halo jump. Their job was to find, secure and mark a tactical landing zone for the main force of *Operation Witham*, a tried and tested operational procedure that had worked well on previous ops. They knew nothing about their travelling companions and it was planned to stay that way.

The Hercules reached its operating altitude of 28,000 feet as it thundered south. They could hear nothing as the aircraft neared its destination but they felt the rear ramp drop and the rush of freezing air that invaded the hold. Then the ramp was raised and they knew that the boys from G had jumped.

The Herc banked to the southeast and the container was finally opened by a crewman. Inside the hold was velvet black with just a narrow line of infra-red lights. They already had their chutes on and a Parachute Jump Instructor double-checked each man's equipment. Their huge packs were strapped behind their knees and they hobbled towards the rear of the aircraft just as the ramp descended once again. The PJI held up five fingers. P minus five; five minutes to jump off.

★   ★   ★

Ricky's mind raced back over the previous few hours. It had been too quick, the planning and the ragged rehearsals for the assault which had taken place hidden behind a sandbagged enclosure surrounded with white tape and hastily scrawled signs which read *'Danger – Unexploded Bomb – Keep Clear'*.

The plan called for an attack inside a reinforced concrete complex which had just two known access doors and was buried deep in the mountains. Stu's brick would lead the assault and enter the complex from one door with another team led by Tonka Taylor covering the second. Two further bricks, commanded by Bill Cowley, would act as a firebase supporting both entry teams. No one really knew what to expect inside the complex but they had photographs taken by the Americans of previously raided and destroyed complexes which complied with a general layout; enough to give them an idea of what they might be up against.

With Stu's permission he had attached himself to his brick as they were a man short but he had two personal problems to overcome. The first was that he was a newcomer who had not yet got on the other men's wavelength. Second, he was an officer, a Rupert, and not very high up the ladder of esteem in the troopers' eyes. Cowley would run the show and unless things went badly he was there just to add legitimacy. He knew the troopers would not relish his presence.

His stomach muscles contracted involuntarily at the thought of the close-quarter fighting to come. Now combat was so imminent he could not help thinking had he done the right thing; not so much for himself but the other three men who were now reliant on him.

He fingered the bluey in his pocket. Somehow he would find the time to sit and write a letter to Gill. It would be his first and it might be his last and he wanted her to know how he felt. She might tear it up, she may already have another man but what he had to say had to be said. He would take the consequences however they came at him, should he be alive to do so.

★ ★ ★

The PJI held up two fingers; P minus two. Keane crushed his buddy's kyalume glow stick, velcroed to the back of his helmet, and had his own crushed in turn. It was the dark of the moon and the green light from the kyalumis was the only way they could keep in visual contact with each other on the freefall descent. He was nervous now and checked his kit over again, making sure the pack was positioned to his satisfaction and his C5 carbine was hung where he could reach it quickly should the DZ below them turn hot. They were jumping into the unknown, into an area called the Dasht-i-Margo, the Desert of Death, away from any known centres of habitation but close enough to the mountains to get to their RV within two night's tab. That was the plan, but everyone knew even the best laid plans...

The maps they had were next to useless as topographical detail was non-existent and they were relying on aerial photographs. The DZ looked smooth and inviting but...

Keane shook off the negative chain of thought. He saw a vague shape looking in his direction and gave him the big O; everything peachy. He got a thumbs-up in return. Whoever it was seemed nervous too, he could swear he saw the thumb tremble. Maybe just the vibration as the Herc dropped to 27,000 feet on its final run.

Time to switch on, concentrate on getting off the ramp cleanly, concentrate on body shape and procedures. Check straps, check bindings, check everything.

Green light; let's get the hell off this Herc.

★ ★ ★

The insertion had gone like clockwork, the approach tab had been hard going but it had been accomplished with the minimum of fuss. Two guides had rendezvoused at the agreed time with mules which were loaded with heavy weaponry and ammunition they had not been able to carry. The guides had come most of the way by truck along the Kandahar to Quetta highway before walking for two days to reach the RV. One was called Haji who greeted Stu like a long-lost brother. He was slightly built, dressed in tribal robes of shalwaz kameez and a round lamb's wool baqul on his head. He looked too young to carry the AK47 with which he was armed, a look mitigated only by the sparse beard covering his jaw.

Stu saw Keane's quizzical look and mouthed "I'll tell you later."

The final approach across the Pakistan border had been achieved in secret. They were hidden on high ground opposite the main entrance to the al-Qaeda complex as the sun rose in the east painting the mountains with a rose-tinted glow. Two General Purpose Machine Guns, mounted on tripods in Sustained Fire mode were zeroed onto the buildings. It was still dark although it was possible to see some Taliban and al-Qaeda fighters moving around inside the walls.

The compound was enclosed on all sides with an open area to the front of the buildings floored with hard-packed dirt. It appeared like the exercise yard of a prison. That was the impression uppermost in Ricky's mind. The knot in his stomach had tightened to a painful ball and he did his best to ignore it and the constant feeling that he needed to defecate.

He was as prepared as he could be but the unknown was ahead of him and like a child in the dark he feared what might be lurking in the shadows under the roots of these mountains.

As he watched more Taliban were joining their comrades in the open air. Now at least ten men, some were even exercising in a lethargic way. Maybe Arabs or Chechens from the old Soviet Bloc as the Afghans themselves rarely broke their stylish languor for anything as boring as physical jerks.

Time dragged. Every second seeming like a minute, every minute an hour. Cowley was holding back waiting for the signal that the attack on the drug distribution centre in Helmand was underway. Then all enemy eyes would be firmly fixed to the west and the attack here should be a complete surprise.

Everyone was psyched up. He could hear Stu's heavy breathing. Sponge and Pete were on his right, disciplined, lying still but he could hear their breathing too. Adrenaline was pumping in massive doses, heart rates were soaring. He could hear his own blood thumping in his ears like the drums of a heavy metal band. Another minute dragged by; or was it an hour? Time had elasticated.

Cowley's voice sounded in his ear, an excited, "stand by" then "go, go, go!"

From behind he heard the first blast of machine guns. It was as if the whole hillside rippled with small explosions as the firebase opened up with everything they had. The compound floor was lashed with tracer and soon became a boiling cauldron of red hot flying metal.

Cowley's voice sounded in his ear again: time to move. Stu led them out along a narrow gulley. Up ahead they could see two guards scramble from a gateway in the wall to stand like statues with their AK 47s in their hands but with their mouths open.

Sponge and Pete carried 66mm anti tank rocket launchers the tubes already snapped open. They knelt together, aligned the crude sights and depressed the rubber firing pads. The first the two guards knew of the attack was when the rockets screamed past them to explode inside the gateway. One was caught in the blast and fell the other turned sharply but was cut down by Stu who was already racing towards the entrance with the others close behind. Two fragmentation grenades were tossed in to finish the work started by the 66s.

Stu and Ricky dived inside closing on the main building. The complex had been built like a Norman castle with its doors in line. The door to the building was heavy hardwood with a steel plate bolted to it. Ricky carried a frame charge but he discarded it. The door was ajar. He kicked it open and Stu tossed in a frag grenade. They charged in behind the blast, hosing rounds through into the room beyond. There was a body on the floor, torn to shreds like a playful dog's favourite toy. Pete and Sponge followed close behind under cover of the automatic fire. Inside it was pitch black. Any lanterns which might once have burned had been extinguished by the blasts. They could still smell the kerosene tang along with fouler odours. Night vision goggles were clipped down and whined as they warmed up.

All four men had crowded in and Stu tossed a stun grenade into the next part of the complex following close behind the multiple concussions. Pete and Sponge were pushing past Ricky to get through the narrow opening. The room widened out into another, slightly larger than the first. Two men were on the floor clutching their ears and keening. Two quick bursts from MP5s silenced them. Here the passageway turned to the left to form a natural defensive position. Just beyond they could hear excited voices and the rush of feet. Enemy reinforcements.

The soldiers hugged the walls and waited for the enemy to round the corner. Six of them, all carrying battered AK47s. They were cut down as they entered. Some managed to loose off rounds and ricochets started to fly, bansheeing off the walls, careless of friend or foe.

Two more stun grenades went into the next room. It was a barracks with kit everywhere. Enemy fighters were milling around, disorientated by the concussions. One oil lamp still guttered weakly at the far end and threw soft shadows over the walls. Ricky had his C5 in his shoulder. He triple tapped shots into a body and watched it fall. He swung left, aimed at another and pulled the trigger. *Nothing.* The nearest enemy was kneeling on his bedding, pulling back the cocking lever on his Kalashnikov. The room was full of stench and blood-curdling screams. The man was rising to his feet, the muzzle of his rifle climbing with him. Ricky pulled out his K-Bar and launched himself, screaming like a lunatic. Fear was gone, adrenaline was rushing fuelling his aggression. The noise and the stench was mind numbing, it was all just a blur, Ricky's brain was flooded with fight chemicals. All conscious thought had fled his mind it was now pure savagery and muscle memory. He gripped the man's kameez and punched the K-Bar forward into his chest, blade flat to slide between the ribs. The man went down dragging Ricky with him, his fist locked around the knife's hilt like it was welded to it. Work the blade left and right to let in air, a sharp tug and it was free, punching forward again, this time upwards, under the rib cage, exploding the enemy's heart. Knee on the man's chest and pull hard. The K-Bar came free with a sucking noise audible above the cacophony of the dying.

Ricky was covered in blood but he did not know it, neither did he care, bloodlust had taken all of them, he could hear it in the words drumming in his earpiece, elation, triumph; kill-crazy.

All four men were still fighting, clearing the barracks hand-to-hand. The enemy, hardened and brave fighters, were overwhelmed. It was now pitch black to them, all lights had been extinguished. All they knew was that devils from hell were among them and they were powerless to save themselves.

Next target? There wasn't one. The only people left standing were troopers and there was a light up ahead, a rectangle of sky. Voices were all talking at once on the chatter net, the adrenaline rush loosening tongues. It brought Ricky back to sanity.

They pushed forward, switching off NVGs as the light became stronger threatening to flare out the goggles. Fresh air, clean and untainted.

They took up all round defence positions, covering their arcs. Stu was on the radio reporting to Cowley. They were higher up the hill. It was an unmarked and unguarded entrance camouflaged by rocks and impossible to spot from the air; a rat run.

All four of them were, blinking in the strong light, checking themselves for wounds. They were all covered in blood but it was not theirs. None of them had sustained anything worse than minor cuts and bruises. Then they stared at each other, blood was already drying on them, turning brown as it congealed. It was thick and it stank of an abattoir.

Ricky threw up behind a rock. The smell nauseated him.

"You okay, boss?" It was Sponge, his voice rough but his eyes belied his tone.

Ricky nodded. "Some ride."

Sponge offered a lopsided half-smile. "You did all right."

Ricky looked at his hands, so much blood on them and he was still clutching the K-Bar. "I can't open my fingers."

Sponge slithered over and prised the fingers apart, letting the knife drop to the ground. He picked it up and offered it back. "C5 jammed?"

"Thanks," Ricky said, wiped the blade on his trousers and slid the filthy weapon into its scabbard. "It happens. Not as often as the M16s though." He looked around "Where's Pete?"

"Taking a dump. It affects people in different ways."

"You?"

Sponge smiled the weak smile again. "I've got nothing left to dump."

Stu strolled up followed by Pete still zipping up his fly. "Everybody in one piece?" Stu asked.

"Stirred and shaken but otherwise healthy," Ricky said.

"I've got some splinters in me arse from a ricochet." Sponge said. "It stings a bit but no real harm done."

Stu tried hard not to laugh. "Bet that made your eyes water."

"How is Tonka's brick?" Ricky asked.

"Same state as us," Stu said. "They're okay."

"That was one hell of a fight," Pete said.

Stu nodded. "Bloody mediaeval. Now I know how they must have felt at Agincourt."

"*And gentlemen in England, now abed, shall think themselves accursed they were not here*," Ricky murmured.

"Henry the Fifth," Stu said.

Pete raised an eyebrow. "I'm impressed. At least two of us know their Shakespeare."

"D'you really think the buggers back home'll give a toss?" Sponge said.

"Coupla days in the press maybe then it'll be back to who's shagging who in la-la land," Pete added. "Now there's a thought." He rummaged in an ammo pouch and came out with a half litre of vodka in a plastic duty-free bottle. "Bin savin' this. To shagging in la-la land." He took off the cap, raised the bottle and swigged a good mouthful before offering it round.

Ricky got a call on the chatter net from Bill Cowley, requesting his and Stu's presence. Cowley was on the patrol radio to HQ Bagram and he pulled a face as he eyed the bloodstains that coated the front of their DPM suits.

"Bad news," he said. "Predators have picked up pictures of a small group that got away. The pics have been enhanced back in DC and they think that one of these guys could be bin Laden..."

"The ever-elusive bin Laden," Ricky said.

"...and they want you to go after him."

Chapter Three

Cowley dropped the radio mike and pointed at a map spread out on the ground before him. "The bastards are heading north, paralleling the border."

"They want *us* to go after them?" Stu repeated.

Cowley gave him an *'are you with us'* glare. "They say the information that bin Laden was here is solid so the Yanks tasked the Predators to the op. The Predators can't get a missile lock on the targets, they keep disappearing in the rocks so all they'll be doing is ventilating a few metres of mountainside with the Hellfires. Unfortunately for us the Pakistan government don't know we're here and haven't sanctioned our cross-border incursion, so we can't call on them for help either.

"A Special Ops chopper is on its way to collect me and my support bricks and any intel we can turn up in them buildings. We have to be quick because the Taliban have called Quetta on their mobiles and there's a couple of lorry loads of supporters on their way here.

"But it also means there can be no choppers for you until the lot you're chasing move back into Afghan airspace. 'Fraid it's shanks's pony for you boys."

"They've got a head start so we'd better get some plans together," Stu said.

"Go and get your men prepped while Ricky and me finish up the briefing," Cowley said.

Stu left at the run as Cowley turned back to Ricky with a sour look on his face. "The Old Man's spitting tacks that we didn't get bin Laden. He's spitting tacks that the Yanks are trying to muscle in on the act. He's spitting tacks that we let eight men waltz out of that cave complex without so much as a by-your-leave."

Ricky was about to open his mouth but Bill stopped him with a raised palm. "I know that's unreasonable. There's bolt holes and rat runs all over the mountain and we couldn't cover all of them but the Old Man sees it as a slight on the Regiment. He really wanted to get bin Laden and finish this thing. If one of those men out there really is bin Laden then we need to get him and he wants the Yanks to know we are serious about getting him to keep their Rangers, Green Berets, or Delta Force from queering the pitch. Okay?"

Ricky nodded "What about guides; in case we run into some locals who want to use us for target practice?"

"Already done. There'll be one waiting for you at the top of the valley. Keen lad, he volunteered. Good luck."

There wasn't much more Cowley could add. It was a straight chase through the mountains to try and catch their quarry. Every minute spent now putting their action plans together would see the al-Qaeda fighters slip further and further away but it would also increase their own chances of survival.

Sleeping bags, lots of water, high protein rations and a big medical kit were vital. They also needed the right sort of weapons and ammo. Minimis were light machine guns and could put down curtains of fire but the 5.56mm ammunition lacked penetration at distance. Heckler and Koch G3s were more powerful, consequently the 7.62mm ammo was heavy but they could punch through most things and one bullet anywhere in the body was enough to fell even the strongest opponent. That decided it for him. The support bricks had four HKG3s for general usage, plus three SG1 sniper versions with Zeiss variable power telescopic sights. They were fitted with bipods and made good support weapons in full auto mode. Each man would also be armed with a 9mm Sig Sauer pistol and K-Bar fighting knife.

They had to move fast and that meant lighter loads, anything not completely necessary would have to be discarded in favour of essential equipment.

He had been thinking on his feet as he walked the short distance to the laying up point where Stu had already prepped the men with the news. Tonka's brick was there too, sitting close by their burly leader.

They all looked at him expectantly. "What's the news, *boss?*" It was Sponge who laid the emphasis on with a trowel.

The enemy were three hours and twelve minutes ahead of them.

★ ★ ★

The guide who met them at the top of the pass was Haji. He had found a goatskin water bag from somewhere which he wore across his back. Stu had given him a skeleton-order webbing harness with magazine pouches for his AK47 and a day sack. These were his prized possessions and all that he carried. Next to the well-loaded troopers he looked tiny.

Ricky had tried to pare down their equipment but he had no idea how long the chase would last and they had to carry everything relative to their own survival.

The mission was explained to Haji who listened with his head cocked to one side. He was shown aerial photographs of the area and Ricky pointed out where they were sitting and the direction in which their quarry had gone.

"They're headed towards the Afghan border up towards Kandahar and they are about four hours ahead," Ricky explained.

Haji thought for a moment. "There is another way."

"Show me." Ricky gave the photograph to him.

Haji traced his finger over a mountain crest. "There is a track here."

"Where does it cross the path the Taliban have taken?"

Haji moved his finger further along. "Here."

"I estimate that's about fifty clicks, boss," Stu said.

"As opposed to about ninety clicks for the enemy," Ricky said. He turned back to Haji. "Is there anywhere they can leave the track they are on before they reach this point?"

"There are many tracks they could take, many caves to hide in but area is bad for them, many more enemies as they go north." He shrugged expressively and jabbed his finger on a spot on the photograph. "There is a caravanserai where the tracks meet."

Ricky pulled a face. "What d'you think?"

"Six of one," Stu said. "We've got a race on our hands to catch them from behind. They're used to the terrain. But climbing over the mountain means we have to cope with more difficult going. They'll stop five times a day to pray but so will we because Haji is very devout too."

"I hadn't factored that into the equation, thanks," Ricky said. "Tonka?"

"I've been doing some rough calculations in my head. They've got a four-hour start, more the longer we sit here gassing. From the photos we know they're moving at about three clicks an hour, that gives them a lead of twelve clicks. If we manage five clicks an hour it will take us six hours of hard walking to catch up with them. Taking into consideration Haji's prayer stops at twenty minutes a time that extends to eight hours. Five minutes break every hour adds another forty minutes. That's a total of nearly nine hours at the best possible rate, always supposing we can keep up the pace. These guys are lightly armed and carry next to nothing. They can go all day if they have to without faltering. We'd be hard pushed to catch 'em."

"Okay, let's look at that," Ricky said. "They have ninety clicks to cover to the junction at three clicks an hour. That's a total walking time of thirty hours plus prayer time of let's say four hours. We'll all have to rest up overnight so there's no advantage to be gained there. Our route is fifty clicks and we're climbing for twenty of that at an average of let's say one click an hour, that's twenty hours plus two hours for prayers. We can use those for meal breaks too so we don't have to add any extra time. Downhill for thirty clicks at an average of three clicks an hour that's ten hours, plus prayer time of say an hour, that means we should get to the track junction just a couple of hours ahead of them. I reckon Tonka's right, we don't have a choice."

"Damn, that's cutting it pretty fine. There's no leeway for slippage or accidents," Stu said.

Tonka rocked his hand from side to side. "Same applies to them."

"Okay, that's it," Ricky said. "Brief the boys and be ready to move out in ten. I don't have to say time is of the essence, do I?"

Tonka and Stu were already walking away and he got just a hand waved in acknowledgement.

Ricky found Sponge who had the patrol radio and he called up Cowley to notify him of their decision. He got the nod and a promise to keep him informed about the al-Qaeda group's progress. He also got a reminder of how important it was to catch this particular group and that was something he did not need.

Ricky cut the transmission as an overloaded mule went by making its way down to the designated landing zone for the fast approaching Special Ops Chinook. He smacked himself on the forehead. He was brain dead, why had he not thought of it before. He called up Cowley again. "D'you have any spare mules down there, Bill?"

"Mules...dozens of the buggers the Taliban left behind, all milling around in a great big herd."

"Can you get a couple up to us? It'll have to be quick."

"Wait one." He could hear mush in the background and then Bill came back on the air. "We can manage three with the Afghan handler who came in with Haji. We'll get them up to you by 1600 hours."

"We'll have moved on. Tell him to keep going until he catches up with us. He'll be able to travel much faster than we can and it shouldn't take long."

"Wilco. I'll tell him you'll pay him twenty dollars so that he doesn't lose interest and wander off. Good luck."

The going was easy for the first two kilometres with gentle slopes on a zig-zag road and they made good time. The road was busier than Ricky had imagined with mule trains passing them at regular intervals laden down with sacks. Each mule train had its own armed escort some of whom eyed the westerners with ill-disguised hostility. Ricky asked Haji about it but the young man shrugged as if he did not know that the sacks contained opium on its way from the poppy fields of Helmand to Pakistan on the first stage of its journey to the processing factories of the west.

Stu was up alongside him. "I thought the Taliban had put a stop to opium smuggling," Ricky said.

"Some, maybe, but The Stan is still the world's biggest supplier. It's their big earner. What pisses me off is that the

CIA and our own government turn a blind eye to it and the Pakistanis are actively engaged at a high level," Stu said.

The mules caught up with them at Haji's afternoon prayer stop. The Muleteer, an aging Tajik with a long white beard who had a venerable Indian-made Lee Enfield No.4 .303 rifle slung over his shoulder on a multi-coloured strap, joined Haji on his knees facing east to make his cycle of prostration.

The SAS men quickly loaded the three mules with their bergens and other kit, breathing sighs of relief and stretching cramped muscles as the 30 kilo packs were dropped onto the complaining animals.

They marched for another two hours, always uphill until Haji stopped and pointed to a narrow trail leading off to the right. "We go this way now."

Ricky eyed it dubiously. "Will the mules be able to manage that?"

Haji nodded.

Ricky looked at his watch; nearly four hours gone already but they had made good time up to now. Other mule trains had grown fewer and fewer the higher they had climbed and now people were passing on foot carrying belongings on their own backs. Straggling lines of refugees making their own way to the safety that Pakistan was thought to hold for them.

Ricky called Stu and Tonka over. "We'll take a break here for Haji's evening prayers. It's going to get tougher from here on in so make sure the men have got themselves sorted and get some scoff down their necks. There's a stream running through the culvert we just crossed. Take the chance to fill the water bottles but don't forget the purifying tablets as the water looks pretty shitty.

"We go fully tactical from here. Stu I want you and Pete to take point, Sponge and the radio will stay with me. Tonka you and yours will help with the mules and detail two men as tail-end charlies. We'll rotate every hour. Questions?"

There were none. They all knew what had to be done, it was ingrained in them.

Ricky checked with Haji that the mules and the Muleteer were in good shape before he settled himself down to clean his G3 and get some rations down. Water was always a problem, it was heavy and they needed a lot of it. It paid to keep the water bottles topped up whenever they had the opportunity. Purifying tablets made the water taste like liquefied Germoline but heated with a sachet of coffee or tea and it became almost palatable.

The climbing became harder and as the altitude increased the wind developed a keen edge but at least now it was not so dust laden. The track narrowed in places so that they had to walk in single file, pulling and pushing the reluctant mules with them. At other times they were faced with a sheer drop on one side where the track clung precariously to a cliff.

Ricky checked his watch constantly and his hand-held Megellan GPS. According to the readout they were making less than a kilometre an hour and the time gained earlier had now melted away. If anything they were running behind schedule.

Stu was on point with Pete a few paces behind. Up ahead the track crested and he could not see more than a few metres. He signalled Pete to stay and edged up to the crest to peer over. On the other side of the crest a group of Afghans walked purposefully along the track 300 metres away. They were well armed with AK47s, RPG 7s and at least one RPK 74 light machine gun.

Stu scurried back to Pete and they both ran back along the track until they found a place to conceal themselves. Stu got on the radio to Ricky and reported what he had seen.

"Any idea who they are," Ricky asked.

"Negative, boss, but they sure look warlike."

"What's the track like up your way? Any place to hide three mules and a handler?"

"There's a small notch off to the left just as you pass two large rocks overhanging the track. You could get them in there but there won't be room for everybody."

"Roger that. We'll try to keep out of their way but be ready for action in case it goes pear-shaped on us."

"Okay, boss. We'll stay concealed and let them pass. If the worst comes to the worst we could give them a nasty beasting up the jacksy."

Ricky grinned. "Roger that."

The Afghans were walking fast, defying the thin air. They seemed to be tactically aware as they had scouts out to the front and a rear guard a couple of hundred metres behind. Thirty-two men all armed to the teeth.

The mules were not completely concealed. A sharp-eyed Afghan could spot them if he happened to look in that direction. They were not the quietest of animals either, huffing and puffing like thirty-a-day men. Ricky stayed with the muleteer and Haji, the rest of the patrol had climbed the steep wall of the pass and were hidden amongst rocks further up the slope. Sponge's voice intruded in his ear. The Afghan scouts were approaching along the track. Two men, both armed with AK47s.

"Standby," Ricky whispered.

A mule snorted and Ricky shot it a hate-filled look. The muleteer mumbled something in Tajik to calm it. Ricky wondered if they could sense fear because his stomach was performing somersaults.

The two scouts strode past, still going at a fair lick, their AKs cradled in their arms as if they were expecting action.

The main party came next filing past one by one. Ricky held his breath for a lifetime but they seemed to get away with it.

"Trouble, boss," Sponge murmured in his ear. "The lead scout's found fresh mule droppings about two hundred metres along the track. He's put his hand in the shite and he's saying something to the other scout. Stuff must still be warm. They're waving back at the main group. Now he's hunting for tracks and pointing this way. They'll know they didn't pass any mules up to now and it won't take them a second to work it out...yep they're turning back."

"Roger that, Sponge. Standby." Ricky took a deep breath and walked out of the cleft onto the track facing the Afghans who were rushing back towards him. He knew that behind him the two Afghan tail-end charlies were closing up. He was the corned beef in the sandwich. He motioned for Haji to join him. Ricky had his G3 slung across his chest and he kept both hands resting lightly on it but well away from the trigger. He could swing it into action if necessary but at the moment it did not pose a threat. He pulled down his shamag and raised his goggles. He wanted to present an open and friendly face to the Afghan leader who was now striding towards him.

Ricky raised his hand in the universal peace greeting. "In'shallah." He turned to Haji. "Find out what they want."

Haji went into rapid-fire Tajik. By now the rest of the Afghan group had piled into the cleft including the two scouts. Ricky could feel the two tail-enders standing a few metres to his rear. They made a neat target for the men above, all the little piggies in one sty but he doubted whether he and Haji would survive an exchange of fire.

"He wants to know what our mules are carrying, Mr. Ricky."

"Who are they?"

"Mujahideen. But I think they are bandits too."

"Tell him that all we have is our own supplies but he would be welcome to share our food with us."

Haji translated and the Afghan nodded and spoke some words back. He was looking around but did not see the hidden men. Behind him his group were getting restless.

"He wants to know what we are doing here and where we are going."

"Tell him we are helping the Afghan people to rid themselves of the tyranny of the Taliban and it is imperative that we move on quickly."

The story was passed on but the Afghan did not look impressed. "He wants to inspect our mules," Haji said.

"What's he really want?"

"I think they are looking for opium."

"Okay, Haji show him the mules."

Haji led the man into the cleft and he came out a few seconds later leading a mule by its halter with the old Tajik muttering into his beard following with the other two.

"He says there is much more here than would feed three men," Haji said.

"Say everything is needed."

"I think he wants to take the mules and the food, Mr. Ricky."

"Isn't stealing a crime in these parts?"

"It is their way. To them it is not stealing, it is a tax on travellers. This man is a chieftain, he has much face to keep. He says you have so much and his people are hungry."

"Tell him he can have one mule now and I'll arrange for some clothing and food to be sent to his village," Ricky said.

Haji looked at Keane doubtfully. "You can do this?"

"Yes." He called on the chatter net. "Everyone except Tonka show yourselves now. Slowly, don't get them nervous. Tonka keep the Chief covered."

The soldiers stood up showing their weapons but pointing them away from the Afghans.

"Tell the chief that we are more than three and we need the supplies we have if we are to fight the Taliban."

The Afghans were shuffling nervously and muttering. It was like watching stitches unravel.

"Sponge call up AWACS. I want an aircraft to overfly us now."

He turned to Haji. "Tell him I am a man of my word. Tell him I have the power to do what I say I will do. I have ordered an American fighter plane to come to show I have the power to do these things." He called Sponge again. "Sit rep, Sponge."

"AWACS have tasked two F14 Tomcats for a flyby. ETA two minutes."

"Thanks, Sponge. Haji tell the chief that as he is such an important man we have two aircraft to salute him and they will be here soon."

Ricky looked at his watch. Time was slipping by and they were well behind schedule. The last thing he wanted was a full scale war with these people. He checked his watch again. Trust the flyboys to be late.

"Sponge...?"

"Look to your left, boss."

Ricky could see two minute specks in the distance looking like midges. There was no sound but the specks grew larger by the second. The two US Navy Tomcats arrowed across the sky and rocketed past. Then the sound hit them; a solid wave of noise that crushed the senses. The Afghans covered their ears with their hands and rolled their eyes skywards, their heads ringing from the scream of four Pratt and Whitney jet engines.

The Tomcats stood on their afterburners and looped over for a second run. Ricky shot a glance at the Afghan chief. He now looked mightily impressed.

The Top Cover leader barrel rolled over their position and with a waggle of wings the two fighters disappeared into the cloud over the mountain tops.

"Trust the flyboys to grandstand," Sponge said in the stillness that followed. He took a radio message and flipped his prezzle switch. "Pilot asks if there's anything else you need, boss."

"Just tell him thanks for the flying display." He turned to Haji. "Find out where the Chief wants his supplies dropped."

Haji unrolled the map and aerial photograph Ricky handed him and haggled for some minutes before he made a mark on the map and handed it back.

Ricky read off the coordinates to Sponge. "Contact Bagram HQ and ask them to organise a supply drop to this MR soonest. Give them the background, Sponge. Tell them these people are starving up here and it's damn cold too."

The Afghan chieftain took a pace towards Ricky and raised his hand. "Tell your man, Tonka, not to shoot please, old chap. I am Abdullah"

"You speak English?" It was a nonsensical thing to say.

Abdullah smiled. "I went to Cambridge and lived in London for some years, naturally I speak English. When my father died, killed by the Taliban, I came home to lead my people but as you have heard we are suffering from the recent droughts and poor harvests. We have come here from the north but instead of fighting the Pashtus and Taliban my warriors spend much of their time searching for food or money with which to buy it. I am most grateful for your offer of help."

Ricky grinned. "Glad I could be of service. Trouble is we need to get moving now as we have a tight deadline."

The Afghan looked at the sky. "It will be dark very soon and it may snow. Tomorrow I and some of my warriors will assist you in your mission and guide you. This path is not the quickest way. We know of paths that will save you time but you will not be able to take the mules, the paths are too steep and narrow, but my men will help you carry your loads."

"I'll leave the mules in your safe keeping," Ricky said tactfully.

Abdullah smiled again. "Of course, they will be perfectly safe with us. The old man too. I think the climb will be too arduous for him."

"He was beginning to slow us down," Ricky confided, "but he is a willing helper and he deserves our respect."

They left the old man with the mules. Ricky had given him some small gifts and the promised twenty American dollars as a thank you together with some food so that he would not be a burden on Abdullah's supplies.

Now the troopers made better time but a gnawing worry still nagged at Ricky. They were nearly an hour behind schedule, night was drawing in and with it a deepening cold.

Chapter Four

S now had hit them as they struggled with the thin air at three thousand metres above sea level. Even the hardy Tajiks were suffering under their loads as the biting wind whipped through their tattered clothes. Ricky checked his watch and the GPS against the aerial photographs. They were behind schedule but could not continue in the teeth of the blizzard. He hoped that their quarry was having an equally hard time down in the valley but instinct told him that this was a forlorn wish.

They found shelter in a cave large enough to hold them all. The troopers had instantly got their hexy burners on the go and soon hot tea was available for everyone, the water made from melted snow so that they did not have to use their precious supplies. The cave was freezing but the heat from the burners would raise the temperature above zero once the cave mouth was sealed to keep the wind out.

The Tajiks, Haji included, were praying in a corner towards what they hoped was Mecca. The dark and the swirling snow made direction finding impossible. Ricky helped them with the compass he had in his breast pocket.

"How are we doing, boss?" Stu asked. He handed Ricky a mug of tea.

Ricky sipped it and grimaced, the tea was only lukewarm. "We've used up all our spare time. Only one good thing going for us is that it will get darker earlier in the valley and lighter later so maybe we can make up lost time with an early start in the morning."

"Reckon the snow'll ease by then?"

"Typical isn't it," Ricky said, "it hasn't rained for two years in these parts but suddenly we get snowed on. Could blow for days but we don't have the luxury of staying in this cosy chalet for après-ski. How is everyone shaping up?"

"Few blisters, cuts and bruises. Sponge is worrying me. He's had his arse out of the door long enough to get frostbite. Imodium doesn't seem to be working for him."

"What do you reckon?"

Stu shrugged. "Probably picked up a bug. I'll make sure he gets plenty of fluids down him."

"Right. Keep me informed."

"Sure. Look, I've been puzzling about something. How come the Yanks came at the run as soon as you whistled?"

"We get priority tasking," Ricky said.

"Even in Pakistani airspace?"

"They just got a little lost, I expect. The Pakistanis won't complain too much, not with all the aid they get from the States.

"What's with you and Haji?"

"I met him on a previous tour a few months back. We got into a fire fight with the Talibs and were pinned down by a heavy machine gun. Haji risked getting his head blown to Kandahar to take it out with an RPG." Stu had a faraway look; remembering. "It was pretty heroic considering his mate had just been gutted trying to do the same thing. Those heavy DHsk rounds tore his insides out."

"It's not easy to handle an RPG."

"It seemed like a bit of a lucky shot, I guess, but it did the trick."

"I'm impressed," Ricky said, "they sure start young around here."

Stu had a small smile on his lips as he strolled over to where Haji had finished his prayers and was sipping from a plastic beaker. "Are you fit?"

Haji looked up. "We are all very cold, Mr. Stu." He waved his hand to where Abdullah and the others were clustered together for warmth but still their teeth were chattering like castanets.

"I'll dig out some space blankets but I'm afraid we don't have enough sleeping bags to go round. Best we can do is to double up a bag while someone's on guard duty. That way everybody'll get a turn.

"Why do you people put up with all this, Haji? Surely you'd be better off back home with your families. We get paid for this, this is our job but why are you involved?"

"It is very simple, Mr. Stu. The Taliban are very bad. They cut of my wife's fingers for wearing nail polish. Then they beheaded her for listening to radio. She wanted to learn English too but the Taliban do not like women to have education. They must wear Burqa and stay home with children."

"You had a wife?" Stu said. "But you're only a kid yourself."

Haji pulled himself up to his full height. "I am a man. I have been a man since I was fourteen. I have two fine sons who are with my brother."

"I'm sorry, Haji. I did not mean to insult your manhood. Things are different where I come from. I'm thirty four and I'm still not married."

Haji relaxed back into a squat and he nodded. "People tell me these things. Your ways are different, that I know."

"So where did you learn English?"

"My brother is importer. He wanted me to help him run business so he paid for tutor. I began learning when I was four. Maybe we can start to work again, when the Taliban is gone."

Stu nodded his sympathy. Life in Afghanistan was tough even in the good times. What with the drought and the scourge of the Taliban the people had been having an even harder time. He had been bemoaning his misfortune at lack of promotion where Haji had lost a wife and a whole way of life but complained about nothing.

"I'll get those blankets for you."

"Mr. Stu?"

"Yes, Haji?"

"Will we catch the Taliban tomorrow?"

"Yes. I think so."

"If Allah wills," Haji said.

"If Allah wills the snow to stop," Stu said. "Maybe you could pray for that, Haji."

Haji grinned suddenly, his teeth white in the gloom. "I already have prayed for Allah's help, Mr. Stu."

"I admire your faith." Stu ambled over to where Abdullah was squatting with his robes wrapped around him. "We're digging out some extra blankets for you, okay"

Abdullah threw his chin in Haji's direction. "You trust him?"

The question surprised Stu. "Sure he's worked with us before. He's solid. Why'd you ask?"

"He is not Tajik. Maybe Pashtu like the Taliban. Never trust a Pashtu, that's what I say."

"He says the Taliban killed his wife"

Abdullah nodded. "That's possible. They kill many women. But still be careful, my friend."

Stu gave him a sideways look and went to find Sponge who was fiddling lethargically with the patrol radio. "Any news?"

Sponge shook his head. "Can't raise anyone. Must be the atmospherics."

"When was the last time you had contact?"

"Four hours ago. Before the blizzard started."

"You've checked all the connections and the batteries?" Stu said.

Sponge gave him a pained look. "Go and fuck someone else over."

"Abdullah thinks Haji is a gook," Stu said.

"Based on what?"

"His dislike of Pashtuns."

"They all hate each other's guts," Sponge said. "Part of the territory."

"How's *your* guts?" Stu asked.

"Pure liquid gold, mate. Even the water's going straight through."

"How d'you feel?"

"How d'you think? Like a wrung out dishrag," Sponge said.

"If you want, I'll take the radio tomorrow."

"That's my job until you peel it off my dead body."

"Just asking," Stu said and grinned. "Seriously...if you need anything..."

"Yeah, yeah, stop honking, you're like a bloody old woman."

"Haji reckons it might stop snowing tonight."

"Hope it keeps fine for him," Sponge grunted.

"It could mean an early start in the morning so get as much sleep as you can. It could be tough going tomorrow."

★ ★ ★

The snow did stop in the early hours but it was deep and unthawed by the rays of the rising sun that seared painfully into their eyes like laser beams from a myriad mirrors. The path was narrow and well defined at this point but snow had drifted chest deep in places. Tonka, big and strong, took point but as strong as he was he soon tired in the thin air and was replaced by a smaller but no less determined soldier.

Keane rotated the point every fifteen minutes to keep up momentum, taking his own turn when the time came. They were making good progress and the mountain crest was in sight bathed in brilliant orange light. It was still well below freezing and his fingers had gone numb. The tireless Stu had slithered up alongside him and pulled off his gloves for him. His fingertips were waxy looking and as white as the snow. Stu made him stuff his hands inside his jacket under the armpits and the fingers throbbed with pain as circulation returned.

"You've got to watch the frostbite," Stu yelled above the wailing wind that decreased the temperature by twenty degrees. "You'll end up losing your fingers if you're not careful."

Keane nodded. Fingers were the least of his worries. He had not been able to feel his toes for half an hour.

"Where's Sponge?"

"Dropped to the back. The pace is too much for him in his condition but he's buggered if he's going to give up that radio," Stu said.

"He's not much use to me back there. I need comms with me."

"You tell him. He won't listen to me."

"You take charge up here. We've got to keep the speed going. I'll have a word with Sponge."

Ricky found Sponge struggling with a Tajik on either side 200 metres behind the main group.

"You look done in."

"Had to stop for a crap. I'm all right."

"You don't look it. Let me have the radio."

"Bollocks, *sir*."

"It's an order, Sponge. Hand it over."

"You're not gonna pull rank up here...are you?" Sponge's face was flushed, he was running a temperature in spite of the cold.

"You're sick. You know how much time we have. I'm taking the radio, you follow on with the Tajiks."

Sponge pushed out an arm to barge past but slipped and ended on his knees. "Get me up."

"Don't argue, trooper," Ricky said. "You'll need all your strength to get over this mountain." He pulled the patrol radio from Sponge's shoulders and hefted it onto his own back. He used hand signals to show the Tajiks that he wanted them to take care of Sponge. They grinned and nodded. It was relief for them but the trooper was taking it with an ill grace.

"You're treatin' me like a kid."

"You're holding us up." He felt bad about it but he needed to get the message through the man's thick head. At last Sponge nodded and sat down on the track with the two Tajiks rotating like satellites around him.

Ricky breathed a sigh of relief and turned, following the path through the crushed and stained snow which had frozen into solid ice. The extra weight of the radio slowed him down and it was nearly thirty minutes before he caught sight of the tail end of the column as it disappeared over the crest. It was almost time for their first enforced rest period and he pushed on as fast as he could to catch up with the others.

Stu had found a sheltered spot where they had some respite from the biting wind. They were all suffering from the cold. Most had the beginnings of frost nip in their extremities and he and Pete made the rounds making sure that everyone buddied up to check each other's skin for the tell-tale white patches.

He could see Keane labouring up the track and went back to help him the last few dozen metres.

Ricky's first thought was for his men. "How's everybody?"

"A couple of minor cases of frost nip, some sunburn believe it or not, and exhaustion but otherwise just great." Stu said

"It's all downhill from here and we're only half an hour behind schedule. We should be able to make up some time," Ricky said.

Stu grimaced. "Sometimes it's harder going downhill."

"Have the others had some hot fluids?"

"Yeah. We saved you some. It'll be pretty stewed by now but still as hot as it gets at this altitude."

"Have the weapons been checked?"

"Couple had jammed up but they've been cleared now. The sun seems to be doing its job, the snow's starting to melt lower down."

"You'd make someone a really good butler, you know that, Stu?"

Stu grinned. "Multi-tasking comes easy to some blokes. C'mon let's move up with the rest before they start thinking we want to be alone together," It was said with a hint of bitterness. Stupidity like that had got him in trouble before. In a roundabout way it had led to the death of the only woman he truly cared for and it was ingrained in his consciousness. He would never let it happen again, not even in jest.

The other soldiers watched as Ricky and Stu crested the rise and slithered down the slope towards them.

"Where's Sponge?" Pete asked.

"Following on with the Tajiks," Ricky said. "He was in no condition to continue at our pace."

"I'll take care of the radio," Tonka said. "I'm an ex-scaley and I've kept up to speed."

"That's one slice of good luck," Ricky said. "We need to re-establish contact and soon."

Tonka dropped the radio off Ricky's back into the snow. "Give me a couple of minutes."

"That's all we've got," Ricky said.

Tonka nodded. "I'll try to get some intel on the targets but by the looks of that mist rising in the valley, we'll be lucky to get a sighting."

"Where's the brew?" Ricky asked.

Stu pointed to where the Tajiks were huddled around a hexy burner. Abdullah looked up as he approached and held out a mess tin half full of brown liquid. Ricky gulped it gratefully.

"Message, boss," Tonka called. "They've lost the target's trail. Couldn't get anything up this morning due to the weather."

Chapter Five

S tu had been right. Going downhill was a lot harder on the feet and legs than climbing. Ricky's feet were ablaze with pain each time he placed one on the ice covered track or stubbed a toe against a snow covered rock.

There was still 10/10 cloud cover over the valley but the Americans had information relayed from the infra-red sensors in spy satellites that cruised below the ionosphere that showed a group of people just about where the al-Qaeda party were expected to be. The bad news was that they were making good time.

The race was on and it would be touch and go.He checked the coordinates on the GPS and did a quick mental calculation. At the speed the enemy were progressing he reckoned they would be at the track junction fifteen minutes ahead of the troopers. They had one more planned prayer stop but if they were to carry on without pausing they would be ahead of them by five minutes. That really was cutting it fine but it improved the odds a little. If al-Qaeda got any sort of a head start they might never catch them as they were all now in various stages of shit order. He called a halt, placing his hand on his head for an O Group.

Haji was standing behind them as Ricky outlined his plan and he suddenly thrust his way forward. "I will come too, Mr. Ricky. Allah will forgive me this once for missing a prayer."

"Okay, Haji. We'll leave the bergens with Abdullah and take belt kit and day sacks with as much ammo as we can carry."

"I too will come," Abdullah said. "My men will stay with the packs."

Haji looked crestfallen as if his grand gesture had been trumped but he nodded. "Just along the track is a sheltered spot I know of, they can wait there."

"Tonka, call in. Ask for regular updates on their position," Ricky said.

"You got it, boss."

They found Haji's sheltered spot and said rapid goodbyes to the Tajiks. Now the going was easier and they were below the snow line but the wind was getting stronger, piercing their combat suits. Soon they would be walking through the thickening cloud that was beginning to roll up the mountainside to meet them. They were still at 1500 metres altitude with close on five kilometres to go to reach the track junction. Normally that would take them less than an hour but these conditions were far from normal. Still they cracked on at a quick pace. Ricky had given himself a pain-numbing jab and now he could feel nothing. He gritted his teeth and kept concentrating on putting one foot in front of the other without toppling over.

Then the sleet hit; douches of wind-driven icy water that soaked them through in minutes and turned the track to minor waterfalls. They had to slow the pace or risk breaking bones on the treacherous going. Visibility had closed right down and they could barely see ten metres through the swirling mist and sleet.

The ground was levelling out but the sides of the pass were getting steeper as they walked through a narrow defile. Ricky called Haji to him.

"According to my calculations we're nearly at the junction. What's the ground like there?"

Haji shrugged as if he did not understand the question. "Just like here...rocky with...."

"No, I mean tactically. Do we have cover or is it open ground?"

"This track drops steeply in another 300 metres and the sides of the pass become so close that you can touch them both with either hand. Then we reach the valley bottom and ground is flat for maybe 500 metres to where tracks cross. It is well used by mules and camels. There is little to hide behind. A river ran through there but is now dry. It was nothing but ditch along western wall of valley the last time I came here."

Ricky called Stu on the chatter net. "Take Pete and recce ahead. We're looking for anywhere to set up an ambush but it'll have to be quick, there's no time to dig in."

"Wilco, boss."

Somewhere up ahead Stu and Pete tabbed through the mist. Water had taken the line of least resistance and channelled down the pass up to twenty centimetres deep in places and flowing fast. It was obvious that the track was part of a dried up water course that had cut its way through the rock walls over eons. The snow melt water was building up into a torrent but the trail was still passable.

Ricky had one eye firmly glued to his wristwatch. They were ahead of schedule but only just. It would be a close run thing with no room for error.

"Message, boss." It was Tonka intruding into his ear. "They've lost the trace from the satellite. They think the targets have gone to ground. There's other traffic too. A camel train moving up from the south and some vehicles moving down from the north."

"Holy shit," Ricky sighed. "This doesn't get any better. Stu, where are you?"

"At the base of the defile. It's pretty narrow here but we've got a view. The good news is we're below the cloud, the sleet has stopped and we've got good visibility across to the east wall of the valley. The bad news is the dry river bed is now a pissing torrent with all the melt water and we have to ford it to get into the valley proper."

"Can you suss out a position for us?"

"It looks pretty dire from here, boss. The valley floor is as flat as a pancake but strewn with tennis ball sized boulders and rubble. It looks like solid rock and there's not even a fold that I can see this side of the track. The only cover is the rim of the east bank of the river that's about a metre above the water level at the moment but it's too far from the track for an effective ambush."

"Is there anywhere that the river is closer to the track?"

"Yeah," Stu replied. "About 400 metres to the north the track swings into the river and there's a couple of shacks close to the bank; probably a caravanserai but there's no one about at the moment. Maybe they moved on when the river dried up."

"Nobody else around at all?" Ricky asked. "We have a satellite report of vehicles and a camel train in the area."

"Nothing I can see."

"Okay, Stu. You and Pete stay put and keep your eyes peeled. We'll be with you in a minute or two."

Ricky and his group broke through the low cloud and saw the valley for the first time. It was worse than Ricky expected, it was moonscape with hardly a scrap of cover, bush or scrub to be seen.

"Nice place for a holiday home," Tonka said. "Nice bit of waterside. Few trout in the summer; can't wait."

Ricky was examining the ground through his binoculars. "We'll set up a support group here with the SG1s. There's no other cover worth speaking of and the high ground gives a good field of fire.

"The rest of us will move up along the river course in the lee of the east bank until we reach those shacks. Those will be a magnet for anyone coming into the valley and still within effective range of the support group. That's where we'll set up the ambush.

"Stu, you look comfortable already, you'll act as support and observation with Tonka and the SG1s. I want to know as soon as anything moves below. I'll leave Abdullah and Haji with you. The rest of us are in for a cold and wet few minutes."

"Better if I leave the radio with Stu and Pete, boss," Tonka said. "Better if we don't split my brick up, we're used to each other."

"Fair enough. You have your own set of actions-on so you'll have to fill me in but we can do it as we move; we're running out of time."

Tonka grinned melon-sized and got onto the chatter net. "Larry, Aitch, you know what to do, get going. Digger take the rear."

They slid and stumbled down the steep slope to the west bank of the river where the rocks were large enough to crouch behind. The stream was only about four metres wide but it was running fast chest deep. Larry already had a safety line wrapped around his waist and he pushed himself out into the torrent picking his way over the uneven river bed. He made it to halfway before a rock rolled out from under his foot and he was washed downstream clawing frantically for a hand hold on the slippery stones. He found his footing as the river turned to the right, shallowing on the eastern side enough for him to dig a foot into soft gravel. He pulled himself out and lashed the safety line to the only large rock available.

Aitch went next using the safety line as a handrail and made it in quick time. Ricky followed. Aitch pulled him ashore as he staggered the last few metres. Already Larry was in a secure fire position covering their crossing from the rim of the east bank.

Tonka and Digger, a soldier on attachment from the Australian SAS, moved past crouched low sliding down the steep bank as they stumbled along but keeping their heads below the rim until they found a suitable fire position. Then Ricky and the first two troopers moved off, leapfrogging Tonka and Digger. In this way they covered the distance to the rear of the shacks in just a few minutes.

Ricky dug out a small groove in the bank so that he would not create an outline and slid his binoculars along it. He studied the shacks for several seconds. Both buildings were more or less rectangular. They were dilapidated and in need of repair. One looked like an accommodation building made of rocks that had mud and mule droppings forced into the cracks for insulation. The windows had wooden battens nailed over them and the door, which was positioned on one corner faced away from them. Its corrugated tin roof was buckled and held down in places with old rope. Rusty flattened-out tins had been nailed over some of the gaps but it looked far from weatherproof. The second building looked more like a stable with a wide door and only one small glassless window. Not so much attention had been paid to the roof which was slapping up down with the wind. It was at a 45-degree angle from the first building with about five metres space between the closest points. A low flat-topped dry stone wall ran from the corner of one building to the corner of the other. It did not seem to serve any useful purpose.

"Home from home," Tonka whispered in his ear.

"Looks deserted," Ricky whispered back. He checked over the place again looking for any signs of life but found none. Something was bothering him but he could not pin it down.

"Time for a CTR. Stu, any signs of movement from up there?"

"Negative, boss," Stu responded.

Tonka nodded, he had the message too. "Larry, Aitch, check it out."

The two troopers slithered over the rim and snaked their way across the fifty metres of open ground to the rear of the accommodation building. They were about halfway there when Ricky realised what was bothering him. One of the patches of tin on the roof was gleaming silver.

No sooner had Ricky realised the significance of the shiny metal than the door at the far corner banged open in the wind and a man came out. He was staring to the north and did not see Larry and Aitch scuttle quickly to the lee of the wall. Ricky let out his breath in a silent whistle. A freshly repaired roof had to mean there was someone nearby but this was too close for comfort.

The man had a pair of binoculars in one hand, a Russian made walkie-talkie in the other and an AK 74 over his shoulder, the short barrel and flash hider obvious. He raised the glasses to his eyes and stared for long seconds at the head of the valley before putting the radio to his lips and yelling into it at the top of his voice. It was some Eastern European language. Croat, Ricky decided although the accent was almost unintelligible.

"If he screams any louder he won't need the radio," Tonka whispered.

"Yeah, but who's he screaming at?" Ricky said

Tonka nodded north. "There are vehicles coming through the pass into the valley."

Ricky refocused his binos. "Four trucks, looks like Toyota pick-ups.

Two have got weapons mounted."

An Australian voice whispered into his ear. "Someone comin' up from the south, skipper, camels and mules, coupla dozen of 'em."

Ricky squirmed around and peered through the optics. He studied the caravan for long seconds. "There are some black turbans with them. That's why our little group vanished, they've hooked up with the merchants."

"You're sure it's them?" Tonka asked.

"Who else dresses like Ali Baba's forty thieves? Besides there's a white turban in amongst them; tall guy with a beard."

"It can't be...surely," Tonka breathed.

"Could be why the Brass was so keen for us to catch this bunch."

"There's a lot of firepower there," Digger said. "Most of those blokes in the caravan are carrying weapons."

"Not much chance of air support either," Tonka said, "Not with this clag over the valley."

"Radio in the contact," Ricky said. "Tell them we're standing by for orders. You'd better get Aitch and Larry back too. They're gonna be exposed in a few minutes."

★　★　★

Now they knew what the low wall was for. The muleteers used it to unload the bulging hessian bundles that the mules and camels carried. More opium.

The trucks too had arrived and the drivers were giving high-fives to the men who had filtered out of the shack.

The black-turbaned Taliban seemed at ease with the Slavs, like old friends, hunkering down by the trucks as the work went on around them.

Ricky and his men, still thigh deep in icy water, dared not move. They were awaiting word from the Head Sheds who no doubt were conferring with London, with the Americans, and possibly now with the Pakistani High Command. As usual negotiations seemed to be taking forever.

Ricky could no longer feel his feet, they were dead weights at the end of his legs and he wondered about his ability to walk let alone run. He had dropped his head below the bank in case he was spotted by a sharp-eyed Afghan and Stu was giving them a running commentary from his position in the cleft.

There were upwards of fifty men around the shacks, more than they could comfortably cope with, even with the advantage of surprise. Ten to one was not good odds, even with the bankers of Stu and Pete supporting them with covering fire.

Tonka seemed to read his mind. "Bit more than we can chew, boss?"

"Maybe," Ricky said with less doubt than he was feeling. "What are your boys carrying in those day sacks?"

Tonka grinned. "We split a few things between us. There's a couple of 66s. Aitch kept hold of his C5 with some HE grenades. Digger's got half a stripped down Minimi and I've got the other half. Larry's got the box mag and ammo. Plus the usual assortment of smoke and frag grenades. What about you?"

"Two 66s and an MP5SP, two smoke and two frags."

"Enough to give a good account of ourselves, whatever the odds," Tonka said.

"Looks like the traders are dropping off and will be on their way soon. With any luck we'll only have the Slavs, the Taliban and al-Qaeda to contend with," Ricky said.

"What's the plan, boss, if we're given the green light?"

"Take out the vehicles with 66s and the C5. We need to disable those heavy machine guns they're carrying right at the start. It also helps that the Taliban and al-Qaeda are grouped around them and we can target them at the same time. Then an assault behind smoke under covering fire from the cleft and the Minimi. Two take the left hand field and the barn. Two take the right field and the shack. Stu and Pete will cover the killing ground to the right of the shack with the SG1s. Nice and simple."

Tonka pulled a face. "Biggest problem is incoming from the traders as we're concentrating on the vehicles. Stu and Pete will need to keep the traders' heads down big time."

"With any luck the traders will have moved off by then but if not that's where the Minimi will come in handy. Glad you had the foresight to bring it."

"The G3s are okay but they don't have the rate of fire. Just seemed a sensible precaution," Tonka said. "Digger's assembling it now."

"Looks like the traders are ready for a brew," Stu's voice drifted into his ear. "They're settling the camels down."

"Shit!" Ricky mouthed.

"Wait one. There's something else," Stu continued. "You're about to have company. Two lads are heading your way with buckets."

"Anything from H.Q.?"

"Not yet, boss," Stu confirmed.

"How we gonna play this?" Tonka said.

"Our original orders were to seek and destroy the al-Qaeda group," Ricky said. "They still apply. Stand by."

"Roger that," Stu's cool voice came back.

Ricky pulled the silenced MP5 from his day sack and checked it. "How far are the bucket boys, Stu?"

"Hundred metres and ambling. You've got about a minute."

"Get into any cover you can find," Ricky told Tonka. "Hopefully they'll not spot us. Have the boys got their tasks sorted?"

"Yeah, they know what to do. Give me your 66s we may need them."

Ricky slid him the day sack. "Don't waste them. We have to take out those trucks."

Tonka gave him a pained look then scuttled away giving last-second instructions to his men over the chatternet.

Ricky steeled himself. Here was a problem. The traders, technically, were non-combatants. If he had to shoot them he was committing murder but if he hesitated they would raise the alarm before they were able to mount an attack thereby losing the element of surprise, something they relied on heavily given that they were so vastly outnumbered.

Now he could hear footsteps crunching on loose gravel and snicked off the safety, setting the change lever to single shot, he wanted no wild bursts.

He pressed himself against a boulder. Covered as he was with mud and filth he blended into the riverbank. The two traders were young. Ricky could just see their faces over the rim of the bank as they approached. They were laughing at some joke one had told the other. The taller of the two suddenly stopped and raised a hand to shield his eyes, staring at something intently. Ricky's heart lurched; had he been spotted? The Afghan still stared at some point in the distance. Finally he shrugged his shoulders as if what he had seen had no significance. The shorter man tugged at his sleeve, rattled his bucket in an unmistakeable message and they continued towards the stream. Neither spotted Ricky as they slithered over the bank to fill their buckets. They both bent forward and as they did so a sudden rush of water pushed Ricky's legs from behind the rock. Just for a second the closest man froze. Then Ricky's moral dilemma was solved as the man snaked a hand down to his belt for the Makarov pistol stuffed there. He also opened his mouth to scream but it was choked off instantly as two bullets went through his head. The second man also reacted fast, turning to throw his bucket, stepping forward as he did so. He too fell flat as Ricky shot him in the chest and throat, right in the killing T, severing the spinal cord and dropping him in a crumpled, dying, soundless, heap.

Chapter Six

There was a sudden whoosh as Larry fired the first of the 66s. Trailing a swirling tail of smoke it streaked towards the vehicles and impacted on the cab of the closest truck with a loud bang that sent men scattering. In the distance the sharp cracking of G3s could be heard and two lines of tracer were curling towards the vehicles and the men now running in all directions. Aitch let loose the second 66 and that too was a direct hit but on an unarmed truck that leapt on its suspension and rolled onto its side gushing flame from a ruptured fuel line.

The angry rattle of the Minimi started up and tracer was stitched through the running men. There was no cover except for the two buildings and many were making for them in the teeth of the vicious hail of bullets.

"Let's go, boss," Tonka yelled in Ricky's ear. Smoke grenades hit the ground twenty metres in front of them and started spewing white. To the left Larry and Aitch were charging forward. To the right Tonka was half over the low river bank one 66 tube snapped open in his right hand the other dangling from a strap around his neck.

Ricky pushed himself to his feet and crawled over the rim in Tonka's wake. They were getting incoming now, high velocity bullets were cracking past their heads as the opposition got organised but it was still wildly inaccurate.

The white turban was rallying black turbans to him and getting some command together. They would be a major problem soon. A man had climbed onto the back of the second gun truck and was jacking a round into the breech of the DHsk mounted there. He started to fire into the smoke but a G3 tracer round knocked him over the tailboard into the dirt.

Cursing at the top of his voice Tonka broke through the smoke and reached the near corner of the shack. He threw the 66 onto his shoulder, peered through the plastic sight and pushed the rubber firing button. The rocket curved in a graceful arc right into the gun truck's fuel tank which exploded with a mighty roar.

Aitch was tossing a bomb from the C5 at the small group of Taliban. It fell short and he had attracted their attention. The return fire was sharp and organised forcing him to duck under cover of the low wall. He crawled a few metres to the left, popped up from behind a sack of opium and sent off a second round. This landed smack in the middle of the group killing two and scattering the rest. White turban dived for the shack with tracer from the Minimi tracking his movements but never able to catch up with him.

Aitch blew a hole in the stable wall with his last remaining bomb and Larry tossed in two fragmentation grenades. The stable rocked with a double blast that lifted part of the roof. The door at the far end burst open and four men spilled out firing as they ran. Only two made it as far as the shack. Aitch hosed the inside with his C5. No one else ran out.

Incoming was getting thicker, bullets snapped and whined past, kicking up dust and vaporising chunks of building. The traders were shooting from behind their animals and the fire was getting more accurate.

The al-Qaeda fighters, Taliban and Slavs were grouped around the front of the shack out of sight of the Minimi and the covering G3s which were concentrated on the traders.

"Boss!" It was Digger's nasal twang sounding in Ricky's ear. "Minimi's jammed and the IAs haven't worked."

"Can you clear it?"

"It'll take a while. Coupla minutes maybe."

"Ditch it. Use your M16. We need cover now."

"You got it."

"Sitrep, Stu," Ricky said.

"We've got the traders pinned down for now but ammo's getting low and we're reduced to sniping. We won't be able to hold them if they decide to rush you."

"Can you see the targets?"

"Negative," Stu replied. "No eyeball."

"Larry, Aitch, sitrep," Ricky shouted.

"We've cleared the barn and we're on the far side of it. Reckon we can enfilade the targets from the corner but we'll be exposing ourselves to the traders," Aitch said.

"We're in the worst position, boss," Tonka said. "We can't advance along the left side of the hut as we'll be sitting ducks for the enemy. Round the right side the traders will get us."

"That only leaves over or through," Ricky grimaced.

"Through it is then," Tonka said and patted the last 66. "Get back."

Ricky flattened himself against the low wall as Tonka crawled a safe distance from the building. The missile impacted on the rotting timber of a low window and went straight through without detonating the warhead but the far wall was more solid and the high explosive blew a hole the size of a barrel, firing molten metal onto the open ground beyond.

Tonka heard the roar and the shrieks of injured men but it was so much background noise. He raced in behind the rocket and tossed a frag grenade through the fist sized hole in the wood, jumping to one side as the 4-second fuse counted down. The window splintered outwards, enlarging the hole so that a man could squeeze through. Tonka pushed in the muzzle of his G3 and let go a long burst. He gestured Ricky forward and through the hole, shoving him hard from behind with his free hand.

The only light inside the hut was that which spilt in from the gaping holes in both walls. It took a few seconds for Ricky's eyes to adjust but he could see a shape crawling in through the far end. He pumped rounds out of his G3 and watched the man drop as the high velocity bullets flattened him.

The inside of the hut was like a dormitory with bunk bends lined up in rows along the walls. Personal belongings were spread around and coffee cups littered a rickety table in a clear area near the door. Tonka had managed to push his large frame through the hole and he tapped Ricky on the head to let him know he was there.

Ricky put a thumb up and shuffled forward towards the gaping hole in the far wall. There was a renewed burst of firing from outside and then a cacophony of voices all screaming "dry, dry" as the clips ran out on their automatic weapons. Digger, Aitch and Larry were all down to using pistols.

Ricky checked his ammo. He had only three rounds in the G3 plus a mag for the MP5SP but that was sub-sonic and only good for a few dozen metres.

Tonka had been watching him. "I've got half a mag, boss. Let's get it done."

Ricky nodded. They had to get the last of the al-Qaeda and Taliban fighters, especially white turban, and worry about the traders later. "Door'll be covered. It's got to be the hole."

"Toss out the last frag. I'll cover," Tonka said.

Ricky wriggled forward, unhooked the grenade from his webbing and closed the split pin that had been spread to prevent it accidentally pulling out. He was two metres from the hole. It was close enough. He hooked his fingers through the ring and pulled, holding the lever down with his thumb, the pressure from the spring surprisingly strong. He flipped the lever and counted two before tossing the grenade, just as a Taliban fighter dived through the opening. Tonka fired and the man was already dying but the grenade hit him on the head and bounced into a corner. Two seconds left on the fuse. Ricky dived headlong behind a bunk. The explosion was shattering in the confined space and blew out another piece of wall. Ricky felt a sharp stabbing pain and then the roof fell in.

★ ★ ★

The man in the white turban was standing to his full height while others cowered on their knees around him. He had only three fighters left and he had to motivate them in order to secure his own escape. He was calculating. He knew that the rifle fire from the cleft could not touch him, he was hidden behind the shack. The rate of fire had lessened too and he suspected the attackers were low on ammunition. This had allowed the traders to intensify their support and keep the enemy soldiers by the river bank and behind the stable pinned down. For the first time since the battle began he had the upper hand but he needed to galvanise his men. They were brave fighters but the attack had taken them by surprise just when it had seemed that they had reached safety and a ride over the border on the drug trucks. After the slaughter at the complex it had damaged their morale and they were afraid of the ferocity of the enemy.

"God is great," he screamed. "Death to the infidels...God is good."

It worked like a charm as it always did. These simple, devout, men were true believers.

"God is great" they chanted in unison and leapt to their feet, faces glowing, as fervour overcame fear. The cry was taken up by the traders who rose to their feet and ran en-masse towards the shack.

An al-Qaeda fighter thrust his AK47 through the hole in the wall and blasted off rounds on full automatic. Then he climbed through closely followed by the others. They emerged towing Ricky and Tonka by the heels, dumping them unceremoniously in the dirt and kicking the bloody bodies.

The traders had arrived and were standing in a semi-circle ululating and waving their guns in the air. The bravest ran forward and launched kicks at the two British soldiers before darting back into the throng.

White turban ripped the guns from the soldiers' hands, then pulled off their shamags and radio wires. "See this is your enemy. This is the face of the great Satan, beaten by the warriors of God. You should not fear these devils they can be killed by the righteous."

He kicked Ricky's supine body for emphasis. It brought him round and he groaned.

Just for a second white turban was dumbstruck. The infidel was alive which cut the impact of his speech. He pulled a long bladed tribal knife from beneath his robes. "The honour is to be mine. God is great."

Ricky was coming-to quickly but he could not move, his muscles would not respond. He could see the light glinting on the wickedly curved blade *'Roll on your rifle and blow out your brains,'* Rudyard Kipling leapt unbidden into his mind. But he had neither the means nor the will; he was not about to join the exit club.

All shooting had stopped. Most of the traders and what was left of the al-Qaeda fighters were grouped around the two British soldiers. Ricky could not tell whether Tonka was dead or alive. There was blood on his face that he could see with his peripheral vision. Perhaps he was the only one still alive. The others would not have left them to their fate voluntarily; not for one second.

For now it was just him. Him, white turban and the vicious looking knife he was waving above his head. His intentions were obvious. Ricky was about to lose some vital parts of his anatomy and the man was about to enjoy it.

He felt his legs being grabbed and he was dragged away from the building into the centre of the ring of traders, all ululating, dancing and waving their weapons in the air, loosing off rounds skywards.

Ricky was flat on his back and he could see specks before his eyes. He blinked to clear them but they remained obstinately there. Not just there but moving, circling in graceful slow motion. His brain was fuddled, it wasn't making any sense. Spots before the eyes swam; they did not circle.

His mind was dragged away from the problem as white turban moved in with his knife held in front of him like a man roasting meat at a barbecue.

He stabbed forward and downward into Ricky's thigh. The blade went deep into the muscle but he did not feel it.

In fact he could not feel his legs at all. He looked at the blade as it was twisted in the wound. He looked up at the man who had surprise on his face so comical that Ricky burst out laughing.

The mob was now silent, the man's spell broken, his authority diminished in a shocking heartbeat.

"God moves in a mysterious way," Ricky said in Arabic.

The man's lips drew into a thin determined line. He was a Saudi and he understood the words. "His ways are a mystery to all men," he replied in perfect English.

"But you are about to discover that at first hand." He held the dagger raised above his head primed to plunge into Ricky's chest.

Now Ricky did scream as agony shot through his body. The knife was raised again but the blade never fell. A red poppy blossomed on the man's forehead and he dropped like a sack of opium from the back of a mule.

It was as much as the traders could take. Their leader was dead, the charismatic holy warrior too and the will to fight left them. They melted away like the snow had earlier under the meagre warmth of the sun. Mules and camels were kicked complaining to their feet. Their dead were dragged away to be buried later, the wounded loaded onto already heavily burdened animals.

Ricky's eyes were still open and he could still see the spots only now they were larger and had wings. Vultures circling, drawn by the smell of fresh meat. How could they know so soon that death had descended on the valley? Scavengers, so cold and merciless some would not even wait for their victims to die. There was no reasoning with them, they were pitiless, self-interested, hungry. Their sole concern now was the cleaning up of man's offal from the gutters where he cast it.

The Saudi had fallen with his face towards Ricky and he remembered it. It was a strong face; had been a strong face before the round had mashed the features. The white turban looked like the Japanese flag with a red rising sun at its centre. Ricky studied the face as he grew colder; before the al-Qaeda fighters carried the body away; before he blacked out.

The face was not bin Laden's. It had all been for nothing.

Ad Unum Omnes
All for one

Note: 2 - Appended.

That was the beginning, at least the end of the beginning. A normal if complex operation for the British army's special forces which did not achieve its final objective; the capture or death of Osama bin Laden, the ostensible head of the multi-faceted and widely diverse series of Muslim terrorist organisations known collectively as al-Qaeda.

Much of what follows is hearsay, as such not admissible in a criminal court of law. Some is verbal evidence given directly to me by persons who were in positions of importance or of command but who did not wish to jeopardise their careers by giving formal or written evidence; and the odd whistle-blower. Some of it is inevitably conjecture based on solid information but without the benefit of first-hand knowledge (one can deduce such things from happenings, before and after an event, which can be historically proven). Thus reported conversations of several meetings which were known to take place at the Ministry of Defence and Home Office, which preceded certain events, are informed guesswork based on knowledge of the subject matter of those meetings and the characters of those present at those meetings which is a matter of record. As there are holes in the chain of events it must be assumed that certain meetings were held in secret but, like undiscovered astral bodies, their existence is betrayed by the effects they have on events surrounding them.

All this information formed part of my due diligence, taken to court but not submitted as it was not provable in legal terms. However, I lay it out here because it has a bearing and does much to determine the background to the case, the motives for it being brought and the mindset of those officials involved.

AFP.

Lincolns Inn

PART 2
First Contact

Ed Lane

Chapter Seven

"You do get yourself into some scrapes."

Ricky eased himself up in the bed, tossed the *Daily Telegraph* to one side and smiled towards the figure in the doorway. "Am I glad to see *you!*"

Gill Somers sauntered in and returned the grin. She was tall and slender, maybe thinner than he remembered, and her gorgeous red hair had been cut short into a fashionable and expensive style which was now stunningly and illegally blonde, at least it should have been illegal for the effect it had on him. Her skin was smooth with a pale olive tan courtesy of her Basque mother. In most measures she was a beautiful woman, one that turned heads, especially dressed as she usually was in designer clothing, a habit she had learned from her wealthy Basque cousins. But there was more to her than that. Gill had a degree in chemical engineering and combined beauty with a first-class brain.

Was it imagination or were the lines around her mouth deeper than the last time he saw her and did her eyes hold the troubled look of a combat veteran? The thousand-yard stare the soldiers called it. It was muted with Gill but there all the same, seeing hidden scenes that played out in the mind's eye on a continuous loop that only time could dim.

"Have they left any interesting bits?" she said as she eyed the dressings over his leg.

He grinned again but it was harder work as his own nightmares flashed back to haunt him. "Most of them."

"Can you tell me about it?"

Ricky patted the bed. "Let me tell you a story, little girl."

Gill sat and cocked an eyebrow. "I've heard all about men like you."

"Met a few too, I'd guess."

"None in the same class as you. But tell me all; all that you're able to anyway."

Ricky ran through the tale, as much of it as he could remember before he passed out and as much as he was allowed to tell. "I came round in this hospital a week ago. A couple of the lads have been in to see me. It's not too far from Hereford to Selly Oak. They filled me in on what happened after a Saudi stuck his butcher's knife in me.

"The blokes had run out of ammo for the G3 rifles and the range was too long for much else. All they could do was watch from a distance as they didn't have time to get closer. The two working the flank were completely dry, not a single round of any calibre to their names and they were facing a couple of dozen heavily armed locals.

"One of the bloke's, a lad called Sponge, was suffering badly from dysentery and he had followed on behind the rest of us on the approach. In his weakened state it took him a while to get to the fire fight but he arrived in time to size up the situation and hand his ammo to Pete Cooke who then put a bullet through the Saudi's head just as he was about to take another slice out of me."

"So what exactly did they hack off?" Gill asked.

Ricky pulled a wry face. "I've lost a couple of toes on my right foot due to frostbite that wasn't treated quickly enough. I've got concussion, a lump of grenade in my shoulder, a deep five inch gash on my right thigh and two broken ribs plus a few stitches where the Saudi tried to hack through my body armour.

"The frostbite's my own stupid fault but the upside to that was I had enough pain- killer in my legs that I couldn't feel it when the guy stabbed me. In fact I was so surprised that I laughed at him and that really pissed him off. Pissed him off so much that he got careless."

"Careless and dead," Gill said. "How often those two words go together. Did anyone else get hurt?"

"Only Tonka."

"I know a Tonka. Big sergeant. He's been with the Regiment for years. What happened to him?"

"He was with me when the Taliban got us and had the stuffing knocked out of him. He's okay now though and living it up in the main ward. He was out cold all through the stabbing routine and the locals thought he was dead meat. He sleeps like the bloody dead by all accounts."

"So everyone else is okay?"

"Yeah. The usual cuts and bruises plus a few mental scars. Par for the course."

"Stu called me. Told me you were in here otherwise I'd never have known. I thought you were still in Colchester," Gill said.

"Need to know. Sorry. There's no way I could tell you," Ricky said. "I'd almost forgotten you knew Stu. Memory's going. Must be the concussion."

"It happens like that sometimes."

Ricky whistled silently. "I'm a wreck," he added with a cheerfulness he did not feel.

Gill took something from her shoulder bag. "I don't want to add to your troubles..."

"But you will anyway."

She smiled lazily and opened a bluey. "Did you mean all this? Or was it you thought you were going to die so what-the-hell?"

Ricky coloured. "Where did you get that?"

"Medics found it in your combat suit when they cut it off. You may not know this but it was touch and go for you for a while. Exposure, loss of blood, shock and a nasty little infection from the knife blade nearly did for you. They forwarded it as a matter of courtesy. I'd have come sooner but I've only just come off ops myself."

"You're supposed to be driving a desk at MoD."

Gill grinned. "Need to know...sorry."

Ricky choked back a laugh. "I deserved that." But it did explain her haunted look, her thousand-yard stare. Her ops could be dangerous deep cover stuff. He forebore to ask. He knew she would tell him nothing he could not guess for himself.

"You're not going to change the subject," she said and waved the bluey gently from side to side.

"You shouldn't mock the afflicted..."

"Did you mean any of it?"

"Yes!"

"Which part?"

"All of it."

"When were you going to send it?"

"I don't know. It's about version sixty," Ricky mumbled, "I could never get the wording quite right, or the timing, something always cropped up."

"So, what now? What do you expect me to do?"

Ricky shrugged and grunted as his ribs twinged. "It's how I felt, how I still feel. How I've felt since two seconds after meeting you."

"You never said anything..."

Ricky tried a shrug again but winced at the thought. "You were always busy, professional, I didn't know how you'd react. You've never said anything either. I didn't know if you felt the same way. You may have a bloke, I don't know."

"You think I'm easy? Lots of men, a bit of a bed-hopper?" Gill asked.

"Don't put words in my mouth. I've never thought that of you."

"Not even when I was screwing a mass murderer?"

Ricky was shocked and his mouth dropped open. "You didn't know that at the time. It was your private life. I could never hold that against you, ever."

"You didn't think I was whoring for the job?"

"No! Definitely not. It was just one of those things, like a holiday romance that went wrong."

"You don't know what it means to me to hear you say that," she said and. leaned forward to touch his cheek.

Just then a male nurse came in with a cloth-covered tray in his hand. He stared at Gill, sharp annoyance etched on his face.

Gill took the heavy hint. "Looks like time's up. We'll talk about this some more when you get out of here."

"Can't we talk about it now? Just a little chat? Charlie will wait."

Gill cast another glance at the nurse who was tapping his foot. "You've waited so long a few more days won't make much difference."

"But you do feel the same way as I do?" Ricky asked. It was a poorly masked plea.

She leaned forward and planted a gentle kiss on his forehead. "We'll talk about it when you've recovered."

★ ★ ★

The major from the Army Adjutant General's Corps had ridden the train to Birmingham New Street and then taken a taxi to the NHS Selly Oak Hospital. He begrudged the time it had taken; he was a busy man with much to do. Time was when he could have visited military casualties in a military hospital in Woolwich or Aldershot, much closer to his MoD office in Adastral House alongside Whitehall, or to his own regimental headquarters at Portsmouth. Now all the military hospitals were closed except for one in Plymouth and the specialist Headley Court in Surrey which dealt with crippling injuries for all three services. Sign of the times. Draw a line and move on, no point in complaining about it. *Crack on.*

He smiled; a thin creasing of the lips. The jargon of the front line regiments amused him, so full of derring-do and gung-ho. *Crack on!* The mere term conveyed speed and an element of danger. The snap of a high velocity round past an ear.

He felt a vague twinge of...what? Jealousy? He had worn the uniform for twenty years and the most danger he had faced was missing the train from Deepcut in the mornings. No, jealousy was unthinkable, perhaps a touch of contempt for the brainless mantras of the infantry. The mudlarks who could be the bane of his life with their silly macho antics. He had little sympathy for them. Mostly they deserved what they got.

It was in this frame of mind that he entered the private hospital room of one Major Ricardo Keane.

Ricky was still in bed and cocked a quizzical eye at his surprise and uninvited visitor. He was marked as military, even in civilian clothing. The tie gave it away, the trim figure, upright bearing and the moustache that in most other walks of life had died out as a fashion item in the nineteen-seventies.

"Can I help you?" Ricky asked.

"Phelps, Major, AGC. You're Keane?"

"As ever," Ricky said and appeared amused at his own joke. "What can I do for you, Phelps?"

Phelps had not twitched a lip at the over-used play on words. "I've got a few questions for you."

"Ah! Must be about the decorations I've recommended for my men. Good of you to come."

"I have to ask you about the operation in Afghanistan."

"Wait one. I'll need to see your ID and I'll need to speak with the Regiment. They will have to give me clearance."

Phelps cleared his throat in annoyance. "No need for that. Here's my authorisation, and my ID." He handed over a sheet of paper neatly folded in a leather wallet which also contained his laminated ID card. "I trust that's in order?"

Ricky read every dot and comma then handed them back. "They seem fine but I'd be happier if I called the Regiment."

"If you must. I had hoped to get this over and done with quickly."

"Won't take a minute," Ricky said and fished out his mobile from a cabinet. He punched in a number and was put through to the duty officer who put him on to the adjutant.

"Danny? Listen I have a Major Phelps of the AGC here. He wants to ask questions about the op in The Stan. What's the SP?"

There was a long drawn out intake of breath at the far end. "He's got clearance. His office rang the Old Man yesterday. You can tell him what he needs to know."

"And...?"

"Just be careful, okay, mate. And don't tell anyone I said that."

"Yessir. Thanks." Ricky smiled as he collapsed the handset and looked at Phelps. "Seems you're kosher."

"Naturally. Now can we get on?"

The questioning was detailed and as thorough as the Intelligence Officer's debrief the previous week. Phelps however was far more interested in the fire fight at the end of the pursuit and went over the details several times asking the same questions from different perspectives. After two gruelling hours Ricky was saved from further tedium by Charlie once again stomping in with his medication.

Phelps did not hide his look of irritation but packed away his papers and cassette recorder. "If I need to know anything further I'll call back another time," he said. "But, hopefully, I won't need to bother you again."

"Amen to that," Ricky said. "Not about decorations is it, Phelps?"

★ ★ ★

Tonka came in to say goodbye. "I'm off now, boss. The MO's signed me off for light duties so I'm back to 'H' to find out how much they've missed me."

Ricky held out his hand. "It was good serving with you...and fighting with you."

"Same here, boss." Tonka took the fist and pumped it. "You here for much longer?"

"Dunno. They haven't told me anything. It can't be much longer though. I'm hobbling around on sticks already and the headaches have more-or-less stopped battering the back of my eyeballs."

"Yeah, that's the problem. There's always a price to pay when you enjoy yourself too much. It was fun while it lasted."

Tonka turned to leave but Ricky called him back. "Has anyone been to see you, other than Slime on the debrief?"

Tonka pulled a face. "Yeah, couple of tossers from the AGC wanted me to expand on my story, mainly about the fire fight at the caravanserai. A lot of nonsense I call it."

"Any particular reason?"

"Digger and Aitch were visiting the other day. Seems they got the third degree too. They reckon the two goons who interrogated them were SIB."

"AGC covers a multitude of sinners," Ricky said, "including the Military Police Special Investigations Branch. But why should they be interested?"

"You know, I hadn't really given it much thought up until you mentioned it. Does seem a bit cock-eyed. Maybe it's normal practice now for ops on foreign soil. Don't forget it took place on Pakistan territory. Maybe they've complained, you know, letters in the diplomatic bag, ruffle a few post-imperialist feathers. The Casevac boys made a hell of a noise getting us out with that Chinook. Must have shaken them up in Hyderabad. They'd have known about our incursion all right, al-Qaeda will have made sure of that and the local politicians will be playing hell with their government to do something about it."

Ricky smiled. "You're probably right. It's been mainly about the fire fight in Pakistan. They didn't seem that interested on the walk in from Afghanistan."

"Well there you go; mystery solved. You take care of yourself, boss. See yuh."

After Tonka had left the subject would not leave Ricky's mind. Even if it was about an illegal cross-border operation the fact that the SIB was involved meant someone, somewhere, was investigating. Where there was an investigation charges could follow. As the senior man on the op it was his head on the block. It was not a comforting thought.

Chapter Eight

"I think we have a case," Phelps said. "A good case. I believe it is time that charges were sought."

He looked around the table and sensed the satisfaction that emanated from the man from the Foreign Office. "We have taken statements from all involved and it seems unequivocal. Major Keane shot two Pakistani boys in cold blood. He himself has admitted it. That together with the testimony from the eye-witness should be enough to gain a conviction."

The man from the FO toyed with his spectacles that lay on a pad in front of him. "You're sure, major? We don't need another fiasco at a court martial. The government of Pakistan are adamant that these killings on their soil should be punished with the utmost severity. We have a great need for their co-operation in these troubled times and it would be disastrous if we let them down."

"I'm as confident as I can be under the circumstances. All the stories tally in all but minor details which is normal with witnesses," Phelps said. "It is beyond doubt that Keane shot and killed two non-combatants going about their business in their own country. Additional charges against others yet un-named may flow from this."

"Where do we go from here?" Stan Hathaway was from the Policy Focus Office based in the depths of Downing Street. A small man, stocky with a forceful manner, who was not a Civil Servant but one of a legion of special advisors. Phelps did not like him. The man had too much power and used it too forcefully for his taste. In short Hathaway threw his weight around with a bully's relish.

"We have a set format for these things. My findings will go to my boss the Provost Marshall who will decide if it warrants further action. If so he will take it to Director Army Legal Services who, if he concurs, will take it to the Attorney General who has the ultimate say in the matter.

"Should the Attorney General agree to pursue the prosecution the matter is handed back to me. I will then take it to Keane's commanding officer who will inform him of the charges. Keane will then be formally charged with the offences.

"From then on the matter will be handed to Colonel Prosecutions UK who heads the Army Prosecuting Authority in the United Kingdom which is outside the chain of command and as such not subject to the pressures of higher authority."

Hathaway had a look on his face halfway between a sneer and a grimace. "Seems a fucking roundabout way to goes about anything. Can't we cuts it short and get on with it?"

"I'm afraid that's impossible. These actions are enshrined into the Army's Code of Conduct and are part of UK law. It's how it must be treated or there is no locus standi," Phelps said. "I have to tell you that this happens as a result of the European Convention on Human Rights, Mr. Hathaway. The European Courts have upheld the right for service people to be tried by an independent body which is not influenced by the chain of command."

"Ha bloody ha. Bet you just loved sayin' that," Hathaway sneered.

Phelps showed his palms and shrugged. "It's out of my hands, we must follow procedure."

Hathaway was beginning to get hot under the collar and the man from the FO took his opportunity to leave. He had no wish to get on Hathaway's notorious bad-side.

Hathaway looked around the table at the various clerks and writers who were taking assiduous notes. "You lot can leave as well," he snapped. "I need to have a private word with Major Phelps."

It was a measure of his reputation that no one turned to Phelps for confirmation but left without demur. Hathaway waited for a few seconds after the door had closed behind the last man. He seemed to have regained his composure and he was almost pleasant.

"Look, Phelps. I don't needs any hassle, OK? I've been asked to look after this case, make sure it goes through smoothly and we gets the right result at the end so we don't want any cock-ups, right.

"You've done well so far, I can see that, but you don't seem to have grasped how important this case is.

"See it's not just the Pakistan government that's hoppin' about. The news has filtered through to the big Pakistani populations in the Midlands and their community leaders are puttin' pressure on their local MPs, some of them, sitting on slender majorities, are shittin' themselves as they relies heavily on the Muslim vote. They in turn are puttin' pressure on the government. It don't like to be pressured, not by its own side, so it wants somethin' done and done soon. Not just that, it wants it seen to be done and it wants it seen that the government takes this sort of thing seriously.

This is real-politik, Phelps, not the shabby worries of the FO. This is the way things really work.

"Seems there's not much you can do about skippin' out a couple o' stages but you have to make sure that none of the buggers involved sits on the file. It's got to zip up the line like a fairy on roller skates. I'm relyin' on you to keep the pressure on your military bods.

"You have to make sure that all the paperwork is up to scratch so that no one has the opportunity to slow it down by returning it for correction and you have to sells it like it's ice cream in mid summer and your freezer's broke...*hard and fast*. You do this well and there's no telling how far you could go, know what I mean, Phelps? You clear on this?"

"Perfectly clear, sir. But you need not worry. I happen to believe that this is a righteous case, that Keane is as guilty as sin, and I'll do my best to ensure that he gets the punishment he deserves."

"He *swiftly* gets the punishment he deserves," Hathaway added with a sly grin. "Good man, Phelps. I'll sees to it that the right people hears about your work. Keep it up."

★ ★ ★

It was a bombshell. Ricky had been expecting something, but not this. This was way beyond the scope of his imagination. *Unlawful killing*. It was the same as murder, was murder; he was being called a murderer. He felt sick at the thought.

The Old Man had done his best to appear sympathetic but had hardened his face when Phelps had read out the official arrest caution. Most of what followed had gone over Ricky's head. He remembered being told he was not to leave the camp, that he was to live in a room at the mess until his court martial, which according to Phelps would not be far in the future as the next Session was less than two months away and a Trial Judge Advocate had already been nominated. He was told to find a lawyer and appoint an Assisting Officer who in days gone past would also have pleaded his defence but now performed more mundane roles and was a shoulder to cry on if it was needed.

There was only one person Ricky could think of to fill that role. Gill would be the ideal person. She was aware of the pressures on Special Forces, she had personal experience of the work, she was easy to talk to but much more importantly he would be close to the woman he loved. If it would be allowed.

He wasn't sure of the finer points of etiquette with regard to 'Assisting Officers', perhaps one had to come from within the Regiment to which they were attached and Gill was serving at the MoD. But he was confident he had the right to choose his own friend if the person was available.

All this passed through his mind as he was escorted back to his room at the mess. He was still hobbling with the aid of a stick which he hated but the pain was still too great to be without it. But it was the mental anguish that hurt more. The army he loved had kicked him in the teeth. Whatever the outcome of the trial his military career was over. Given that physically he would eventually recover enough to continue his service, the stigma would follow him. In his state of mind he doubted his own fortitude to cope with it. If he was found guilty it would all be over anyway.

Back in his room, a depressing basic and functional four walls, albeit with en-suite facilities, he pulled out his mobile and speed-dialled Gill. Just talking to her would give him the vital lift he needed.

★ ★ ★

Gill was there the next day, her clearance gave her access to the camp and she was escorted by the adjutant to Ricky's room. A formal request had been made and tentatively approved by the Regiment for Gill to act as Ricky's Assisting Officer.

She did not come empty-handed. She brought a large basket with flowers to brighten up the room, a bottle of good Islay single malt whisky and a bundle of newspapers.

She threw them on the bed. "Have you seen these?"

He shook his head and unfolded the *Guardian*. The headline screamed at him, *'Army Officer slays Pakistan Two.'*

"Where the hell did this come from?"

"The *Sun's* worse," Gill said. "It seems someone has been briefing the press."

"Can they do that? Surely it could jeopardise my chances." Ricky flapped open the cover of the *Sun*. *'Trigger-Happy Tommy'* the headline screamed in 120 point type. "Jesus. They can't do this to me, surely they can't."

Gill took his hand and squeezed it. "I don't like the look of it. This is politics at play. Someone's got it in for you. They've been very clever and not mentioned you by name and have quoted informed sources but it's a determined attempt to blacken your character by association. At the same time it's letting people know that justice is about to be done," she said.

"The government?" Ricky said. He barely moved his lips.

Gill had to strain to hear the words but nodded her agreement. "It's a safe bet. And, at a shrewd guess, close to the top too, I'd imagine. This wouldn't have been leaked without someone senior sanctioning it."

"Maybe someone here leaked it," Ricky said.

Gill shrugged. "Maybe but I think you have to assume the worst, that the government is about to throw you to the wolves."

"It's the same with my old boss, they're trying to get him too," Ricky said, bitterness coating every word.

Gill withdrew her hand from his. "Look, sit down, Ricky. I have something serious to say. This isn't like your boss's case. There they're trying to prove that he is guilty because of the behaviour of the men under his command and not through his own actions. There's an argument as to why stop there? Why not try the Brigade Commander, or the Divisional Commander, or the Secretary of State for Defence? I don't think there's a court in the land that will convict him because it will beg too many questions of the upper echelons.

"In your case, according to those newspaper reports, it is because of your own actions that you are being tried and that makes you a much softer target. If they find you guilty, you'll be stripped of your rank and you will spend time in Colchester Military Prison. How much time will depend on the presiding Judge Advocate but military sentences can be far more severe than civilian ones."

"Hold up!" Ricky protested, "I've not been tried yet and you've got me banged up already."

"I'm just asking you to face the facts. You seem to be sleepwalking into this without a clue what you are going to do about it. The adjutant tells me that the trial is barely eight weeks away. That's uncommon haste and barely gives you time to put a defence case together. You need a solicitor and a barrister, a good one, and you need one now. So pull yourself together, get your arse in gear and get going."

"Oh, gee, thanks for the pep-talk, mom."

"Treat it as a joke if you like but that's not going to win you any lollipops, sunshine."

"Okay, I'm sorry. I have been a bit down recently. No excuse. But with you here it will make things easier. You've already bucked me up no end."

"That's just the point, Ricky. I shan't be here. I can't get involved."

"Oh, great! You're worried about your precious career. Frightened that some of the mud will stick to you?"

"It's not that. I just can't be seen to be involved. It's best if I'm out of the way."

"Well thanks. Thanks for your support but don't let me hold you up," Ricky said, disappointment etched deep on his face. "You certainly get to know who your friends are when the chips are down."

"I'm sorry I can't be here for you..."

"Just go, okay! And you can take your flowers with you. There's enough of a stink in here already."

Gill did not argue further, he was too upset to listen. She left and heard the flower vase smash into the door behind her.

★ ★ ★

It was Ricky's lowest ebb. His physical injuries and mental scars combined with Gill's abandonment dragged him down. He wasn't too proud to try to find some solace in the whisky she had brought but he knew alcohol wasn't the answer and gave up after two glasses.

Gill was right about one thing, however much it pained him to admit it. He needed to get off his arse and start fighting back. For too long he'd wallowed in a trough of self-pity which was unlike him and due probably to the emerging symptoms of PTSD which manifested themselves in mood swings, shaking limbs and dives into deep melancholia. Then and there he decided it wasn't going to beat him and he started work on his defence.

He had been working for just fifteen minutes when his mobile warbled. He checked the window which read *'number withheld'* and all but decided not to accept the call.

Then his newly regained sense of adventure kicked in and he pressed the green button.

"Major Keane?" It was a feminine voice, soft and musical, full of cadence.

"This is Keane. Who are you?"

"You don't know me, major but I know of your situation and I may be able to help you."

"Keep talking," Ricky said. Questions were already bouncing off his frontal lobes but for now the voice was enough. Maybe an actress, she had the stressed-honey vowels of a voice-over queen.

"My name's Ann FitzPatrick and I am a barrister. Your solicitor called me, asked if I had seen the newspapers and would I be interested in defending the case. The answer to both those questions was yes, if you wish me to act for you."

"There's a few things I don't understand," Ricky said, one of them being who the hell his solicitor was, he had not appointed one, "but in principal I'm in agreement."

"Good. When can we meet? I understand that the hearing has been set for next but one Sessions. This is an unrealistic timescale and I will apply to have the court martial postponed until we have had time to assemble a reasonable defence. But just to be on the safe side we should proceed with all possible speed. Can I see you tomorrow?"

"I'm not going anywhere," Ricky said. "It will have to be here in Hereford as I'm confined to camp."

"Yes, I know. I have already applied for a visitor's permit to be waiting at the main gate when I get there tomorrow morning. Arrange for a suitable room to be made available for us. We'll need it all day and it will be a tough day for you. Please be prepared for that, major."

"Call me Ricky." She was very sure of herself. Already he was putting an imaginary face to the heavenly voice and hoped he wasn't going to be disappointed. He filed his questions for the next day and clicked off.

★ ★ ★

It wasn't often that Stu visited the Green Dragon. The place held too many memories, dark memories. It was where he had met Judy and it was where they had been making for when she had stumbled under the wheels of a speeding taxi. The thought still made him shudder with guilt. It had been partly his fault, as he had been scrapping with another man and Judy had tried to get out of their way.

Toff had been a good-looking trooper with a way with women and a sore loser when Judy had preferred to spend her time with Stu. Full of beer and hurt pride he had ambushed them in the street, out for revenge. The problem was that Toff, out of his head, had not remembered a thing the next day but the guilt still lay like a pall of pain on Stu's shoulders.

Toff was now out of the Regiment and out of the army. A casualty from an operation against ETA, the Basque separatists. Coincidentally it had been Ricky Keane who had commanded that op. What goes around comes around.

He found the man he was looking for in the bar and sat up on the vacant stool beside him.

"Seen this?" Stu slid his copy of the *Daily Express* along the bar.

Bill Cowley cocked an eyebrow and read the headline. "Yeah!"

"Is that it then?"

Bill swivelled around to face him, nursing what was left of his pint. "What do you want me to say?"

"How about it's a travesty and someone ought to be doing something about it. How's that for starters?"

"It may be a fucking travesty but which bastard is going to be daft enough to stick his stupid neck out and do something about something that reeks of politics? That all right with you?" Cowley took a final swig from his now empty glass and waved it at Stu. "Mine's a pint."

Stu beckoned the barman and another drink materialised.

"You not drinking?" Cowley asked as he sampled the fresh beer.

Stu shook his head. "This has got me fired up."

"Why? The bloke's a Rupert. Let the Ruperts worry about it"

"You're not looking beyond the bottom of that glass, Bill. If they can do it to him they can do it to us, there were eight of us on the op and each one of us did for a few Afghans and traders plus a few indeterminate Eastern Europeans. Once this goes ahead, and let's say he's found guilty because the cards seem well and truly stacked against him, what's to stop them coming after the rest of us?

"And that's just the top ten per cent of the iceberg. What docs it mean for future ops? How will the blokes feel if they know they could end up on the wrong side of a court martial for taking out some raghead? How can we be seriously expected to operate under those conditions?"

"I was looking at it from the point of view of this case," Cowley said. "Seems Keane slotted these blokes without justification. If that's right I can understand the hoo-ha. It's not as if it was accidental collateral damage is it? There's got to be some rules of engagement and we have to abide by them."

Stu snorted. "I can't believe you're saying that, Bill. You're all for waving your card in the middle of a fire fight or a black operation? I really don't believe it. You've been in the Regiment for years, you know the score. We're asked to do things that most others would have nightmares about and we're good at what we do; the best. If we have to worry about who's looking over our shoulders the edge is going to go. We have trouble getting recruits through Selection now and that's how it should be but imagine if Keane gets convicted how the applicants will start drying up. Nobody wants to get sent to fight with both hands tied behind their backs and with no support from the chain of command."

"So, what are you suggesting?" Cowley said.

"It's not rocket science. We are the regiment which takes on all the shitty tasks that no one else can handle. We're at the sharp end most of the time but what with The Stan and Iraq the green army is getting a lot of shit too. But we're the ones who're involved in this. It's one of our own who's being shafted, albeit he's a Rupert. And we are the only regiment that relies heavily on senior NCOs to run it. Without us it can't function as a unit. We should get our heads together and pass a message on to management that we are not happy with the situation and we would like immunity from cases like these, starting with this one."

Cowley gave him a hard look. "Why me?"

"You're the senior warrant officer in the Reg since the RSM took a smack during *Op Witham*. People listen to you."

Cowley sighed into his pint and lowered his voice. "I can see all sorts of trouble coming out of this but I do think you have a point. It's worth flying a kite or two to see which way the wind's blowing. Tell you what, young Stu, I'm a bit pissed so the brain cells aren't firing on all cylinders. Let me give it some thought and I'll get back to you.

"Word of warning though. Let's keep this between us for now. We don't want something like this getting out before we're ready or we could be done for mutiny."

Chapter Nine

'Honey' was the word that kept repeating itself in Ricky's mind. Ann FitzPatrick had turned out to be every bit as edible as her voice. Honey blond hair tied back with a silk bow, honey-coloured complexion seemingly basted by the sun of the most fashionable ski resorts. And that voice; smooth, soft, pure as sunshine. It sounded better in real life. The mobile had tended to add a hard edge that was not there in face-to-face conversation. Or perhaps he was letting the vision cloud his memory.

She had taken off her jacket and hung it over the back of a chair revealing a peach coloured blouse which was just a little too tight across an impressive bust and gaped slightly at the buttonholes.

The adjutant had found them a room at the back of the mess. It was an under-utilised storeroom with items still in dust-covered cardboard boxes, unpacked since the move to Credenhill from the old Bradbury Lines. It was private and it was theirs for as long as they needed it. The adjutant at least was showing some sympathy if not outright support.

There was a table and two chairs. From somewhere the mess manager had conjured a coffee-maker with cups, powdered milk and sugar. No spoons though. Ricky wondered whether it was an oversight or if the man had been ordered not to supply anything that may be construed as a weapon.

Ann, he was permitted to call her that, had a clean foolscap pad on the desk with several ball-point pens of different colours. There was also a discreet digital voice recorder which was switched on as soon as she had taken it from her briefcase. She had not asked if he would permit its use but what the hell, she was on his side; maybe.

The first few minutes had been spent in idle chit-chat. She had poured them both coffee and given him the opportunity to admire the rear view. Great legs under a knee-length black skirt stretched tight across boyish hips below a narrow waist that spoke of hours at a gym somewhere. The rear view was as great as the front and that was saying something. Her face was a picture of smooth skin mottled discreetly by a smattering of becoming freckles, rosy lips and a slim nose of exactly the right length.

Ann did catch him staring and smiled. She was used to this and she used it. In her profession a beautiful face could get you places a double-first at London and Cambridge could not. But she had those too; Politics and Law. She had briefly considered a career in the former but had shied away from the thought.

She put down her coffee cup and picked up a pen. "Shall we start?"

The case had intrigued her from the beginning. Not from what little she'd read in the newspapers but a telephone call from an old friend who was in the know. She specialised in political law but it was profoundly boring and so had branched out with pleasing success into criminal matters. Over three years she had taken on twelve court cases and won them all. She was the risen star of her chambers with a reputation beyond her thirty-two years and a partnership to match.

She had not been quite straight with Ricky. There was no solicitor to begin with. She had subsequently bullied and charmed one of her contacts into taking on the role for the sake of the system. Solicitors were meant to instruct council, not the other way around but it was an ancient convention with which she played fast and loose when it suited her. Ricky was still staring at her. "Well?"

He grinned boyishly and pushed back his hair to cover his embarrassment. "Ah, yes, sorry. I didn't expect a barrister to look quite like you."

"It's a cross I have to bear. Now can we start?"

"What do you want to know?"

They ran through the basics. Full name, current address, rank, service history and decorations. Then they hit a brick wall.

"You have to tell me about this operation," Ann said.

"I don't know where I stand on that. It's classified."

"Look if I'm going to defend you I have to know the full story. I've been told that due to the sensitivity of the matter parts of the trial will be held in camera and much of this will not be in the public domain." She handed him a typewritten letter. "It's signed by your commanding officer and gives you permission to confide your story to me. I on the other hand have signed the Official Secrets Act on arriving at this establishment today."

Ricky slid the letter back to her. "If the boss says it's okay, that's good enough for me."

Ricky had an impressive turn of phrase when he put his mind to it and for over an hour she was lost in the dust and cold of Afghanistan, living the hardships and facing the danger with the man opposite her. He did not over-emphasise his own part but told it matter-of-factly. The attack on the complex had him squeezing his eyes closed as he relived the horror, the flashbacks coming thick and fast but he continued on. This wasn't just another debrief, this was real again and the emotion showed through with the anguished twist to his mouth, the clenched and trembling fists.

"Would you like to take a break," she asked after a daunting passage.

The eyes said yes but he shook his head. "I'd like to crack on now I've started or I might not be able to start again. This is very cathartic, much worse than I imagined it would be."

"Just take your time. If you want to stop we'll get another coffee and talk about something else for a while. Anything you're comfortable with."

Ricky gave her a taut grin. "I'll be glad when it's over and the story is out of my insides. Then maybe part of me can begin to heal. Not the raw part, not that part that now hates the army for allowing me to be dragged into the gutter. I'll not go quietly, I've determined that. As feeble in mind and body as I might be, I'm ready for the battle and it's going to be one hell of a fight."

★ ★ ★

Stu was tidying away some kit with Sponge and Pete when his mobile trilled out the *'Ride of the Valkyrie'*. Embarrassed, Stu flipped the cover as quickly as he could. It was Cowley.

"We're havin' a few jars at my place tonight. Come over around seven."

That was it. Cowley being cagey was not lost on Stu.

"Da, da, de, *DA*, da," Sponge grinned. "What was *that*?

"Don't be so pig ignorant," Pete said. "That's the regimental march of the Paras and you will stand to attention when it's played."

"Oh kiss my arse. And there was me thinkin' it was the *Hokey Cokey*," Sponge laughed. "But what I'd like to know is why our esteemed leader has it on his mobile. Is he gettin' just a teeny-weeny bit homesick for the Para Depot?"

"I got a special offer ringtone, okay. Sorry to have inflicted it on you. I hear your boys prefer *Greensleeves*."

Pete laughed.

"What?" Sponge said, aggrieved but not knowing why. "What's with this *Greensleeves*?"

"Some other time" Stu said grinning. "I've just been invited to a piss-up."

"Oh, great. What time and where?" Pete said. "I could do with a piss-up after all the crap that's been flying around."

"Not you, you're not invited. This is more for the older wankers amongst us."

Pete pulled a sad face. "Ours not to reason why. Probably because all the old farts can't stand the pace us youngsters set. I'll try hard to hide my disappointment. Changing the subject, I take it you two have both got letters from the Army Prosecuting Authority?"

"Yeah, I'm being called as a witness but we're not supposed to discuss it. That's what it said," Sponge said.

"Bollocks to that," Pete retorted. "It's crap. We talked about it before the case was brought, didn't we? If we all use the same phrases when we're describing things it's only to be expected, right? We all serve together, we live together, we fight together, we get pissed together, we're in it together, right?"

"All for one," Stu murmured.

"Yeah! That's it," Sponge said. "All for one and one for all, that's it, ennit."

"That's it, Sponge," Stu said, "Is that how you boys feel? D'you think we should back Major Keane or let him stew?"

"It's a no-brainer," Pete said. "We can't let the bastards grind him down. He might be a Rupert but he is one of us and he pulled his weight on that op, more than pulled his weight. He's a good lad, for a Rupert."

"I wasn't so sure about him to start with," Sponge muttered, "but he did okay. Right little Dervish he was."

"He's earned our respect and our support," Pete said. "We'll do what we have to do and if that means comparing notes before we give evidence, so be it."

"There's a bit more than that to it," Stu said. "You've already given statements so you can't wander too far from what you've already said without making yourselves look like turnip heads, or worse, liars. The best thing you can do is stick to the truth, stick to your stories no matter what crap they throw at you, okay?"

"Yeah, you're right, Stu," Pete said. "Those lawyers can tie you up in knots once they sense you're changing your story."

"Do the rest of the lads feel the same way as you two do?"

"Not so much. Then *they* weren't there, but there's a lot of anger about him being thrown to the wolves. Some of the guys are wondering what it's all about. Here's us standing up for democracy, fightin' the good fight, in the front line against global terrorism, and what thanks do we get? We get gang-banged by SIB. What's the point?" Sponge moaned.

"That a general opinion?"

"Everyone I've talked to thinks the same," Pete said. "Some of the blokes are thinking of chucking it in as not worth the candle any longer. Others, a minority, don't give a shit as long as there's a fight at the end of it. Those are the adrenalin junkies, not the thinking bayonets."

"Let's keep this conversation to ourselves for now," Stu said. "Especially let's not talk about the case where ear holes are wagging, just to be on the safe side. You never know who's listening."

★ ★ ★

It was standing room only in Cowley's small front room. Stu had a can of lager thrust into his hand and he glanced around at the faces as he ripped off the top. Cowley motioned him to a space behind the door and he took up a position leaning against the wall and sucking on the cold beer.

"Right, gentlemen," Cowley said. "You're all busting a gut to know what this is about so I'll tell you. But before I start is there anyone here who doesn't think that Major Keane has got the shit end of the stick?" He glanced around the serious faces and got nothing but nods. "That's what I thought. I've sounded a few people out who aren't here tonight for various operational reasons and it's virtually unanimous. The big question is, what can we do about it.?"

"Do we know if there's any substance in the charges?" One man asked.

"That's immaterial," another said. "From what I hear it was a combat situation, kill or be killed and no one should be hung for that."

Cowley tilted his can at Stu. "This man *was* there. Did you see anything that could be construed as a criminal act, Stu?"

"No sir, I did not," Stu said. "We were carrying out the orders we were given and protecting our own lives as best we could. When it kicked off everybody and his brother was shooting at us and we were shooting right back. We didn't have the firepower to win the fire fight and it came down to every bugger for himself but from where I was I honestly did not see Major Keane commit a criminal act and I was watching through a six-power scope. All he did was defend himself."

"That's good enough for me," Cowley said. "But the court martial will have to take care of itself. What we are here to discuss is something far more serious. It's nothing less that the revision of our Rules of Engagement and the protection of our soldiers from criminal charges laid against them as a direct result of combat.

"I'm not talking here about the man who goes off and cuts some poor sod's throat for his gold teeth, or rapes someone behind the cow sheds, they can have the book thrown at them for all I care, but the soldier who is fighting for his life and the life of his comrades must be secure in the knowledge that he has the full support of the government at all times. That is something that has been missing recently and it's damaging confidence and morale."

"What do you propose to do about it, Bill?" Someone said.

"That's what we are here to discuss tonight. My initial feeling is we take this to the Old Man and let him kick it upstairs."

"They won't take it seriously," another man said. "Brigadier SAS Group may be sympathetic and agree to pass it on but it'll just get stashed away in some file at the MoD."

"Cynic," Cowley said and it raised a small laugh. "But he's right. The most we can expect is someone from Division coming down to pour oil on troubled waters, soothe us, pat us on the back and usher us back into our boxes."

"Now who's being a cynic," the first man said.

"With good cause. No, what I propose, and we can all kick it around to get the rough edges off, is a multi-layered campaign that will start with the Old Man and move all the way up to the Chief of the General Staff if we have to. After that, if it doesn't work...well, we'll see. This is far too important for half measures."

Note: 3 - Appended

I *'ve received discovery from the prosecuting counsel and the evidence against my client appears damning. And yet. I have heard his side of the story and I have little doubt that he is a sincere, honest and courageous soldier who was doing his duty as he saw fit within the parameters of the orders he had been given.*

I took on this case as another opportunity to enhance my reputation as a serious defence barrister. Now, much to my amazement, I find that I am emotionally involved; a historical first. No one hearing his tale could have failed to be moved. That he is suffering mental anguish over the lives he has taken is obvious, as obvious as his physical wounds.

That the case is being brought is due to a complaint levelled by a Pakistan citizen that his two younger brothers were murdered as they went to fetch water from a stream. That they were shot mercilessly without warning and they were unarmed.

The story is given credence by an eye-witness, one Sayyid al-Shamrani, who had been employed by the British as an interpreter. His account differs from the accounts given by my client and by the soldiers nearby in that he claims the victims were shot without provocation and without the need. He says his position on a ledge above the plain where the Pakistan traders and the al-Qaeda group were resting gave him an ideal view of the circumstances.

Apparently Mr. al-Shamrani is due to fly into the country for the court martial, hence the haste in hearing the case. My argument that his visit should be delayed to allow me more time to build my defence has been met with the claim that the situation in Afghanistan is so fluid it may be impossible to get him for another time. The Trial Judge Advocate has ruled thus on it. It is a point with which I do not agree but have to concede as I have no evidence to the contrary and it is a pivotal piece of evidence in the case against my client.

I need to know more about Mr. al-Shamrani. I need to know of his background, how he came to be working for British forces in Afghanistan and his political allegiances. This will not be easy to discover. I have no knowledge of the country or its people other than that which I have read in the newspapers or seen on the TV. I don't know, but I know a man who will.

From what I have read of the opposition's case I believe that this will be a difficult one to win and it may well turn out to be the first defeat of my career.

Before today this may well have caused me to regret being so foolhardy as to take this case without proper consultation but now I am committed and I believe in the innocence of my client. In all conscience I cannot abandon him as others have done. Win or lose we are in this together.

AFP.
Lincolns Inn

Note 4 - Appended

T *he powerful Dictionary computers at GCHQ in Celtenham
are linked to the American owned Copperhead computer
which runs the Echelon system for the National Security Agency,
linked to GCHQ's listening station at Menwith Hill in Yorkshire.
Echelon is programmed to pick up on keywords such as names and
phrases in telephone conversations, e-mails, faxes and telexes and is
said to have the ability to scan 56,000 channels at any one time.
These messages are then automatically recorded and human operators
alerted as to the time, place and contact details of both the sender and
the recipient of the message. One such keyword was <u>al-Shamrani</u>. It
had been placed there by the Secret Intelligence Service on the advice
of the Central Intelligence Agency.*

*Targeted intercepts selected according to a list devised by the
various organizations signed up to Echelon, in this case the British
Security Service, are sent automatically to the GCHQ centre in
Palmer Street in London.*

*I was totally unaware that this system had the capabilities to spy
on every electronic communication in the country. It is not aimed at
the military but at ordinary businesses and individuals. When I first
learned of it I was horrified at the illegality of the system and its
ramifications for the rights of the individual to privacy. But this was
just the first of many such systems that I was to learn of in the
following days. Surprising, worrying, frightening, terrifying, what*

the government does in the name of security. Whose security? The public's, or the government's?

AFP.

Lincolns Inn.

Chapter Ten

"Hi, Ann. It's Richard, Richard Wells. You called me."
"Hi Richard, thanks for ringing back."
"No problem. You're lucky to have caught me though, I'm just off to Afghanistan for two months, embedded with the Americans. It should be fun."

"I think your talents are wasted as a journalist," Ann said. "You should have continued your work as an historian, that's what you were trained for."

"Not much money in that and far less excitement," Richard laughed. "I'm really enjoying this. Maybe I'll go back to history when I'm too old to enjoy myself quite so much, or the *Independent* kicks me out."

"Just be careful. I'm learning that Afghanistan is a very dangerous place. Which brings me to why I called you. I know you've written a book about al-Qaeda. Can I pick your brains?"

"Why not? Me saying no never stopped you before. Fire away."

Ann suppressed a smile. It was true, Richard had always been a fount of general knowledge which she had tapped into many times. "Have you ever come across anyone called al-Shamrani?"

"Al-Shamrani? Rings a bell. Hang on a second while I get my notes up. Al-Shamrani, al-Shamrani...yep, here it is. Al-Shamrani. There was an al-Shamrani associated with al-Qaeda a while ago. The one I'm thinking of was a member of the Farooq Brigade and close to bin Laden. He was involved in bombing the National Guard building in Riyadh back in '95 and the Saudis dealt with him by hacking off his head. Al-Shamrani is a Saudi tribal name, as far as I can figure it anyway."

"Not Afghan then?" Ann asked.

"Definitely not originally. Of course some al-Shamranis could have emigrated to Afghanistan. By that I mean moved there to fight in the Jihad and stayed to raise a family. The off-spring could be termed Afghan but they they'd still be quite young as al-Qaeda has only been in Afghanistan since bin Laden was chased out of Sudan in 1996 and the Taliban made him welcome."

"So you're saying that any grown up al-Shamranis in Afghanistan are likely to have gone there to fight for the Taliban, al-Qaeda and bin Laden?"

"That's a safe bet," Richard said. "There's always anomalies but why else would a Saudi give up the good life?"

"Thanks, Richard. You've been a great help."

"Really? In that case you can buy me dinner when I get back, a big one, I'll be twenty pounds lighter by then."

"You turn sideways and you'd disappear anyway. It's a deal. Stay safe."

"You bet. Bye."

Ann had recorded the conversation. She gave the disk to her secretary to transcribe and mused on the possibilities. It seemed that Sayyid al-Shamrani was not all he appeared to be.

★ ★ ★

The call was intercepted. The details were passed to 'F' Branch of the British Security Service and its spreading domestic surveillance empire. A file was opened and resources allocated. The hare was running.

Phone bugs were put in place, hidden surveillance cameras and microphones installed and computers hacked into as the mighty secret apparatus of the State applied itself to the task. Soon the file began to thicken as intelligence came in.

The initial recording went to MI5's case officer, from there to his contact at the Home Office who called Stan Hathaway who agreed to a meeting at Thames House. When he arrived he was not in the best of moods.

"Bit of a fly in the ointment, the case officer said. "Keane's barrister has dug up some dirt on your star witness."

"So?"

"Seems he's working for al-Qaeda, or has in the past."

"Shit," Hathaway whispered the word like it was another poor news day.

"What are you doing about it?"

"What do you want me to do about it? The intel has just come in, we haven't yet taken a view on the ramifications but it probably means your witness's testimony is worth squat."

"What do we know about this Sayyid wotsisname?" Hathaway asked.

"Only what it says here. One of his distant relatives was al-Qaeda in the past and was executed by the Saudis for blowing up one of their installations. SIS is in the loop and they're making enquiries. I don't think there's much doubt. "FitzPatrick's informant is one of the best in the business. We've used him ourselves from time-to-time."

"Jesus. Does it get any worse?"

"I'll say again. What would you like us to do?"

Hathaway eyed the man from under his bushy eyebrows. He knew what he was being asked. "Options?"

"Few. You could drop the case as it seems to hang on this man's testimony. You could go ahead and hope for the best. You could play the fool and say you were duped and sling al-Shamrani in jail as soon as he sets foot in the UK, or we could go on the offensive."

Hathaway grunted this was more his style. He had never run away from a fight and the soft options were really no options at all. "How? No, don't tell me, I don't wants to know. Just make sure nothing comes back to you or me. Clean and clinical, okay?"

★ ★ ★

"Walk with me," Ricky said.

Ann cocked an enquiring eyebrow. "Are you allowed out?"

Ricky nodded. "Anywhere in the camp, otherwise it's an escort at all times beyond the perimeter and I can't be bothered with that."

He led her out into the cool air. "Place get's claustrophobic."

"Is that all?"

He pulled a face. "Maybe you'll call me crazy but I get an odd feeling of intrusion lately. Nothing you can pin down. It's just like you've suspected someone of pawing through your knickers drawer."

"You think the prosecution would stoop to eavesdropping? Come on, surely not."

"I don't know." He thrust his hands in his pockets. "Maybe. I wouldn't put it past them. Somebody's obviously taking an interest in me.

"You know, when I was lying in the dirt with the Saudi waving his knife around, I saw vultures circling. Way up in the sky to start with but getting lower all the time. I don't know how they do it, how they smell death so fast. Now I'm feeling the same. It's like the vultures are circling again but these are far more dangerous."

He was down again and not the way Ann needed him. "I do have some good news," she said and told him about al-Shamrani.

Ricky whistled softly. "Son...of...a...bitch. The bastard was all over us like best mates and all the time he was stitching us up."

"It would seem that way but I've been over the transcripts of your men's testimonies and could find nothing that would suggest he was on the opposing side."

"No, he seemed kosher. Stu Dalgleish said he'd met him before and he'd lent a hand in a fire fight with the Taliban. Even took out a machine gun that was causing them grief. Why would he do that?"

"That's not in my notes. I'll have to get back to Sergeant Dalgleish and get him to enlarge on the subject. Is there anything you can think of that might help? Anything that happened during your operation?" Ann asked, fishing for more.

"Fraid my memory's shot in parts. There was something though...let me think. Yeah, one of the Tajiks. It was Abdullah, he told Stu he didn't trust Haji because he wasn't a Tajik. I put it down to tribalism but it seems he was proved right."

"His family name is Saudi," Ann said, "and his given name is Sayyid.

Ricky whistled tunelessly. "Afghan-Arab. Those are the real hardliners. Al-Qaeda pros. A lot of the Taliban are just local tribesmen with little military training but the Arabs have been through the al-Qaeda camps. All Sharia hardliners, just like the Pathans. Everybody called him Haji though. Must be a nickname.

"I've just remembered a couple of things. Haji led us over a mountain but at a crucial point he was taking us in the wrong direction. If it hadn't been for Abdullah we would never have caught the al-Qaeda group. He also knew that the weather was going to close in. Maybe he hoped it would stop us. It's conjecture but now we know what we know things are starting to add up."

"Could you have caught the al-Qaeda people any other way?" Ann asked.

"Doubt it. It was possible but not probable. When Haji mentioned the shortcut I jumped at it."

"So it was Haji's idea to go over the mountain."

"Oh yes," Ricky said. "The cunning bastard, I can see it all now. I was led by the nose." He grinned his boyish grin and for the first time since she had met him Ann saw the man he really was. But the clouds settled on him again too quickly. She tried to lighten the conversation, take it away from the case for a further moment of respite.

"Ricardo is an odd name for a British soldier."

He snorted. "Not these days. Little league of nations we are. There are some really good blokes with monikers that sound as alien as someone from *Star Trek*. Funny names but good lads; good soldiers. And most with a British accent you could cut with a knife. Geordie, Scouse, Cockney, Tyke, Welsh, Irish and not forgetting the Scots. They're all good lads to have with you in a scrap."

"But Ricardo? You're as English as Stilton cheese,' Ann said.

"I was actually born in South America. Colombia to be exact. My dad was a coffee grower. He and mum moved out there before I was born."

"Why did you leave?"

They were passing a low brick wall and Ricky stopped and motioned Ann to sit. His leg was giving him gyp and the foot was not far behind in the pain stakes. "I usually tell everyone it was because mum got homesick but the reality was that we barely escaped with our lives. The Medallin Cartel, the big cocaine smuggling gang, came up with the bright idea of shipping their drugs out with coffee to fool the sniffer dogs in the States. Most of our coffee went to the US, it was a big market for Arabica beans with the North American Roasters, huge for us and huge for the Cartel's drugs too.

"Dad wouldn't have it and said so. That didn't go down too well with the Cartel bosses and you've heard what they can do if they get pissed-off with someone.

"We were tipped off by a friend of dad's in the Coffee Growers Federation and we got out just in time with enough cash to get ourselves from Quibdo to Arauca on the Venezuelan border without leaving a trail the Cartel's tame police could follow. Using credit cards is a dead giveaway.

"Naturally I thought it was great fun, not having any inkling at nine years old what would happen if the Cartel caught up with us. Dad was a natural at it. Escape and evasion? He could have written the book on it.

"Anyway, to cut a long story short we managed to get back to the UK. Dad sold his share of the business to his partners and we set up home here. He's a canny old bugger, my dad, he had salted away the best part of his salary in a British bank all the time we were over there so we weren't short of a bob or two and survived extremely well until he managed to land a job as a coffee broker.

"Which brings me to something I've been meaning to ask you. Who's paying for your services?"

The suddenness of the question caught Ann unawares. She thought she had prepared herself for this moment, had known the question would be asked eventually, but it still dropped like a bombshell. Her silence dragged on for what seemed to her like minutes. She had to say something. She really did not want to lie to him. "There are a few cases I take each year pro bono. When your case was brought up it caught my imagination."

"So you're doing this for free?"

"I expect to win and that will enhance my reputation and bring its own rewards."

"But this case will be held mainly in camera. Is anyone going to hear about it?"

"There will be plenty of interest believe me. The papers will be all over the bits that can be reported. Whoever's leaking to the press will make sure of that. The news will get around in legal circles too," Ann said, still flustered. "That's where the majority of my work will come from." She was prevaricating and he could tell but the truth had to be withheld from him; for now.

He stood and walked a couple of strides before turning. "Shall we go back?"

She did not want to leave it on a low note. "Was that why you joined the army? The memory of your exciting escape from Colombia must have left a powerful impression."

"Now you come to mention it maybe it did have a bearing. That and being brought up in the open air." He was limping now and trying not to grimace. He had left his stick behind in a fit of machismo and was now suffering for it. Ann came alongside him and slipped under his arm. She said nothing as she took his weight.

He could see the top of her blonde head as he looked down and felt her strength take the strain. This way they made their slow way back to his room where she helped him into a seat.

"Thanks." It was all he said.

Ann just nodded, making little of it but had to admit her heart had beat a little faster at the feel of his hard body against hers. It was something she would have to watch.

★　★　★

Bill Cowley was sitting uncomfortably in the Colonel's spartan office fiddling with a spoon balanced on the saucer of a coffee cup he'd been handed.

Colonel Tim Bailey was just stirring three sugars into his own cup before turning to face Cowley. "What's up, Bill?"

Cowley was nervous. It was an alien emotion and it disturbed him. He did not know Bailey well but was sure the other man could sense his nervousness and he did not want to show any weakness that could be utilised. He had requested this meeting and as the senior warrant officer he was granted one without delay. It had to be important. "Bit of a problem, boss."

Bailey sipped at his cup and raised an eyebrow. "I sort of guessed that. What kind of problem?"

"It's over this case with Major Keane, boss. The boys don't like it, too close to home. They figure if the government can charge an officer then chances are they'll be next."

"Major Keane has admitted to killing two civilians. You know we can't be seen to condone murder. It's bad PR for the army at the very least. These things have to be seen to be done."

"Yeah, just like every other trial of this kind. On and on until they get the result they want regardless of the truth of the matter," Cowley said bitterly. "There are always witnesses with axes to grind."

"You think that's true in this case?"

"I've heard what our boys have to say about it and I can't see a case to answer."

"Then it will all come out in the wash," Bailey said.

"Maybe it will and maybe it won't. It depends on how much the government wants a conviction. They can load the dice pretty heavily. That's the problem as the boys see it. There's no trust there, no trust between the Toms and the suits. They'd like some official backing; they'd like it formalised so that soldiers in action, in a hot zone or fire fight can't be charged for defending themselves or their mates whatever the circumstances."

"I'm no lawyer, Bill but I can't see how that can be done. It'll give carte-blanche to a few hotheads who can't control themselves. It would be a killer's charter."

"I can see that in some circumstances but there should be a system in place that can deal with those situations," Cowley said. "The onus must be on our boys being able to fight without having both hands tied behind their backs. Northern Ireland was one thing. It's part of the United Kingdom and it makes sense to have a code that reflects that. Abroad it's different. People have different ways and they think and act differently. Take The Stan. Patrols are often fired on by insurgents and then the locals all join in. It's tribal and us Brits are just another tribe. Everyone's got a gun and everyone uses us for target practice. None of them are innocent bystanders. Yet all they have to do is put their weapon down and suddenly they're non-combatants. Well it won't wash any longer. It won't wash with the men outside and it won't wash with the rest of the green army."

"What do you want me to say, Bill? We're soldiers, we put up with it and crack on. Always have and always will. It's our job, it's what we're paid to do."

"Look, boss. I know this is difficult but we must find a way around this. The politicians have to be convinced that they can't treat us like an extension of the civilian world. All that human rights stuff may be okay for them but it shouldn't be allowed to take precedence over tactical considerations, it shouldn't be at the expense of needlessly endangering the lives of service people by making unworkable rules and then punishing soldiers who ain't able to abide by them.

"I don't think any of the government has a day's service to their names. They don't know what any military service is like, let alone being on the FEBA or stuck in a fire fight with the Taliban without enough ammo or support to win it. Someone ought to be telling them and it can't come from the Toms. It's got to come from high up in the chain of command."

Bailey could see Cowley's point of view, in fact he endorsed it, but he was in no position to sympathise, his situation was invidious. However much he agreed with his soldiers he could not be seen to be actively supporting them. Discipline had to be maintained. "I hear what you're saying, Bill."

"Will you pass it on, boss? We need to know something's happening and soon."

"I'll discuss it with the Brigadier at our next meeting. But don't push it, Bill. These things take time."

Bailey didn't know it but time was in short supply.

Chapter Eleven

Stu had gone covert. His years working undercover in Northern Ireland had taught him all the tradecraft he needed to stay out of sight. It was possible he was already being watched, if not it would happen as time passed, as the security services took an interest in him.

He had walked into this with his eyes open. He had not taken much persuading; he had leapt at it. His career was on the line, even maybe his life if things got really rough but his career was going nowhere and risking his life was what he did for a living; no change there, then.

He had taken a few days leave and a lift into Hereford, then onto a bus to London, so far so good, no sign of a tail. The bus had stopped at Leigh Delamare Services for a break and he had checked the people off it and back on again. There was no one remotely resembling a follower amongst the senior citizens and college kids who used the cheap service midweek. But he really wasn't bothered yet. For now they could follow all they liked. Maybe there was one on the bus, one of the kids with a 2-way radio disguised as an MP3 player. Maybe there was a tail car following in case he switched rides. It was a matter of professional pride that he could spot them but that was all. He would assume they were there.

At Victoria Coach Station he bought a ticket to Peterborough and waited around for the service to board. The bus had a front and rear entry. He boarded at the front and took his seat next to the rear door. At the last minute he left his seat and leapt out of the door just as it was hissing closed.

He ran out of the bus station, along Buckingham Palace Road to the tube station, watching his reflection in passing car windows and shops, looking with his peripheral vision to see if anyone had panicked and rushed to follow him.

He dived down the underground bought a ticket at a machine and made for the Victoria Line. The station was crammed with surveillance cameras and he knew the feeds could be intercepted.

It was getting busier, building up for the rush hour which suited him as the trains were more frequent and the crowds would help to mask his movements. He strolled along the southbound platform as a train entered the station and its doors slid open. He squeezed on board but stood just inside the door with his head out glancing along the platform as if watching for a friend. Again at the last minute he stepped off the train and looked to see if anyone did the same. No one did but the cameras at either end of the platform would have made close physical surveillance superfluous and the lack of reaction meant nothing. The train pulled out as a rush of people entered the platform trying to catch the departing service. There was an almost audible collective groan as they realised they had missed the train and a general milling around as they sought seats or somewhere to stand to read the *Evening Standard*. Stu mingled with them sauntering to the exit that led across to the northbound platform to join another crowd that was gathering as a rush of oily air signified a train was approaching. He let himself be propelled across on the tide and onto the northbound train.

He got off at Green Park and turned into the Park itself where he found a secluded bench. He pulled a baseball cap from his pocket and put it on with the peak low over his eyes, turned his reversible jacket inside-out and balanced a pair of ancient Ray Bans on his nose. The lenses were unfashionably big and covered a large part of his upper face.

He spent a few minutes studying where the traffic cameras were sited and which way they were pointing. He now knew he wasn't being physically followed but cameras were an easy option for watchers and trackers and difficult to avoid. He waited until the closest camera had turned to peer south down Piccadilly and walked out of the park and into the elegant Jermyn Street, home of the famous London shirt makers. Jermyn Street paralleled Piccadilly. It wasn't so overlooked but just as busy with office workers on their way home.

With his baseball cap low over his eyes and his ancient Ray Bans hooked in place nobody paid him much attention. Half the capital wore dark glasses after nightfall, the kings and queens of cool and the don't-mess-with-me hardcases, all hiding their inadequacies behind tinted shades. Baseball caps too were de rigueur, even amongst the elderly and the tourists that thronged the place at all hours. His was nondescript and of uncertain colour, nothing that would stand out.

He bought another ticket at a machine in Piccadilly Circus tube station and took the Bakerloo line one stop to Charing Cross before changing once again, for the hell of it, to the Northern Line for the short ride down to Waterloo.

Now his jacket was tied around his waist like a French tourist, the baseball cap back in his pocket. Expensive Safari shades had replaced the Ray Bans and a red check Jordanian-style scarf wound loosely around the lower half of his face to help fool the facial recognition technology of the ever-present cameras.

Another ticket bought at a machine, this one to Surbiton but he left the train at Kingston, walking the short distance along Kingston Hill until he reached Ladderstile Gate that led into the wide expanse of Richmond Park. It was fully dark now with few lights but he kept to the track using a small Maglite. He then switched it off and slid into a stand of trees to see if anyone had followed him. He had the place to himself; after fifteen minutes he was satisfied that the occasional passer-by was just that and he kept undercover threading his way through the trees to the RV 300 metres from Robin Hood Gate.

He checked his watch. He was right on time.

A shape detached itself from behind a nearby tree but it was only a deer grazing and he relaxed. Then a twig snapped behind him and he turned. "You'll have to do better than that, boss."

"It was worth a try. Glad to see you're on the ball."

Stu grinned in the dark but got serious. "Where do we go from here?"

The night shrouded figure shrugged. "We had to have this meeting to get the ground rules sorted. From now on it will be too dangerous to contact each other directly. Phones, e-mails, texts et cetera are all out and we'll use dead letter drops around Hereford so that you don't have to travel too far in future to find them."

"This is going to be big, boss. We'll have all sorts of shit down on our heads when this gets going," Stu said.

"Maybe it won't be necessary. Maybe the government will see sense and we can ditch this but I doubt if they're that reasonable."

Stu stared into the darkness as another deer blew through its nostrils. "I've set the ball rolling. Everyone's waiting on the response from the chain of command but it's in hand. We're ready to move as soon as you give the word."

He paused and watched the black shapes of more deer slowly munching their way across the open space fifty metres away. It was a good sign; where there were deer there were no hidden watchers. "You sure you're okay with this, boss? It's a big burden to carry."

"It's time something was done and I can't see any other way out than this, Stu. It's going to create a helluva stink but I can't see any alternative. I've laid out the plan of action." A hand came out and pressed a small USB flash drive into Stu's palm. "It's coded and ready to burst transmit on receipt of the codeword. Keep it safe. For communications we'll use the regimental intranet when we're on the start line. Code is Valkyrie, that's why I sent you the ringtone. It has to be played on a Quicktime player to get the file to unlock."

Stu smiled in the darkness. "Very apt, boss."

★ ★ ★

Tim Bailey, the acting commanding officer of the 22nd Special Air Service Regiment, was a privileged man and he knew it. Most half-colonels would have given their back teeth to command the most professional and feared army unit in the world. Probably their canines and incisors too. It was that prestigious and a job open only to few on their way up the greasy pole of the chain of command. His turn had come after his predecessor had taken time out attending a course at Camberley and he was determined to make the most of his brief chance until the man's inevitable return.

Many famous generals had commanded the unit before him. Big shoes to fill and under normal circumstances he had no qualms about following in those illustrious footsteps.

The Director SAS Group was a Brigadier and long-standing colleague. They had served in the Regiment together, albeit the Brigadier had been a squadron commander and he a lowly subaltern at the time but they had got on well. He too was new to the job and finding his feet. He was a man with much to prove and ambitious with it. His plum job was his stepping stone to higher command and he was determined to come through with his unblemished record intact. Now his instincts for self-preservation were wildly semaphoring their danger signals like a scout on speed.

"You say you want me to push this request for a review of ROE upstairs, Tim? And intercede on Keane's behalf?"

"It's not me, boss. I'm merely passing on the message from the men. I have to say I do have a lot of sympathy for their point of view."

"As do I, Tim, as do I. But you of all people must know that it's not that simple. Throughout its history the Regiment has had to fight for its existence. I'm led to believe that it was almost disbanded under Harold Wilson's government back in the '60s and if it had not been for the PLO terrorist attack on the Israelis at the Olympics in 1972, which gave it the spur to become the world's leading anti-terrorist unit, it may well have gone then. The powers-that-be have never understood how to properly use the Regiment in its traditional role and what they don't understand they axe.

"The point is Special Forces are at a crossroads now. In a way the family silver has been sold off. The government has hired out the Regiment to other armies and police organisations the world over to train them in counter-terrorist and counter-insurgency tactics and how to be the world's best bodyguards. This expertise was the Regiment's stock in trade and, now it's been shared, its value to our government has decreased to the point where once again there are whispers that the Regiment has reached its sell-by date."

"I've heard that too," Bailey said. "Not from outside but from sources within the Regiment. Some of the old hands think the same way. They don't advocate it but they can see the writing on the wall. The Special Reconnaissance Regiment will eventually take over a lot of the tasks that the SAS do now and we will be helping to train them to do it. That really only leaves the counter-terrorist and fire-fighting roles and many police forces are now pressing the Home Office to take on CT themselves rather than calling us in to help out."

"Yes, some of the police forces are getting a little above themselves, sometimes with disastrous results. But it also doesn't help that a member of the Det was involved in a major cock-up recently. That didn't go down too well in high places.

"So you see, Tim, now's not the time to rock the boat. This business with Keane is unfortunate but it must run its course without any interference from us. It may be unfair to Keane but he is an experienced officer and should have been aware of the consequences of his actions. I'm afraid it will be up to the court martial to decide his fate.

"And there's your own career to consider. You're acting OC at the moment. I assume that you would like to make it more permanent at some time in the future. So you need to manage this, Tim. I know that some of the senior men can be bloody-minded on occasion but you are in command and you'll need to get them to wind their necks in over this. It won't do you or the Regiment any favours otherwise."

Bailey could see the way the wind was blowing, reinforced, if reinforcement was needed, by the Brigadier's use of third-party language. He was distancing himself in favour of a head below the parapet approach. It was understandable but not something that he could admire. It was politics. Sometimes a man just had to stand up for what he believed in and damn the consequences.

"I hear what you're saying, sir but I would be failing in my duty to the men if I did not press the ROE problem with you."

"Very, well. I can't see any harm in raising the question with Division. That's the best I can do. Don't hold your breath, Tim. I can't see much coming from this."

* * *

Hathaway was not a happy man. The information collected on those connected with the trial was inconclusive. Some of the soldiers had been away on operations but the ones who weren't had not been under a strict surveillance regime and that worried him.

The MI5 case officer, who Hathaway knew as Smith, looked at him across an array of computer equipment where he was hunkered down alongside two technicians who were wearing headsets and boom microphones. Both were chatting away in technospeak to others on the net. As he stood he tapped one of them on the shoulder and got a nod in return.

Smith was middle-aged with close-cropped hair combed into a Caesar fringe that made no attempt to hide his growing bald spot. He was average height and his solid build attested to his past as a successful field officer. Smith may or may not have been the man's real name; Hathaway didn't much care at this point in time, although he might well make it his business to find out if the man failed to perform to his expectations. "Well?"

"We've got FitzPatrick sewn up tight," Smith said. "Telephone taps, cameras and audio bugs in her chambers, her computer logged into our surveillance net, just about everything she says or does is recorded. We have the whole of her current defence case on record. There's nothing there that we don't know about."

Hathaway grunted. He had always felt it was a weakness of the British legal system to allow the defence full discovery of the prosecution's case without a quid pro quo. He did not know how many laws were being broken here but it was a very satisfying position to be in. He was sure that their spying would be covered under terrorism legislation somewhere in the small print.

"What about the witnesses, these other soldiers who were on the patrol with Keane? What are they up to?" Hathaway asked.

"Not seen as a high priority. Their statements have been given to the SIB and there's not much they can add to them now."

"I don't trust anybody," Hathaway said. "There's no knowing what they might be getting up to while our backs are turned. I need to knows that they're not being privately briefed. I need to knows who they see, where and when. I don't wants no slip-ups in this case, the government's depending on you to make sure this is all tied up long before it goes to court."

"That's going to cost more money," Smith said, "a lot more money. Surveillance is expensive. We don't have the personnel to cover all these guys without calling in some additional help from freelance agencies. Are you sanctioning that?"

"Look, Smith, this is your operation and important eyes are on you. You have to do what you has to do because if this goes tits up it'll be your head on the block, mate."

Smith had dealt with people like Hathaway before. Good at promising carrots and waving sticks but never very good at leaving a paper trail. If he did what Hathaway was demanding his fingerprints would be on it and not Hathaway's. If any shit was to fly he would collect it, not Hathaway.

"I'd really need written authorisation for expenditure of that kind, you've no idea what the bean-counters are like here."

"Get real," Hathaway sneered. "You'll digs the money up from somewhere. Raid the coffee fund, take a loan out on your pension rights. You really don't have a choice."

Smith nodded again, a signal to his techie to turn off the recording equipment. That was good enough for him. Whatever recoil there might be he had covered his back. He'd like to see Hathaway talk his way out of the recording that had just been made.

He looked at his techie. "Call up all the mug shots of the military witnesses and cross reference them to any unusual recent sightings. Anything outside their normal areas." He turned back to Hathaway. This might take a while. I'd offer you a coffee but it seems we can't afford it now."

"Ha bloody ha," Hathaway said. There was no venom in it, he had got his own way.

"We have a sighting on one," the techie said after an hour. "Victoria coach station. The FRS picked him up yesterday."

"That's facial recognition software," Smith said. "Not all the bugs out of it yet but it's useful stuff."

"That's funny," the techie murmured.

Hathaway's nose twitched. "What is?"

"This bloke's just employed a classic counter-surveillance technique. Why would he bother?"

"Which man is it?" Smith asked.

"Sergeant Stuart Dalgleish, currently attached to 22 SAS from 3 Para."

"What's he doing now?" Hathaway asked.

"He's legging it along Buckingham Palace Road. Now he's crossing and running into the Tube."

The techie spent another thirty minutes tracking Dalgleish along platforms and up and down escalators before he eventually lost him at the exit to Green Park Station. Several more minutes fruitless checking the feeds to roadside and bus lane cameras failed to turn up the target. "Sorry, sir. We've lost him."

"Shit," Hathaway swore softly. "What's he up to? He must have something to hide acting like that. I know the bastard's SAS but he wouldn't normally act like that, would he?"

"Not unless he suspected he was being followed and that hints at a guilty conscience," Smith said.

"I told you it was important to keep tabs on these men," Hathaway said. "Christ, there's no telling what they've all been up to."

"Full surveillance from now on it is then," Smith mumbled. "I'll contact a few bodies and get them organised."

"Do that and do it soon," Hathaway said. "Let's keep the lid on this. I don't wants any nasty surprises."

He left them to it and Smith hunkered down once again behind the computers. "Do you still have the recorder on?"

The techie shook his head. "Turned it off when you told me to."

"There's a bulb still lit on the camera."

The Techie pulled a face. "Must be a fault." He hit a button on his keyboard and the light went out. "There you go."

Smith stood to his full height and stretched. The camera bothered him slightly. Maybe someone should take a look at it. He'd ring maintenance in the morning.

In a small room at the Falconbury Orchard Hotel in Hereford his image, together with that of Hathaway and the techies was carefully saved to a USB drive.

Note 5 - Appended

*T*here is a housing development opposite the gates of Credenhill. It is set back across an open car park but some of the properties overlook the distant main gate with its fencing topped with rolls of razor wire. Many of the houses are owned by military personnel, some away on attachment or on accompanied tours which meant the wives or partners go too, leaving the family home empty or leased-out. It was one of these which was quietly occupied and the "To Rent" sign taken down.

They were an odd couple but the neighbours had no real qualms about the newcomers.

Over the following few days they may have had cause to wonder briefly why the curtains were always kept closed and why there was a succession of visitors at odd hours but there was nothing unduly worrying about the comings and goings, just family and friends helping them to settle in.

AFP.

Lincolns Inn

Chapter Twelve

In the back bedroom an array of visual and audio equipment linked to lap-top computers took up the space meant for the happy couple's double bed which was stacked against one wall. Collapsible picnic tables held a variety of used coffee cups and pizza boxes, some filled with part-eaten food. The new 'mistress' of the house sat well back inside the room with her feet up on a packing case and one eye pressed to the eyepiece of a 60-power telescope mounted on a solid carbon-fibre tripod. Alongside her, mounted on a similar tripod, was a state-of-the-art digital DVD camera with telescopic lenses linked to a laser powered directional microphone. The set-up was wired directly to a lap-top with a high-speed broadband connection to the computers at Thames House.

She was in her late thirties with brown hair cut very short in a mannish style highlighted by a wide streak of crimson running the full length of the right side of her head, Her nose may once have been broken as it was thickened across the bridge. Her eyes were blue and guileless and her mouth wide and generous. She looked both comfortable and dangerous; comfortable because of her mumsy face and open countenance and dangerous because the extreme haircut promised something racy beneath. The haircut was a mistake on this job and she knew it. It set her apart and got her noticed. If she had the time she would have found herself a wig but there had been no time to prepare for this emergency job.

Her 'husband' came in with a coffee cup in his hand.

"That mine?"

"Fuck off! Get your own. Anything happening?"

"Shit's happening all over the world and we're stuck in this feckin' place keeping tabs on some nasty boys." She affected a southern Irish accent when it suited her. "You know who lives over there don't you?"

"Don't give a shit. Just another job as far as I'm concerned." He was a large-boned ex-copper from the Met called Ken. An ex PT17 firearms officer who was learning surveillance on the job. Mo Maurice was mildly disgruntled at having to babysit a novice but he was all that was available in the time they had to put the twelve-man surveillance team together. He had his talents, she was sure.

"If you don't know, I'll tell you. Over there is the home of the 22nd Special Air Service Regiment. The feckin' Sass. And we have to keep surveillance on them. It's a monster, Ken, a feckin' monster. If they find out we can expect not just to get caught but to get a good kickin' into the bargain. What those blokes don't know about surveillance and counter-surveillance isn't even worth writing on the back of the proverbial.

"So, what are you saying?" Ken asked. "Maybe we should jack it in and get out of here?"

"That would be sensible. That would be more than sensible but it doesn't pay the bills does it? The boss says to watch out for some blokes and we'll do it to the best of our ability. What I'm saying is that we have to be as professional as they are if we're not to get sussed."

"And what makes you such an expert?"

Mo had spent a tour with the Det in Northern Ireland in the mid 1990s watching the hardcases and terrorists at close quarters. There, if you got sussed, you were likely to end up tortured and dead so you didn't make mistakes. Since then she had been a soldier of fortune working close protection for a variety of clients, most of whom she hated and wouldn't have minded being given the good news; apart from the damage it would have done to her professional reputation. Then she had signed on with the agency and got involved with all sorts of government work. It was regular and paid well even if the hours were manic when on a job. She had been married twice and divorced twice because of it.

She wasn't about to share her life story with a stranger so she said, "because I *know* what I'm doing, dickhead."

She took her eye away from the telescope for the first time since Ken had entered the room and rubbed it. "Your turn, I'm going cross-eyed."

"What do I do if I spot someone on the list?"

"The camera is linked to FRS. It's recording automatically. You just need to be aware if you suspect one of the targets is on the move and radio the boys in the mobiles to give them the SP. They'll need to know the make of any car, the colour and the index number. How many up is useful too and in which direction they're turning when they leave the camp. That's about it. Just remember not to get too close to the window.

★ ★ ★

Ann FitzPatrick drove into the outer car park at Credenhill, retrieved her briefcase from the back seat of her

Mercedes and blipped the car closed. She turned towards the main gate and two men climbed out of a car nearby.

"Miss FitzPatrick?"

Ann turned, a quizzical half-smile forming. "Who's asking?"

"Can you come with us please?"

"Sorry, I'm here for a meeting."

"We know, just get in the car, quickly please."

Her briefcase was pulled from her hand and a strong arm reached around her and moved her forcibly towards the car which was parked with its doors open and engine running.

"What are you doing?" It was all that she could say in the time as she was pushed with surprising ease onto the back seat of the car. One man climbed in with her and the other slid into the driver's seat and had the vehicle moving before the doors were closed.

Now Ann was becoming frightened as the car exited the car park. "Who are you?" She pulled her elbow free from the man's grip.

Neither man replied. The driver's eyes were constantly on his mirrors and he steered the car along country lanes at ever-increasing speed. Suddenly he veered left into a narrow lane and braked hard. Ann was pitched forward and by the time she had regained her balance the doors were opened and she was manhandled into a second car with two other men. This too took off with spinning wheels and the rattle of gravel under the wheel arches.

"Where are you taking me?" her voice was steady and it surprised her as her stomach was doing flip-flops.

The driver glanced into his mirror at her but did not reply. She could not see but his foot was on a switch in the footwell and he started to speak. It was a jumble of words and numbers and Ann could make neither head nor tail of it. "Are you speaking to me?"

"Relax," the man next to her said.

They drove further this time but once again they screeched to a halt alongside yet another car and she was pushed and dragged from one vehicle to the other. Her head was in a whirl and she did not immediately recognise the man sitting next to her on the rear seat.

"Sorry for the drama, ma'am."

She looked at him now. "Sergeant Dalgleish?"

He grinned. "Yes. You wanted to talk to me again. Privacy is a bit lacking in the camp of late and I thought it would be better if we got away from there."

"Why the cold war spy stuff?"

Stu grinned again. "Yeah, it may seem a bit OTT but we had to make sure we're not being followed."

"That's a little paranoid, isn't it?"

"No ma'am, it's very paranoid and for good reason. Don't forget I've been in this business for years and I know what can be done. By the way, your office may be comprehensively bugged. I had one of the lads sweep Ricky's room and we found a couple of audio devices. It's becoming standard practice."

"Standard practice for whom?"

"The Security Service. They've put MI5 onto this," Stu said.

"Who has?" Ann was beginning to become perplexed.

"Someone in the government. This case is important to them and they want to keep tabs on how it's going."

"I've never heard of anything like it."

"Get used to it. It's going to happen a lot from now on," Stu said, guessing it would become a self-propagating prophecy.

"There's such a thing as attorney-client privilege. They can't do that."

"They can if they don't think they'll get caught. You complain and the kit will disappear into thin air and you'll end up looking like an over-reacting menopausal woman. It won't do much for your credibility.

"We've left Ricky's bugs in place. We don't want them to know we're on to them. Just remember to take it easy with the delicate stuff when you're in there. What you have to realise is they managed to get bugs placed into one of the most secure facilities in Britain so your office would be a doddle."

"I don't understand this; at least I do but I'm not sure how to cope with it."

Stu patted her hand but took his own away when self-consciousness overcame him. "Sorry! I can help you there though, give you a few tips. You know about double-entry book-keeping? Maybe you should try something similar. Have a dummy case for the peepers to look at but keep all the explosive stuff outside the office.

"Work on a standalone computer. Keep the files and the computer somewhere really safe. It's not a hundred percent certain to fool them if they catch on but it will be okay as long as they think they're locked into your real files."

"This is all getting very silly. This is Britain, they shouldn't be able to do these things," Ann muttered.

"Times change, ma'am. 9/11 changed them. I'm all for keeping the country secure but when it's used for someone's political expediency, where it's nothing to do with terrorism, then it's an abuse of power and has to be dealt with."

"Hear, hear, Sergeant Dalgleish, I can identify with that."

"It's Stu, ma'am. You're not one of these human rights obsessives, are you?" He said it with a twinkle in his eye which was not lost on Ann.

"Different chambers. But I can't deny there's plenty of money to be made in that neck of the woods."

Stu grinned. She was sharp and he liked that. "What did you want to ask me? With all this I'd nearly forgotten the reason we met."

Ann pulled her briefcase to her and took out her recorder. "It's something Major Keane said that needs clarification."

"About Haji?"

Ann nodded, "Hmm, yes. He said that you told him about a fight with the Taliban where Haji helped you."

"That's right. We had just initiated a contact with the Taliban and called in an air strike. It was a bit of a nightmare and one of the lads took a whack from shrapnel. We were trying to sneak our way out when Haji opened up on a couple of Taliban soldiers. God knows why he did it. My thoughts at the time were that he was trying to help us escape and his inexperience, coupled with his hate for the Taliban, got the better of his common-sense. He subsequently told me his wife was murdered by the Taliban mullahs for listening to the radio, so it sort of made sense that he should lose it big time. Now maybe I think he was trying to let the Taliban know where we were and he miscalculated the reaction.

"They opened up on us and all hell let loose. We were pinned down by a heavy calibre machine gun and Haji took it out with an RPG...er Rocket Propelled Grenade. Russian-made. Afghanistan's full of them."

Ann pursed her lips and then smiled. "It's okay, you don't need to explain all the jargon. What I don't know I'll find out later. We have good sources.

"So he hit the machine gun and took it out of action which did...what?"

"It allowed us to disengage and withdraw out of the immediate line of fire. Haji was shit-scared, I know that much but he stood up and gave the gun the good news. It was especially brave considering his mate had been taken out by the same gun a couple of minutes earlier."

"Is it true to say that you would all have been killed, including Haji, if he had failed to silence the gun?"

Stu pulled a thoughtful face. "It's a good bet we would all have bought the farm. The Taliban were all over us, the Minimi had taken a hit and were losing the fire fight hands down. I guess all we could expect was a couple more minutes before we were overrun."

"And Haji would know that?"

"As well as anybody."

"So he was saving his own skin as well as yours?"

"Of course. Ahh, I see what you're driving at. Question: Why would Haji kill his own people? Answer: Because it was him or them."

"Major Keane has told you about Haji?"

"Yeah. Bastard was screwing us from the start. I'm especially upset. It's not often I get so comprehensively conned. I thought he was for real and I trusted him."

"He's the opposition's star witness and they're flying him over for the court martial. Can you remember anything else that might be of use?"

"Why's he so important?"

"Because he says he saw Major Keane shoot two unarmed civilians. He says he was in an ideal position to observe what went on."

Stu looked thoughtful again. "From what I remember he was certainly in a position to see the fire fight but I don't know how he came to get closer than the support group. Where does he say he was?"

Ann knew this part by heart. "On a ledge above the caravanserai. He says he was only fifty-metres away from the action."

"If he was, I didn't see him," Stu said emphatically.

Ann looked pleased and laid her own cool hand on his. "That's just what I need to know. I have to discredit him so that his statement is worthless."

"In that case I have another idea," Stu said.

★ ★ ★

The full-colonel was a pen-pusher from Division. He sat in the Old Man's office as if he owned it, lounging back in his chair and polluting the atmosphere with an expensive cigar.

Tim Bailey wrinkled his nose, found a saucer that could pass as an ashtray and slid it across the desk to the man. He was balding, a little overweight, his office job conducive to late breakfasts, long lunches and four-course dinners. He had not lost it completely, not yet, but Tim would have loved to have been a fly on the wall at the man's next medical assessment. He was brushing a fine dusting of ash from his lapel and speaking in an accent that wasn't quite Home Counties. Tim put it somewhere north of Watford.

"The Divisional Commander has asked me to come along and help you to sort out this little mess you seem to have got yourself into."

It immediately rubbed Tim up the wrong way. People who knew him well knew that the quieter he spoke the angrier he was and when he was angry he was best placated or avoided. Now his voice was low and soft. "What little mess would that be, colonel?"

"This problem with your men and the ROE. It's not something that's negotiable you know. All the Rules of Engagement are determined by the MoD and vary according to theatre. They've worked well in the past."

"The past is another war," Tim said. "Things change and the Ministry just has to keep up with the times. It's no use them clinging to outmoded, not to say dangerous, notions of behaviour."

"Steady-on, Bailey. That's a bit strong. I'm not sure the general would approve of that attitude."

"Perhaps the general would care to come to explain it to my men. After all, they are the ones who suffer from the poor judgement of others."

"All that lions led by donkeys guff again, is it? It won't wash in this day and age. We're all professionals now, you know."

Tim shook his head. "I'm not suggesting otherwise. It's not the military aspect that's at fault. Every serving officer knows that the ROE are prohibitively restrictive in certain circumstances and do put the lives of troops at risk. We know that and we're asking for the people responsible at the MoD to recognise the fact."

"So you're not going to budge on this issue?"

"In all conscience I can't. The men want the ROE revised or be given an excellent reason why they can't be. At the moment I'm not in a position to give them that answer, are you?"

"This is not doing your career prospects any good, you know," It was meant to sound like advice but Tim took it as a veiled threat. His voice was so low the colonel could only just hear it. "You can't get round this with bluster, colonel. It won't work with me and it certainly won't work with the kind of men who make up this regiment. Go back to Div and get me someone who can talk sensibly on the subject. Good day, sir."

The colonel who was not as foolish as he made himself seem sat in his car and speed-dialled his office. "Kit? Frank. Looks like there's going to be a big bust up with the SAS and these bloody ROE. I think we need to kick this upstairs and hope they can draw the sting before it blows up in our faces. It's not looking good. Yes, I'm on my way. Be with you in an hour or so. And yes, I know I'm mixing my bloody metaphors."

★ ★ ★

Ann put down her briefcase and perched on the edge of a functional table. She had not seen Ricky for over a week and it surprised her how down he now looked. "Feeling the pressure?"

"You could say that. I haven't heard from you for a while. I thought you might have given up on me too."

She smiled, offering support and sympathy with a twitch of the lips. "No chance...look...I have something serious to ask you."

"Something difficult, I can tell."

Ann looked him straight in the eye. "Have you considered pleading guilty?"

Ricky's face hardened. "Why? I'm totally innocent."

"Because you'd probably get a lighter sentence if you copped a plea...and it's my duty to advise you of what might be in your best interests."

"Going that badly, huh?" Ricky grunted.

"The prosecution has a good case. It will be difficult to fight."

A light came on in Ricky's eyes and she could see his back bristle. "Fighting's what I do best. If you're not up for it get me someone who is."

Ann gave him a silent thumbs-up and smiled. "I thought you'd say that but I have to give you the best advice I can. We may not win this case. It's a risk."

"So's life. What's new."

She leaned across and kissed him silently on the cheek. He pulled back, a surprised exclamation forming but she quickly put a finger on his lips and mouthed, "walls have ears."

Chapter Thirteen

Smith turned away from the bank of computers and grinned at his techie. "We've got the bastard just where we want him. Typical bloody gung-ho type, doesn't know when to roll over. If he took his lawyer's advice he'd be better off but he can't see when he's stitched up tighter than a virgin's fanny."

The techie grunted and manipulated a miniature joystick. "You gonna tell Hathaway?"

"I'll run it by him. What did you make of the lawyer in the car park?"

"She had an appointment to see Dalgleish but she was picked up by a couple of heavies and taken to see him off-campus. He brought her back in another car and the FRS picked him out. It couldn't have been a very satisfactory meeting 'cos she's now asked Keane if he wants to give in. Maybe Dalgleish couldn't give her what she wanted. Maybe he told her something she didn't want to hear."

Smith hummed to himself as he thought, an oddly tuneless little ditty. "Dalgleish was the one dodging around London recently, wasn't he?"

The techie nodded. "Yeah, strange that."

"Now he's managing his meetings with FitzPatrick. What have we got on him?"

The techie manoeuvred the joystick and punched a button. He read from his monitor. "As you know he's a Para but been with the SAS for over twelve years, he's part of the establishment but still only a sergeant. Can't see any reason for that, his record's spotless and he won a Military Medal in the Gulf. Done his share of sneaky-pete-ing. Worked undercover in Ulster and South America and done his watch on the Special Projects Team. Some close-protection work too, in Spain. There's only one question mark against him and that involved the death of his girlfriend a while or so back. He took some time off for compassionate leave then and his psyche reports show it badly affected him for a while. He's done both Air and Mountain Troops. A bit of an all-round hard bastard if you ask me."

"With a weak spot," Smith said.

"It must have been love," the techie said. "Otherwise it was out of character."

"Does he have any technical skills?" Smith asked.

"Don't they all, especially if they've been on the counter-terrorist and counter-insurgency teams and he has. He'll be up to speed on all the electronics measures and counter-measures."

It struck a chord with Smith. He still had not had the errant camera checked. He did not know why it bothered him but it did. "Keep a very close eye on Dalgleish, he's beginning to worry me."

★ ★ ★

Major Phelps and two plain clothes military policemen met Haji off the plane at Heathrow and ushered him through customs and immigration with only the most cursory of checks. Haji was wearing western clothing; a suit with the jacket fully buttoned at the front, as was his white shirt, tieless but buttoned right to the collar. He was bareheaded and it looked as if a demon barber had hacked at his hair at some recent time leaving him with clumps that stood up all over his scalp like the spines of a hedgehog. He looked young and bewildered. Phelps approved. It would not help if he came across as a hardened Mujahideen.

"Good trip?" Phelps asked.

Haji nodded, a taut smile on his lips that had been a fixation since they had met him but his eyes were hunted, barely still for a second, as if searching the crowds for enemies. Phelps knew the trip had been awful. There were no direct flights from Kabul and he had made the overland trip in the back of a pick-up truck to Lahore and then by train to Islamabad and the Air Pakistan flight to London. It had taken the best part of a week.

"Please, where are we going?" They were in a car on the way to Yorkshire. The court martial was to be held at a legal centre in the Catterick Garrison. Haji would be billeted there until the trial.

"Don't worry, Mr. al-Shamrani. Just sit back and enjoy the ride. It'll be a few hours so you might just as well make yourself comfortable," Phelps said.

He opened his briefcase and buried himself in some papers. He had seen FitzPatrick's contention that claimed al-Shamrani was al-Qaeda. It was probably a defence ploy but he would take it seriously enough to keep the young man under close supervision for the time being. He did not want to enter into conversation with him. As far as he was concerned al-Shamrani was just a means to an end. A tool to be used.

He was pleased the way the case had unfolded. FitzPatrick's apparent acceptance of the strength of the prosecution's case pleased him too. It meant he had done his investigative work well and that in turn would please Hathaway. A guilty verdict would be the icing on the cake.

He glanced quickly across at Haji. His head was turned away as he watched the English countryside slide by, what countryside he could see beyond the shoulders of the M25. Phelps idly wondered what was passing through the young man's mind.

★ ★ ★

Haji was looking at the passing scenery but not seeing it. His mind was elsewhere. His briefing, where he had received his final instructions at a madrassa in Lahore, had been thorough. His commander had facts at his fingertips and constantly repeated them until Haji was word perfect. Not since his training at the al-Farooq camp in eastern Afghanistan had the work been so intense and potentially so rewarding.

He had volunteered as an interpreter after attaching himself to a Tajik warlord's entourage and fighting, albeit deliberately ineffectually, against the Taliban in northern Afghanistan. Only slowly had the Tajiks come to accept him but never fully trust him. That he could speak English, Arabic, Urdu, Pushto and Tajik undoubtedly helped to bring him to the warlord's attention as an aid to his business with the drug barons of Pakistan which ensured that Haji's life was not threatened by suspicious tribesmen.

Once America, the Great Satan, had invaded Afghanistan to oust the Taliban he had gravitated to Kabul and offered his services to the Crusaders in the hope that he could gain information and pass it on to his superiors in al-Qaeda. It had worked far better than he had hoped. The Americans paid in dollars which financed his brother in setting up a small business in Kabul selling carpets as a front for arms dealing and drug running. The apparently respectable facade of the shop gained him credence, first with the Americans and then with the British who paid less well and were apt to be more suspicious. In the end he was accepted and used by both armies in sometimes covert operations where in some cases he had been able to forewarn the al-Qaeda leadership of imminent raids. He had even managed to warn Sheikh bin Laden in time to save him from an American attack. A last minute warning sent via Islamabad to the Saudi holy man in the Sarlath Mountains had jammed in a welter of sudden messages. He had risked discovery and it had been a wasted warning which got through too late for many in the complex but now he could exact revenge for those dead brothers.

They had given him this big responsibility to take the fight to the enemy. He knew what he had to do. How to do it was the question. If the infidels were to keep a close watch on him it might be difficult so first he had to earn their trust. At least allay their fears and lull them into believing that he was no danger to them.

First this trial. Once that was over perhaps the infidels' vigilance would lapse, once he had played his part and was of no further use to them. A visa had been issued in Kabul which was valid for three months. As a useful tool of the British he hoped he would be allowed to travel freely inside the country. His commander had said that this would be the case, that British security was lax but he had not bargained on this escort.

He had important work to do. He did not know where the infidels were taking him but he did know his contacts were in London. Their names were burned into his memory. He had instructions for them and a message of support from the Sheikh himself. Important work indeed, work that could not be allowed to fail.

He turned to face the man alongside him. A man whose name he did not know.

"Sir, I need to stop."

Phelps glanced up, surprised. "Why?"

"Sir, I have to pray, it is time. I need water for wadu and I have to face east for rak'ah."

Phelps let his breath out in a controlled hiss, not trying to hide his annoyance. "If you must, you must, I suppose." He tapped the driver on the shoulder. "Did you hear that, Michaels? Stop at the next services. Perhaps we can all take a leak and get some coffee whilst we're there. Make the most of it, eh?"

They were on the A1 just passing through Sandy and Michaels knew of a fast food place where the manager was a friendly soul who would find a quiet space for the man to pray in private.

It was better than Haji hoped. The room was a small storeroom which was used by the cleaner, another brother, who had helpfully marked the eastern wall. It had a small sink in one corner for the wadu, the ritual washing, and a faded rug rolled up beneath it for him to kneel on for his cycle of prostration alongside a galvanised bucket and mop.

Haji smiled at Michaels, who had made the arrangements for him and accompanied him to the room, and thanked him. He had no doubt the man would stand outside until he was finished his prayers and escort him back to the car. There was no other way out of the room with just a small skylight to brighten it. Haji waited until the door was closed before pulling a mobile from his body belt and calling the number he had been given. He was beginning to relax. It was going to be much easier than he imagined.

★ ★ ★

Now that the court martial was so imminent Hathaway had taken it upon himself to review both the prosecution's and the defence's cases. He liked the prosecution. It was rounded, neat and complete. FitzPatrick's defence was standard, almost dilatory. For someone with such a large reputation she had shown little imagination in putting together the defence of a client who stood to lose everything. But he had discovered that the beautiful Ann was a demon in the courtroom, thought on her feet, and could charm a jury with her voice and film star looks. Unfortunately for her there would be no jury, simply a board of hardened army officers and a civilian Judge-Advocate who knew on which side his bread was buttered. FitzPatrick could be as eloquent as she liked it would do her no good without the facts to back her up. All the facts were on the side of the prosecution and they would be hard to counter.

Hathaway had paid particular attention to the list of questions that Fitzpatrick wanted to ask al-Shamrani. They were all intended to give the impression that the man was a member of al-Qaeda and therefore could not be trusted as an unbiased witness. Hathaway had made sure the prosecution council was carefully schooled by Phelps so that all the points could be countered as they were raised. The prosecuting counsel had no idea that he was being briefed on notes stolen from the defence. He was of the type old-fashioned enough to report such behaviour to the Law Commission if he had an inkling of what had gone on. It was right to have someone with an unblemished reputation to mount the prosecution. That way there could be no charges of bias levelled at the inevitable outcome.

Politically this was excellent. His advice had been passed to higher echelons that the outcome was not in doubt and that they could reassure the Midlands MPs that justice would be done. They in turn could pass the message on to their troubled constituents. An altogether satisfactory situation. And yet...

FitzPatrick bothered him. Why was her defence plan seemingly so lax, so lacking in vibrancy? Perhaps he should let Smith investigate further, just as a precaution. Too much was riding on this to allow mistakes.

Hathaway left his armchair to pour himself a Guinness from a pack left under the sink. He abhorred the modern fad of ice-cold beer, which in any case warmed up far too quickly to be savoured properly and led to a faster downing of pints. Good business for the breweries, which was also good news for the Chancellor as the tax take grew correspondingly but not, he feared, good news for the loyal beer drinker.

He lived in a small flat in Lambeth just a few stops away from Westminster on the tube. Now it was growing fashionable, time for him to consider moving on to a less trendy area. It would not do for his working-class image to be tarnished by association with the metropolitan elite that was now populating the streets around him.

Hathaway smiled to himself. He hadn't done bad fer a workin' class lad. It was something his father always said of him and he had adopted it as his personal mantra. His dad was a hero. One of the old school communist trade unionists. A cutler by profession he had been a shop-steward for the National Union of Steelworkers. A man who, if he could not persuade you of the rights of an argument would hit you round the head with it.

He felt the slogan kept his feet on the ground in the heady atmosphere of power politics in which he now played a role. Through his boss, Tom Gannon, he had the ear of senior ministers. More importantly he had the trust of the government, which was more than could be said of two-thirds of the current Cabinet. It would be a cold day in hell when Stan Hathaway gave away his position of trust and it paid to be careful.

* * *

Smith took the call from Hathaway. It wouldn't hurt to double check on FitzPatrick. He arranged for her apartment to be searched thoroughly, just to make sure she wasn't hiding anything of relevance. Most of the work would be done while she was out of her Kensington apartment but some of necessity would take place at night so that her briefcase and personal effects could be examined while she slept. It was a risk but if the operator was discovered it could go down as a failed burglary. Nothing ventured, nothing gained. His people were professional enough to be in and out without detection.

Now he had other things on his mind. The report on the camera had come back from the engineers. The camera itself was fine but they had swapped it out just to be on the safe side. The wiring too was in good condition without any sign of tampering. That too had been replaced. The worrying thing was the computer log for the camera. Its operation had been over-ridden from a remote location. How that was possible Smith had no idea, his technical knowledge was sketchy at the best of times, but happen it had. The good news was that the remote site was being tracked. Whoever had intercepted the feed had routed the signal halfway around the world through remote servers, bouncing it off various satellites until it had reached its final destination. He was still awaiting that answer.

The techie next to him was still punching keys and fiddling with the joystick on his control unit with an intense look on his face. Smith had always taken the techies for granted. They were part of the furniture; useful but not particularly interesting. This techie was a little out of the ordinary and it had not occurred to Smith before. He was older than the average. Usually they were straight out of college with a degree in computer nerding and lived on the internet morning, noon and night. This man was more substantial, it looked as if he might have a life outside of computers, he wasn't such a sad bastard as some of the others, at least it seemed that way to Smith as he watched him work.

He had noticed that some of the women found him interesting too, often cornering him by the coffee machine during the breaks. The techie seemed to enjoy the attention as much as the women enjoyed lavishing it on him. A ladies' man, albeit one with a pronounced limp. A gimp with a limp and an eye for the girls. Yes a lot more interesting than your average techie geek and good at his job otherwise he would not be working for MI5.

"Found anything?" Smith had tired of his amateur psychological profiling and was getting impatient.

The techie angled his head sideways and grinned at him without taking his eyes off the monitor. "Soon. A few more minutes. This guy is good but not as good as he thinks he is. He's left me an electronic trail to follow but hasn't realised it. Usually when you end an uplink the trail goes cold but in this case he's routed it via commercial ISPs and they keep a record."

"So where does that leave us?" Smith queried.

The techie hit another key with a flourish. "It leaves us innnn...Hereford. The coordinates put it right slap bang on a hotel on the outskirts of the town."

"Oh god," Smith sighed. "I hope this isn't heading where I think it's heading."

The techie handed him a piece of paper with a name and phone number on it. Falconbury Orchard Hotel,

Falconbury Lane. That's the phone number. Want me to call it?"

Smith nodded. "Yes. Find out who was staying there at the time of the transmission." He wandered away to the coffee machine as the man made the call. No sense in hanging over his shoulder while he did the mundane stuff. He drew himself a paper cup full of dark brown fluid and sniffed it. It didn't smell much like coffee. Come to that it didn't taste much like coffee but it was hot at least. He wandered back to the console. "Well?"

"We're in luck. It's only a small hotel and it wasn't particularly busy that day. We've got a list of four names that the hotel's faxing through for confirmation."

"Anyone stand out for you?"

"Only a Mr and Mrs John Smith," the techie said with a grin. "Common name, huh."

"Someone shagging someone on the side," Smith grunted. "Anyone else?"

"The other three are men. The hotel receptionist thinks they were reps. They get a lot of them mid-week."

"Check them out," Smith said. "You've got all the details, yeah?"

"Addresses, phone numbers, vehicle registration numbers, the works. I'll get onto it."

"Now!" Smith said.

The techie flashed him a look. "Of course, now."

"Right. I'll be in my office. Ten minutes, yeah." It was not a question but an instruction. He'd see what the man was made of. Was that a look of annoyance the man had given him? Aspirational for a humble techie to get hacked off with an operator. Theirs was to do and do quickly without argument or discourse. This man was truly outside the mould. Maybe he fancied himself as an operator too; but not with that limp.

His coffee was now lukewarm and he scowled at the cup before flipping it still a quarter full into the waste bin where the dregs sprayed over the side onto the polished floor. Smith glared at the mess. He did not like this turn of events. Firstly he would have to report the intrusion to his superiors and that would bring the house down. MI5 infiltrated? The press would have a field day if they ever got to hear of it. Then there was the content. How was he to explain why he had been secretly recording a meeting with a representative of the powerful Policy Focus Office? Otherwise known in government circles as *People Fucked Over*. That in itself was career suicide unless he could come up with a good enough reason; covering his own arse wouldn't qualify. And finally, what did the hacker intend to do with the information he had lifted. Why had he taken the trouble to hack into the Security Service's computer systems? What had he to gain? It went to motive. Was it a terrorist cell seeking ways to outwit the service, or something else?

There was a tap on his doorframe. It was the techie. "Got something for you, boss. One of the indexes came up on a cross check with the eyeball operation at Credenhill. It's a car that picked up FitzPatrick a few days ago."

"Who's it registered to?"

"It's one of our Security Service reg plates."

"Don't mess about, "Smith snarled. "Who's it signed out to?"

"You."

★ ★ ★

Mo flashed her ID card at the pretty young receptionist. "One of my colleagues phoned you yesterday about some recent guests." She smiled. "You remember?"

The girl's smile back was a little unsure. "About some guests during the third week of February, was that it?"

"That was it," Mo agreed. She took a computer printout from her pocket. There were eight pages, each one with a photograph on it and the names blanked out. "Do you recognise any of these faces?"

The girl shuffled the pages across the reception desk and studied them. A nice surprise for Mo. Most people only gave ID pictures a cursory glance before denying any knowledge of the subjects. It was safer that way but this girl did not seem to be bothered. Either that or she was too naive to understand the possible consequences of a positive ID.

"This man. I recognise him. He's Mr Smith."

Mo craned her neck to see the face. Stu Dalgleish. No surprises there. "Do you see Mrs Smith here?"

"I never saw Mrs Smith. She came late and it was dark. Mr. Smith had already booked in for them both."

"So maybe Mrs Smith never actually existed?"

"Oh, she was there all right. One of the cleaners found her perfume the next day. Very expensive stuff too. We tried to ring the number Mr Smith had given but it was unobtainable."

"What happened to the perfume?"

"The cleaner took it home. No point in wasting it."

Mo pulled a face. Any help the bottle might once have been was now useless.

"Do you remember the brand?"

"Chanel...I think, but I can't remember which one."

"That's fine, no problem." She handed over a card. "If you think of anything else give me a call."

Outside it was coming on to rain. Mo turned up her collar and walked to the car. She didn't mind the rain as long as it didn't run down her neck. That really pissed her off.

In the car she pulled out her mobile and speed-dialled Smith. "It was Dalgleish at the hotel. He was the one that intercepted your feed. He had a woman with him. Ten-to-one it was FitzPatrick. She left some expensive perfume behind. She looks like a Chanel kind o' gel."

"I don't like this, not one bit," Smith said. "Why would FitzPatrick get involved with tapping the British Security Service? I don't get it."

Mo gagged on a laugh. She could see the funny side of the tapper tapped but she doubted if Smith would see the joke. "Who else, then?"

"Check it out, Mo. Take a couple of your team off the Credenhill eyeball and get down to Kensington. Turn FitzPatrick's place over. If she was with Dalgleish she may have left some evidence around. Check everything thoroughly, briefcase, laptop, the works."

"What about Dalgleish?"

"Time to stop pussyfooting around. Let's find out what he's up to. Pick him up when you get back and we'll have a talk with him."

Chapter Fourteen

It was mid morning and the hangar was packed. Every man who was on-site or otherwise unengaged on ops was there. Even Slime, the Intelligence Officers who manned the Kremlin Intelligence centre had deigned to put in an appearance.

Tim Bailey had entered with the usual understated way of the SAS. With him were several civilians, some of whose faces were familiar, and the Brigadier SAS Group. Cowley had called them all to attention in their seats and the hubbub died instantly.

"Morning gentlemen," Bailey said. "No doubt you're wondering what this is about so I won't beat about the bush.

"We as a regiment have asked some difficult questions about the Rules of Engagement and how they apply to soldiers in contact with an enemy in the theatres in which we currently operate. I know that none of you are happy with the status quo. There would seem to be a good reason to revisit the ROE, especially in the light of one of our men being charged with unlawful killing in a battlefield situation. Now I cannot go into that as it's sub-judice and some of you here are testifying at the court-martial so it is definitely out of bounds for this meeting.

"However I'm delighted to tell you that the Secretary of State for Defence has agreed for one of his ministers to come here this morning from Whitehall to give us the MoD's side of the story with regard to ROE and the thinking behind them. Please hear him out and I'm told he will take a few questions afterwards. Minister..."

★ ★ ★

It had been a rough ride for the minister as his lawyerly arguments had not found much support amongst the soldiers and he was not in the best of moods as he made his way to the officers' mess after the meeting accompanied by his staff and various hangers-on. One of these was Hathaway who had elbowed his way into the act to make sure that his stake in the court martial was not undermined. Hathaway did not trust the minister, he was not a safe pair of hands, but he hoped his presence would help to keep the man on-side and on-message until after the trial was safely concluded.

The minister, whose name was Simon Oakley, made desultory conversation with Bailey as they walked but his mind was on other things. He was a scholarly-looking six-footer, slim, almost emaciated, with rimless spectacles and the donnish air of a university professor. Defence had not been his choice of portfolio, preferring welfare or education but he had accepted the junior minister's post as a step up the ladder to heading up his own ministry and a seat at the Cabinet table. He had little resonance with the armed forces, his own background as left-wing firebrand and fully paid-up member of the Young Communists as well as the de rigueur membership of CND and Amnesty International, ill-fitted him to see eye-to-eye with military aspirations. Added to that, a sense of his own importance had not sat well with the, to his mind, disrespectful way he had just been treated by his subordinates. He was unaware of the Regiment's ethos of free-speech and Chinese Parliaments where each man had the right to speak his mind no matter what rank or position held. It was more democratic than the Parliamentary whip system.

Oakley was used to getting his own way and detested counter-argument with a passion. He was also known as a narrow-minded bigot with a spiteful streak although he would deny that with a venom usually reserved for his most hated political enemies.

He had not come to Hereford with an open mind. Neither had he come to build bridges. His objective was to lay down the law and put these tin soldiers back in their box. Firmness of purpose was his watchword. One could not have the rank-and-file dictating to high command; it was unthinkable.

"Interesting meeting, Minister?" Bailey asked.

"Not quite what I was expecting, Bailey. I thought this unit would be more disciplined."

"It's a Regimental tradition. The men are allowed to have their say."

"I don't have this problem with the Guards."

"No, sir, you wouldn't. But as it happens our G Squadron is drawn mainly from that Brigade and is officered almost entirely by them."

"I noticed that this regiment does not seem that inclusive," Oakley said, looking around.

"I don't understand, Minister. How do you mean inclusive?" Bailey asked.

At his elbow he felt the Brigadier shuffle and nudge him with a whispered "You don't want to go there, Tim." But it was too late they were already there.

"I don't see too many black faces around. Nor women. Not welcome in this mess?"

Bailey bristled. "Excuse me, sir, with respect. This regiment is open to anybody that can make the grade. It is one of only three units in the British forces to have a selection process, the other two being the Parachute Regiment and the Royal Marines. It is no coincidence that all three units are the ones most utilised in difficult situations. Our Selection process is of necessity the toughest to pass. Only those with a particular bent for Special Forces have the aptitude and the physical and mental strength to pass. We have our fair share of Fijians, Tongans and Samoans. It is the same criteria for them as it is for everyone regardless of sex, race or colour."

"Hmm, so I've heard." The Minister ruminated for a moment. "It still seems strange to me that so few ethnics or women make the grade. Tell me, who is it that does the selecting?"

"I think you already know the answer to that, Minister. We have our own training cadre and Selection is run by highly-experienced officers and NCOs."

"So it's a club for the boys. It seems no different to the Freemasons. To get in you have to be approved by the members. I think the system is degrading and loaded against minorities. I think the system should be changed and I shall make it my business to see that it is in the very near future. You must be open to all. There should be quotas. In this day and age I find it unacceptable for there not to be women and minorities represented in any government organisation, regardless of any wholly artificial entry criteria."

Bailey's voice had dropped to just above a whisper. "You're suggesting that we are biased in whom we choose to serve with this regiment and you are further suggesting that we should ease the selection process to allow others in, who might not be able to reach the standards we currently require? Have I got that right, Minister?"

The minister sipped his sherry, enjoying the silence and the audience he had created, everyone waiting on his next words. He noticed Hathaway waving but chose to ignore him. He spoke as if to a child. "Colonel Bailey, inclusivity is my watchword and should be yours."

Bailey, very carefully, put down his glass. "In that case, Minister. If that is all you have to say I bid you good day. Gentlemen?"

Without a word every officer present put down their glasses and filed out of the mess leaving only the minister, his entourage and the Brigadier.

The minister glanced at Hathaway, who had gone red in the face, and threw his arms wide. "What the fuck have I said?" He was secretly pleased with himself. He had deflected the talk from ROE and given the self-righteous, class-riddled, army stuffed shirts something else to think about. They were not going to change the ROE on his watch under any circumstances.

His miscalculation had not yet sunk in but the look on Hathaway's face was arousing a tiny tic of concern.

"I'm afraid, Minister, you've well and truly put the cat amongst the pigeons," the Brigadier said. "Lunch, anyone?"

★ ★ ★

Stu snapped closed his mobile and took a deep breath. *'Stand by, stand by'*. The mission was on with a vengeance. He had heard about the happenings in the officers' mess and had expected the call. His laptop was open and running on his desk. He took the USB drive he had been given off his keyring and plugged it into the laptop. He was already online with the regimental intranet and he prepared the files from the USB for uploading. His finger hovered over the return key. All he had to do was hit the button and the world would change. It was an awesome responsibility which he took seriously. If ever there was a time to reconsider this was it. Like a drowning man was said to see his life flash before his eyes, Stu now reviewed his. The successes, the failures too many to count, the highs and the lows. He was sad to note that the lows outnumbered the highs by at least two-to-one but then life in general sucked. Nobody could expect to live their entire life in a rose garden and the course he had taken with his had supplied more than an average share of manure. But it was his life and he had lived it the way he wanted. If he could have changed anything it would have been to expand the brief time he had spent with Judy into something altogether more permanent. But even that had a brighter side. A debt to be repaid. One that was now in the process of being collected. He was not a fatalist, not in any sense that fatalists would understand, he believed you made your own luck, or had the ability to recognise opportunities and take advantage of them when they arose, but life did seem to him now to have a certain direction, had a will of its own. Yet! It depended on him pressing the button on the keyboard, so free-will was still paramount in this scheme. But was it free-will? Had he been drawn in or had he entered of his own volition? Were his strings being pulled or was he dancing to the tune of his own trumpet? At the bottom of it did he believe he was right to do what he was about to do? Did it accord with his sense of natural justice? Yes on both counts. His finger hit the return key and he watched the progress strip run along its bar. It took very few seconds as it was encrypted and zipped. Now every Regimental Sergeant Major in the British army had a copy of Valkyrie and needed only the decryption code to open it.

His mobile warbled the familiar tune and he jumped. His nerves were getting frayed. He could feel the tension in his shoulders. This was beginning to get to him. He flipped the top open. "Hi."

"Hello, Stu." It was Ann FitzPatrick. "I've had some trouble with my hair."

"You have?" Stu grimaced and looked at his watch. This was bad timing but he'd promised. He still had twelve hours of his leave remaining. "I'll be there in three hours. Sit tight."

He grabbed his car keys and made for the car park inside the perimeter fence. He needed to see the damage for himself, talk to Ann where they could not be overheard; find out what of importance she had left in the apartment and work out a plan of mitigation. He hoped to god she was as clever as she seemed or Ricky was for the chop; big time.

He had shown Ann how to mark her doors with fine hairs wetted and placed between the door and the frame forming a near invisible bridge that would stay in place until the door was opened. Most operators placed them low down alongside the skirting board but he had told Ann that was where any trained intruder would look so hers was put in the top edge on the hinge side where it was hidden by the angled joint at the corner of the frame. Whoever had entered Ann's apartment was either an amateur or a slipshod pro who did not think a civilian would take such precautions and had not looked hard enough for the telltale. It told Stu much about the opposition. It was a good bet that the section head at Box had brought in contract labour as in-house talent would not have missed it. Contract labour was not a good sign. It either meant that Box was getting panicky or that they wanted to deal with the situation on a deniable basis. The first thought was bad enough, panicky people made bad decisions, but the second was worse. It was an unknown quantity with unknown qualities. Their brief could cover a multitude of sins and if they had been briefed to take the gloves off it could get very nasty. Very nasty indeed.

★ ★ ★

Mo watched through the telescope as Dalgleish's car exited Credenhill's main gate and got on the radio. "All mobiles this is control. Player One is exiting main gate and is complete." She read the index number to the operators in the three cars parked at the egress points from the area. "Silver VW Golf, turning right, right, right. Follow and intercept as convenient. Player is not thought to be armed, I say again, player is not thought to be armed. All mobiles confirm."

"Mobile Two confirmed. I have eyeball." That was Jason and Cedric, two good lads she had worked with before.

"Mobile One, confirmed. We do not have eyeball but are moving to intercept." Ken and Derek, two unknown quantities which made her nervous but then she was always like that on operations.

"Mobile Three confirmed. We are complete and on our way." That was Barry and Dwain on the wrong side of the airfield to be much use as yet. They would come into play if the chase proved longer than anticipated.

"Roger that, Three. All mobiles radio check every two, I say again, every two minutes."

Mo got a chorus of Roger that's and settled down with a large scale road map in front of her, tracing her finger along the A480 the main route from the area looking for a spot where the interception could safely take place. She assumed until she heard otherwise that Dalgleish would be heading east towards London and that was a bitch. The only easy way in and out of Credenhill was by chopper, the roads were a mess all the way to the junction with the M4.

The radio burbled. "Control, Mobile One. We have eyeball. We have exited ahead of Player One and are travelling east, east, east on four-eight-zero. Copy?" It was Ken doing his Met thing, or maybe something he'd heard in a film.

"Roger that, One. Two, do you still have eyeball?"

"Affirmative, Control. We are about two-hundred metres behind Player One. We also have eyeball on Mobile One."

"Control, this is Three. We are approaching alpha four-eight-zero now. Taking a left, left, left onto four-eight-zero. We are about one click behind the pace."

"Roger that, Three."

Mo checked her map they were approaching the junction with the A4103. Another left turn would take them through the northern edge of Hereford itself or maybe he would continue on to the A438 which might prove problematic as it passed through the centre of the town. Maybe that's where he was headed.

The thought had just crossed her mind when the radio snapped on. "Control, Two. Target's gone left, left, left on alpha four, one, zero, three. Mobile One has missed the turn and is continuing south."

"Roger that," Mo said. That was the problem with a front tail. "Mobile Three, close up to Two. Mobile One, go left, left, left, on alpha four, three, eight, across two, that is two, roundabouts then right, right, right on alpha four, one, zero, three. Toe down, blues on, confirm."

"This is Mobile One, wilco." It was Ken again, now in WWII fighter pilot mode. Where the hell did he get it from? Still, he should enjoy the chase with his flashing blue lights that were hidden behind the grille of his Volvo. It would be like old times for him. With luck she could get Mobile One back into play as they had three sides of a rectangle to negotiate when the others were going straight along the top edge.

Now Mo was sure that Dalgleish wanted to by-pass Hereford and was probably heading for the M50. If it was her she would take a right off the A4103, to connect up with the A438, by-passing Ledbury to get to Junction 2 of the motorway and then a quick zip up to the M5. It was a roundabout route but far quicker than following the old 'A' roads. And it seemed Dalgleish was in a hurry as Mobile Two had just radioed in and they had already reached the roundabout connecting to the A4103. He was flying. It was what she needed.

★ ★ ★

Stu was moving as fast as the traffic allowed. The Golf GTi was a quick and nimble car and he made the most of its capabilities. He kept a watchful eye on his mirrors and was mildly concerned with the blue BMW that was mirroring his moves albeit several cars back. He squeezed onto the A4103 between two tipper trucks with 'Motorway Maintenance' signs decorating the backs and sides. The front truck was slow away from the roundabout and he fumed at the delay. He noticed the BMW had moved up to the truck behind him. Close enough for him to make out the M3 badge on its grille. He relaxed slightly, probably some marketing manager late for an appointment.

He passed the truck at the next opportunity and saw the BMW do likewise but overtake both trucks in one move to close up to his tail. Stu slowed down a little to give the car the opportunity to pass which it did.

There was another car, a Saab, making ground fast from behind, tagging past the trucks in quick succession and tucking in behind Stu. He slowed again but this time the car slowed with him and he could see he was catching the BMW that had overtaken him. It had slowed down and he was now the filling in the sandwich. Blue lights came on in the grille of the car behind and a STOP POLICE sign came up from the rear parcel shelf on the Beemer in front which was turning into a layby.

Stu groaned. Fifteen years motoring without a blemish on his licence and now this. He tried to think how much over the limit he had been travelling. With luck it would be just three points and a £60 fine. He just had to be nice and talk his way out of anything heavier.

He watched in his mirror as two men got out of the Saab and one from the passenger seat of the BMW. Mob handed, perhaps they were going to throw the book at him. He'd just have to grin and bear it.

Then a third car slid to a halt alongside, splashing loose gravel. Its door burst open, a man wearing a balaclava jumped out and pointed a handgun at him. "Out of the car, now. Out, out. Keep your hands in sight."

Stu's brain went into hyperdrive. "Hey I was only speeding."

"Shut-the-fuck-up." His door was wrenched open and the pistol pushed hard against his temple. It was a Sig 226, a good reliable 9mm pistol, one he used himself after his faithful old Browning High Power had been replaced. Smart pistol; stupid move from the gunman. The man on the opposite side of the car who had opened the passenger door was now in the direct line of fire. Not good team work but swiftly remedied as the second man moved to his left behind the door pillar.

"Get a grip," he heard the man say but the gunman was running on adrenalin. "Hands behind your head, hands behind your head. get out of the car, now."

Stu couldn't comply, his seat belt was still fastened and his hands were now behind his neck. "I can't..."

The pistol jabbed forward hard into his head. "I said get out."

"The seat belt's still fastened," Stu yelled.

"Undo it, undo it now. Use your left hand, keep the right where I can see it."

Stu complied. The seat belt slid across his chest and snagged on his right elbow which was now level with the pistol at his head. He moved his arm and the gunman pulled away to let the belt through. Stu snapped up his right hand, caught the man's arm below the wrist and smashed it against the roof sill. Then he pulled the man inwards and hit him hard on the bridge of the nose with the heel of his left hand breaking the bone. Without a pause he turned the man's pistol against his thumb to flip it from his grip before using it side-on as a club on the man's jaw.

All this had taken less than two seconds and the other three men, who were now clustered close to the VW's front wings, were slow to react. Stu palmed the pistol grips and flipped off the safety.

"Back off!" He eased out of the VW and shuffled backwards to the Saab which still had its engine running. He reversed it quickly as the men pulled their weapons but he spun the car in a handbrake turn and accelerated away.

"Mobile Two, receiving over?" It was a female voice issuing from the speakers hidden under the dashboard. Stu felt for the switch by his clutch foot. It was there, where he would have placed it had he been One-Up. He trod on it. "Hello, sweetheart. I'm afraid Mobile Two's gone foxtrot."

"That you, Dalgleish?"

"Big mistake you've just made, sweetie."

"Won't happen again. Count on it."

"Ahh. I can see your boys are tagging along. Should be an interesting few minutes."

The radio went dead and he knew they had changed frequencies. He did not have the time to fiddle with the radio to log their conversations, he had to drive hell-for-leather to keep out of trouble.

The car was unfamiliar to him, the seat was in the wrong place and so were the mirrors. It would not be an easy drive. He was able to adjust the rear-view mirror but the door mirrors and seat could only be moved together and it was impossible at the speed he was travelling.

He hit a few switches, steering one handed eyes glancing ceaselessly at the rear-view. The blues came on together with the two-tone klaxon. Traffic was light but it would help him clear the way. Somehow he had to lose the following cars. He slalomed past a white van and found a clear straight stretch of road. He was touching ninety but the two chasers were closing on him. He accelerated harder, the Saab had some guts and leapt forward widening the gap. He felt for his mobile, pulled it out, flipped the top and hit speed dial. There was a bend coming up fast and he needed both hands on the controls, stick shifting down to fourth and then third before accelerating hard through the bend. Another clear stretch and he reached for the mobile as a tinny voice echoed from the passenger seat where he had dropped the phone.

"Boss?"

"Yes."

"I'm in deep shit. Someone's after me. They're armed. Probably Box, or hired help. Maybe they've twigged us. I've got a Beemer and a Volvo on my tail."

"Where are you, Stu," The voice now cool and calm. A safe haven in a raging storm.

"Somewhere on the A4103. I'll try to circle back to Credenhill..."

He threw the handset back on the seat as a three vehicle convoy came into view ahead of him. They pulled to the left as much as they could to let him pass but one was a low loader carrying a mobile home that took up the whole width of his carriageway. There was oncoming too; no way past. He mirror-checked the chasers who were fast closing up, their blues and twos going in mad synchronisation.

Now he knew where he was, approaching a place called Five Bridges. A junction loomed and he slammed the brakes on hard before executing a tight left turn. The Saab coped beautifully but the BMW behind didn't have the traction and broadsided past the turning. The following Volvo had more time and wallowed into the turn like a harpooned whale.

This road was much narrower with twists rather than bends and Stu made the most of the Saab's power. The following Volvo had the power but not the manoeuvrability and was falling back, baulking the BMW which had caught up.

Stu left the phone on the seat and shouted above the roar of the engine and the blasting horns which he didn't have time to turn off. "Heading towards Much Cowarne. I'll hang a left there and get onto the A465 back to Hereford." He was unable to hear an answer or even knew if the message had got through. He shot a glance at the mirror. The BMW had got past the Volvo and was closing up fast. The road straightened and Stu took the chance to shout a few more words at the mobile sliding around the passenger seat. "Valkyrie must go, boss. These bastards must have some intel otherwise they wouldn't be risking their necks like this."

There was a sharp right-hand bend looming. He was over the ton on the approach and needed to scrub-off speed. He trod hard on the brakes, the pedal thudding against the sole of his shoe as the ABS hit overload. He double-gated the gears and slipped the clutch hard. The deceleration was far too severe for the following driver to cope with and the BMW slammed into the Saab's rear. Stu's head snapped back against the restraint and he lost his grip on the wheel as it kicked left. The black and white chevrons were straight ahead and the car cut through like a snowplough on a juggernaut. It hit the verge and launched itself over the hedge and into the field beyond. The car bounced across the ruts and into a tree. Behind him the BMW had flipped and rolled. The last thing Stu remembered before the airbag blew and he blacked out was a roar of exploding petrol as the BMW's fuel line ruptured.

Honesta turpitudo est pro causa bono
It is right to do wrong for a good cause

Note: 6 - Appended

I have to admit to my growing concern. At first I had thought Stu Dalgleish's assertions about the Security Service had been somewhat fanciful but had complied with his wishes. Not to do so would have been pig-headed.

With the discovery of the missing tell-tales it now seemed all too apparent that his suspicions were justified. Under normal circumstances I would immediately inform first the police and then the legal authorities but I have no confidence that the police would have been anything other than disinterested and the Law Society would demand to see proof to back up my 'wild' accusations. Apart from a small sector of the legal profession which make a good living from suing the police no one in legal circles wants to believe that the authorities could stoop to such dealings. Not only am I now aware that they do but I have the awful feeling that it will get worse in future if nothing is done to contain it.

My dilemma is how now to proceed. Do I assume that the intruders have found what they were looking for or will they return a second time? It has been well over three hours since I called Dalgleish and there is still no sign of him and I can get no response from his mobile phone. It is a measure of how much I have come to rely on his advice in these matters that I am afraid to make a decision in my own right. A week ago there would have been no problem; now…

I do have a fall-back position, one that I am reluctant to take as it has inherent dangers of its own. Everything is crossed that MI5 haven't yet found where I am keeping my real casework and these appended notes. Perhaps I am stupid even to commit these things to paper but I need the release and it helps to order my thoughts.

AFP.
Lincolns Inn

PART 3
Counter Move

Chapter Fifteen

The boot in Dalgleish's ribs prodded again, hard, and he opened one eye. He was supine on a rough cord carpet and the single unshaded light bulb dangling from a plastic ceiling rose was blinding. He closed his eye with a low moan.

The boot again, this time even less gentle, delivered with the sort of force that suggested its wearer was less than happy. Dalgleish became more aware as a bout of nausea left him. His arms were secured behind him and he could feel the bare flesh of his back. He was naked. It shouldn't have surprised him but it did, especially as the boot's owner appeared to be female.

"You with us yet, dickhead?"

The voice could have been pleasant if modulated but it held the gritty aggressive tone of a hardcase.

Dalgleish opened the eye again, blinked rapidly to clear his vision and turned his head away from the light. "Just about."

Rough hands grabbed him and he was pulled from the floor and rammed onto a hard-backed chair as his arms were forced upwards to fall behind the seat effectively pinioning him to it. The fog was slowly clearing both from his sight and from his brain but he wished he was back to unconsciousness as what he saw didn't appeal. Two men, both masked, stood either side of him and he could feel the presence of the woman behind his back. He had recognised the voice, the same woman who had been directing the chase. Not good news; she seemed like a professional. The room looked like a suburban lounge. It had flowered wallpaper, a television and a three-piece suite pushed back against one wall. The heavy curtains were drawn but there was no light filtering through at the edges so he'd been out cold for at least an hour.

"Feeling better?" The voice had softened. Now she was mum tending an injured child.

"What do you want?" Dalgleish knew what they wanted. It was best to cut to the chase and save a whole lot of pain.

"I see you're not one for foreplay, Stu."

"I know the score."

"Of course you do, sweetie. You've done all the RTI training. No doubt you've got all your cover stories worked out, all that disinformation clever enough to be almost believable but which would take time to confirm and give your buddies a chance to pull off a rescue or get you off the hook. Trouble is we're not all that trusting here and there's an awful lot we already know. There's just a few details that we need and we'll know if you're lying."

She stepped around from behind him and showed him her masked head and the hypodermic. "Just a little concoction stolen from the Russians. Pretty feckin' effective at eliciting information but it eventually turns your brain to mush."

"What do you want to know?"

He could imagine her thin smile behind the balaclava. "Tell me about your meeting with the lovely Ann."

"Where are my clothes?"

"You've only got one chance to talk, Stu. I'd make the most of it if I were you. This infantile stalling will get you nowhere."

"There's something in my pocket that'll help you," Dalgleish said.

"We've been through your pockets. We've also found and destroyed the tracers. Nobody's coming for you. You're on your own."

Dalgleish shrank in the chair and nodded. "Right. Just needed to be sure.

"We found the bugs hidden in Major Keane's room so I thought it was better to meet his Brief somewhere we couldn't be overheard."

"Why were you looking for bugs in the first place?"

Dalgleish managed a cynical grin. "Because *we* don't trust anybody. There's been too much garbage in the press for someone not to be sticking the knife in."

"Who's *we*?"

"The blokes who were on the op with Keane. We all think this case is a stitch-up."

"And you're doing what about it exactly?"

Dalgleish pulled another face. "We got our stories together. No harm there, we know what we know."

"And the chat with the lawyer?"

"She'd heard that the prosecution was bringing over an Afghan called Haji. I've met him and she wanted some background on the bloke. I told her he seemed an okay sort to me. Even got us out of a tight spot in a fire fight with the Taliban. I couldn't help her much."

"Did she tell you Haji was suspected of being with al-Qaeda?"

"She did." Dalgleish gave out a short snigger. "I didn't believe it. I think she's clutching at straws. As I said, I wasn't much help."

The woman held up the hypo and inspected it, giving the plunger a little push to send a tiny fountain of liquid spurting from the needle-fine tip. "Tell me about the other meetings."

Dalgleish started almost imperceptibly. "What meetings?"

"Don't be coy, Stu. The meeting at the Falconbury Orchard Hotel, the one with Ann FitzPatrick, and the meeting in London where you took such great care over not being followed. You know."

"You've made a mistake there. I was in London, yes, and I did practice some anti-surveillance moves just to keep my hand in but I didn't meet anyone, just went to the pictures."

"I told you about fibbing, Stu," the woman whispered. "Don't take me for an idiot." She pressed the plunger again right under his nose and he could smell the alcohol stink of the drug.

"Okay, I did meet Ann. I helped her with some security advice about how to tell whether anyone had been in her apartment. That's where I was going today. She rang and told me the tell-tales had been compromised. I was going to see for myself."

"What else?"

"She wanted to know how she could keep her computer files safe. I was going to help with that but your boys stopped me."

"Yes, thanks for that. One of my men is in hospital with second degree burns. Another wants a quiet chat about broken noses. I may let him have a few minutes with you if you keep trying my patience. The Falconbury Orchard?"

"I suppose you want to know about the computer hack? It wasn't difficult. We work with MI5 all the time and it was a piece of cake once we'd dropped a Trojan onto the mainframe hard drive. It didn't come through the firewall so no alarms were set off and it was just a matter of monitoring internal communications until something came up that we could use."

The angle of the woman's head suggested interest, like a bird eyeing a worm. "Like what?"

"That guy Smith. He had a habit of recording meetings and you can't mistake the mouthpiece from the PFO, he's in the papers often enough. I bet Smith was covering his own arse but it gave us an inkling of what was going on behind the scenes. The government really wanted Keane's head on a pike. We just wanted to even the odds a little."

"And *was* it Ann FitzPatrick who was with you?"

Dalgleish laughed. He made it sound like an embarrassed schoolboy caught playing with himself. "It was just me."

"And the bottle of perfume found in the room?"

"I left it there on purpose, for the hotel staff to find. At the back of my mind I figured there was a possibility that you'd trace the link and I figured it might throw you off the scent if you were faced with a Mr and Mrs Smith."

"Was that meant to be funny, Stu? That 'throw you off the scent bit'. Did you just make that up? And why Smith? And why use his car's VRN? What were you trying to prove?"

"Okay, okay. I wanted Smith to know we were on to him. So that he'd ease off Keane but I guess it was just wishful thinking, eh?"

"Guess so. I'm going to leave you to stew for a while, Stu. Maybe give you time to think over what you've told me. That okay?"

"I've told you everything..."

"A few minutes, right?"

Mo met Smith outside. "Did you get all that?"

Smith nodded. "Sounds plausible."

Mo grunted and dragged on a freshly lit cigarette. She let the smoke curl down her nose. "He's lying faster than a second-hand car salesman."

"How so?"

"I've trained with these guys. They don't have just one cover story but two or three. They give them up only as the need arises. We've put him under no pressure yet. He can tell us what he likes with just enough truth in it to get by."

"But he's let out a lot already. It's stuff we can use. We know that FitzPatrick knows we've been bugging her and maybe we can use that against her. Dalgleish may think he's being clever but it's self-defeating."

Mo eyed Smith dubiously. "You think he let that stuff out by mistake? Dream on. There's another tale buried underneath all this and I'm going to dig it out of him."

Smith nodded his mute assent. "Let me know what you get as soon as you get it even if you have to kill him in the process."

Mo nodded. "That Russian stuff you gave us. Does it really work?"

Smith shrugged. "They say it does but it's never been tested over here. I don't care if you fry his brains, just get me what I need to know."

★ ★ ★

Gill Somers had heard the sounds of Stu being taken and his mobile phone crushed beneath someone's boot. No chance of finding him through the embedded satellite location chip. This had forced her hand and Stu was right, it was time to press the button and go with Valkyrie. It would be a rough ride sure enough. Her laptop was open on her dressing table, the code ready to send.

She regretted hurting Ricky's feelings but if he was to be saved desperate measures were needed. Maybe he would forgive her one day; maybe not. Maybe the hurt was too deep and trust gone forever. Maybe what she was about to do would alienate him even further. Was it right to do wrong for a good cause? Was the cause sufficiently important to warrant the damage that was about to be done? She thought so and others did too but it was a massive step with massive dangers and no one would emerge unscathed.

It was her plan, her decision. Now she had an inkling of how the US president might feel with his finger on the nuclear trigger. Would he soul-search as much as she or was taking on the presidency something which came with a greater level of certainty? It was something that had to be faced, part of the job that came with no assurances. But not for her. She wasn't elected for this, had not been prepared for it. Maybe it wasn't quite as catastrophic an action as bringing down the holocaust of nuclear war but in its own way it would be almost as damaging to those involved with lives and careers like flotsam floating on the tide of disaster.

Then there was Ann FitzPatrick, her old friend from University who had jumped at the chance to defend Ricky in spite of the dangers to her reputation. Ann had always been up for a challenge, especially if the money was good. Gill's house, a gift from her father, was worth over a million pounds but she would sacrifice it, and the memories it held, for Ricky.

Stu's disappearance had thrown Ann and now she was wobbling under the pressure; in need of a steadying hand. The procedure was there. If Ann kept her head and followed her instructions there was a good chance they would keep ahead of the game.

Gill eyed the blinking cursor on the screen and hesitated, much as Stu had, even though she knew the time for procrastination was gone. As tough as Stu was, MI5 would eventually get what he knew, everyone gave it up in the end. Before that could happen it was time to give them something else to worry about. She hit the return key hard and 'file sent' came up almost immediately. It was amazing how something so small could cause so much damage.

Chapter Sixteen

It wasn't fear so much as a feeling of impending doom that clouded Ann's mind. Would the watchers from MI5 think it strange that she was making an unscheduled trip to her gym? Would they think it odd that she was no longer waiting for Stu to show up? Given that her phones were tapped they would know she was expecting him. On the other hand she *was* a woman unused to being kept waiting. Maybe pushed to impatience by her monthly cycle. There could be a dozen reasons but would MI5 accept the less-than-obvious? It was a gamble but so was everything now.

The gym was a modern one, off a main road in Mayfair. Expensive and discreet, she shared its services with sportspeople, movie stars and a fair sprinkling of London's rich socialites. It wasn't her only weakness but it was by far the most expensive. Her electronic membership card gained her access to the lobby where a muscular young man in a tight-fitting tee-shirt stood guard over the inner luxuries behind frosted glass doors that led first to the locker rooms and then to the various equipment and treatment rooms.

"Hello Darren. Nice evening."

"Hi Miss FitzPatrick. Yeah, looks nice but I ain't seen much of it from in here."

Ann smiled and crinkled her nose in sympathy. "I can imagine it gets a little claustrophobic at times. Don't they have anyone to relieve you?"

"Yeah, one of the personal trainers gives me a break every couple of hours, unless they have clients to look after, then I have to wait."

"It's good to know there's always someone on the door. I'd hate to think any Tom, Dick or Harry could get in," Ann said.

"Not much chance o' that, miss. There's close-circuit TV too. If there's any trouble I'd have a couple of the lads in here in double-quick time. That's what you clients pay for and we take your security very seriously."

"Glad to hear it, Darren. Have you had any problems recently?"

Darren was torn between passing the time with a beautiful woman and giving out any information that could be misconstrued. "Nah we never have no bother, miss."

"Never?"

"Well once in a while some punk'll try to talk his way in but we send him on his way, y'know?"

"Not many people can get one over you, I bet."

Darren grinned. "Not any, miss. I even tossed out the people who came to fix the security cameras before the boss cleared it with their company."

"When was that?"

"Couple of weeks ago. I was suspicious see cos we hadn't had any trouble with the cams. Turns out it was a standard maintenance visit so no problem."

Ann gave Darren an admiring glance. "I'm very glad to hear you're on the ball. Keep it up, Darren." She pushed her way through the glass doors leaving Darren preening himself on her praise.

That was too easy. Had Darren been briefed? Was she becoming paranoid? What advantage would MI5 gain by her knowing they had been here. None that she could fathom, unless the tactics were now to throw her off her stroke, keep her looking over her shoulder, afraid of her own shadow. If so, it was working.

MI5 here too. What had they done and where had they done it? Those were the burning questions. And what had happened to Stu? His failure to show up, or even to call, was becoming ever more ominous.

Her locker had been opened. The tell-tale was missing. Nothing but gym shoes and a swimming costume there for them to rummage through. But how clever had they been? There were no cameras in the locker room. None officially but it wasn't beyond the bounds of possibility that they had installed a feed in one of the ventilation ducts overlooking her locker. Assuming they had, she would change in the ladies'. No, *No!* That was a giveaway. It was necessary to bite that particular bullet and act as she had always done.

Now the fear was turning to anger and anger to resolve. The bastards couldn't do this to her, make her feel like a helpless child. If they wanted a fight she would give it to them. She took a water bottle from her hold-all to drink but the bottle slipped from her fingers and splashed on the tiled floor.

In a corner was a small walk-in cupboard where the cleaners kept their materials and clothing in a metal locker. The locker was freestanding with a gap between it and the wall just wide enough for her to get her fingers through to grasp a key taped to the back wall. It was for a car left permanently in the underground car park at Park Lane. It belonged to an Arab client of her chambers who used it on his infrequent visits to Britain. It had not been moved for nine months and the boot of the Rolls Royce held a multitude of secrets.

Ann picked up a mop and made a play of wiping the floor by her locker before returning the mop to its closet and making for the gym. So far, so good.

★ ★ ★

Smith came in unheard and made Mason jump so much his artificial hip went into spasm. "Don't do that."

"What?"

"Creep in like that. I nearly deleted a whole morning's file."

"You're getting sassy, mate. I'd cool it if I were you. Have you got anything worth bothering over?"

Mason grinned to himself. If only Smith knew. "Nothing. FitzPatrick's at her gym. Nice body, very nice. She likes to keep in shape."

"There was nothing in her locker." It wasn't a question.

"A pair of sweaty trainers and a wrinkled swimsuit she'd forgotten to wash the last time she used it."

Smith curled his lip. "Like I said."

"She did have a dodgy conversation with Dalgleish a few hours ago. Something about her hair being out of place. Some sort of code if you ask me."

"I know about that," Smith said. "We've got Dalgleish and he's talking; singing like a canary. Won't be long before we wring everything out of him. Got the right woman on *that* job."

"Meaning..."

"Pull your socks up, laddie. You're falling off the pace and it's been noticed."

"Moi? I'm the best you've got. It's this useless kit you give me to work with."

"Why didn't you spot the incursion? Dalgleish tapped into our computer links," Smith snorted.

"It didn't come through the firewall otherwise I'd have found it," Mason said.

"It was done manually from within. That's what Dalgleish said."

"I'll pull up the visitor logs for the past couple of weeks."

Smith snorted again. "Make it quick." He needed to speak to Mo. It seemed as if FitzPatrick was on the level. Concern over her lacklustre defence was just that, a mild concern. If she was hiding anything then Dalgleish would know and that intelligence would have to be dug out of him one way or another. It was belt and braces but he had to be sure. The trial was just a few days away.

★　★　★

Ken twitched the curtains open and peered out into the night. "Something's up," he said nasally and fingered the disfiguring dressing across the bridge of his nose. "The bastards are on the move over there." He inclined his head towards the gates of Credenhill. "All sorts of stuff pulling out, must be a real flap on."

Mo nodded absent-mindedly, she had more to think about than SAS night manoeuvres. "This stuff's not working." She held up the syringe, now half empty.

Ken grunted and gave Stu's trussed figure a full-blooded kick on the thigh. "Gi' me five minutes with him. I'll make the bastard talk."

Mo cupped Stu's chin in her hand and turned his head from side to side. "He's not responding. I expected him to be bouncing off the walls but not comatose. He can't talk if he's unconscious."

"He's faking," Ken said with certainty. "Better give him the rest."

"You're a bright spark and no mistake. It'll fry his brains if not outright kill him. Then he'll be no good to us."

"Give it to him anyway. It might work but we haven't lost anything either way, cos he's not talking right now."

"These truth serums aren't what they're cracked up to be," Mo said. "It depends on the questions whether you get useful answers. You can get as much shit as you can truth. This stuff is a variation of SP 17. It's mixed with pure ethanol to loosen his tongue but it just ain't working."

"So why are we messing around?"

Mo sighed. She really did not want to hurt Dalgleish, not permanently, but now she had little choice as the half-dose had not worked. Perhaps Ken was right and it was time to go the whole hog, especially as Smith was pushing for results.

"Tighten up that ligature on his arm. I need a good vein."

Ken put a vicious twist into the rubber tubing around Stu's bicep and he stirred. "There told you he was faking."

Stu's eyes flickered open but appeared unfocused. His mouth drooped open and saliva ran in a thin stream down his chin.

"Hello, Stu. With us are you? How many fingers am I holding up?" Mo said.

Stu's eyes did a 360 degree swivel before centring on Mo's fist. "Sssh Threee."

"Is your name Dalgleish?"

"Yeesssh."

"Do you serve with the SAS?"

Stu did not reply and his swivelling eyes wandered to the window.

"Are you serving with the SAS?" Mo repeated patiently. From habit Stu would fight not to answer that one. She tried another tack. "Do you know Ann Fitzpatrick?"

Stu's mouth had now formed a slack grin. "Yeeesssh."

"Do you know her well?"

"Nooo."

"Is she hiding something?"

Stu did not reply and Mo knew she would have to find a better way of phrasing the question. "Does she talk to you?"

Stu's eyes were again on the window where Ken had left a crack between the curtains, his grin even slacker and wider.

"Does she talk to you?" Mo repeated.

"Yeeesssh."

"Does she tell you secrets?"

"Secretsss. Plenty secretsss."

Mo looked across at Ken and winked. "Now we're getting somewhere."

"Does she talk about the trial; Major Keane's trial?"

"Yesssh."

"Does she have any secrets about Major Keane's trial?"

"Issa secret."

"What is, Stu? What's a secret?"

"Valkyrie!"

"Sounds like a codename," Ken grunted.

"Shut up," Mo snapped and gave him a savage look, "you'll break the chain."

"Stu," she cooed, "what's Valkyrie?"

"Ride. Greensleeves, sssecret."

"He's associating, regaining some control, we've lost him," Mo said.

"What's this Greensleeves stuff?" Ken asked.

Mo didn't take her eyes off Stu's face. "As I said, he's associating. *Ride of the Valkyrie* is the regimental march of the

Paras. *Greensleeves* was the slow march of the old Women's Royal Army Corps before it was disbanded in '92. I can't see the relevance of that but Stu obviously sees a connection. May be relevant, may not. Time for a second dose, it's kill or cure."

★ ★ ★

It had been a hard day at the office. Hathaway kicked off his shoes and made straight for the under-sink cupboard and his first Guinness of the day. He opened the bottle and checked his watch. Nearly midnight. What would his old dad have made of all this overtime without double-bubble? It was worth it to be at the centre of power in the country, to be part of a cosy team near to the centre of government, to kick around ideas and make decisions, big decisions, on how the country was run, to make policy on the hoof. It was better than sex. Being honest with himself he wasn't a first rank player, not yet. He still had his boss between himself and the inner sanctum but that was fine, he and his boss were like-minded. They were a team.

He wandered into the small sitting-room and flipped on CNN to check on the rest of the world's news. It paid to keep informed, especially on how the world viewed Britain and its politics. Not that there were many friends out there who weren't after a handout.

The war in Afghanistan was going well. CNN was showing a clip of a newly re-opened school where girls were once again receiving an education having been denied it under the Taliban's rule. Bloody mediaeval, the Taliban. Hathaway was glad he had helped in the decision to go to war alongside the Yanks. It was a righteous cause and it didn't do Britain's reputation any harm in the States.

Hathaway opened his laptop and settled on the settee to type up some notes for the next day's press releases.

It happened fast. The door burst open and four masked men raced in. Before he could move Hathaway was thrown face down on the floor, his laptop spinning down with him. A knee was pushed hard in his back and his arms were wrenched up and taped together. A foot pushed his face into the rug so that he couldn't breathe; old dust stung the back of his throat as he tried to drag in a ragged gasp. A hand grabbed his hair and pulled hard. The knee was still in his back and the movement was excruciating. Duct tape was wound dextrously all around his head covering his eyes and mouth with just enough space left for him to breathe through his nose. Then he was hauled to his feet and carried head-first from the flat and down the stairs. Cool air hit his neck and he was rushed across the pavement and thrown bodily into the back of a vehicle with a solid metal floor. He heard a door slide shut and a voice yelled a command that had the van roaring away. Hathaway's blood ran cold. The voice had spoken in Arabic.

★ ★ ★

Simon Oakley settled into the comfortable back seat of his ministerial Prius and congratulated himself on another triumphant meeting. Of course he had been preaching to the converted with the brothers of the Trades Union Congress but it still gave him a warm feeling of shared values. He closed his eyes and let his head fall back against the restraint. He was half-asleep when he felt the car's petrol engine fire up. It shouldn't have happened. The short ride to his London home could have been accomplished solely on the battery motor.

He opened his eyes and peered around. "Frank, where are we?"

"Frank he off sick, minister. I drive you."

"Well you're going the wrong way. You've missed the turning." Oakley could only see the back of the driver's head. Long unruly hair on which perched, ludicrously, a peaked chauffeur's cap which was two sizes too small.

"It okay, sir. We had call from Whitehall. You wanted back there."

"Why wasn't I informed personally?" Oakley said, half to himself. He pulled out his Blackberry to check his messages. No signal. Oakley gave it a useless shake. "Damned things, never work when you need them. Who was it that called?"

"Whitehall."

"I know but who at Whitehall?"

They had turned down a quiet street behind Covent Garden. The car in front stopped suddenly and the driver hit the brakes hard. Oakley was thrown forward as the doctored clasp of his seatbelt pulled free and he hit the back of the front passenger seat with stunning force. The Prius's doors were wrenched open and Oakley was dragged roughly from the vehicle and onto the cold hard road. He looked up and saw a face hidden behind a chequered Palestinian scarf before a sack was pulled over his head and there was a sharp prick of pain in his arm.

Chapter Seventeen

M o bit her lip. This was beginning to get out of hand. The additional dose of the drug had now rendered Stu unconscious but not before he had been able to expand on Valkyrie. There was something bad there, something deep, but the clues were too few to work with, not until Stu came round again – if he ever did. She'd get no bouquets if he died. In spite of what Smith said MI5 would pull the plug and let them all swirl down the nearest drain. MI5 would like the world to believe they were whiter than white and that's why they used deniable sources like her. But there were some seriously bad people populating the service and she had no illusions about them. Smith was one.

Ken was fiddling with a coffee mug with his back to the window. "I still think he's shamming," He didn't really believe it but it was something to say to fill the empty air. He could see the creases in Mo's brow and felt the storm clouds gathering. "What's up, Mo?"

She ignored him with a slight shake of the head that said '*do not disturb*.' Ken flicked the dregs from his mug onto the stained carpet and levered himself off the windowsill. "I'm gonna get another coffee. Want one?" Again the shake of the head. Ken grunted and made for the kitchen.

Mo watched him go but did not see him. There was too much going on in her head and all of it frightened her. She had tried ringing her boss at the security company but he was enjoying himself at a high-octane bash and wouldn't take her call. *Useless bastard.* He of all people should know that in this business it was 24/7. But the money and power of the A-listers he now mixed with had turned his head. It was big business now with lots of overheads and that required hours of networking and pressing flesh. All to the good but operational needs should be paramount. Mo made a mental note to take her pay and sign off the company's books after this job. It was getting decidedly risky.

She did not want to call Smith but someone needed to take control of the situation and quickly. Her mobile window read 'No Service' and she frowned. There was a crash from the kitchen and the lights went out. "Ken? What are you doing in there, you stupid bugger? Get those lights back on."

The door flew open. Two men, masked and dressed in black charged into the room their HKMP5 SPs in the shoulder streaming laser beams. One went left, one right and cleared the room. A third man came in close behind and landed on Mo with his full weight. He ripped out plasticuffs from his belt and trussed her like an oven-ready chicken.

"House clear," Pete's voice sounded softly in Tonka's earpiece as he finished securing the woman.

"All sorted?"

"No problems," Pete responded. "The two blokes asleep in the bedrooms were no trouble and the one in the kitchen went down like he'd been hit by a Challenger. All three secured and ready for transport."

"Get the medics in. Stu looks in a bad way and I want him casevac'd soonest. I'll keep the woman in here for now. I want everything documented and photographed before we go and it's got to be quick so get to it."

* * *

Mo's breathing was impaired by the thick hood that sucked into her mouth every time she took a deep breath. She shook her head in a futile attempt to clear it. She knew the man's voice. "It's Tonka, isn't it? Long time no see, big boy. Can you take this hood off? I'd like to get an eyeful now."

"No can do, Mo. Not even for old times' sake. We had some good ones back when, didn't we, girl?"

"Cost me my first marriage, you did, you big ape."

"Takes two, Mo. And there wasn't much else to do some nights with South Det."

"When you weren't pissing up the wall in the mess or hanging a kid's dumper truck off your dick, you mean," Mo grumbled.

Tonka smiled slowly. "Keep that to yourself. I've been trying to live it down since then."

"You married now then?"

"No. Never got around to it. Too much to do, no time to do it. You know how it is. Besides I've seen too many marriages go down the swannee in the Reg to want to go through that myself. Haven't got the guts for it," Tonka said.

"What happens now then? How'd you get on to us?"

"We've been keeping an eye on you for a while now but you went a bit too far with Stu. Couldn't let you carry on like that. Hope you haven't done him any permanent damage," Tonka said. His voice was still light but Mo did not mistake the underlying message.

"Yeah, me too. He's a good lad."

"The medics have got him now. It's down to them but I wouldn't want to be in your shoes if he turns up his toes."

Mo pulled a face under the hood. She knew the score. "Are my other blokes all right?

"Just worry about yourself. We're gonna be moving you out soon and I don't want any dramas. Will you keep quiet or do I have to put a muffler on you?"

"I'll come quietly, guv. Honest!" Mo said.

"Just as well. I wouldn't want to mess up that pretty face. Nice hair too; very you."

"I wasn't sure about the hair," Mo said. "Was it that that gave the game away?"

Tonka laughed. "Partly. You did stick out a bit. But I liked it."

"Any chance? After this is over, you know, of going for a drink or something?"

"I wouldn't mind," Tonka said, "if this pans out okay. We'll see. But don't go thinking I'll go easy on you until then. You ain't out of the woods, Mo. Not by a long chalk."

★ ★ ★

The mobile phone was in the dead letter drop, just as Stu had said it would be. Ann passed the spot twice to make sure there was no one nearby to intercept the call. The package wrapped in plastic and securely taped was in a hollow log on Wimbledon Common. It took a few seconds to open and she glanced around nervously, expecting unwanted company at any time. Stu had told her about the abilities of MI5's A4 to watch without being seen but he had also told her that the job had been contracted out and that the private company people were less well-trained. Any followers should be easy to spot as they did not have the logistics to do the job properly. She hoped it was the case as she was no expert at spotting tails.

The phone had a number preset in its memory and she called it. It rang only twice. "Yes?"

It was Gill and Ann was pleased but also disappointed. She hoped it would be Stu. It struck her as odd that she should miss him so much.

"Please be quick," Gill said.

"I've had visitors, can't move without bumping into them. Can't make the boot sale. I'll leave that to you. Meet you at the event."

"You're a quick study."

Ann could feel the smile in Gill's voice and was reassured. "Any news...?"

"I'll be there. Hasta luego."

The phone cut off. Ann had been walking slowly as she made the call and reached a bench. She sat and slowly looked around. There were now one or two walkers and a young couple two-hundred metres away pushing a buggy. Ann removed the SIM from the phone, dropped it on the floor and ground it under her heel until it was almost unrecognisable. She walked away and dropped the phone into a bin on passing. She glanced behind at the young couple who were now seated on her bench fussing over a child in the buggy. She smiled. Maybe that part of life had already passed her by.

The young man with the buggy reached in and turned off the scanner.

"Did we get it?" his companion asked.

"Yeah for what it's worth. Anything left of the SIM that we could use?

The woman moved the plastic with a toe. "It's totally fucked. Nobody could get anything off that."

"Thought they said she was an amateur. Somebody's been briefing her."

The woman shrugged. "Let's get that phone message back to Thames House. Then it's not our problem anymore."

* * *

Smith swung into the techie's cubicle with an urgent walk that hinted at his uncertain state of mind. "Do you have the entry cam videos sorted yet?"

Mason wheeled his chair around to face him. "Yeah. I've been through hours of the stuff but nothing stands out. Nice pics of you though, coming and going. You're a busy boy these days."

Smith ignored the jibe for now. He was getting fed up with the techie's backchat and would get his revenge in time. But now was not the time nor the place.

"Anything else I should know about?"

"Just had a mobile phone conversation radioed in from FitzPatrick's watchers. The phone was picked up from a drop and she destroyed the SIM immediately afterwards. She's really been given the SP."

"Fuck!" The word was spat out like bad lobster. "What was the gist of the call and who was it made to?"

Mason played back the call.

"Who's the other woman?" Smith asked.

"Thought you'd ask that but the trace proved negative. It was a pay-as-you-go mobile with no account details. Just use and dump the SIM."

"So we have nothing useful?"

"Well now we know there's someone else involved. We know that FitzPatrick's on to us and from the content of the call they've got something to hide," Mason said.

"But we don't know who this new woman is, where she is or what it is she's hiding, do we?" Smith said.

Mason shook his head with a doleful expression on his face. "No, sir, we don't."

"Keep digging around in FitzPatrick's background. There must be someone, somewhere in her past she trusts enough with this job.

"No, forget it. I'll get someone from 'F' branch to do that. I want you to concentrate on keeping tabs on FitzPatrick. Do we have anything useful from the outside help?"

Mason looked glum again. "I can't raise them right now. The computer links are down as well as the mobiles. There must be some sort of communications tower failure in the area. I'm looking into it."

Smith's gut churned out a message that he hadn't felt since the Cold War days. He hadn't liked it then and he didn't like it now. He hurried back to his office with its window overlooking Millbank and the oily reaches of the Thames. His seniority gave him access to such luxuries but he wondered how long he would be able to hang onto it should this one go pear-shaped. The Director General was beginning to take a personal interest, having been advised by one of the Service's myriad contacts in Whitehall of the delicacy of the situation. DG was not one to disappoint or to take disappointment lightly. Smith wondered again whether it was too late to off-load the case onto a minion but he had allowed himself to be dazzled by the prize and become too hands-on. It was a mistake, he now realised. Years of being part of an untouchable clique which was a law unto itself had lowered his natural guardedness, had breached his armour of invincibility. Getting out of this with his career intact would be something to which he would apply his maximum attention. In the meantime he would shoulder boulders uphill to stop this case from going south and he would re-double his efforts to find a scapegoat in case success eluded him. First he needed to cover his back with Mo and her team, to scrub the slate clean; cut them loose.

His desk phone rang suddenly and he snatched it from its cradle. "What?"

It was Mason. "Just had a wire from Special Branch. You're not gonna like this?"

What now? "Get on with it, man."

"One of the defence ministers has been taken off the street near Covent Garden. It's Simon Oakley. Local plod received an anonymous phone message calling it in. Witness said the snatchers were wearing Arab head scarves. Oakley was bundled into a dark saloon car. Oakley's driver and car are missing too. That's all they've got right now."

"When did this happen?"

"Couple of hours ago. Special Branch was only notified after the local plod realised what they were dealing with," Mason said.

Smith slammed down the phone and picked it up immediately to call GCHQ in Palmer Street. "George, it's Smith. Have you heard about Oakley?"

"Negative. What's happened?"

Smith took a deep breath. "He's been snatched and it looks like some Arab organisation. Anything shown up recently? Any increased comms or other noise?"

"Nothing. It's been particularly quiet over the past few weeks. The Taliban and al-Qaeda licking their wounds in Pakistan is the majority of the traffic. We've had no inkling of any action on home turf. This is out of the blue."

"Better get your boys on the lookout for traffic now. We don't have much to work on except someone thinks the Arabs were wearing Palestinian headgear."

"Could be someone wants us to think they were Palestinians."

"Conjecture," Smith said. "I tend to agree with you but I need hard facts. Get on it, George. This is major league and we've been caught with our pants down."

Smith had hardly replaced the receiver when the phone rang again. DG's secretary. DG wanted to see every branch head in one hour.

Smith gathered his thoughts. This would be about Oakley, not about the Keane case but it was a distraction when he least needed it. He spent time gathering his portfolio and making further calls. DG would expect some progress to have been made and it paid to put wheels in motion. He accomplished as much as he was able and turned to leave. The phone rang again. Smith was tempted to ignore it but his instinct told him otherwise. "Yes?"

It was Mason. "You won't believe this, boss. They've snatched Hathaway."

Smith sat heavily in his chair and banged his head three times on the desk.

Chapter Eighteen

It was late but the Defence Estates Police guard checked her pass and allowed her in. Ann was escorted through a strangely silent Credenhill to Ricky's room. He was there polishing shoes that already had a mirror-like sheen to the toecaps. He stood as she entered and was pleased to see a spark in his eyes.

He moved to greet her and kissed her lightly on the cheek.

She sat on the room's one chair and he resumed his seat on the end of his bed. She glanced around at the orderliness of the room and his Number 2 dress uniform hanging on the handle of the closet, the two parts of a Sam Browne belt, also highly polished, dangling around the shank of the hanger by its buckles. "Very smart. The medal ribbons look good."

"MoD seat polishing, Battle of the Circle Line, Order of the paper-clip counters, etcetera. Nothing to get excited about." Ricky said.

Ann was no expert but she recognised the white and blue colours of the Military Cross ribbon. She knew Ricky's military record by heart so the others must be campaign medals for Iraq and Afghanistan with Northern Ireland thrown in for good measure. Ricky was no armchair warrior.

He noticed her looking around the room and pre-empted her next question. "They're moving me up to Catterick tomorrow for the court martial, that's why the room is so tidy."

Ann smiled. "I did wonder, it's not usually this organised."

"Clean, you mean. One has to do one's best. I'd hate to be called slovenly on top of everything else. Why are you here so late?"

She was prepared for the question and decided to give it to him straight. He had earned her honesty. "I wanted to see how you were bearing up. Just a few hours to go and some people have been known to go to pieces. I like to try to give them some backbone but you obviously don't need it."

Ricky smiled. "I got over my rocky patch a while ago. I'm ready for this. I want to clear my name."

"I won't try to bullshit you." Ann grimaced as if the word itself had left a sour taste in her mouth. "It will be a hard fight and there's no certainty that we will win."

"I like tough odds. Makes life more interesting."

Ann nodded but she could see her words had hit a soft spot. He'd measure the size of the problem in his mind and measure his ability to deal with it also. Ricky was a fighter and he would be fine. She stood to leave. "That's all I came for, unless you have anything you'd like to ask?"

"Is it me, or is it very quiet out there?"

"Seems to be but I really wouldn't know with what to compare it."

"Not just me then. This place usually bustles at all hours. Must be a flap on," Ricky said.

He sounded wistful and Ann gave his shoulder an understanding squeeze. "This one's not your problem. Get some rest."

"Yeah, goodnight, Ann. See you in court."

Her police guard was waiting for her outside. "Colonel's compliments, ma'am. Could you spare him a few minutes?"

Tim Bailey was in his office and she was shown straight in. He greeted her and showed her to a chair. Ann shot him a quizzical look.

"Miss FitzPatrick, thank you for sparing me the time."

"Not at all, Colonel." She waited to see in which direction the conversation would go. It was his move.

"As the Regiment's commanding officer I'm responsible for the men under my command. In effect that means on and off duty, here and abroad. Whatever they do reflects on the Regiment, the army in general and me as the guy in charge. I wouldn't want you to think that that would prejudice my behaviour in any way against Ricky Keane."

"I'm glad we got that out of the way, Colonel."

"I'm not being very direct, am I?"

"From what I hear that's unusual for you."

Bailey smiled and it crinkled the skin around his eyes. Visible signs of aging that were growing faster. This business was aging him by the minute. "Is there anything I can do to help your case?"

That surprised her. "What could you do?"

"In all truth there is little I can do inside the courtroom but I can make sure that anything you need will be supplied."

"That's very kind, Colonel..."

"Tim, please."

"...Tim. But aren't you putting your own career on the line by backing a potential criminal?"

"Have you noticed how quiet it is outside?"

Ann nodded. "It does seem rather desolate."

"That's because yesterday night every trooper, NCO and Warrant Officer in two Sabre Squadrons pulled out to I know not where. All I'm left with are the senior officers, the training squadron, the signals unit and elements of HQ staff who are needed here. Virtually the entire Regiment not actively engaged has gone AWOL. That's my career killer, I've got nothing left to lose."

"I have two questions. Do you know *why*? And why are you telling *me* this?"

Bailey pursed his lips, stood to walk to his desk, opened a drawer and pulled out a bottle of single malt. He waved the bottle. "Can I offer you one?"

Ann shook her head. "This has nothing to do with me, you know."

"Possibly it has more to do with you than you realise. To answer your first question." He paused to pour a good measure. "On the surface it's to do with trust. The men no longer trust the government to look after their interests. The Regiment is making a point. Technically it's mutiny but if I were to show you the training schedules every one would show a legitimate reason for the squadrons to be away. Only that's not really the way we do things. This is a deliberate withdrawal of labour to make a protest."

"And, will it work?"

Bailey shrugged. "This will be like detonating a Hydrogen Bomb under the MoD. There will be massive amounts of fallout and a lot of collateral damage but I cannot see the government giving way to this type of blackmail short-term. Long-term it may have the desired effect but many of the men currently serving will not be around to benefit from it, including me.

"As to your second question. I believe that the underlying cause of this is the arrest and trial of Major

Keane. It was the spark in the powder keg. The only way it can be prevented from becoming an explosion that will resonate throughout the army as a whole would be if you won your case. Will you be able to do that?"

"I haven't lost yet, Tim"

"That's not what I was asking."

"Do you know that during the process of this case MI5 have gone out of their way to obstruct me? That Major Keane's room is bugged, that my chambers and telephones are bugged, that my every move is watched and reported upon, that my home and personal effects have been broken into? Do you know I have no idea who I can trust, Tim?"

Bailey kept a level gaze over the rim of his glass. "I had an inkling but no idea it was that serious."

"Trust me on that, Tim. I have no proof but I can surmise that my defence case is in the hands of the prosecution who will know every move I am going to make and will have counter moves already in place. In short, Tim, I have been hamstrung from the very beginning. And you ask if I can win?"

"So, I ask again. Is there anything, anything at all, I can do to help? This is no longer about one man but an entire service and I would do anything up to and beyond giving my own life to prevent a meltdown of the army."

"Do you have contact with the Sabre Squadrons?"

"That's why the signallers stayed behind, I'm sure."

"Then there might very well be a lot you could do. I'm going to have to trust you, Tim. Please don't let me down."

As she was escorted to the gate Ann was distracted by a helicopter taking off. "What's that?"

The policeman didn't bother to turn. "Colonel's chopper, ma'am. He's off somewhere in a right tearing hurry."

Ann bit her lip and hoped she had not put her trust in the wrong man.

★ ★ ★

Hathaway had been conscious for most of the journey. A bumpy ride for the first hour until he was carried into a light aircraft. Another captive had been thrown in with him. He could feel the weight of a body against his but whoever it was did not move and barely breathed. Hathaway thanked his stars for small mercies. But could his own plight be much worse?

The small plane landed with a thump and they taxied first across grass and then ribbed concrete until the plane came to a halt. Once again he was carried head first up an incline and into what smelled like a fuel tank. He was dropped into some netting and securely lashed. He could hear Arabic being spoken all around him as the second body's feet smacked against his skull as it too was lashed down. Another aircraft, the stink was aviation fuel. This one was much larger and sounds echoed around a cavernous fuselage. Orders were given and Hathaway heard four big engines start up and soon the whole plane was vibrating as the engines were run up for a surprisingly short take-off. In seconds the plane was in the air and climbing at an acute angle.

Someone came and said something in Arabic then the tape was pulled away from his mouth and water dribbled in. They weren't going to be allowed to die from thirst. But there was a much more practical reason as Hathaway soon discovered as vomit rose in his throat driven by the stink and the irregular motion of the plane. He heard the other body groan; at least he was still alive but, like Hathaway, probably wishing he was not.

He had lost track of time. They could have been in the air for minutes or hours. He had vomited three times and the acrid taste filled his mouth and made him gag again. No more water had been forthcoming. He had tried to shout above the din but had received nothing but a kick on the shoulder to add to his discomfort. In lucid moments he had tried to analyse why. Why him? It wasn't as if he was high profile in the anti-terrorist war. He was close to the top of government but could be replaced without undue trouble. It eluded him. Maybe he was just in the wrong place at the wrong time, perhaps a would-be terrorist had mistaken him for someone else.

But these people seemed high-powered, well-briefed, well-funded and well-equipped. Would they make such a mistake? What did they hope to gain? The government would not make deals with terrorists, not normally, only when it was costing the country's taxpayers and big business more than the government wanted to concede. Not in his case. As a bargaining chip he was next to worthless.

A change in engine note brought him out of his reverie. The plane was about to land and he might soon have answers he would rather not have.

* * *

The situation had escalated far faster than Smith had thought possible and was going way over-the-top. Now Cobra, the government's crisis response committee, was involved with the Home Secretary in the chair. Around the table of briefing room 'A' sat the heads of both MI5 and MI6, the Commissioner of the Metropolitan Police, a man Smith did not know from GCHQ, the Chair of the Joint Intelligence Committee and, freshly arrived from Hereford, the acting OC of the SAS.

Smith was bored. The Home Secretary was embroiled in an argument about the political fallout should it ever become public knowledge that a defence minister had been so easily taken off a London Street. The Met Commissioner was getting it in the neck, poor sod.

Now it was MI5's turn to get a roasting and the ever-present question was *WHY*? Why hadn't the Security Service seen this coming? Smith's DG, a smooth operator in this environment was spreading the responsibility over the entire anti-terrorist network without making any apparent accusations against any one service. It was a masterly act and Smith silently applauded. DG nodded to Smith. Now it was time for some better news as Smith's enquiries were beginning to pay dividends.

"Gentlemen," Smith said, "we are beginning to get intelligence back from various enquiries we've put in hand. Although we still don't know who is responsible, leads are beginning to surface. The minister's driver was held at gunpoint at home, bound and gagged whilst his place was taken by one of the terrorists. Special Branch has a team of Scene of Crime specialists at the driver's home going over it with a fine tooth comb. The phone call that was made to the police after the attack on the minister was traced to a pay-as-you-go mobile and that call had been made from within two hundred metres of the scene. The caller withheld his details which is not unusual in these circumstances as members of the public are loathe to become further involved. However, his description of Palestinian type headgear should not have too much relevance placed on it.

"CCTV cameras around the area are few and thinly spread which may be why the terrorists chose that location. We do however have several shots of a dark saloon leaving the area and are in the process of tracking its movements. This inevitably takes time but we should soon have a good idea in which direction it was ultimately headed. The minister's Prius was dumped in Battersea and taken by joy riders until seen by the police heading towards Balham. A chase ensued and the vehicle crashed. The culprits were detained at the scene but appear to have no connection with the minister's abduction. Apparently the car was left with its doors agape and the keys in the ignition; it being too much of a temptation for these young men to refuse. The car is being recovered as we speak and will be subjected to thorough examination."

"Do you have anything of a more positive nature?" The Home Secretary asked. "It seems to me that this is getting out of hand. There are too many people involved something's bound to leak."

"The Prius will not be connected to the minister's disappearance, Home Secretary," the Commissioner said. "There were no outward markings on the vehicle and the House of Commons seal had already been removed from the windscreen. It was the VRN that gave us the clue. The two thieves concerned would not know that."

The Home Secretary blew out his cheeks. "That at least is one small mercy."

"Then we have the case of Mr. Hathaway," Smith continued. "We do not know of any reason why Hathaway was abducted. There doesn't seem to be anything connecting the two cases."

"They were together at my RHQ a few days ago," Bailey said. "Might there be a connection there?"

Smith did not want to go down that route. "No, Colonel. That's pure coincidence and just speculation."

Bailey was not to be put off. "Even so, it is a connection when there appears to be no other."

Bailey was mischief-making, Smith could feel it but, and there was that word again, *WHY*?

The Home Secretary turned his face towards Smith's DG. "Look into it. Now can we get on?"

Smith folded his portfolio and sat back as the DG caught his eye. Smith felt the gooseflesh rise on his neck. That was a look he'd hoped he'd never see.

Chapter Nineteen

The English language version of Al-Jazeera was up on the big plasma screen in Mason's cubicle. "This came in this morning."

Smith stared at the images. Hathaway and Oakley were bound and hooded. They were kneeling in front of three masked men wearing Palestinian shamags and carrying AK47s in various aggressive poses. A banner behind read in Arabic and English *'Shuhada: Martyrs of the Jihad'* in white on a green background. There was a graphic depicting an exploding hand grenade in black, red and white. "Who are these people?"

Mason froze the recording. "Shuhada means martyr in Arabic. Nobody's ever heard of Martyrs of the Jihad. They must be a new group. MI6 is doing some background checks," Mason said.

"What do they want?"

Mason set the video rolling again. One of the gunmen stepped forward and pulled the hood from Oakley's head so that his face was clearly seen. He began ranting in Arabic. A caption began to roll from right to left across the bottom of the screen. *'British imperialist Crusaders must leave Afghanistan or these men will die. It will not be a martyrs death. They will be beheaded like common thieves as they have stolen the lives of many brothers with their Crusader ways. British government is given three days to publicly issue a withdrawal order and to apologise to the Afghani peoples. There will be no further warnings.'*

"Don't want much do they," Smith muttered.

"Standard operating procedure," Mason said. "Given time they'll settle for a couple of million dollars."

"It's time and money we don't have. And this lot sound serious."

On the screen the man doing the talking grabbed Oakley's thinning hair, pulled his head back to expose his throat and drew a wicked looking knife from a scabbard on his belt. The knife was laid against Oakley's bobbing adam's apple.

"Three days...or he dies," the man said in heavily accented English. The screen went black.

"The government aren't going to like this," Smith said. "There's no way we're going to meet those demands. Do we have any clues as to who these people are, anything at all?"

Mason grinned. "I do have some good news. GCHQ, MI6 and we have put together some interesting stuff. We tracked the car that took Oakley from the outskirts of west London, along the M3. It came off at the Fleet exit and was next seen at Blackbushe Airport in Hampshire. There was one take-off at that time. It was a Sky- Van and the flight plan was filed to Southampton.

"From Southampton we got intel that the Sky-Van landed shortly before a cargo plane registered in Libya took off. The plane had landed at Southampton for an unscheduled stop caused by a fuel problem, or so the pilot said. It had filed an onward flight plan to Morocco but there is no record of it having landed there. Satellite pictures from the area, and we were lucky here as the bird was doing its sweep at the time, show a similar aircraft overflying Yemen and approaching Sana'a airport."

"Christ, they could be anywhere," Smith said. "The Yemen is full of al-Qaeda supporters and training camps. We'll never find them."

Mason grinned again. "We had another stroke of luck there. And this is where GCHQ comes in. One of the kidnappers used a mobile from the scene of the attack on Hathaway and it registered with GCHQ. It was used again two hours ago at a place just north of Sana'a. We have the rough coordinates. MI6 have an asset in the area and he's been sent to recce the place. With a touch more luck we'll have the hideout pinpointed by the end of today."

* * *

For the second time in two days Tim Bailey rode his helicopter to London together with his senior intelligence officer. The meeting was scheduled at MI6's HQ on the banks of the Thames. The area was officially known as Vauxhall Cross but Tim had heard it called, somewhat pretentiously, Riverside. They were expected and shown to one of the computer suites where a senior officer called Blake awaited them. With little preamble he started a briefing on the Covent Garden affair as it was beginning to become known.

Bailey had been briefed by his IO on the way down and listened carefully as Blake quickly outlined the current intel. It was becoming obvious what Blake wanted. "You're asking for a rescue plan?"

Blake nodded. "Can you do it?"

"All our assets are currently engaged. Even so it will take days to plan and get assets in position."

"We have two days," Blake said. "Are you saying you can't even attempt it?"

"It's an impossible timescale, even if we had the assets to hand, which we don't. Then again Yemen is a hostile country we can't count on them for help, in fact the government there is just as likely to take pot shots at us as the bandits. What do you think, Mike?"

Mike Quentin was scanning the aerial photographs and sketch maps displayed on wall mounted computer screens. "How good is this intel?"

Blake looked and acted like the head of a public school. He squinted at the muscular, fresh-faced, SAS man over the top of rimless spectacles with his chin on his chest. "GCHQ provided the coordinates and one of our own assets confirmed the likely location in this group of buildings here." Blake used a laser pointer to highlight the buildings in question on a satellite image with a circling motion. He stopped the pointer on one particular building. This is where we think the hostages are being kept. Our asset has seen men entering and leaving the building carrying what looks like bowls of food."

"And if he's wrong?" Bailey asked. "We would need confirmation before we go in guns blazing. What if it's a home full of women and children?"

Blake shrugged. "It's the best we can do in the timescale. The terrorists have threatened to execute both men at dawn their time in two days. Pressure's on with this Bailey, I've got my orders directly from 'C'. He is watching this with an eagle eye, as is the government. Oakley's a minister for god's sake. We can't let them get away with this."

"So the government is willing to send us in at half-cock, risking the lives of under-prepared troopers and possible civilian casualties for the sake of two men, both of whom happen to be part of the establishment. Is that right?"

"Oh don't get so self-righteous, Bailey. It's about the message it will send not to mess with us. We will just have to accept collateral damage."

"And that's the official government position?"

"Bailey, you are being deliberately naive. You know that cannot be the case. We in operations just have to bend the rules occasionally, especially if the cause is just."

"I've been thinking," Quentin said. "If we could appropriate a suitable aircraft we could get some spare bodies from the Kremlin out to Muscat to run the show. One of our squadrons is on exercise there with two Pumas from 33 Squadron RAF and one Hercules. We could use the Herc to drop a stick into Yemen. The extraction could be by Puma. They would have to use Saudi airspace to overfly and refuel in the Ar Ru'b' al Khali desert. Then it will be a pretty hairy low-level dash there and back across Yemeni territory from the Saudi border. Sana'a is pretty heavily populated and sneaking in and out quietly is a real no-no.

"Both choppers fly out from Muscat carrying spare fuel and a couple of ground crew with a pump. On the way back one carries the assault team blades with the hostages and the other the spare fuel. We could do it but those choppers will need to be in the air soon to be in position for the pick-up. It's got to be close to a 2,000 mile round trip for them. They average around 140mph and have a range of about 400 miles. That's three refuelling stops out and three back, bearing in mind Sana'a is around 2,200 metres above sea level, the Puma will need more fuel to climb. It's do-able but we'll need the blessings of Saint Chris."

"That's settled then," Blake said with a thin smile. "I'll leave it in your hands, Bailey." He turned away and did not see the look Bailey directed at his IO.

"Send everything you've got to Credenhill, Blake," Bailey said. "I want it there by the time we get back."

"And you shall have it, dear boy," Blake murmured, "you shall have it."

★ ★ ★

Oakley was kept hooded and apart from Hathaway. He knew Hathaway was there he had heard him calling for water and occasionally screaming at their captors. Oakley was never very good at physical resistance. He just succumbed to whatever indignity was thrust upon him. Surely these men had good reason for doing what they did. He thought he was in no real danger. The government would procure his release but he had to admit his bladder had given way when the knife had been held against his throat. He could still feel the sore spot where the blade had nicked the skin.

Apart from that he had not been brutalised which was a blessing. He was not good with pain and doubted he could withstand much of it. That his captors were capable of the utmost brutality he had no doubt. During the night, he assumed it was night, some poor soul in the next room had been given a dreadful beating. Her screams had rung in his ears. She had pleaded in some language he did not understand but he could feel the fear and the pain in the words. He felt for the woman, for the indignities and pain heaped upon her. It sounded as though she was raped repeatedly. The thought brought bile to his throat. It was unconscionable. How could civilized people do that to another? A small voice in his head made him squirm. It said at least it wasn't him. He'd read reports on African militias whose ganja raddled soldiers repeatedly and viciously raped other men before mutilating or killing them. Privately he thought death was the kinder option but even that made him cringe.

As the thought passed through his mind the door to the room swung open and another bundle of humanity was flung in. He could not see but he heard the grunt and whimper as the body hit the floor. The door was slammed shut without a word from the captors but the new arrival began sobbing quietly and scuffling slowly across the floor to the far wall.

Oakley swallowed, his mouth dry and foul but he managed to ungum his tongue. "Are you all right?" It was a stupid question for many reasons. The woman was patently not all right and probably did not understand him anyway. There was just a mewl of fear in response. "I won't hurt you, I couldn't I'm tied up and hooded too. There's nothing I can do to hurt you?"

"Or help me," The voice was barely feminine, raw from screaming and the accent was heavy. "You're British?"

Oakley nodded and tutted. How could she see such a movement? "Yes, my name's Simon. What's yours?"

The woman did not reply immediately and Oakley sank back into the huddle that had been his recent posture. Maybe she did not want to talk although he craved some companionship, any companionship as long as it wasn't his captors.

"I don't suppose it matters that you know," she said finally. "I've given up everything else. I'm Miriam."

"That's very..."

"Jewish...yes, I know."

"I was going to say very pretty." Oakley heard the woman groan again as she shuffled her body around on the floor. She began whispering in the same language that had filtered through the wall. Praying or cursing he could not be sure. "Are you badly injured?"

"I would be better dead," the woman said. "I have no life, no future. I have been soiled and desecrated. There is nothing left." Her last words were no more than a whisper. Oakley could almost feel the life force ebbing away from her. "You shouldn't give up, you know."

"I thought I would be prepared for this. I thought…but I was wrong. Nothing can prepare a woman for what has befallen me."

"In a short while this will only be an unpleasant memory. You sound so young, your whole life is ahead of you."

"What do you know, you're a man." There was thinly veiled contempt in the woman's voice. "You do not have to live with the stigma or the memory of the filth inside you. You are like the others. A woman's body is there for you to do with as you will. It is not, Mister Simon, it is *NOT*."

The last word was said with such venom it made Oakley recoil. He was about to apologise when the door slammed open again. The woman wailed in despair as she was dragged out. Oakley screamed too, screamed at the guards to leave her but his words were ignored. The screams carried to him from outside and then trailed off to a whimper punctuated by a single gunshot and then silence.

$$\star \quad \star \quad \star$$

Hathaway heard the shot. It was right outside his cell and he wondered who had paid the price. It hadn't been Oakley, the voice had been too feminine and they still had a day left to the deadline. Even so his stomach lurched and his anus twitched when the door slammed open and he was forcefully lifted from the floor into a chair. His hands were bound in front so that he was able to feed himself when the food did come, which was rare but now they were fastened to his thighs by a chain that was passed over his wrists and beneath the seat so that he could not lift his arms but was able to sit upright. The hood was pulled from his head and he blinked in the strong light that was glaring from arc lamps. He blinked again and turned his head, on either side stood a guard with a rifle, their faces concealed behind shamags and their eyes shielded by sunglasses.

"Meester Hath-way." The voice came from behind the lights from a shadow he could not penetrate. There was another movement and a video camera was slid into place on a tripod between the lights. Hathaway screwed up his eyes and stared at the lens. "It's Hath-A-way."

"Meester Hath-HER-way. It is time to send another message and we require you to dictate to the camera."

One of the guards leaned around him and thrust a handwritten card under his thumbs. It was printed in capital letters so it was easy to read. A hand switched on the camera and motioned him to start. He looked back at the lens and licked his lips.

"I have less than twenty-four hours left to live. If you value my life and that of Mr. Oakley you will comply with the wishes of the Shuhada: Martyrs of the Jihad.

"We are being well-treated but we know that our lives are at stake. Already, one Israeli..."

Hathaway paused and looked beyond the camera. "I can't read this."

"Read it or you will be dead sooner than you feared."

Behind his back one of the guards cocked his Kalashnikov and Hathaway nodded. "We are being well-treated but we know that our very lives are at stake. Already this morning one Israeli...whore...has been executed. I know, I heard the shot and the screams. Please help us. Get us out of here...please. These people mean it.

"They have a case, we should look at what we've done to Iraq and what we're doing in Afghanistan. Maybe we should think again, take a good look and review our involvement. We owe it to these people."

Hathaway had gone way off script but he heard a chuckle of approval from his tormentor.

"Veery good, Meester Hath-her-way. Better than my poor writings. You truly are a master of your craft."

"I just want to get back home."

"And Meester Oakley?"

"Him too, yeah, but whatever you need, I can help, right."

"What I need is not in your power to give."

"When I get back. I can put over your case for you, better than anyone. I have an in with the government, people in high places, I can help to change their minds but it'll take time. I have to get back first."

The man behind the camera laughed. "With or without Meester Oakley. You are a brave man with other people's lives, Meester Hath-her-way. They are of little consequence to you, no!

"Here we fight for the weak, those who cannot fight for themselves, We are martyrs to a greater cause and we do not as dismissively as you trample the lives of the innocent. Yours is a potent weapon and should be used with the utmost caution. I hear your words Meester Hath-her-way and so will the world."

Oderint Dum Metuant
Let them hate as long as they fear.

Note 7 - *Appended*

I am ready, as ready as I'll ever be. With the mini revolt within the SAS I was doubtful that some of my witnesses would be available for the court martial hearing but I have been assured that they will be there.

I have also been assured that my real case file will be delivered to me on the morning. The trial is due to start at 10-o-clock and I will need everything in my hands. However it is dangerous to have the files on or near my person before then as anything could and might happen to them. I have one or two surprises for the prosecution, at least, I hope they will be surprises but in this current climate of fear and mistrust it is difficult to be sure.

One thing more is exercising my mind and that is the condition of Stu Dalgleish. I have been told that he is safe and in a safe place. I have also been told that he was physically abused and not yet able to accept visitors. That worries me, it worries me unduly and the last thing I need right now is something else to worry about. I was counting on him as a star witness for the defence.

Tonight I will brief Ricky once again. A final briefing as we have been over most things many times before but there is still a niggling worry that he will be unable to hold his own in the courtroom. He still suffers from occasional bouts of depression and also bouts of anger caused by the manifestation of PTSD symptoms. He can normally control it and I have my fingers crossed that he will not allow the prosecution's cross-examination to upset his equilibrium. My opponent is well known for being able to get under the skin of hostile witnesses. I have great admiration for him. I hope he will underestimate me.

Can I win? I am not confident as I believe the verdict has already been decided.

AFP,

Enfield Country House, Arrathorne, Wensleydale.

Chapter Twenty

It was not an easy target. Sana'a is an ancient walled city, the very name itself means 'fortified place'. It is up at 2200 metres and surrounded by small towns and villages. It is the capital of Yemen and houses a large number of troops plus part of the considerable defence units of the Yemeni air force. Whoever had picked this place had done them no favours.

"Quite a poser," Bailey said.

Mike Quentin grinned. "Wouldn't be fun if it was easy. We have the heli payloads worked out and the fuel consumption. The difficult bit, as I said, is after crossing the Yemeni border. It's a couple of hundred clicks across Yemeni territory across a heavily cultivated and populated part of the country. We'll need to refuel before we cross and hope to god there's enough gas to get the chopper back to the dump before the tanks run dry. We'll only need the one chopper for the final run, the other will act as a Forward Support Base on the Saudi side of the border. We've decided to repaint one of the ships in Yemeni air force colours which may stop the locals from texting the Yemeni high command. And it will be at night so that's a help all round."

"So it's feasible?" Bailey asked. "It can be done."

"It's lucky that we had a squadron in the region doing all that additional desert training we've been asked to do."

"Get on with it, Mike."

Quentin grinned. "Right. With no accidents or pure bad luck the blades will be in and out of Yemen inside five hours. The whole thing should be conducted in total darkness. The entry team will use muffled weapons and hope that they get the terrorists before they can open fire. If the balloon goes up they could be in for a bumpy ride back. The Yemenis have a cracking air defence set-up. With luck we can box a way round it."

"What are the options for the insertion?'

Quentin chewed his lower lip. "We have two. We could take a leaf out of the terrorist's book and have make-belief engine trouble for the Herc. It can then fly in to Sana'a International at low level, if they'll give us permission, and the blades can Lalo out on the final approach. That's risky as they may be seen and the Yemenis could impound the Herc. Alternatively we could overfly on a commercial route at 24,000 feet and the boys can Halo onto the target. The down side to that is we'd ideally like MI6's asset on the ground to mark out a DZ and police it. We don't have time for that so we'd need to drop in blind."

"Risks either way," Bailey murmured. Quentin was cocking an eye at him and he nodded. "Halo it is then. Give the GO."

★ ★ ★

Now that the rescue attempt was in SAS hands Smith was able to relax and concentrate on the forthcoming trial. Now things were containable and with the outside assets out of the loop he could use MI5's own 'A' Branch to great advantage. FitzPatrick had been tracked to a small country hotel in Wensleydale. She had booked the best room and another for her two female staff. 'A' Branch had a couple of agents in one of the other rooms. The hotel provided free WiFi and they could use this, it made tapping e-mails so much easier.

It all seemed set fair but why was his gut still plaguing him? *The other woman.* Who was it on the end of FitzPatrick's mobile? And they had never really ascertained who had left the bottle of perfume behind at the Hereford hotel. It was still a mystery and Smith did not like mysteries, not unless he was controlling them.

He raised his contact in 'F' Branch on the squawk box. "Come down, Freddie, with anything you've got on FitzPatrick's contacts."

Freddie Simmons was one of those men who were instantly forgettable. Anyone who passed him in the street would have trouble recalling anything about him. It was a valuable asset in his role of internal surveillance of all kinds of subversives. In his time he had infiltrated the Unison Trade Union and the Animal Liberation Front as well as a group of Irish Loyalists, the Ulster Defence Association, and that was how he'd won his promotion to section head. He rarely made eye contact, preferring to look at people's mouths which gave him an air of submission but allowed him to calculate with some degree of accuracy if they were lying. He came into Smith's office quietly and sat with his hands resting on a plastic file. "Smith!"

Smith nodded and pointed with his chin. "What's in the folder?"

"We ran thorough background checks on FitzPatrick. Her family have a house in Woking. Mother and father still living but reside for most of the year on the Costa del Sol.

She sees them infrequently and since her career took off doesn't call them all that often. She's not close to her parents due to some shenanigans when she was younger; drink, drugs and young tearaways. She could be a bit of a rebel in her younger days and dad, being a magistrate, wouldn't put up with it. So young Ann was shuffled off to Benendon to teach her some manners. It caused a bit of friction in the family."

"Not short of a few bob then?" Smith asked.

"Family has independent wealth. Granddad invested in North Sea Oil and Gas, made a fortune and got out before the bottom fell out of the market."

"No sisters?"

Simmons shook his head. "No siblings of any hue."

"What about work mates?"

Simmons rotated his head slowly once again. "She doesn't make close friends at work. She had a disastrous affair with a male colleague some years ago and the bastard stabbed her in the back over a promotion that she should have had but he got after putting the boot in with the partners. She has since eschewed any close working relationship male or female except for her junior but from what we have been able to ascertain it is purely professional and they don't see each other socially."

Smith stood up and paced towards the window. It was a grey day and vestiges of mist hung over the water. He could not see the mock Egyptian facade of Vauxhall Cross from where he stood but imagined that people were using the tunnel under the Thames to travel back and forth to Whitehall. An extra few hundred million on the development costs but why should he care. He turned to face Simmons.

"Isn't there *anyone* close to her?"

"She shared a room with another girl when she was up at London. Young kid, very bright, got into Uni at the age of sixteen. There were a few years between them so FitzPatrick took the kid under her wing for a while. Kid's name was Somers, Gill Somers. She's now working at the War Box attached to the Royal Logistics Corps. Got a great record. There's a Masters Degree in chemical engineering before she joined the army. A year at Sandhurst then attached to the Airborne Division before passing Selection with 14 Intelligence Company, the Det. Worked undercover for the Det in Ulster, worked in Spain for MI6 and again recently against dissident IRA units in Northern Ireland. Got a couple of gongs too. Balls of steel and a brain to match by all accounts."

The light was now in Smith's eyes. "That name rings a bell. I've heard it or seen it in a report somewhere recently. We may have hit the jackpot. It's a coincidence and I don't believe in coincidences any more than I believe in Father Christmas."

Simmons grunted. "Looks like you should. You've just got your Christmas present early."

"Where is she now?"

"Right this minute we don't know. She took a week's leave and we can't yet trace her. We're working on it."

Smith punched a button on his squawk box. "Mason. Where'd I hear the name Gill Somers?"

"Somers, boss?"

"Yes, Somers. S...O...M...E...R...S, and Gill, like in fish. Probably short for Gillian."

There was a pause and Smith could hear Mason hitting computer keys.

"Oh yeah. Captain Gill Somers was listed as Major Keane's Assisting Officer but she declined. Didn't want any of the shit to stick to her, I reckon."

"Oh my god! She also knows Keane?"

"Looks like it, boss," Mason said. "What's the problem?"

"I'll get back to you," Smith said. "Meantime dig up anything you can on her service record." He flipped the switch closed.

Simmons grunted. "I've tried that. MI6 have put her full records into escrow under the thirty-year rule. We can't touch them without a letter from the Holy Ghost and Six are very touchy about it. No joy there."

"I'm getting a very nasty feeling about this, very nasty. Thanks, Freddie, give me what you've got. I need to take this to the top."

★　★　★

Gill's mobile vibrated in her pocket. She read the window and punched up the text message. MI5 were on to her. Well it had to happen sooner or later. But the timing was awful.

It would not take long for them to locate her. She had used a major credit card to rent the hire car and they would soon track the transaction, get the VRN and find her image on the myriad roadside cameras on the route up to Yorkshire. That was a minor concern and she would need to be more vigilant. She glanced out of the hotel window, ignoring the view across Herriott country, to check on the Vauxhall in the car park. It appeared untouched for now. She would bring the case file in from where it was hidden beneath the spare wheel and carry it with her at all times. It was the safest option. Once MI5 had put Gill Somers together with Ann FitzPatrick it would be no holds barred. FitzPatrick's tall, beautiful, blonde clerk called Julia Mendez and Gill Somers were one and the same person.

Gill shared the room with Ann's junior, Sissy Hamilton, who would now have to be let into the secret. It would not be an easy meeting as Sissy was already upset at having to share a room with an unknown and untried clerk and to be told that she had been kept in the dark about some extremely relevant case notes would increase her anger. She would assume she wasn't trusted and that hurdle would have to be overcome. On top of everything else Ann did not need internecine conflict in her defence team. It needed to be handled carefully.

Sissy came out of the shower room with a towel wrapped around her head and another knotted over her bust. She was a round-faced urchin with short cut hair, blue eyes and a devil-may-care slant to her mouth. Her opinions were strongly held and often voiced. On their brief acquaintance Gill had developed a liking for her un-attorney-like bearing and forthright manner. She was Gill's superior in the great legal scheme of things but she would have to be made to follow instructions for the time being.

"Ann's taking us to dinner, Sissy. Can you hurry it up a little?"

"First I've heard of it. Why didn't she tell me herself?" Sissy started to rub her hair with short irritated motions. "I'm her junior, for god's sake. Nothing but a bloody mushroom, that's me."

That made Gill wince. If ever there was a truism that was it. If Sissy was already feeling that bad the next hour would be dynamite. "I passed her in the hall. It was an off-the-cuff decision. They don't serve evening meals here so we have to go out for one."

Sissy sighed. "Pity you didn't think of that before you booked this place. Now I have to get dressed up. And someone has to drive which means no wine with dinner." The look was pointed and a heavy hint. It played into Gill's hands.

"Don't worry I'll drive. I rarely drink anyway so it's no hardship."

"How long do I have?"

Gill pulled a face "Twenty minutes?"

Sissy nodded. "All right, I can make that."

Gill breathed a sigh of relief. All she had to do now was persuade Ann that they needed to brief Sissy away from the hotel which was undoubtedly bugged and do it without alerting the watchers.

They drove out into the country, Ann in the front with Gill and Sissy grumpily in the rear. Gill kept away from towns and drove until she found a small car park at the end of a foot path. There were clear views all around and she nodded in satisfaction as she switched off the engine.

"What gives?" Sissy's air of irritated boredom had evaporated. "Aren't we going out for dinner?"

"We are," Ann said, "but there are some things you need to know about this case and Julia and I thought it best that we had some privacy."

"What things? It seems pretty straightforward to me. We don't have a cat in hell's chance of winning and the only thing puzzling me is why you agreed to take the case, Ann."

"That's a long story and it's for another time. Right now Julia has something to show you."

Gill handed over the real case file, uncomfortable with her assumed name but going with it. She didn't want Sissy sidetracked.

Sissy took the bundle. "Is this what I think it is?"

Ann nodded. "It's our defence, our real defence. I've had to be extremely careful because our files have been read by people advising the opposition. My understanding is that the government are pressing hard for a conviction and MI5 have been intercepting my phone calls, e-mails and faxes to give the prosecution an advantage."

"Whoa! MI5? This is getting deep. What makes you think that and why wasn't I made aware of it?"

"That's down to me," Gill said. "I've been advising Ann on security aspects. It's no reflection on you but everyone in the chambers had to behave perfectly normally to make MI5 think that we knew nothing of the incursions. No one else knows except the members of my security team and Ann. It's best that way and it's enabled us to keep the defence strategy secret."

"Well, that's a relief then," Sissy said bitterly. "I thought it was because you couldn't trust me."

"I trust you, Sissy," Ann said but I did not want to put you in a position of having to lie to the Security Service should they come asking questions."

Gill had been watching her rear-view mirror and saw a small car pull into the side of the road about three-hundred metres away. "Just hang on a second." She fitted a small plastic plug into her ear. "Raider one."

"We've seen them, boss. Moving up now."

In the mirror Gill saw a grey Range Rover pulling up beside the small Ford. Pete and Digger would take the watchers' eyes off the ball. "Okay, everything's cool. You can carry on."

Sissy turned in her seat. "What's happening?"

"Some uninvited guests," Gill said. "My people are having a quiet chat with them. There's nothing to worry about."

"This is so weird," Sissy moaned.

"You'll get used to it," Ann said, although she knew it was a lie.

Gill started the engine and pulled away. "Now that the competition is otherwise engaged we can talk more freely while we drive. You need to be fully prepared for tomorrow."

"What I need is to get out of this car but we're in the middle of nowhere. I'm not sure I want to be part of this, Ann."

Ann swivelled in her seat and clutched Sissy's hand. "Hear me out first, Sissy. You might want to change your mind."

Chapter Twenty-One

The assault team leader was beaming infra-red pictures onto a large wall screen in the computer suite at Vauxhall Cross where Blake had briefed Bailey. He sat now on the edge of a desk with one leg dangling, swinging to and fro like a nervous tic. The same picture was being beamed into the Kremlin, the SAS's intelligence centre at Credenhill, the Cabinet Office and to Thames House. The picture was fuzzy and broke up often. They also had a comms uplink but it too was intermittent. So much for the millions of pounds spent on kit. It never seemed to work properly when it was needed.

Blake's DG, or 'C' as he was known, was keeping a watchful eye on events from his office, a fact which made Blake more than usually nervous. He knew that this operation had been hashed together and he more than anyone knew of the myriad reasons why it might not be successful.

Blake stiffened as he watched the grey-green images on the screen. Sana'a was surprisingly built up with some impressive architecture and this was not helping the infil. What did help was that the target buildings were outside the city's walls in a more sparsely populated area. More sparsely was a matter of degree.

The high-altitude, low-opening parachute jump had gone exactly to plan although the Herc's takeoff had been subject to delays and dawn was just minutes away. That did not auger well for the extraction. The Puma had left on time but had landed inside Yemeni territory in order that they should arrive on target on time and not ahead of time which would be disastrous for the element of surprise. It was a dangerous move but one that had to be done as the chopper did not have the fuel capacity to fly back and forth.

The green shapes were closing in on the target building. The highly trained SAS soldiers were observing radio silence and working on hand signals watched through their night vision goggles. They were stealthy and silent and had not yet been challenged. The entry was seconds away when the scene disappeared from view.

Blake realised he had been holding his breath and gulped in a huge lungful of air. It eased the pain in his chest but not the tension in his neck. Now it was in the hands of the gods...and the SAS.

★ ★ ★

The muezzins were sounding the call to morning prayers as dawn brushed the eastern sky. That was how Hathaway imagined it in his mind as he was still hooded. The sound was real enough but the vision was all in the brain. Would this be his last dawn? Their time was up and he could feel tension in the guards who had kept him company all night.

There was a scuffling by the door as several sets of footsteps entered the room. Hathaway had his hood pulled off and could again see the rough plaster of the walls and concrete floor. The roof was wooden slats resting on rough-hewn beams. Hathaway blinked as his eyes grew more accustomed to the gradually strengthening light that was seeping through one sack-covered window. There was another scuffle and Oakley was marched in. His legs were not working properly and he was supported by two men in the usual shamags and dark glasses. Oakley too had his hood removed. He saw Hathaway and gave a weak smile although he did not meet his eyes. Instead he focused on the banner which was stretched across the back wall with its Arabic and English inscriptions and the graphic of an exploding grenade.

The last man in was big, rotund almost. He was wearing a grey suit with a white shirt buttoned to the neck, a shamag and black designer sunglasses. He said something in Arabic and one of the guards erected a video camera on a tripod.

The video camera was running. Both Oakley and Hathaway were kneeling in front of the green banner. To the left and right were armed gunmen.

Hathaway took it all in. He had had several convivial conversations with the big terrorist since the last video had been made and he could not believe that his life and Oakley's were actually going to be taken. The man had seemed so civilised that Hathaway had warmed to him and ventured to see the man's point of view. *Perhaps he would help when he got back to the UK. Give their cause a little free publicity, lean on a couple of editors in the national press to give them coverage whenever they could. He would write a game plan for them.*

His newfound friend was standing behind him and he did not see the large hunting knife that the man pulled from its sheath. It glittered in the arc lights and reflected back from the camera lens. The reflection caught Hathaway's eye but he did not recognise it for what it was.

It is not easy to sever someone's head with a knife. The flesh and muscle has to be sawn through and the fifth and sixth cervical vertebrae separated before the head falls free. It is bloody and gruesome, noisy and extremely painful until the spinal cord is finally severed. Hathaway's captor knew this and as it was for the camera, and ultimately the whole of the world, he would make as much theatre from it as possible. There was to be no voice-over. The images would be all. He enjoyed his moment, showing the blade and making sawing motions behind Hathaway's head. Then he stepped forward to flashes of blinding light.

From nowhere black-clad men poured through the door. A muffled muzzle poked through the sackcloth at the window and ripped out rounds. All four of the guards went down in seconds without retaliating.

"Simon, Stan, get down, get down."

Hathaway stared open mouthed, still on his knees his self-defence mechanism numbed, even as his eyes recovered from the strobe. The big man was the only one left on his feet. Machine gun muzzles were swinging onto their last target. "NO," he screamed. That's as far as he got as three weapons ripped out rounds and the man fell twitching to the floor.

"You bastards," Hathaway screeched. "He was a friend, he was harmless, you didn't need to kill him."

One of the soldiers skipped forward, rolled the dead man onto his back and tore his jacket open. Strapped to his chest was a canvas belt with four slabs of C4, a battery and wires running across his chest and down his sleeve to a detonator switch in the palm of his hand. The soldier said nothing but made sure Hathaway was aware how close he had come to obliteration. How close they had all come.

Oakley was already strapped to a stretcher. Still protesting, Hathaway was wrestled onto another. There was a sharp prick in his arm and he no longer cared.

The room emptied as quickly as it had filled. The final shot on the camera was a black gloved hand covering the lens. The attack had lasted just twenty-three seconds.

★ ★ ★

In three locations in London there were sighs of relief as the troop commander's gasped success message was passed. The blades had retrieved the hostages and were airborne in the Puma. No alarm had been raised and they were successfully boxing around the known AA missile sites. At Credenhill Mike Quentin got the first high five ever known from the regimental commander. It looked like they had cracked it.

★ ★ ★

In the killing house in Hereford the five terrorists were rolling on the ground with helpless laughter as the tension left them. The rescue had gone off without a hitch. An edited video would be sent to Al-Jazeera and the message would be passed. You don't mess with the British. You might hate us but we scare the shit out of you too.

Cowley took off the shamag and ruffled his thinning hair. "Good stuff lads. That should keep the bastards guessing."

Sponge eyed the fake blood drying slowly on Cowley's jacket. "Is it goin' to work, boss?"

"Why not? As far as the world is concerned Oakley and Hathaway were snatched by terrorists and the SAS did what it usually does. Not too far-fetched a story, laddie. The big question is will MI5 and MI6 swallow it. If they start to analyse the animated film sequences and find out that we never did raid into Yemen in Pumas then we could be batting on a sticky wicket but I can't see them getting into it too deeply and our lad inside MI5 will have covered our tracks as best he can. Anyway in a couple of weeks it will be academic. None of them will admit to having the wool pulled over their eyes, will they?"

Sponge turned to Cruncher who was tidying up brass blank cartridge cases. "What's academic mean?"

Chapter Twenty-Two

For a General Court Martial the court comprised of a board of four officers under a president who had a casting vote in the event of a hung decision and a Judge Advocate often a civilian magistrate or, rarely, a High Court Judge. It was a mark of the importance the government placed on this trial that the Judge Advocate General had appointed one of the latter who sat in splendid isolation on a dais beneath the Royal Coat of Arms in full robes and wig. His name was Reginald Jeffreys and Ann hoped that only the surname and not the temperament could be associated with James II's notorious 'Hanging Judge'. But she felt it was not a good omen.

Both the prosecution and defence counsels were also fully attired as if in a civilian courtroom. Ann and her opponent had gone through the normal pre-trial hearing, legal sparring that decides on what basis the trial will be held. Sometimes the judge's rulings could take days but Ann was not surprised that all the rulings were given on the spot in favour of the prosecution. The die was cast in no uncertain terms.

The judge retired until the defendant had been escorted in and the public and press had taken their places. The press outnumbered the public and there was an unseemly scramble for seats. Ricky had asked his parents not to attend and they had complied with his wishes so there were no relatives to cater for. He was wearing his service dress uniform and had chosen the SAS buff beret and winged dagger badge rather than the blue and red dress cap and flaming grenade of his parent regiment. Although she was aware of the protocol Ann was saddened to see that his medal ribbons had been removed showing just a line of stitching on his left breast. The highly polished Sam Browne belt was also missing and she wondered whether he knew that his hard work on the leather would go unrecognised and had been simply passing the time. The military were strange creatures but surprisingly endearing at times.

The judge re-entered and took his seat on the bench. He waved a limp hand at the Court Orderly as an instruction for the Board members to enter. The room came to attention and the uniformed participants saluted the president who returned the salute and greeted the judge.

Jeffreys was wearing half-moon spectacles and he looked over the top of these at the president before inviting the Board to take their places at a table on and below his left. It was an ostentatious display of superiority as if he was rubbing the army's nose in the mire. Jeffreys was obliged to be independent from the military but he was really playing to the press crowded at the back of the room.

There was another rustle of movement and a few murmured apologies as another uniformed figure entered the court through the public door, saluted and stood beside the seat immediately behind Ricky. It was the seat reserved for his Assisting Officer but the place had hitherto remained empty. Ricky turned to glance over his shoulder and his jaw dropped as Gill gave him a deliberate wink.

Jeffreys gave her a hard punishment stare. "The defendant will remain standing all others may now sit whilst I read the convening order and identify the members of the Board. If the defendant has any objections to any member of the Board he may state these at this time."

Ann rose to her feet. "We will have no objections, M'Lord."

"In that case the oath can be administered. All stand. Service members remove your head dress."

The oath was administered to each of the Board members in turn. Once finished, Jeffreys directed that each member be provided with a copy of the Charge Sheet. He glanced at Ricky as if seeing him for the first time. "Are you the person named in the heading of the Charge Sheet?'

Ricky nodded, "Yes, My Lord."

"A simple yes will suffice. Were you at the time of the offences in the place specified at the time specified?"

"Yes."

"Do you plead guilty or not guilty to the charges as specified?"

"Not guilty."

Jeffreys looked disappointed perhaps hoping for an early lunch. "The defendant may sit." He waved his hand at the prosecution's table. "Are you ready to proceed, Mr. Howerd?"

The prosecuting council rose to his feet in a rustle of silk gown and bowed. "Yes, M'lud."

"Miss FitzPatrick?"

Ann also stood and bowed, a slight tilt of her head. It was as far as she would go to register her disapproval of the situation. She wondered just how much the judge knew of the behind-the-scene dealings. He would have thoroughly briefed himself on the legal aspects and would have received his no doubt carefully phrased instructions from the Lord Chancellor's Office. His input was crucial as the Board would rely on his legal advice in coming to their verdict. She would have to place sufficient doubt in their minds to overcome any biased summing-up by the judge. It was going to be a hard fight on a battlefield where the enemy had all the heavy artillery on its side.

As this passed through her mind Ann was half-listening to Jeffreys reminding the press that reporting restrictions were in place and they were only to report on the legal aspects of the court martial and no names were to be mentioned under any circumstances. Jeffreys' enjoyment of putting the press under restriction was obvious.

Sissy had her head buried in the secret brief. So much was new to her and the court martial proceedings had left her much in awe of the uniforms and pageantry. But now they were entering territory she understood and the familiarity calmed her. She made notes on post-it yellow slips and attached them to relevant pages for Ann to see. She doubted whether Ann had missed the ramifications of some of the evidence but belt and braces was always the rule with her boss. Two heads are better than one. The tone of Jeffreys' voice prompted a memory and she leaned to whisper in Ann's ear.

"Rumour has it he doesn't like the press's current freedoms as he's often been criticised by newspapers for his liberal treatment of offenders and apparent disregard for the views of the victims. He would seem to be an ideal choice of judge to give Ricky a fair hearing but a long-held belief in pacifism doesn't endear him to the uniformed services."

Ann nodded slowly and whispered back. "We'll need to be very careful with him."

Sitting on Sissy's right Ricky had heard part of the exchange and pulled a face. Ann looked across and gave him a 'don't worry smile'. Sissy hoped her boss was as confident as she looked.

* * *

The C130 Hercules was on its final approach to RAF Lyneham in Wiltshire. Hathaway, still strapped onto a stretcher, was now awake and feeling like death. Whatever concoction the medics had given him had left him with hangover-like symptoms. A soldier was sitting beside him checking his vital signs and gave him a thumbs-up. "All right, mate?"

Hathaway nodded and the soldier smirked. "Soon be back in the land of milk and honey. You've had a good sleep, shoulda done you some good. After what you've bin through it's the best thing."

"What happened?"

The soldier feigned a frown. "You don't remember? Not to worry that's not unusual under the circs. Memory should come back in time. Good job the boys got you out when they did. Another few minutes and it could have got nasty."

"How's Mr. Oakley?"

"He's still sleeping it off. He'll be as right as rain when he wakes up. Heads up, we're just about to land." The soldier squeezed his shoulder and went off to strap himself into a canvas seat nearby.

Hathaway couldn't see much from his position and couldn't crane his neck far enough to get a decent view along the fuselage but he could hear several voices and cheerful banter. He checked his wristwatch, the time and the date. It was 3.30pm and the trial had started that day. It was the first real thought that had not been about himself since his kidnap. It said more about his character than he cared to admit.

"Is that you, Stan?" It was Oakley, his voice weak and quavering, not at all his usual bumptious, self-assured manner.

"Yes, Simon. I'm here. You okay?"

"I've got a terrible headache. Where are we?"

"Just about to land back in Britain. It looks like we made it in one piece."

"Did you hear the woman, Stan? The Jewish woman. They tortured her all night and then they shot her. It was..."

"I heard the screams and the shot. Bastards. We'd have been next if our boys hadn't come in when they did."

"Perhaps they should have taken them alive. There was no warning and it was extremely violent."

Hathaway sighed. "You wouldn't say that if you'd seen what I saw. One of them was wired up with a suicide bomb. Given warning he could have blown us all to bits."

"Still..." Oakley said, "it *was* very violent."

"I'm just thankful we got out alive. I don't think compassion comes into it with those terrorists. They lives by the sword and dies by the sword. It's justice of a sort and I'm grateful for it," Hathaway said and found he really meant it.

At the front of the aircraft Mike Quentin also checked his watch. He had begged a ride on the Herc, which to all intents and purposes was on a training exercise and piloted by one of their usual Special Forces crews. It had been in the air for just an hour, long enough to get the drugged 'hostages' from the killing house in Hereford, into the air for a few circuits of Brize Norton and finally on to Lyneham.

The flight plan that he and the pilot had concocted had the aircraft inward bound from Qatar and the final approach was as if they had indeed flown from the east. There was an ambulance waiting on the tarmac to take Oakley and Hathaway to a nearby hospital for a check-up before they would finally be released into the hands of MI5 for a thorough debrief.

Quentin grinned to himself. The original plan he had been given had not allowed for the SAS to come out of this with any glory but with the colonel's permission he had cemented in the gaps. The plan would not stand up to intense scrutiny. If MI5 decided for any reason to investigate deeply they would find the fictitious flight plan did not match the aircraft's mileage log. Not much they could do about that as it was a pen and paper job. If it had been on computer they could have fiddled the figures to match. C'est la Guerre. Who would be interested enough to notice?

The thump of the wheels hitting concrete brought him out of his reverie. The plane came to a halt very quickly and the huge rear ramp was wound down letting in a gust of cool air. At the rear of the fuselage soldiers were already lifting the two stretchers for the walk down the ramp and into the waiting ambulance. He could see quite a crowd on the apron. Uniformed men, police and several civilians crowded together like penguins on the ice at the South Pole. There was an audible 'aaahh' as the stretchers were carried out and slid into the ambulance. Two men in plain clothes climbed in with them and the vehicle roared off with blues flashing.

The crowd eddied but did not break up. The remaining blades were walking off the ramp in single file. Quentin attached himself to the end, kept his head down and sauntered out.

"Major Quentin?"

Mike glanced up to see Blake walking towards him with his hand out.

"A job well done, Major."

Mike shook the proffered fist. "Luck went with us this time but I wouldn't want another one like that for a while."

"Yes, indeed. Lack of real intelligence can pose real dangers," Blake said.

"I've got a lot on, Mr. Blake..."

"Oh, yes, sorry to hold you up. I just wanted to congratulate you. What would we do without the SAS, eh?"

Mike nodded and waved himself away. He took a half-look over his shoulder. Blake was still watching him as he walked and it gave him a hollow feeling in the pit of his stomach. What had he meant by his pointed remark? And what might he suspect?

* * *

"What can I do for you, Tim?" The brigadier handed Bailey a tumbler half full of neat scotch and sipped his own.

It was early but what the hell, it might ease the pain. "I've come to offer my resignation," Bailey said.

The brigadier raised his eyebrows. "At this moment of triumph? I'd have thought you'd be out celebrating after that tour-de-force in Yemen. That was text book stuff."

Bailey looked sheepish. "Indeed, Brigadier, text book. I couldn't have written it better myself."

"So what's the problem, Tim?"

"Just the small matter of two whole Sabre Squadrons, the Special Projects Team and the duty Counter Terrorist Team going missing."

The brigadier stopped with the tumbler half-way to his mouth. It was hard to surprise this man but Bailey seemed to have achieved it. "Two whole squadrons, you say? And you've mislaid them."

Bailey nodded. "They just waltzed out one night taking vehicles and weapons with them to I know not where."

"Jesus Christ, Tim, this is serious."

"And it's my responsibility, sir, hence the resignation."

"What's this about? Not this Ricky Keane stuff, is it? I thought we'd got around that."

"It's not just Keane. After Oakley put up such a poor show at the briefing the men just do not trust the government to do what's right over ROI. None of them want to be put into the same position as Keane. As usual the SAS is the spearhead, this time for the entire army. I hear every army regiment, the RAF Regiment and the Royal Marines are behind them waiting to see how this pans out. It could develop into a major mutiny. The senior WOs and NCOs have played their hand and they're holding a few aces, it seems to me."

The brigadier sat heavily. He could see his own career sliding ever more rapidly down the tubes. "What can we do about it?"

"So far this has been kept quiet. I don't know how much of this you want to hear but the Yemen job was a phantom cover operation for the fact that we have no cover from the Regiment. If a real emergency arises we could be well and truly stuffed."

"The Yemeni operation was a fake?"

"From beginning to end. Oakley was taken because he's a prat who needed to be taught a lesson. Hathaway because he's been the government's hit man on the Keane case. Neither man left the country and neither has been hurt other than a few bruises and a couple of pin pricks. Mentally no more than any soldier would suffer on a normal escape and evasion exercise."

"Just the small matter of kidnap, aggravated assault and false imprisonment," the Brigadier said caustically. "And you're right I really don't need chapter and verse, that will make me an accomplice after the fact."

"*If* it comes out, sir. At the moment the SAS are heroes. Tracks have been covered and it will be in no one's interest to investigate further. MI5 and MI6 will spend a little time chasing down a non-existent terrorist organisation but that will be a dead-end. The general terrorist population will think twice about kidnapping Brits in future. It was such a mess for the terrorists that al-Qaeda will fall over themselves to claim it wasn't them which nobody will believe and it'll dent their credibility.

"It has bought us time to try to sort out this other mess. What are we going to do about the Regiment's withdrawal of labour?"

"This isn't a bloody union strike, man. It's mutiny; it's against every Queen's Regulation in the book."

"You could try throwing the book at them, sir but I don't think you'd get past page one."

"We're not about to wash our dirty linen in public, Tim. We'll keep it in-house for as long as we can. There's no point in kicking this up to Div, they'd have even less clue on how to deal with it. Keep your resignation in your pocket for now and we'll work together on this."

"For now, sir?"

"It's your mess. I'll have to accept your resignation eventually, along with a few others I should imagine. Right now I need you to work out a plan and implement it. At least you'll save your reputation if you pull it off."

"And yours, sir, and yours."

"You've bought some time, Tim. Use it wisely. Oh, and you weren't here, I haven't seen you. Okay?"

Bailey nodded. He was on his own in spite of the protestations of support. Succeed in solving the problem and he would have to resign as surely as if he failed but the prize was his reputation and that was worth fighting for.

Incidit Scyllam qui vult vitare Charybdis

Between a rock and a hard place.

Note: 8 - Appended

*W*ent the day well? Not really. The ground rules have been set much in favour of the prosecution. The General Court Martial Board is comprised completely of senior officers. The President is a full colonel with two lieutenant-colonels and two majors making up the Board, the army equivalent of a jury. It is their role to decide on a verdict and a more po-faced lot I've never yet seen. Yes it's a serious occasion but to a man they have failed to make eye-contact with either me or Ricky. A sure sign that they may have already decided on a verdict in their own minds.

It would have been pointless to object to the constitution of the Board as they would merely be replaced by men of similar persuasion. Ricky had said these were not fighting soldiers but from some of the support arms who were never likely to see the outside of an office let alone a battlefield. Remfs he had called them, whatever that may mean, or 'The Tail'.

He seems to have accepted the situation philosophically. 'The Tail has a role to fulfil as much as the fighting arms. We could not do our job without them doing theirs', he'd said, which was magnanimous. Respect from a fighting man for those who toil in the backrooms. I just wonder whether that respect will be reciprocated or whether petty inter-unit rivalries will take centre stage.

The courtroom is like a stage. The judge is the old ham who insists on speaking the best lines. The prosecution is the hero there to see justice done and we the defence the villains whom everyone loves to hate. Simplistic? Maybe but this is real life and the consequences are serious.

It was a great pity that Ricky's respect did not extend to Gill. He refused to speak to her throughout the morning. The hurt must run deep. She is a fiery character in her own right and I can see his refusal to acknowledge her is beginning to chafe. Dissension in the ranks. I don't need it and it will have to be confronted soon. I am having a smaller but no less acute problem with Sissy who now has to get used to the notion that Julia is now Gill and an army officer to boot. She is having trouble coming to terms with the multiple layers of deception. She will have to get used to it and quickly.

The prosecuting council has outlined his case with his opening remarks. He is yet to call witnesses. These are few but could be deadly. I am much looking forward to cross-examining Mr al-Shamrani for he is the lynch pin of the prosecution's case.

On the other hand I dread putting my defence witnesses on the stand to be cross-examined by my opponent. That may be where our troubles truly start.

AFP,
Hartfield Country House, Wensleydale.

PART 4
End Game

Chapter Twenty-Three

Smith rubbed his eyes with the heels of his hands and sighed. Amongst other files, all neatly lined up with their edges square to the desk, he had the transcripts of Oakley's and Hathaway's debriefs. They were pretty thin fare. Neither man had much in the way of hard evidence that could help to identify the kidnappers. For much of the time Oakley had been in a drug induced sleep or had his head covered with a hood. Hathaway was more use in that respect but even he was light on detail.

One thing that bothered him was Oakley's obsession with the murdered Israeli woman. He had been on to his counterpart in the Mossad at the Israeli embassy but the man had denied losing an agent recently. Maybe the woman wasn't an agent but then who the hell was she?

He left the reports on his desk, pushed himself to his feet and walked to where Mason was re-running the video of the SAS attack. "See anything useful?"

Mason shook his head. "Doesn't matter how many times I run it there's nothing here that we don't know already. The sound was muted on the tape so we can't even get a voice print from it."

Smith pulled a face and frowned. "Isn't that unusual? These blokes like to hear the sound of their own voices, especially if they think they're going to be all over Al-Jazeera. Their fifteen minutes of fame."

Mason turned and squinted over his shoulder at Smith to give him a hard look. "Not that unusual. They sometimes alter the voice electronically but they know that we can now clean it up so it's just another step along the route to anonymity. These blokes didn't want to get caught as they had no intention of letting the hostages live. This was about the message, not the words. They really had no interest in the government's response. Rubbing its nose in the dirt, the embarrassment it caused, sheer snookery *was* the message."

Smith grunted. "What makes you such a fucking expert all of a sudden?"

"Don't know an awful lot about me, do you?"

"I know you're a cheeky bastard. Anyway, what I came out to ask was have you got any further with tracing the missing Israeli woman?"

"How do we know she's an Israeli?"

"Oakley said she had a Jewish name and she was speaking in Hebrew. She said her name was Jewish."

"And Oakley's an expert in linguistics, is he? Would you be able to distinguish Hebrew from Serbo Croat?"

Smith looked bemused. "Are you saying the woman was a Serb?"

"No. I was just pointing out that Oakley could have been wrong. We only have his word for it that she was an Israeli. As the Israelis are denying it maybe we should be looking elsewhere."

"The terrorists had Hathaway read the claim that she was an Israeli whore."

Mason grunted a laugh. "I'd put about as much stock on that as I would on the Mossad's denial. We have nothing but conjecture and hearsay. Not a lot to go on."

"I was hoping it would be a lead," Smith said. "Oakley is obsessing on it and we need answers."

"Oakley can obsess himself in the shower with both hands. We've got jack shit."

"He feels connected to her, feels her pain. He needs to exorcise the memory."

"Give me strength," Mason said. "What's the soft bastard doing in the MoD if he can't hack the realities of life?"

"That's a question for the powers-that-be to ponder on and not for the likes of us," Smith said. Mason had voiced what he had been thinking. It was unlikely Oakley would survive the next ministerial re-shuffle. He wasn't made of the right stuff. "Show me the assault video again. Run it through on slo-mo."

"Why? I've been through it a dozen times. I'm getting a bit sick of watching the glory boys in action."

"Just do it, will you."

Mason grumbled under his breath but fast-forwarded the video to the correct place then ran it in slow motion. The twenty-three seconds took well over five minutes to run with Smith peering intently at every frame. The large terrorist went down spouting blood before a black gloved hand pulled the jacket open to reveal the suicide vest.

"That's it," Mason said.

Smith nodded absent-mindedly and Mason reached for the off switch.

'No, wait!" Smith yelped. "What's that?"

"What's what?" Mason sounded exasperated as if Smith was trying his patience to the limit.

"That!" Smith pointed at the big terrorist's wrist. The underside was showing a fleshy gap between a glove and the cuff of the jacket. Part of a tattoo was visible. A blue line shaped like a 'V' that disappeared under the sleeve.

Mason peered hard. "Dunno. Could be anything."

"Find out," Smith snapped. He left to return to his own office and the neat arrangement of files. He picked up the file marked Gill Somers and flipped it open. This woman was concerning him more and more. They had tracked her to Yorkshire where she had been posing as FitzPatrick's clerk but she had now reverted to her own name and rank and was sitting in the court room as Keane's Assisting Officer. Not that Keane had liked the idea it seemed. There was some friction there. Smith's agents had noticed a definite froideur between them. Hadn't she turned him down? What was she now doing there?

Then there was the report from the pair from 'A' Branch who had been interrupted as they were setting up a directional microphone in their car. Interrupted by two men who looked like local farmers but who had stopped to ask directions. Men in a Range Rover with false number plates. Men who had kept them talking long enough that they lost the tail on FitzPatrick's group.

So he was back where he started and it was becoming imperative for him to personally pay Somers a visit.

★ ★ ★

The knock on the door was loud and firm. Hathaway was reluctant to answer it. He had work to do to catch up on the time he'd been away. Take all the time he needed, that's what his boss had said but the man's eyes had belied the words. They said don't be a soft bugger like Oakley.

The banging came again and he realised he was procrastinating not from a desire to continue working but from gut-wrenching fear. It was nonsense he knew, terrorists don't knock first…do they…but he could not stop his legs from shaking.

"Mr. Hathaway, it's the police, open up, sir."

The voice sounded distant through the wood but it was a fair bet half the neighbourhood would hear it.

"Coming," Hathaway finally managed. He stood behind the door. "Shove your ID through the letterbox, let me see it."

The letterbox rattled and a leather-cased warrant card slid through. An Inspector Davis, Special Branch.

"Can we come in, sir. It's bloody wet out here."

Hathaway shot the bolts and the safety chain. He could not remember attaching it. Maybe his nerves were shot worse than he imagined.

The two men standing on his doorstep looked typical policemen. Both were average height with plenty of weight under their rain coats. They were bare-headed and water ran in thin rivulets from hair that was slicked to bony scalps. Hathaway handed the warrant card back to the man whose photograph stared stony-faced from its encapsulation.

"What can I do for your, Inspector?'

The two policemen sidled past him into his small sitting room. Davis turned and waved a hand at their rain coats. "Do you mind if we…?"

Hathaway shook his head. They were dripping all over his favourite B&Q rug. "Leave them in the bathroom."

Davis's sidekick gave a crooked grin and carried both coats out as his boss settled himself on a straight-backed chair. "It's more what we can do for *you*, Mr. Hathaway. He took a small padded envelope from his pocket. "We've been going over all the material that the army boys got from your terrorists…"

"Hardly my…"

"...right. *the* terrorists. Some of it's a bit...er...delicate."

"What do you mean?"

"Well, let's say it's probably not stuff that you would like to see out there in newspaper land. You know, cosying up to them, that sort of thing."

"I wasn't cosying up to them. I was fighting for my life."

"We understand that, don't we, Brian? The Stockholm Syndrome and all that."

"Yep," Brian said. He was Davis's sergeant, a younger version of his boss right down to the worn tweed sports jacket and brown brogues. "Nasty, that Stockholm Syndrome. Just look what happened to Patty Hearst and that group...what was it called, guv?"

"The Symbionese Liberation Army. Yeah, that was a bad one. They really got to her...and she was the victim of a kidnapping too."

Hathaway was looking bemused. "What's this got to do with me?"

"We're just saying that we understand the pressure you were under. You had to be nice to the bastards but not everyone will understand. Things look different to those who weren't there."

Davis handed over the envelope. Hathaway opened it to find a sealed DVD jewel case. "This is...?"

"All the extra stuff from the tape the terrorist's made, the stuff they didn't release to Al-Jazeera. Wouldn't want it to get into the wrong hands, would we?"

"Is this the only copy?"

Davis turned on a slow smile. "No, sir. We need the original to further our enquiries. There might be something on there that'll be useful in the future. But we'll keep it safe."

"Thank you, Inspector. Will I be able to claim it eventually?"

"Once we have no further use for it, sir. No problem. Looking out for each other, that's what friends are for, eh, sir?" Davis nodded and Brian went to retrieve the rain coats. "Sorry about the rug. I noticed you were worried about it. Surprising how things can be so easily damaged, especially when you have a soft spot for them."

"Special Branch, is it? Will you ever catch all the terrorists involved?"

"We'll try to make sure they don't bother you again, Mr. Hathaway. We're hoping we got the lot but you never know how wide some of these al-Qaeda cells spread their branches. Mr. Oakley's a fairly obvious target but we're still trying to work out why they picked on you. Don't suppose you have any idea?"

"I have a very responsible position with the government..."

"Hmmm, right. If you were working on something sensitive you wouldn't tell us. Quite right, sir. Still, if you do think of a connection to terrorism, or the Middle East in general, anything, however vague, let me know. G'night, sir."

Hathaway showed them out with a growing feeling that hidden somewhere in the exchange of pleasantries was an important message.

★　★　★

"Why the change of heart?" Ricky asked. "I thought you didn't want to get your hands dirty."

Gill was about to snap back when Ann butted in. "Children, be nice."

It burst Gill's bubble of indignation. If only the big lunk knew half of what she'd done for him but it had to remain her secret.

"I gave it a lot of thought and decided you needed a morale booster. I thought I was doing you a favour."

"We were managing just fine," Ricky said, shades of bitterness still tainting his words.

"Look, I'm sorry I left you to fend for yourself but I really needed to keep a low profile..."

It was Ricky's turn to butt in but Gill held up a hand to stop him "...not for the reasons you're thinking. It was nothing to do with saving my career, or siding with a loser..."

"What was it then...?"

Gill bit her lip. This wasn't the time or the place she had imagined but she couldn't think of a better one right now. She could see he was feeling down after the day in court and the growing realisation that it wasn't an equal fight. He had been prepared by Ann but the reality was something else entirely and it was finally beginning to hit home. His morale certainly needed a boost. "I came because I love you, you idiot."

If she had hit him by surprise with a wet fish he wouldn't have jumped so much. His mouth opened and closed like a landed carp.

"I think I'd better be leaving," Ann said. "It looks like you two have a lot to talk about. See you in the morning...and don't be late."

★ ★ ★

Smith had not enjoyed the train ride. The carriages had been packed, hot and noisy with passengers making inane telephone calls or listening to loud pop music that seeped through their ear phones. If he could hear it god knew what it was doing to their eardrums. His mood on arrival was not the best but it was mitigated on being met by one of the surveillance team in an elderly Ford Mondeo. Smith was buried in his own thoughts for much of the journey towards Gill's hotel but eventually the driver gave a nervous cough to attract his attention.

"What?" Smith said, his chain of thought broken.

"The target's not at the hotel, sir. She's on camp with the lawyer and Keane."

"Am I wasting my time here?"

"She'll be back later. Just thought you might like to stop somewhere for some dinner."

"I gather you missed yours...what's your name?"

"Andy, sir, Andy Galbraith, and yeah I am feeling a bit peckish."

"Are you in touch with the surveillance team?"

Galbraith nodded and pointed to his ear. "Constant. We'll know as soon as she leaves the camp."

"Stop at a pub. You can fill me in on details while we eat."

Galbraith was young and eager. Smith could remember a time when he was both but the job knocked it out of him. He wondered when he had become so cynical but could not pin it down. It had happened over time like a patina on old furniture. And perhaps it added value too. Cynicism was a useful tool at times. Believe nothing you hear and only half the things you see. That was a useful adage. It was related to him by one of the old cold war warriors, one of the Peter Wright era, and he had always used it as a fall-back position. What did the computer geeks call it? The default position, that was it.

Galbraith was munching his way through pizza and chips with a glass of cloudy lemonade to wash it down. Smith hated pizza with a passion that bordered on mania. Even the smell made him feel nauseous. He had opted for a cheese and ham omelette, with chips as a side order he wouldn't eat, and a glass of house red. He could see

Galbraith eyeing up his untouched chips and he pushed them across the table to him. The appetites of youth. Enjoy it while you can. Soon enough the ulcers would bite back, if he stayed the course. There it was again, the thoughts of a cynic.

Smith took a mouthful of wine and pursed his lips. Not a bad plonk for a country pub. Merlot, South African by the flavour. Wine was one of his small vanities. He would amuse others with his skill at identifying grapes and countries of origin. He had no friends, no real friends with whom he could enjoy a bottle of an evening, just colleagues and contacts; another side to the job. He'd had a wife once, and a child but these had fallen by the wayside of long hours, desperately long absences working undercover against one suspicious group or another, and of course the secrecy. It was secrecy that drove a final nail into the coffin of matrimony. He had lost touch with Diana, and little Clara; not that she would be so little now. Eighteen was it? Eighteen years and he had not seen her for thirteen of them. Diana had remarried and moved abroad, France he knew, somewhere in the Dordogne. Young Clara was probably speaking more French than English. He wondered if she remembered him. Perhaps he would see her again, perhaps not. What could he say to her after all those lost years? *'Sorry I was away so much, working for MI5 you know'. 'Sorry I missed your fourth birthday but I was shagging a suspected terrorist in the hope I'd rattle a few secrets out of her.'* Somehow Smith doubted it would work.

"Sir!"

Galbraith jolted him from his reverie. "For god's sake call me Smith."

"Sorry,..Smith. You seemed miles away."

A fast learner Smith acknowledged. "I've got a few things on my mind. What is it?"

"You wanted a run-down on Captain Somers' activities. We've codenamed her Fox by the way."

Smith raised his eyebrows. "Fox?"

Galbraith sniggered. "Have you seen her?"

"Only the picture from her ID card."

"She's some looker. You wouldn't believe she was army. A real blonde bombshell. I always thought they were all fat legs and piss-pot haircuts."

"Galbraith, you have a lot to learn and the first of those is never, and I mean *never*, stereotype people. You can get yourself into a lot of deep water that way."

Galbraith shrugged. "But her file says she's a scientist, a chemical engineer. The odds were on her being like the back end of the Cowes ferry."

"Her file, the bit I can get into," Smith grunted, "also says she's worked with the Det in Northern Ireland and on operations with MI6 for which she was awarded the OBE. She's no dumb blonde that's for sure. The fact that 'Six' have put a 30-year block on the files means that she was working on some pretty hairy ops with a lot of political fall-out. All of which tells me she is not likely to be a pushover.

"What's she been up to around here?"

It was Galbraith's turn to grunt. "Security's tightened up, that's for sure. We tried to get a bug into Keane's room at the barracks but a couple of heavies with Regimental Police armbands saw us off. There's a guard stationed permanently outside Keane's door, done up to the nines in full service dress. Keane has to have an escort to and from the court but someone is always stationed outside that bloody door."

"On whose orders? We may be able to loosen the ties a little with a word in the right ear."

"Don't know for sure. They're not MPs, they're RPs but RPs for what regiment I don't know. But I'll find out."

"Do that. I'd like to know what's being said inside that room. No chance of using directional mikes I suppose?"

Galbraith shook his head. "Can't get close enough and there are too many obstacles in the way."

"What else?"

Galbraith hunched his shoulders as if to ward off a blow. A frown creased his face hinting at an internal struggle but it had to come out. "I don't know about you, Smith but I've got a feeling that we're being played here. Somers turns up pretending to be FitzPatrick's clerk then, as soon as the court martial starts she morphs into Keane's Assisting Officer. I thought she turned that job down. Why'd she change her mind, why the deception and why did two heavies, posing as farmers, interrupt our tail the other night? It seems we can't move now without someone running interference. Something's been bugging me ever since we got here and in thinking about it the penny's dropped. It's like our every move is being watched and circumvented."

Smith stopped with the wine glass part way to his lips. Suddenly the flavour had gone sour. "Do you have anything concrete?"

"Our two farmers had false plates on their Range Rover. Not that that proves anything but it doesn't do much for my gut feeling."

Smith was growing to like young Galbraith. He had thought he was sharp and that was proving to be the case. *Gut feeling? At his tender years?* "Do you have any theories?"

"I think FitzPatrick has hired some heavies to look out for them and they're good. Probably one of the top security companies, the ones that take on jobs in the Middle East looking after diplomats and Arab princes."

"Find out which company, will you. Most of the big ones have government contracts and can be leaned on."

Galbraith nodded and pressed his finger to an ear. "Somers is on the move. If we leave now we'll catch her just as she gets back to the hotel. With her knickers down."

Smith grinned. It was encouragement for Galbraith and his enticing mental picture. Personally he doubted he could catch this woman off-guard quite so easily.

Chapter Twenty-Four

The room was comfortable with its own bathroom. There was a bed with a soft foam mattress which Haji eschewed in favour of a rug and blankets on the floor. It was what he was used to and he did not want to fall into decadent western ways. That did not apply to the shower which he used frequently, luxuriating in the constant supply of hot water. That was one luxury he could not ignore. Water was a precious commodity in the desert; for drinking not bathing.

His captors, for that was how he viewed them, had provided him with reading material in Arabic and English. There was also a television but its evil eye remained off for there was nothing there to entertain him and time passed slowly. He always carried his own copy of the Holy Koran for peace of mind; to quieten his soul. This was now in his hand as he faced the two senior captors. One was the soldier with the small moustache and florid face. Not a stupid man but one stranded in his own bigoted past. The other was a lawyer called James Howerd. Friendly, persuasive and more open-minded. More dangerous too and Haji would not let his guard slip. He knew why he was here, why he was supposed to be here, following the Sheikh's orders but he did not trust the unbelievers; not one millimetre, not one centimetre, not one metre, not one kilometre. They would turn on him like a pack of rabid dogs if they were given any inkling of his true purpose.

"You're quite comfortable, Mr al-Shamrani?" Howerd asked. "If not, Major Phelps will get you anything you need."

"I need for this to be over, Mr Howerd. It is not something that fills me with delight. I miss my home, my country and my people."

"Of course and by tomorrow it will be over. I'm putting you on the stand after Major Phelps has said his piece. After that you will be free to go."

"Go where?"

"Major Phelps's men will escort you back to London. You have your open return flight ticket with Pakistan Airlines, you can book a flight back at your convenience."

Haji nodded. "That is good."

"Now we just need to go over your testimony for tomorrow, to make sure you get everything right."

"The truth is the truth, Mr Howerd. How can I get that wrong?"

Howerd made a half grin. "It's not that. The truth is the truth but a good defence lawyer can make it sound less than the truth and you'll need to be prepared. My opponent is one of the best and you will be tested on your evidence."

"I am ready," Haji said.

Howerd turned to Phelps. "I think he is ready, Major. No need for any final polishing." He turned back to Haji. "You're sure there's nothing we can get you to ease your wait?"

"Nothing, Mr Howerd. I shall pray for victory tomorrow."

The two captors left him to his devotions but not before he saw a uniformed soldier take his place in the hallway outside the room. A soldier with an armband that read RP. Haji had no idea what it meant but he knew the reason for the man's presence. He was free only as long as he stayed in the room.

It was good news that he was to be returned to London. In spite of his protestations he was in no hurry to catch a return flight to Pakistan. He would give the escort the slip and get on with the real purpose of his visit. His mobile phone was still concealed in his body belt together with ten thousand US dollars, enough to fund several attacks on the unbelievers. The Greek mythology he had read came back to him. He was the Trojan Horse.

★ ★ ★

"I'm sorry I can't offer you a drink, Mr Smith," Gill said. "But take a seat. What can I do for the Security Service?"

Smith folded away his credentials and sat on the only chair in the small room to which Somers had moved and now occupied alone. She sat on the bed and crossed her slim legs. He remembered Galbraith's description and inwardly chuckled. A more unlikely soldier would be hard to find. Somers was more like a glamour model with her stylish haircut, a face cameras would love and a body to match. No wonder MI6 had used her. She was honey-trap material. He decided on a direct approach.

"I don't enjoy playing games, Captain Somers. There are important jobs to do. Like making sure this country is protected from all kinds of alien threats and I don't have time to mess around."

"Meaning...?"

"You've been trying to make fools of us. It's a serious offence to obstruct an investigation and it seems to me you've been sticking your oar in where it's not required."

"And what investigation is that, Mr Smith?"

Smith sighed. "You know damn well."

"Oh you mean the illegal surveillance of Major Keane's defence lawyer. I trust you did get Home Office approval for the wire taps?"

That hit home. "It's covered under the Anti-Terrorist Act," he bluffed. "The point is that I've got evidence that you were, and still are, interfering in that investigation."

"Evidence...ahh, yes." Gill got to her feet and raised the cover of her laptop on the dresser. The screen sprang to life. She pressed some keys and the machine whirred. "Talking of evidence I'm just downloading something that might be of interest to you, and writing it to DVD. It'll take a few minutes so please carry on."

Smith's interest was piqued but he could not help a shiver of worry. "What is it?"

"All in good time. Please continue." Gill sat back on the bed and re-crossed her legs.

She was far too unconcerned for Smith's liking. He guessed she would be cool but this was definitely inside the arctic circle. She had taken control and was leading him. That had to be stopped. It was time to try the frighteners.

"I'm considering passing everything to the Director of Public Prosecutions. I dare say you'd soon be ending up in court too. Bang goes your career and your pension. Probably end up serving time too. What do you think you'll get for impeding an officer of the law in his investigations?" First offence, taking previous good conduct into account, what, six months, a year? Could be two, depends on how seriously the judge takes it. As the security of the nation is involved I'd say he'd take it pretty damn seriously."

"What do you want from me?"

"I want you out of my face. This case is important and it needs to run smoothly. I don't want to see your pretty little fingerprints on anything. Clear?"

"And if I don't keep *out of your face*?"

Smith sighed again. "If the thought of losing your career and your freedom isn't enough, there are other ways..."

The computer pinged which took a little of the edge off Smith's threat but it still hung in the air between them. Gill nodded her understanding, rose to her feet and ejected the disk from the laptop's drive.

"Here's something for you to think about, Mr Smith." She smiled as she handed him the disk.

"You remember what I said."

"Good night, Mr Smith."

★ ★ ★

It was all there. *Everything.* His meeting with Hathaway that was taped for his own protection was now a weapon against him. All the twists, all the turns, all the lies, all the deceptions. All recorded for the world to see. If this ever got into the public domain he would be finished. The trial would be stopped and the Service would be cleaning out his Augean Stable for years to come. DG would have a major apoplexy and that alone was not something to contemplate with equanimity.

The worse thing of all was how cleverly it had been spliced together to make it look as if *he* were the traitor. It was all becoming oh, so clear. His car registration recorded at the hotel in Hereford. His insistence on taping the meetings, his comings and goings cut in at just the right places. His fingerprints on the gadget that had been used to hack into the Service's computers. A false but authentic looking degree certificate of computer studies from Exeter

University. Him who didn't know a space bar from a monitor was now a computer wizard and the records to prove it were in the public domain, downloaded from the University's own website.

Given time and the backing of DG he could concoct a counter for all these accusations but would he be given either? If he failed in his task of delivering a guilty verdict in the Keane trial it would not reflect well on the Service in the government's eyes and that meant DG, whose position at times was rocky, would also be in the firing line. Given the choice of DG's own career or that of Smith's, Smith well knew the outcome.

He also knew who it was who had stitched him up. Mason. By all conclusions he was the only one in a position to string this all together. The man was right, he knew little about him, but now Smith would make it his business to find out. If Mason coughed out the full story there would be no way to cover his tracks.

Not that it would matter. The realisation struck him that he had cocked-up big time and the only thing he could look forward to was the chop if this ever came out. The threat was obvious. Somers was warning *him* off or she would make the disk public.

And that was the key. *If this ever came out.* Now it was time to cut his losses. The trial would take care of itself. With luck the Board would decide on a guilty verdict and that would cover his immediate failure. After that the safest course was to remove anyone involved and that would take time and proper organisation.

★ ★ ★

"You realise we could all be arrested, especially you?" Gill said into the mobile.

"Breaching the Official Secrets Act? It's possible but not something I'm going to lose sleep over," Toff Mason said. "I owe you, miss. It's been playing on my conscience for a while and I'm just happy I was able to repay the debt."

"More than repay me, the boot's on the other foot. MI5 is bound to come after you. You'll have lost your job, probably get put inside, and won't have any chance of future employment when you do come out."

"Not to worry, boss. I figure the Service won't come after me too hard. It can't afford to have even more egg on its face. Main worry is they'll initiate a black op. It's happened before and I wouldn't put it past Smith who looks like chocolate wouldn't melt in his hand but he's an evil bastard."

"Thanks for the heads-up, Toff. I won't forget this."

"Okay, so the beer's on you the next time we meet. No chance of a leg-over too is there?"

Gill choked back a laugh. "You never change and the answer's the same. In your dreams, buddy-boy."

Mason laughed in turn. "No harm in asking. Still hooked on Ricky Keane then?"

"Now how would you know that?"

"C'mon, boss. This is your Uncle Toff you're talking to. Y'know, the walking sex machine. I've seen women look at me in the same way you look at him. All gooey eyed."

"I didn't know I made it that obvious."

"Maybe not to everyone. It did throw me a bit when you went off with the Spaniard."

"Something I'd rather not be reminded of, thank you. Real mistake he turned out to be."

Mason's soft chuckle sounded in her ear. "Maybe it's just as well. Getting into bed with an ETA terrorist could have had its interesting moments. But you got him, that's what counts."

"How's the leg now, Toff?"

"It's been fine since the hip replacement. Scuttlebutt has it you got the bastard who shot me too."

"That's something else that still gives me nightmares. Let's leave it there, Toff. What are your immediate plans?"

"A long holiday somewhere warm until this blows over. Don't worry about me I can look after myself."

"Contact me when you decide to come back. We can't let you swing in the wind."

"I never thought you would."

"There is one small thing you could do for me before you go."

"You only need to ask."

The phone went dead as Gill broke the connection. Toff had been a good SAS man until his preoccupation with sex had caught him out. He had been the reason that Stu Dalgleish's girlfriend had ended under the wheels of a taxi in Hereford; part of the reason his conscience had troubled him into helping. The other part had been his heavy-handed and unwelcome attempt at her seduction which she had now forgiven. It was a court martial offence which she had not reported and that was the debt Mason had now repaid in full. She just hoped his premonition of black ops was just due to an over-active imagination.

★ ★ ★

Phelps entered the court room and saluted before removing his cap, identifying himself and taking the oath. His evidence was given in a clear and concise manner. The court learned how the complaint had come via the Embassy in Karachi, how it had been handed to him as one of the senior investigative officers in the Special Investigations Branch of the Military Police, how he had gone about taking statements from witnesses and how he had been informed of and tracked down a native Afghan who had witnessed the entire affair from a vantage point above the action.

Howerd had led him through his evidence with a masterly hand leaving it exactly where he wanted it; the introduction of his star witness.

"I have only one question for the witness, M'lord," Ann said when offered the opportunity to cross-examine.

Jeffreys waved his hand for her to continue.

"I'm obliged, M'lord." She turned left to face Phelps and gave him a winning smile. "Major Phelps..."

"Yes, marm."

"I'm much obliged to you too for such clear evidence. One thing however does occur to me..."

"Yes, marm?"

"...did you ever consider how providential was the coming forward of an actual witness to the action. Did you not think it a little convenient?"

"No, marm, I did not."

"And were you aware that this witness is a suspected member of al-Qaeda?"

"*Objection!*" Howerd was on his feet. "M'lud that cannot be proven it is mere conjecture."

Jeffreys leaned forward and pierced Ann with a ferocious stare."You will confine your questions to the facts, Miss FitzPatrick."

"As your Lordship wishes. I withdraw the question."

"The members of the Board will ignore the question as if it has not been asked," Jeffreys said.

Ann sat and Ricky leaned across to try to catch her eye. Were they scuppered that early?

Sissy gave him a sly smile and whispered in his ear. "How can they forget the question? It's been asked and will stick in their minds. Ann's already put a question mark against al-Shamrani's veracity. Wait 'til she gets him on the stand. Then we'll see some fireworks."

Phelps had been dismissed and Haji was making his way to the stand. He had been well briefed and bowed to the judge and the court. He looked young and harmless, utterly unlike the common perception of an al-Qaeda warrior. He identified himself and gave a promise to speak the truth.

Jeffreys consulted his notes and stared at the back of the court where the press was once again in large numbers. "Clear the public area. This next evidence and that which follows will be held in camera. May I remind the members of the press that reporting is subject to legally imposed restrictions."

Once the room had cleared it took on the hushed reverence of a church. Dust motes drifted in narrow beams of sunlight as it did through stained glass windows. Jeffreys broke the sepulchral silence. "Continue, Mr Howerd."

"Thank you, M'lud." He led Haji through his role in Afghanistan as interpreter and guide to Allied forces, how he helped in small battles, how he had become trusted due to his diligence. Howerd produced several documents from both American and British commanders testifying to Haji's value as an ally in the conflict and introduced them into evidence.

Ann had copies of the documents and they were no surprise.

Then Howerd asked Haji about the gunfight in the mountains, how he had worked his way onto a ledge overlooking the action and how he had been dumbfounded to see a British soldier shoot two unarmed civilians without warning. Two young men, barely out of their teens, there to fetch water for the camels. It was a masterful performance full of nuances; his horror at seeing such an act of murder, his trust in the British betrayed, his sorrow at having a man he had called friend turn into a cold-blooded killer.

Ann had no doubt that had the Board been a jury she would have lost the case then and there. As it was some of the members shifted uneasily in their seats, their faces drawn. It was a worrying sight.

Howerd had finished with Haji and gave her a slight bow. His eyes said your witness. *Pick the bones out of that.*

"Mr. al-Shamrani, is that an Afghan name?"

Howerd had been ready for this. "*Objection!* Mr. al-Shamrani's lineage has nothing to do with this case."

"I beg to differ, M'Lord. It has a great bearing on this witness's credence."

"I'll allow you some latitude, Miss FitzPatrick, but do be careful. The witness may answer the question."

"Thank you, M'Lord. Well, Mr. al-Shamrani, is yours an Afghan name?"

"It is not. The name is Arab."

"So you are in fact a Saudi citizen?"

"I am Afghan."

"How does the name Haji translate into English?"

"Your pardon. I do not understand?"

"Your given name is Saddiq yet you are called Haji. Does it have a meaning?"

Howerd was on his feet. "M'lud..."

"Is this going anywhere, Miss FitzPatrick. Your latitude is very nearly used up."

"Just a minute or two more, M'Lord..."

"Very well, make it quick and I must see the purpose of this line of questioning or I shall overrule it."

"Thank you, M'Lord. Mr al-Shamrani...?"

"It is one who has been on Hajj, the holy pilgrimage to Mecca."

"Am I right in thinking that it is really an honorific. A title of esteem for one who has made the pilgrimage?"

"Yes."

"And you are very devout. In fact you follow Sharia Law as do the Taliban and al-Qaeda?"

Haji's eyes flicked towards Howerd who leapt to his feet again. "M'lud I really must protest..."

"Miss FitzPatrick that is really quite enough."

"I am trying to show that the witness..."

"Miss FitzPatrick..."

"...is sympathetic to al-Qaeda."

"My patience is at an end. You will cease this line of questioning and get back to the case in hand or I shall hold you in contempt. The Board will disregard those questions as they are irrelevant. Do you wish to continue with this witness, Miss FitzPatrick?"

"I do, M'Lord and thank you for your patience. Mr. al-Shamrani how much were you paid for your services?"

"I do not understand."

"It's quite simple. How much money did the Americans and British pay you."

"A little. Maybe fifty dollars American a day."

"So what you were doing was for money and not for any great belief in the cause of ridding Afghanistan from the Taliban's clutches."

"I had to earn a living to keep my children from starving."

"How much are they paying you for giving evidence today?"

"Again I fail to see where this is going," Jeffreys said. He affected weariness in his voice. It was a warning sign.

"Mr al-Shamrani. I'm told that your wife was killed by the Taliban. My sympathies are with you. Can you tell me about that?"

Again Haji's eyes flicked over to Howerd and he licked his lips as if his mouth had suddenly gone dry. Howerd clambered to his feet, mimicking Jeffreys' affected languor. M'lud, please..."

Jeffreys glanced at his pocket watch. "I think we will recess for lunch. Miss FitzPatrick, Mr Howerd, see me in my rooms...now."

★ ★ ★

"Miss FitzPatrick you really are not doing your cause any good. I have noticed that the Board are growing tired at your continual innuendo. It may alienate them further. If you continue with this line I may have to advise them to disregard it altogether."

"I'm grateful for your Lordship's advice. But I do have good reason for taking this line that will become apparent later. My learned friend's case rests largely on this witness's testimony and I must be able to throw doubt on his veracity," Ann said.

Jeffreys turned to where Howerd was leaning against a bookcase twirling his wig in one hand and staring down at a mark on the military issue carpet. "What do you think, James. Will you keep objecting?"

Howerd looked up, a thin smile on his face. "If my learned friend has a point I would like her to get to it quickly. However I'm in agreement with your Lordship and feel that this line of questioning is sitting badly with the Board and is doing her client a disservice. Under the circumstances I can only add my advice to yours. However if my learned friend insists on continuing it can only strengthen my case. If she insists on doing my job for me I shall not object too vigorously."

"There you have it, Miss FitzPatrick," Jeffreys said. "Prosecuting counsel has more regard for your client than apparently do you. Rest assured that I will be monitoring the situation very closely indeed."

Chapter Twenty-Five

B lake stared across the vista of the Thames from 'C's suite on a top floor of Vauxhall Cross. In the distance he could see the Palace of Westminster aglow in warm midday sunlight. Nearer was the Tate Gallery with an exhibition of Japanese art and banners snapping in the stiff breeze like Samurai pennants.

'C' watched him, calculating the message he was about to receive from the hang of Blake's shoulders.

"We're no further forward in tracing the origins of this group, *Shuhada: Martyrs of the Jihad*. Not a whisper amongst our usual sources. Not unprecedented but a little unusual," Blake said. He turned to face his master. "The source we had on the ground in Yemen has not been able to confirm the body count. This group, whoever they were, was efficient in cleaning up its own mess and disposing of its own dead."

"And what do you read into that?" 'C' asked.

Blake pulled two pieces of paper from an inside pocket. "We received a request from the Little Sisters in 'Five' yesterday. There was a fraction of a tattoo visible on the wrist of one of the terrorists. We have been asked if we can identify it." He handed one picture over and pointed to the tiny chevron-shaped mark. "As you know, 'C', we have a library of such logos on file and the computer programs to interpret fragments such as this. The Middle-East Desk collects every known logo from every known source in the region and associated regions but this one eluded us. So we widened the search to other databases. You can see from the fragment that the angle from the point is exactly 45 degrees. With that, the depth of the point and the width of the rectangular section above it we were able to come up with this..." He handed 'C' the second sheet.

"My god!" 'C' said. He was looking at a winged dagger with a scroll across the blade that read *'Who Dares Wins'*. "The SAS?"

"Maybe an ex-member, someone who served with or was attached to the Regiment at some time. It's quite a prestigious attachment. I've heard that some soldiers will have the tattoo even if they have not been badged. Fantasists who would never make the grade but who want people to think they had."

"In this case?"

"If you will bear with me, 'C', I have a theory. It may sound ludicrous."

'C' waved a hand for Blake to continue. "Your theories usually have some substance, fire away."

"It's the void. The nothingness. No trace of this group. No evidence that they were ever in Yemen. Al-Qaeda have denied any involvement, which for once rings true, and no other group of fanatics has come forward.

"So I ask myself who would profit from kidnapping these two men. Hathaway is a spin merchant for the government and Oakley is a less than adequate junior defence minister. What they have in common is the government's interest in the current court martial of a serving SAS officer."

"I see where you're going with this. Do you have any proof?"

Blake smiled. "I suspect proof can be found if we search hard enough to find it but do we want to? Just supposing the SAS set up the whole thing to enhance their reputation and to put a scare into the government at a time when it is proposing a weakening of the Regiment's elitist culture. Just supposing. What would be the value to us?"

"All intelligence is valuable," 'C' said. "I could see where it may come in useful on occasion."

"Precisely," Blake said.

"But what you're suggesting is a monstrous slur."

"Perhaps. It has also drawn my attention to the court martial in question. It seems one of the witnesses is a Haji Siddiq al-Shamrani. We have a marker out on the name al-Shamrani, one of whom was closely associated with al-Qaeda. This man too is suspected of being associated with bin Laden. I believe he will be worth watching."

"And the request from 'Five'?"

"Sadly, nothing found on our Middle-East logo database. Disingenuous but not untrue. I think we need to keep our suspicions close to our chest. Don't you agree, sir?"

'C' slid the pictures back across his desk. "You know what to do with those. This is not our territory so I don't want our fingerprints on it. Keep an eye on al-Shamrani but keep it low profile whilst he's in the country. I don't want Five's DG howling down the phone that we're treading on his toes."

Blake smiled a conspirator's smile. "It's already in hand, 'C'."

★ ★ ★

The DVD on Hathaway's television table was worrying him. The content was worrying but more so was the subliminal message from the Special Branch man; so full of coded words and he should know. He had spent his life in politics devising and delivering coded messages to supporters and opponents alike. *'I think the government would be very receptive to your ideas Mr So and So, and so grateful for your promise of donations to the party funds. I dare say the government could find a use for your talents at some future time.'*

'I can't see any problem with advertising your product here, Mr Doe. Your industry is in a similar position to the party, we could both do with a higher profile but advertising can be so expensive...'

A hint, a nod, a wink, that was how business was done and it worked the other way too. *'The minister is minded to award the contract to Road Construction Inc. They've been so helpful in his campaign to increase speed cameras in this area and you know how strongly he feels about road safety. Perhaps you could make a similar contribution. Negotiations are still finely balanced.'*

He was good at it but all the pussyfooting around was not Hathaway's real style. 'Call a spade a spade' his old dad had said and Hathaway preferred to get straight to the point. *'Do it, or you'll gets no more work from us'.*

'Back off, or sees your little dalliance with your secretary splashed all over the front page of the Sun.'

That was his style. It had made his reputation as a hard man, made him feared up and down Whitehall and in every editor's office in Wapping. So it came hard to be on the receiving end for once.

The more he thought about it the more real the threat became. He was being warned off the Keane case. No more leaning on people. Ease off or have your cowardly antics shown to the nation. It was on video so bound to make both BBC and ITV evening news bulletins. He had bullied them often enough, cowed them into dropping coverage or reducing it to dead donkey status. He had a few enemies there who would be happy to see his reputation as hard man washed away like so much flood borne detritus.

He had a choice. He could carry on doing his masters' bidding, continue to push for Keane's conviction and try to deal with the fall-out as he had always done or he could walk away, let it be known that the government were no longer as eager for a conviction. It did not want to seem ungrateful in the light of his and Oakley's heroic rescue.

Hathaway had some sympathy with that. If it wasn't for them he'd be headless right now. That was another thing his dad had taught him, never be in debt to anyone. Maybe he was talking about money but the cap seemed to fit equally well for his reputation.

Deep down this attempt to castrate him rankled. Whichever way he played it he was likely to lose either his job or his reputation and he valued his job far more highly. The DVD could be positively spun. He had done it for others he could do it for himself. His rep was salvable his job would not be. His boss would see any failure as treachery and he would be out the door in double-time. No real choice then and it was his duty to make sure Keane was dead and buried.

★ ★ ★

Ann considered she had been lucky to get as far as she had with her line of questioning but she had not yet achieved her goal. The advice from her opponent had been kindly meant and it was good advice. Howerd had read the runes and could see into her future.

She had taken Haji back through his evidence but had failed to shake him from his story. She had watched Ricky's shoulders slump with each answer and knew what he was going through, sitting mute in a chair as he relived his actions, taken back by the words of an onlooker.

It was a gamble but she needed a high note now, "Mr al-Shamrani, just one final question. Your wife was killed by the Taliban, why was that?'

She could see Haji start. He had thought the question had been passed over and was unprepared for it.

"What is this...?"

"Why was your wife killed by the Taliban?"

Howerd was part way to his feet. He did not like the look of near panic on Haji's face. "...M'lud?"

Jeffreys was reading his notes and had not noticed Haji's distress. He waved a hand "I'll allow it. The witness will answer."

"Well, Mr al-Shamrani..."

"It was the law. She disobeyed the law."

Ann leant forward and rested on her elbows. She seemed concerned and projected sympathy. "What law was that?"

"Hejab. Seclusion. Women belong in the house or the grave. That is their right."

"And that is Sharia law. The law of the Taliban."

"Yes."

"And how did your wife break that law?"

"She left the house unaccompanied."

"And who informed the Taliban of that, Mr. al-Shamrani?"

Haji's face went tight and he pointed at Ann. He voiced a stream of Arabic before realising no one could understand. Ann could see the whites of his eyes and his pointed hand was shaking. "Women belong in the house *or the grave*."

"No further questions, M'Lord."

★ ★ ★

The Court Orderly was a staff-sergeant serving with the Adjutant General's Corps. He was nearing retirement but enjoyed the sinecure of his post and was not looking-forward to the end of his engagement. The thought of living on a staff-sergeant's pension or finding additional work to cover his outgoings did not enamour him of the idea. That made him receptive to little business dealings on the side. For a few pounds he would pass information to certain parties. Sometimes the press and sometimes others. His name had been handed on by a reporter he frequently helped and he was happy to accept a new income stream. His report to Mr. Blake was concise. Of special interest to the prurient minded was the witness's reaction to being questioned about the death of his wife. Poor sod was probably still in mourning. Them types seemed to wail on for years. Got so upset he did he almost threatened counsel's life. Maybe it just seemed that way. Poor bugger must have put the emphasis in the wrong place, him not being a natural English speaker and all. But it made a good story and Mr. Blake seemed pleased enough. And yes the witness was leaving for London right away in an unmarked Military Police car.

★ ★ ★

Haji was furious with himself. He had let the mask slip and he had noted the stirring of interest on the faces of the soldiers. He was furious with himself but even more furious with the woman. How dare she violate *him*.

More to the point would they understand the significance of the old Pathan proverb he had blurted out? He thought perhaps the damage was limited to merely giving a wrong impression that could be attributed to grief. He had said as much to Howerd before he left in the car. It was as much as he could do to mitigate the damage and he could see sympathy and understanding in Howerd's eyes. *The trusting fool.*

The car drove him straight to Heathrow Airport. He did not need to give his escort the slip, they just dropped him outside Terminal 3 and showed him where the Pakistan Airlines check-in desk was situated. Then they left him.

He made his way into the toilets and bolted himself into a cubicle. He pulled out his mobile and sat on the seat while he waited for his call to be answered. It was, in Arabic, and he replied in his native tongue. "It is the messenger. I need your address."

Details were given to an address in Dollis Hill in North London, also directions on how to get there. Haji was lost in London but the tube service was excellent. He took the Piccadilly Line to Green Park and changed there to the northbound Jubilee Line. He followed his instructions along the tree-lined avenues until he reached his destination at a semi-detached house which had a brass plate screwed to its wall that read in Arabic and English *'The Brotherhood for Mutual Understanding'*. It was one of many front organisations set up by bin Laden. When one was closed down or was discovered by the security services it would reappear as another. Haji grinned as he read the sign. He trusted the Sheikh and understood his needs. It was the mutual understanding of master and servant, each knowing his own place in the great plan of life.

He pressed the bell. He was expected and the door was opened immediately by an elderly man wearing a white turban and flowing tribal robes who glanced hurriedly up and down the street before closing the door.

He greeted Haji warmly. "The messenger of the Sheikh is most welcome in my house. You were not followed?"

Haji shook his head. "No, uncle, they did not suspect me. They let me go about my business, taking the usual precautions of course."

"Some tea, Haji? You must be thirsty."

"It is good to be with one's own family. I feel soiled by association with the unbelievers and crave some closeness to the comforts of home. I thank you for your kindness."

"There is much to discuss but after tea you must rest awhile. There is a mosque close by where we can pray together in good company. Only then will you feel truly refreshed."

"Haji nodded. Already his spirits were lifting.

Out in the street Blake's men made a note of the address and the details on the brass plate.

★ ★ ★

Smith was letting his frustrations get the better of him. "Where *is* Mason?"

A new man was settled in Mason's cubicle. Man? He looked barely old enough to wipe his own backside, one of the new wave of computer geeks recruited by the Service straight from university. They had their talent scouts in all the major establishments. Great at working computers but not experienced for much else. The newcomer turned his head. He looked like a startled rabbit. "He's gone off sick, sir."

Smith grunted made for his office and called 'B' Branch. "I want Mason's files sent up here right away. You know which Mason. The one working for me who went off sick today. What excuse did he give?'

There was a clicking of computer keys on the other end of the line. "He has a medical certificate from Guys Hospital. Seems that his hip replacement has failed. He'll be off for quite a while."

Smith grunted his thanks and slammed down the phone before having second thoughts and hitting the digits for 'A' Branch.

"Jimbo? Smith. I need you to find someone for me, toute-suite. Can do? I'll send his file down as soon as I get it. Cheers, I owe you."

He pulled his mobile from his pocket and hit redial. Galbraith answered.

"Any results on those enquiries, Andy?"

"Hello, Smith. I was just about to ring you. Nothing on the security company. No one will admit to taking on the contract.

"The other question was not so tough to answer. Apparently the accused's parent unit is responsible for dress and security. Keane's opted for his attachment and all the guards are SAS troopers. Doesn't get any easier does it?"

"So who's the boss man there?"

"You'll need to speak to a Colonel Tim Bailey. He's the Acting Officer Commanding 22 SAS."

"Yeah, that's right, I've met him at a Cobra meeting. Thanks, Andy..."

"Smith...before you go..."

"Yes?"

"I've had a thought. What if there is no outside security company. What if the SAS themselves are running interference. It would explain why I couldn't track down a security company."

"If ever you want a decent job come and see me, Andy. I could use a talented bloke like you."

"All part of the service."

Smith put down his mobile and steepled his fingers. The SAS were looking after their own. It made sense and gave him just one target to aim at. He picked up his desk phone once again and asked the security operator to get

Credenhill on the line. He needed to make an urgent appointment to see Bailey.

There was one other call he needed to make but he could not do it from inside Thames House. It was far too delicate for that.

★ ★ ★

In a mosque in Dollis Hill one of MI5's army of informants was relating a sighting to his controller. There was a new young man accompanied by Dr. Saad Abib al Adine, the Director of *The Brotherhood for Mutual Understanding* upon whom he had been instructed to watch and report. The young man had been addressed respectfully as Haji, a holy pilgrim, and appeared to be held in high esteem. Would that be of interest and would the money arrive in the usual way?

It would. The man was thanked and was happy. The report was filed for 'F' Branch and tagged.

Sic Volvere Parcas
So spin the fates

Note: 9 - Appended.

*I*t's been a hard day but a satisfactory one. I beieve I have succeeded in casting al-Shamrani in a new light. His loss of control was an unexpected bonus. I must remember to thank Richard Wells properly when he returns from Afghanistan. His knowledge and insight into the Afghan tribal cultures has been invaluable.

There was another piece of good news. Stu Dalgleish has made a full recovery and will be able to give evidence tomorrow. I'm so happy about that; I did fear for his sanity when Gill had told me what they had done to him. A truly courageous man to have put himself in such harm's way for a friend in need. I shall also be happy to see him on a much more personal level. I've missed him.

Sissy has now come to terms with our situation and has rallied round like a 'trooper'. We are so much more comfortable knowing that members of the SAS are now responsible for our care. What rules were bent I don't know but I'm not going to look this considerable gift horse in the mouth.

I think it true to say that today we turned a corner and tomorrow looks brighter than it did. Still an uphill battle but the incline is lessened somewhat.

The elephant in the room is still Howerd's cross-examination of my witnesses. I toyed with the idea of not putting Ricky on the stand but that would seem too much like an admission of guilt. I shall have to keep everything crossed that he stands up to Howerd's probing. I don't want to play the medical card as it may seem a low trick but his PTSD may cause him to react much like al-Shamrani.

Someone with a guilty secret.

AFP,
Hartfield Country House, Wensleydale.

Chapter Twenty-Six

There was still an awkwardness between them. The past was not so easy to erase. Ricky sat on the edge of his bed while his 'Assisting Officer' sat at the opposite end.

"Did you mean what you said?" Ricky asked. "He looked into Gill's face trying to find a vestige of a lie.

"Is the Pope Catholic?" It was a flippant reply which Gill instantly regretted as a pained look crossed his face.

"I'm serious."

She tried to atone for her mistake "So am I…very."

"Where do we go from here?" Ricky asked. There was a slight hint of pleading.

Gill slid her hand along the rough blanket and touched his fingers. He didn't pull away. "We have a future…if you want."

"My future's a little hazy right now."

"You should have more faith in Ann. She's the best."

A light sparked briefly in Ricky's eyes. "And you would know that…how exactly?"

Gill puckered her lips in a semblance of a knowing smile. "We shared a room together for two years."

"It was you…"

"I got in touch with her when you needed a good lawyer."

"She gets off on deadbeat cases then?"

"Your case isn't as deadbeat as you might think."

"Board thinks otherwise, I can see it on their faces."

Gill squeezed his hand harder. "Ricky, stop this...this defeatism. It's so unlike you."

"It's not defeatism, it's realism. What future can we have if I'm stuffed into a 'corrective facility' for a few years."

"That is not going to happen. I've made a few plans."

"I can guess but I can't let you do it. Your life will be ruined too."

"I've got two whole squadrons waiting on my word, plus the Special Projects Team who have come up with a dilly of a plan to get you out of the country without anyone being the wiser."

"You want me to be chased around the world for the rest of my life?"

"*Us*, Ricky, *us*. I'm in it for the long haul."

"And what about all those blokes out there. The ones whose careers are going down the drain as well as ours?"

"They're all signed up. They know the score and it's about more than just you. You're a scapegoat and you're being used as an example because some politicians in the Midlands fear they'll lose their seats at the next election if you don't get the chop. The blokes out there aren't standing for that because they could be next in line. Don't worry on that score, they can take care of themselves."

"I can't let this happen, Gill, I can't. I want to face the court, I want a fair hearing and I want to clear my name or take my punishment if it's handed out. I can't allow anyone else's life to be ruined."

Gill slid closer until her knees were touching his and his hand was in her lap, clasped with both hers. "Don't be a martyr, Ricky. It's not your fault you're in this position and you shouldn't have to suffer for it.

"I've sold my house in Tunbridge Wells and I've got well over £1 million in the bank. I'd use it all for you but Ann has now waived her fees so the cash is going spare. We could start a new life together anywhere in the world. You just need to give the word."

Ricky raised his free hand and stroked her cheek. "What a lovely thought but I can't let you do it."

"Oh don't be so pig-headed, Ricky. I don't need you in prison. I want you with me. I've waited too damn long as it is. My fault, I know, chasing my own dragons, but I've had enough too. I want out and I want out with you."

"You don't understand, Gill. I killed those two boys and it gives me nightmares. The piper has to be paid."

"Oh, god, Ricky. You don't understand either. My last op, the one in Ireland, I killed a man too. Close up and personal, the worst kind of way where you can smell the stink and watch as he kicks and screams and pisses and craps himself. It finished me. I can't hack it anymore."

She had dropped her head and a tear splashed on their entwined fingers. He had never seen her like this, so vulnerable, so feminine, so close.

"Do you want to talk about it?"

At first she shook her head and bit her lip. "I thought I could hack it but nothing prepares you for the real thing."

"So this is for us? The walking wounded. The casualties that don't make the 'News at Ten'. Cool pair, we are." He lifted her chin and kissed her gently. "If it's for you, I'm in. And bollocks to the world."

"Ricky, you say the sweetest things..."

"D'you know what I love more than a woman in uniform?"

Gill flicked open the top button of her tunic. "A woman out of it?"

Ricky smiled, reached up and slipped open the second button. "You guessed."

Gill undid the third and fourth. "Not difficult. I know the way you think."

He slipped his hand inside and felt the warmth of her breast against his palm. "In that case you'll know exactly what I'm thinking now."

★ ★ ★

The court had the same hollow ring as the day before as the press and public were still excluded. Ann had lost the tingling of optimism that had sustained her through the previous night. Now reality had dawned with the new day.

She called a succession of troopers who had been on the operation with Ricky. One by one Howerd demolished their usefulness as defence witnesses. He was a master of his brief, churning out technicalities as if he were born to it. Larry, Aitch, Digger and Tonka had all been summarily dismissed, their stories unable to be of help. Sponge had arrived too late to see the incident. Pete held firm as he had a clear view from his perch above the battlefield and his testimony that he had seen a weapon in one of the trader's hands could not be shaken.

"Sergeant C," Howerd said smoothly. "How far away from the defendant were you?"

"Bout four-hundred metres, sir."

"And you were armed with an Heckler and Koch G3-SG1, is that correct?'

"Along with a C5 carbine and a 9mm Sig pistol...sir. The C5's not much cop at that range."

"Of course, but it's that particular model of G3 rifle I'm concerned with. It's fitted with a telescopic sight, is it not?"

"Yessir?"

"And that sight has a magnification of six?"

"It's variable up to six."

"And were you using it at maximum magnification?"

"At four-hundred metres? Yes."

"What is the size of the object lens?"

"About fifty millimetres."

"And at four-hundred metres that would give you a field of vision of what exactly...at full magnification?"

Pete thought for a second. "Not sure. You'd have to ask an armourer."

"But it would be a very narrow field, would it not?"

"Bit like looking down a tunnel, yeah."

"And where were you focused at the time the two young men were shot?"

"On the group by the buildings."

Howerd picked up a sketch map of the battle area. "Did you draw this, Sergeant?"

Pete squinted at the paper although he could see it well enough. "Looks like the one I drew for the debrief, yeah?"

"And the measurements are accurate?"

"As far as I can tell. I didn't actually get a tape measure out."

Howerd allowed himself a smile. "Of course not, you were far too busy. M'lud this sketch map matches with others that were drawn after the skirmish and are all entered into evidence."

"I'm obliged, Mr. Howerd. Please continue."

"Sergeant. You have indicated on this map that the distance between the defendant and the area on which you were focused as around fifty metres. Is that correct?'

"About, yes."

"Would it surprise you to learn that we have taken a G3-SG1 rifle to the ranges? With the scope at maximum magnification at four-hundred metres the field of vision is only forty metres across. Which leads me to conclude that you could not possibly have seen the defendant or the two victims at the time of the shooting."

"But I had both eyes open. I could see."

"Yes but without the benefit of magnification at four-hundred metres, how can you be so sure that the victims had weapons on their persons?"

"No further questions, M'lud."

Jeffreys squirmed in his chair. All the talk of killing was not to his liking and he wished it over. "Do you wish to redirect, Miss Fitzpatrick?" His tone of voice distinctly said don't."

"If your Lordship pleases." Ann was beginning to enjoy Jeffreys' discomfort. It was small recompense. Howerd had made a thoroughly professional job of demolishing Pete's testimony. It was no more than she had expected and she was prepared.

"Sergeant!"

"Ma'am?"

Ann pointed at a window. "Can you see that road sign in the street?"

Pete squinted his eyes and stared. "Yes ma'am."

"How far would you say it was?"

"Bout three-fifty, four-hundred metres."

"Can you read it?"

"No, not really, ma'am."

"What can you see?"

"It's a road sign..."

"How is it constructed, from where you're standing? Oh, and cover your right eye."

"Well...it's a single grey post with a triangular sign on top. Red and white with...don't know, possibly a road junction sign."

"It's a crossroads, very good, sergeant. Can you see anything else?"

"Well somebody's wrapped a bit of ribbon around the post, 'bout half-way down. One of them yellow ribbons."

"Thank you, sergeant. That will be all."

Pete pointed to each eye in turn. "One-One on the pulhheems."

★ ★ ★

"Thank you for agreeing to see me so promptly, Colonel."

Bailey nodded and walked to Smith's window taking in the view across the Thames. "I was coming to town anyway but it will have to be quick as I have a meeting with Cobra in thirty minutes."

"I won't keep you, long. Take a seat."

"What's this about, Smith?"

"Your regiment is posting security for the Keane trial."

"What's it got to do with you?"

"I thought we might be able to come to some mutually beneficial arrangement."

"Over what?"

"Please take a seat, colonel and I'll explain."

I'm not planning on staying long enough to get comfortable. What's on your mind."

"I need a few minutes in various rooms in Yorkshire."

Bailey turned, rested his rear on the windowsill and laughed. "Get lost, Smith."

"As I said, it could be mutually beneficial."

"You want me to look the other way while you plot to send one of my officers to prison. It would have to be damned beneficial."

"How about if I could persuade the Ministry that the SAS should be exempt from certain future developments..."

"Such as...?"

"Something along the lines of the equality legislation they're considering. Don't really want them shifting the goalposts, do you, Colonel?"

"That's not in your gift, Smith."

"Not directly but I have contacts and a certain amount of influence in the right places. I could deliver."

"I gather Mr Oakley is hell bent on introducing an element of levelling in Selection. He will be hard to convince."

"Maybe not as hard as you think, Colonel. His recent experiences have given him a new insight on these things. A Damascene conversion–almost–and it won't take much to topple him over the edge into reason."

"And ROE?"

Smith sucked in a breath like a plumber with bad news. "That could be a little more tricky. Oakley still thinks the army should be more like the scouts; all bob-a-job and helping old ladies cross the road."

"You're showing your age, Smith. But there's no deal without the government takes a look at ROEs."

"I'm sure we can come to some arrangement."

"Guarantees?"

Smith chuckled. He had him. "No guarantees but my word I'll do everything possible to get the required result."

"When and how long do you want?"

"Tonight and about thirty minutes. I gather things have been interesting today and the playing field has been levelled a touch. Having an inside track would be valuable."

"You've got it. Between twenty-one hundred and twenty-one thirty hours tonight. Don't cock it up."

"Don't worry, Colonel. My team's led by one of the best."

As soon as Bailey had left Smith called Galbraith. "Andy, I have a little job for you tonight."

★ ★ ★

Hathaway had let his anger build until it got too much to contain. He picked up the phone and dialled Scotland Yard. "This is Stan Hathaway calling from the Policy Focus Office. I want to speak to the top man in Special Branch."

"SO12, sir? There's a duty officer. Would you like to speak to him?"

"Just bloody put me through."

"Chief Inspector Williams here, sir. What can I do for you?"

"I have a complaint."

Hathaway could feel the concern on the other end of the line. A complaint from the PFO was big trouble.

"And what exactly is that, sir?"

"One of your officers threatened me and I want him punished."

Now he could hear the policeman's soft release of breath. So far, Williams thought, it did not sound too serious. Maybe a small misunderstanding, an unintentional giving of offence. Some slight heavy-handedness before the officer realised with whom he was dealing. "Give me a few details, sir and I'll look into it."

"Too right you'll bloody look into it. I want the bastard's skin hanging on the Commissioner's office wall. And if you're not careful your balls will be up there with them. Clear?"

"Can I have the officer's name, sir?"

"Davis, bloody Davis. Inspector bloody Davis and his bloody sidekick Colin somebody-or-other."

Now there was a question in Williams's voice. "You're sure it's SO12 you want, sir?"

"If that's the bloody Special Branch it is. That's what it said on the bastard's warrant card."

"Well, there could be a problem there, sir..."

"Too right, mate..." Hathaway was now catching relief in Williams's voice. "What problem?"

"We don't have an Inspector Davis in Special Branch. There's one up at Hendon but that Inspector Davis is a woman."

Hathaway felt like he'd been hit in the solar-plexus. "I'll get back to you."

He put the phone down. If not Special Branch, then who? Someone out there held the key to his future. Who would benefit from having *him* stitched-up? And who had access to that video? The army. And of course MI5. He could feel Smith's clammy fingers all over this. The man wanted some leverage. He was covering his back; taking some revenge.

Hathaway's boss strolled into his small office smacking a file against his thigh. "How's the trial going, Stan? They're getting edgy on high. They've heard rumours that the defence is putting up a bit of a fight after all. They need to be reassured. You know how jumpy they can get."

"Do they know about...you know?"

"Be your age, Stan. They ask a question and we provide the answers. They're not interested in the whys and wherefores. That's our business. They're too busy to get bogged down in fine print. No need to worry them about that is there? You know what the army say, no names, no pack drill."

Hathaway nodded. The Powers-that-Be did not want to know. It was arm's length. If they knew what dirty tricks this department got up to in the government's service they'd be genuinely horrified; but possibly not too surprised. It was much easier to turn a blind eye and let the hirelings bear the weight and the blame if it all went sour.

"I've not heard that one. Still I never wanted to be a soldier. Couldn't see the point in shovelling other people's shit around the world."

"You do your fair share of shit shovelling every day, Stan."

"Yeah, but I get paid so much better for it. You can tell them not to worry, boss. It's under control."

"Good stuff, Stan. Knew you wouldn't let us down. We're all counting on you." Then he was gone like a mini whirlwind. Hathaway admired his energy. He was feeling drained. One more call to make to the Lord Chancellor's Office, just to make sure Lord Justice Jeffreys fully understood the delicacy of his brief.

Chapter Twenty-Seven

Tim Bailey had his helicopter fly him to Yorkshire for a hastily arranged meeting with Keane and his defence team and an invitation to dinner at the mess. If he was going to play Judas he might as well do it on a full stomach.

He wanted to see how Keane was holding up, catch up on the details of the case with the lovely Ann and to give Smith's people time to do their dastardly deeds.

This was the breakthrough he had hoped for. Something he could present to the men to get them back in the fold before catastrophe could strike. So far they had been lucky and there had been no urgent demands for SAS assistance but their luck would not hold forever.

He now had an inkling where his two missing squadrons had gone to ground but finding them would be needle-in-haystack time, especially if they did not want to be found. They were past-masters at disappearing. Two squadrons could live happily for weeks in seemingly empty countryside. You could picnic in the middle of their position and never know they were there.

He would need to put the deal to Cowley by encrypted burst radio transmission. They would want proof of the government's good intentions and Bailey hoped that Smith would provide something soon that he could sell to the troopers.

Bailey pulled rank and had a small private room set up for the meal so that they did not have to share the large mess table with assorted junior officers, all with ears aflap. The private caterers had laid on a decent three-course dinner and the staff to serve it. He would bear the cost on his mess bill. It was the least he could do.

Keane he knew slightly, Ann he had met previously but he was pleasantly surprised by the accompanying Gill in full service dress and Sissy looking stunning in an off-the shoulder number she just happened to have with her.

Ricky did the introductions. "Colonel this is Miss FitzPatrick, Captain Gill Somers and Miss FitzPatrick's associate Sissy Hamilton."

Ann held out her hand. "Ann, please. So nice to meet you, Colonel."

Bailey played out the charade. "The pleasure's all mine."

Gill saluted and took Bailey's offered hand. "Captain Somers. I've heard a lot about you.

"And Miss Hamilton. May I call you Sissy?"

Sissy blushed bright pink. "You may, Colonel. But what do I call you? I can't keep calling you Colonel all night."

As we're all friends here we won't stand on ceremony. It's Tim.

"I've booked us a side room for a little privacy. Ladies..." He offered his arm to both Ann and Sissy and led them to the table. Ricky and Gill came in together.

The meal was whiled away in idle chatter which left the two soldiers wondering what the meeting was all about but after the pudding dishes had been cleared away, the coffees and liqueurs delivered and the serving staff had left Bailey became all business.

"Well, Ann. How are things looking? Am I about to lose one of my valuable assets?"

"I'm hopeful, Tim. Things went better today than I'd expected. Tomorrow I've got my strongest team on the stand. Sergeant Dalgleish and Ricky himself."

"What's your feeling. Does it go well in general?"

"It's difficult to call. I'd hate to play Texas Hold 'em with the members of the Board. Poker-faced isn't the half of it. But I'm hopeful we're making an impression."

"And you, Ricky. How are you holding up?"

Ricky smiled and took Gill's hand across the tablecloth. "I've got some pretty good support here, boss."

Bailey smiled. "Romance in the air, is it?"

"We're getting engaged when this is over, Colonel," Gill said.

"Planning for the future. I like that but it'll be hard on two serving officers going off in different directions. Sure you're up to it? I'm lucky, my wife is tucked up in a farmhouse near Brecon with three kids. I know that when I get home, which is all too rare these days, she'll be there with a hot meal and a glass of my favourite malt."

"You're a chauvinist, Tim," Sissy said with mock severity.

"No just a happy and contented husband. And thereby hangs the moral."

"We'll work on it, boss," Ricky said. "The thing is I feel I can cope if Gill's there to hold my hand."

"Good luck to you both. You have my blessing if ever you needed it."

"Was there anything else, Tim," Ann said and glanced at her watch. "We still have to go over tomorrow's testimony."

"Ordeal you mean," Ricky said. It was meant as a joke but his laugh sounded hollow.

Ann smiled her reassuring smile and turned back to Bailey. "We're meeting Sergeant Dalgleish at my hotel and I don't want to be late."

Bailey glanced at his own watch and nodded. "Then don't let me detain you any further. My main purpose was a little morale boosting but I can see I'm surplus to requirements."

"It was very kind of you to think of us, Tim" Ann said. "Many others would have thrown Ricky to the wolves."

"Yes, thank you, Colonel," Gill said. "I won't forget it."

"I'm happy to have done what I could. You have my best wishes for tomorrow."

The four left Bailey alone with the remains of his nightcap. What he did he did for the good of the Regiment but he felt a terrible twinge of sorrow that he may have sacrificed the one for the good of the many.

★ ★ ★

Life in the west had been good to Josef Pavlovich. He drove a smart car, wore an expensive Breitling wristwatch, had his shirts made in Jermyn Street and his suits in Savile Row. He was known by sight at many of the best restaurants and nightclubs in London. Yes, many knew his assumed name, but no one, except his clients, knew his business and they could only contact him via telephone linked to the internet. It was safer that way; for him and for them.

Josef was a highly trained and successful assassin. He had once worked for the East German Stasi but now he was a free agent, able to sell his skills for good money.

He chose his clients carefully. There were many traps for the unwary and he eschewed the business of husbands tired of their wives or wives determined to rid themselves of unfaithful husbands. In the main he avoided criminal gangs too. A rich seam for some but too fraught with double-dealing and rapidly changing allegiances. His business was big business and there was no business bigger than government, Josef was a master of the black operation. Wet jobs they had been called back in the old days of the Soviet Union. Then he killed at the bidding of the Politburo in Moscow. Now it was western governments who used his services. Squeaky clean administrations which could not be seen to get their hands dirty.

His forte was accidental deaths. He had studied pathology and had learned much about making a murder look like an accident. He was careful and cunning. Never to date had any of his victims been viewed as other than sad accidents.

The target's apartment was a cinch to break into. He had been lucky. The ground floor apartment directly beneath was empty, a 'To Let' sign nailed to its wall, and he had been able to study the layout from inside. He knew where the bedrooms were and the bathrooms, the sitting room with its television point and the kitchen off the dining area. He had left a side window to the empty flat unlatched and disabled the alarm system so he could get back inside and into the communal hallway without disturbing the police guard on the front entrance. It took just a few seconds to gain entry into the target's apartment.

It was late, gone midnight, and as expected his target was in bed asleep. He took a coil of rope from a paper sack and held it in his surgically gloved hands so that he would not transfer skin fragments that could be traced to him. The only epithelials on the rope would be the victim's. The rope was made of silk, soft and smooth. He had made an amateur-looking job of fashioning the loop but it was still an effective hangman's noose. That was a mere prop. The real murder weapon was a long nylon tie that once tightened could not be released without cutting it though with a sharp knife.

The target slept deeply. He threaded the tie beneath the man's neck, pushed the end through the slot and jerked it tight. The target's eyes opened and so did his mouth. Josef pushed a small orange soaked in LSD into his mouth to stop the choking noise from becoming too loud. He pulled a pillow from the bed covered the target's chest and pushed down hard on it to prevent the target from rising and thrashing his arms around. Josef was a big man and very strong. The skinny target was no match for his weight. He waited as the heels drumming on the bed lost their vigour before hauling the man to his feet and stripping off his pajama bottoms with one hand and a thoughtfully placed foot. He was careful not to touch the target with any great force. He did not want bruises to show in the post mortem but controlled the man's body by gripping the tail of the tie. The target scrabbled at the nylon strap with his fingernails until his strength failed. One final detail was covered by nature as blood pressure engorged his penis.

The target stopped kicking and Josef laid him on the floor, the orange still in his mouth but almost bitten through. He liberally spread some KY jelly on the man's penis and on his hands before dropping the tube into a drawer. The silk rope was first rubbed against the target's body before it went into the bottom of the man's wardrobe together with some Playboy magazines and some very mainline porn videos to which he transferred the target's fingerprints both inside and outside the covers. It was a thorough job.

Sometimes it wasn't enough to kill a man. His reputation had to die with him.

★　★　★

Stu Dalgleish looked every bit the professional soldier in his service dress uniform. The upwardly curved wings, stitched to his right shoulder, were enough to mark him as a member of an elite unit for those in the know. He was composed and calm. Ann felt proud of him, especially knowing what he had put himself through.

She covered his testimony item by item. It did not vary much from the evidence given by the others on the operation but the details were more precise.

"Sergeant Dalgleish, could you point out to the court your position when the two young men approached Major Keane. The Court Orderly will bring you the map."

Dalgleish took the sketch and held it for the Board to see. "Just here, ma'am. On elevated ground overlooking the valley."

"And you had a clear view of the buildings and the river?"

"Yes, ma'am. I picked the spot particularly for that reason. My job was to give covering fire when the attack went in."

"And you were armed with the same version of G3 rifle as other members of the group."

"Yes, ma'am. The SG1."

"The board will forgive me for stressing this but it is important. With a six-times magnification telescopic sight."

"It was switched on to six, ma'am, yes."

"Sergeant Dalgleish, whereabouts were you focused when Major Keane opened fire on the two men?"

"On them, ma'am. I was talking them in so that the boys down there would know how much time they had to find cover."

"Can you tell the court precisely what you saw."

"Yes, ma'am. As I said the two men were walking up to the river where the assault group were taking cover. The two weren't in much of a hurry. Just at that point in the river the bank had crumbled and it had left a small beach-like area. Major Keane was on this, half behind a rock with his legs in the water."

"So he had done the best he could to take cover?"

"Objection, M'lud. Leading the witness." Howerd was half-way to his feet and spoke from a crouch.

"Sustained. Rephrase please Miss FitzPatrick."

"How would you assess Major Keane's position, Sergeant?"

A smile twitched at the corners of Stu's lips. "It was about the best he could do given that all the available cover was taken by the other blokes."

"The two men approached the river. What happened then?"

"They slid down the bank onto that little beachy bit. The bigger of the two bent down to dip his bucket but suddenly stopped for about a second. Then he dropped his bucket and made a grab for a weapon in his belt and Major Keane shot him."

"And the other man...?"

"Well he threw his bucket at Major Keane and he went down too."

"And you saw all this in detail through the telescopic sight?"

"Yes. Ma'am."

"Thank you, Sergeant. No further questions, M'lord, but I reserve the right to redirect."

Jeffreys looked like he was sucking lemons but had to concede. "Very well. Mr. Howerd, I take it you will cross-examine?"

Howerd was on his feet shuffling papers and staring at them myopically. "Sergeant D." He then looked at Stu and smiled. "Thank you for a very succinct summary. I only have one or two questions but I want you to think about the answers very carefully. Did you actually see a weapon pointed at Major Keane?"

"The man went for his belt...?"

"Did you see the weapon?"

"I saw something black."

"The Court Orderly will now show you item ten in evidence. Do you see it?"

The orderly held up an object in a clear plastic bag.

"Yes, sir. It's a mobile phone."

"Yes a mobile phone and it was found near to where the men fell by the Pakistan Army. Is it not possible that it was the phone that the man was reaching for?"

"Why? He could have yelled..."

"Is it possible, Sergeant?"

"Improbable..."

Ann was on her feet. "M'Lord my learned friend is asking for conjecture."

Jeffreys leaned forward and rested on his elbows. "He's asking for an opinion. I'll allow it."

"I'm obliged, M'lud, Howerd said. "Sergeant, I did ask you to think carefully before replying now I ask again. Is it possible the black object you saw was this mobile telephone? Remember you are on oath."

"Not in my *opinion*, no?"

"How can you be so sure?"

"I've been around for a few years. I can tell when someone's going for a weapon or about to make a call."

"You've known the Major long?"

"A couple of years. We've been on ops together. He knows what he's doing so there's a good chance he won't get us killed by being gung-ho."

"Would you say you knew him well enough to solicit a loan from him?"

"What sort of question's that?"

"You will answer the question, Sergeant," Jeffreys said.

"No. I'd never ask him for a loan."

Howerd shuffled another piece of paper and stared at it. "M'lud a fresh piece of evidence has come to light and with your permission I will enter it into the court."

"What is it? Let me see."

Howerd passed the paper to the orderly who handed it up to Jeffreys. He handed a copy to Ann.

"As you can see it is a statement from Sergeant D's bank account. On it you will see a deposit of five-thousand pounds. That money was transferred from Major Keane's account three days ago. If it was not a loan, Sergeant, what was it?"

Chapter Twenty-Eight

Hathaway's boss, Tom Gannon, poked his head around the door jamb. "Have you heard the news?"

Hathaway shook his head then thought for a second "What news?"

"That idiot Oakley's gone and topped himself," Gannon hissed.

"When?"

"Last night. Details are sketchy but it looks like he was playing some sort of bizarre sex game and strangled himself by mistake. His secretary called us when he didn't turn up for work this morning and the duty officer got his plod to break in. Bloody man's had a 24-hour police guard on his front door since the kidnap and he has to go and do this."

"Doesn't sound like Oakley," Hathaway said thoughtfully. "He never struck me as the type for kinky sex."

"Who knows what goes on behind closed doors," Gannon muttered. "Anyway we've got to get some positive spin on this. Not the same since the kidnap, under the weather, terrible personal strain. You know better than me. Put it down as heart failure due to stress and hope to god that the press don't get their hands on the details until we've had a chance to get his successor in place. We'll delay the post mortem for a week or so and get a minister to launch a new initiative on the same day to grab the headlines. Otherwise this won't look good for the government."

"Who've we got in mind as replacement? The press are bound to ask."

"Young Jack Simmonds is next in line. He's a totally different kettle of fish to Oakley. Bit more fire in his belly. It should please the hawks at MoD."

"I'll pull in a few favours around Wapping to keep the lid on this for a while. Oakley's bound to get the sympathy vote due to what he's been through. The editors will play the game for now but we'll have to hope the red tops don't get a sniff," Hathaway said.

"Well that's *your* job, Stan." Gannon peered at him closely. "How are you holding up, by the way?"

"True northern grit. It'll takes more than a few terrorists to puts me off me stride."

Gannon squinted at him with one eye. "Hmmm. If you say so. You've got to be on top of your game this week."

Gannon left and Hathaway telephoned the duty officer for more details.

"Yes, very sad, Mr. Hathaway. Police are there now but initial findings suggest that he accidentally choked himself. It's the old theory that sexual enjoyment is heightened by starving the brain of oxygen. Auto-erotic asphyxiation they call it. We had another MP do the same thing a few years back. Can't see where the enjoyment is myself. From what the police have found it seems like he made a habit of it and just miscalculated this time, tightened the loop too much and couldn't get it undone. Wanted a bigger high maybe. Bit like snorting cocaine, you always want more."

"No evidence of foul play?"

"No. It looks straight-forward. Besides he had a guard on his door all night. No one could have got in. What are you thinking? Terrorists again?"

"It did cross my mind but you've put it at rest. Thanks." Hathaway put down the phone and rested his chin in both hands. The reason for Oakley's death was plausible and more than likely correct but he could not help a feeling of something closing in on him. The fake Special Branch policemen first and now Oakley. Coincidence or not it was beginning to feel bad.

* * *

Ann was spitting tacks. She had asked for an adjournment and Jeffreys had granted her five minutes in his rooms. Howerd was there too leaning nonchalantly against a book case, a slight smile of superiority twitching at his lips.

"I really must protest, M'Lord. Why wasn't I given warning of this 'so-called' evidence?"

Jeffreys raised his eyebrows and stared at Howerd, "Well, James?"

"It was only discovered yesterday. Major Phelps had a search warrant granted on the strength of information received and was able to access Sergeant Dalgleish's bank accounts. And this anomalous amount of money came to light. I am merely seeking an explanation."

Ann's eyes blazed back at him. "Neither my client nor Sergeant Dalgleish has any knowledge of that money transfer. Both of them deny it most vehemently."

"Forgive me for stating the obvious, Miss FitzPatrick, but they would say that."

"You are attempting to impugn two men's reputations. You are suggesting that Major Keane bribed Sergeant Dalgleish to lie on his behalf."

Howerd shrugged. "I merely present the evidence. It is up to the court to interpret it."

"And what if it is false evidence..."

"Be careful, Miss FitzPatrick," Jeffreys said. "If Mr. Howerd is correct then there is a case of attempting to pervert the course of justice to be answered. There may be further charges to follow."

"M'Lord, if we are talking perverting the course of justice there is certainly a case to be answered. I firmly suspect that this money is a plant, part of an on-going dirty tricks campaign designed to see my client found guilty of the charges against him."

"Are you suggesting I would have any part of that?" Howerd spluttered.

"No, Mr Howerd I am not. I have far too much respect for your integrity to suggest such a thing. However, that respect does not run to Major Phelps and MI5, both of whom, I believe, are complicit in plotting against my client."

"That is an extremely serious accusation, Miss FitzPatrick. You will withdraw it or prove it," Jeffreys said.

"With pleasure, M'Lord." Ann pulled a file from her briefcase like a conjurer pulling a dove from a hat. "It's all there, chapter and verse. Illegal phone taps on my chambers and my home. The kidnapping and holding hostage of Sergeant Dalgleish. The breaking and entering of my home. The bugging of my gymnasium, the parts played by Major Phelps, a Mr Smith of MI5...and a Mr Stan Hathaway of the Policy Focus Office. Much of the material was supplied by an active MI5 employee. Also there are written statements from the sub-contracted agents who were ordered to follow and intercept messages from defence witnesses and who were also ordered to arrest, hold and torture Sergeant Dalgleish. I think you will find it is all in order, M'Lord."

Both Howerd and Jeffreys looked dumbstruck.

"It looks like I have been played and you have a case for a mistrial," Howerd said.

"That's a decision for me." Jeffreys looked dazed and not a little nervous. "Miss FitzPatrick. I will need to look into this evidence most carefully before I make a decision."

"If it's of help to your Lordship, I have discussed this with my client and he wishes to get this trial over and done with. Under the circumstances I would also wish that the evidence presented by my learned friend this morning be ruled inadmissible."

"I would have no objections, M'lud," Howerd said. "Do you believe any of the other evidence I've so far presented has also been fabricated, Miss FitzPatrick?"

"I've no reason to believe it has been fabricated other than the testimony given by Mr al-Shamrani which I believe is false, an attempt by al-Qaeda to blacken the name of the British army and the hope of a Pakistan trader for a great deal of compensation for the deaths of his two drug-running brothers."

"That is yet to be decided by the court, Miss FitzPatrick," Howerd said.

"Of course and if we are allowed to continue I will disprove it."

"Very well, Miss FitzPatrick. I will allow the trial to continue and I will rule this morning's evidence unreliable. I am very much afraid there will be serious consequences arising from this matter but for the moment this will stay in this room and will not be mentioned in open court," Jeffreys said.

"As your Lordship wishes," Ann said and Howerd nodded his assent.

* * *

"My next witness could not be here in person, M'Lord but with your permission we are able to contact him by satellite link."

"More surprises? Very well, Miss Fitzpatrick, continue."

Ann waved at the orderly who disappeared then reappeared with two uniformed soldiers pushing a wide screen television and other electronic apparatus including a satellite uplink and camera. The two soldiers quickly and expertly assembled the equipment and established contact.

"Mr Abdullah, can you hear me?"

A robed figure wearing a wide smile appeared as the screen flickered and steadied. There was a pause before the reply came back. "......Yes loud and clear."

"M'Lord this is Abdullah Abdullah, chieftain of a tribe of Tajiks. He too was present at the time of the incident. It has taken a while to track him down hence I was not able to be certain that he could appear until this morning." Ann looked across at Howerd who hid his eyes behind his hand. *Touché*.

"Mr Abdullah was educated at Cambridge and speaks perfect English."

"Very well, Miss FitzPatrick let us hear what Mr Abdullah has to say. You have no objections, Mr Howerd?"

"None, M'lud."

"Mr Abdullah. You have been made aware of the facts of this case have you not?"

".........Yes, miss."

"A previous witness, Mr al-Shamrani, has testified that he was on a ledge overlooking and very close to the gun battle on the day in question."

"......... He was close by me the whole time. I did not trust him so I kept my eye on him."

"What caused your mistrust?"

"He is Afghan Arab. Holy warrior. Trained in the al-Qaeda camps in the mountains. He tried to lead your people the wrong way. The pass he chose would not have allowed your soldiers to intercept the al-Qaeda fighters. And he knew it would snow. He is not to be trusted."

"Would you just confirm what you could see of the incident of which Major Keane is accused."

".......Ah, Major Ricky. Good to see you..."

"Mr. Abdullah...," Ann warned.

"........of course. Very little could be seen from where I was and even less from where the liar al-Shamrani hid. He tried to expose himself to the drug traders and to the al-Qaeda fighters in the valley but I pushed him down. I think the ones with the buckets may have glimpsed him briefly, one looked our way but the exposure was too brief for him to be warned."

"M'Lord, there is a great deal of animosity between the Tajiks, Uzbeks and Hazaras on one side and the Pathans, or Pashtuns on the other," Ann said. "The Taliban are mainly Pashtu. However, Kabul is fast returning to a cosmopolitan way of life which has enabled Mr Abdullah's Tajiks to enter the city to gain evidence. Items twelve to fifteen are written statements from people in Kabul who were neighbours of Mr al-Shamrani while he was married. His wife had been the daughter of a merchant who owned several shops in Kabul and was well-known in the area. These are sworn testimonies, countersigned by a mullah. Each one has an English translation attached. Mr Abdullah can you tell the court to what these documents appertain?"

Abdullah had grown solemn. "........It is the story of how al-Shamrani called on the Taliban to kill his wife. He told them that she was faithless, would not wear the burqa and left the house unaccompanied. The Taliban found her guilty and beheaded her in the street. It was felt that al-

Shamrani wanted to be free of the marriage so that he could pursue his own agenda unencumbered. One of the shops the woman's father owned was given to al-Shamrani as dowry. *His* brother now runs it and it is believed he trades arms and drugs from there."

"And the children?"

".......There were no children. His wife was older and barren."

"Thank you, Mr Abdullah. Your witness, Mr Howerd."

"Mr Abdullah. You greeted Major Keane as a friend. Is there a reason why you should be so pleased to see him?"

".......He saved my people from starvation. It was a bleak winter. Without his help many people would have died."

"And so you are in his debt?"

".......The debt was repaid, sir, in Afghanistan, with my help on his mission. I am a man of honour and so is Major Keane. I resent your implication."

"No further questions, M'lud."

★ ★ ★

"Smith? That info you sent up on Mason. Looks like he's skipped and the bastard will be hard to find."

"How's that, Jimbo? Thought you boys in 'A' Branch could find anyone."

"He's ex-SAS. More tricks than a cart load of monkeys. He'll need to make a mistake for us to get a lead on him. He took the Eurostar to Paris yesterday. Now he could be anywhere in Europe. Cleaned out his bank account and bought a whole load of Euros in cash so he's not planning on using a credit card anytime soon."

"Get his picture to GIGN in France. See if they can get a lead on him. Put some pressure on. Suspected terrorist etc."

"Hope this one doesn't come back to bite you, Smith."

"What's new. Keep this just between us for now?"

"I'll keep it under the radar but you know what the French are like..."

Smith switched off the intercom and called Bailey. "Colonel. Just thought you'd like to know. Oakley's been found dead and you'll be getting a new minister who's far more flexible. I think you'll see an improvement very soon."

"I'm sorry to hear about Oakley. Suicide was it?"

"Best not to go into details right now. It'll all come out in time I daresay. Just remember who your friends are in future."

"I'm not sure what that remark is intended to mean but thanks for the news. I'm sure it will be welcomed amongst the men. I'm just sorry it couldn't have happened in better circumstances."

"Smith, DG wants you. Sounds in a bad mood, I wouldn't hang around."

Smith put down the phone and glanced at the passing messenger. "Any clue?"

The man shrugged. "DG's had a long chat with the Lord Chancellor this morning..."

★ ★ ★

"Major Keane," Ann said, "we've heard everyone's version of that day except yours. What happened?"

"The court's heard about the chase to cut off the al-Qaeda group as it was suspected that bin Laden himself was with it. We managed to get to the valley before them but by then they'd met up with a camel train which was carrying opium for some Eastern European dealers. It was our bad luck that they all came together at the caravanserai.

"We were few in number and now vastly outgunned but our orders were to capture or kill the bin Laden figure. To do that we needed the element of surprise. I had split the group into two parts. One to give covering fire while the other carried out the assault. The covering group was positioned on high ground and the assault group with me in command made its way across the narrow river, which by now was in full flood with snow melt, to just below the two buildings which I hadn't realised were occupied by members of the drug trafficking gang.

"Up to then we hadn't been spotted but that was put in jeopardy by the approach of two men with buckets, straight towards our position. There wasn't much cover so it seemed certain that we'd be discovered."

"Was that when you decided to shoot them?"

"No. I wasn't entirely sure what to do. I had a small hope that they wouldn't see us, me in particular, as the cover I had was very scant and I wanted to keep my weapon dry. I was half-in, half-out of the water and the current was very strong, lifting my legs and threatening to wash me away from the rock behind which I was sheltering. They did not see me immediately but as the older of the two leant forward my body was washed sideways into his field of vision. I saw him start and he dropped his bucket. I hoped he would turn and run but he did not."

"He drew a pistol," Ann said.

"Yes. It was a Makarov, a Russian automatic. I shot him twice before he could fire."

"And the other man?"

"He threw his bucket and was coming at me. I shot him too. I didn't want to..."

"Did you feel that he was also armed."

"I thought it likely, yes?"

"Thank you, Major. Your witness."

Howerd climbed slowly to his feet. "I have just one question. Did you see a weapon in the second man's hand or did you just fire on the expectations that he may have one."

"It all happened very quickly..."

"Please answer the question, major."

"I assumed..."

"Thank you, major. No further questions."

Ann climbed to her feet. "M'Lord, it is perfectly obvious to the court that My Learned Friend is clutching at straws. His main witness has been discredited and he is seeking on the flimsiest of evidence to carry a conviction on conjecture."

"That is for me to decide, Miss Fitzpatrick. The Board will ignore the defence's last statement."

"Ann..."

Sissy was tugging at her gown and she looked at the paper she was offered. "M'Lord, may I continue?"

"If it is relevant..."

"It is, M'Lord. Major Keane, what do you understand by the Military Covenant?"

Ricky shrugged. "I guess it means that the government will take care of us soldiers because we put ourselves in harm's way in serving our country."

"Not a bad assessment, Major. What it actually means, as laid down by the Judge Advocate General, is that soldiers differ from civilian employees because success in military operations, where the price of failure may be death, requires the subordination of the rights of the individual to the needs of the task and the team. *The needs of the task*. That is very telling. Gentlemen of the Board, I submit that my client has no case to answer and I rest the defence."

★ ★ ★

"Members of the Board. You have heard the case for the prosecution and the case for the defence." Jeffreys straightened his robes and looked down at the table below him. "It is the prosecution's case that the defendant did unlawfully kill two men. We have heard from a witness that he saw both the victims as unarmed and were shot down in cold blood without warning. You have heard other witnesses refute that evidence and cast doubt on the veracity of the prosecution's main witness.

"You may discount the defence's entertaining but irrelevant use of the road sign. It does nothing to prove, or disprove, the evidence of a weapon on the second victim's person. It merely proves that the soldier in question has either enviable eyesight…or an excellent memory.

"The defence has sought to portray the matter in the manner of a battlefield encounter where the other parties were combatants and therefore lawful targets. In her summary of the Military Covenant she omitted the phrase *'within a legal framework'* and you must take due note of that *'within a legal framework'.*

"What you have to decide is whether in fact civilian traders, no matter how you may disagree with their trade, were combatants, or merely acting in self-defence from an attack by foreigners who had invaded their land.

"How you decide this has a bearing on the shooting of the first victim. In the second case however I feel the matter is more straightforward. The defendant admits that he shot the man as little more than a reflex action in the expectation that the man was armed. According to the Laws of England that could constitute unlawful killing and if you find as such you must find the defendant guilty of the charge laid against him.

"You should not be swayed by considerations of tactical importance, neither by any implied consideration of avoiding casualties amongst the attackers which may or may not have occurred if the attack had been prematurely discovered. Was it merely a matter of tactical convenience that the men were shot or did they pose a serious and immediate threat to the lives of the attackers? I would hazard that they did not.

"You may now retire to consider your verdict."

Chapter Twenty-Nine

Smith's career was teetering on the edge of an abyss and he needed some good news. Jeffreys, frightened, had complained to the Lord Chancellor's Office and had couriered the evidence that FitzPatrick had collected. DG had blown a fuse; hit the roof in no uncertain way. Not only had Smith broken the rules, broken the law and abused his position but he had also been caught at it. That was breaking the first rule of spying.

DG had reined him in. No longer was he to have carte blanche, no longer one of the favoured few. Now his every action would be monitored by DG's own staff. A humiliating and nauseating state of affairs. Blood would be let and the chief target for the blood- letting was the subject of Jimbo's excitement.

"We've been handed a break."

"How's that, Jimbo?"

"The French spotted Mason on close circuit at the Gare du Nord as he got off the Eurostar. They tracked him to Gare l'Est where he picked up the TGV to Zurich."

"Bloody Switzerland. The Swiss aren't too hot at co-operation," Smith said.

"They helped out this time. The French told them that our man's wanted for bank robbery and that got them moving. Anyway he overnighted in a small hotel on the Seilergraben, the other side of the river from Zurich station. The next morning he caught the Alpine Express to Milan. The Italians had no problem picking him up on camera and he changed trains there and went to Venice. He's currently shacked up in a hotel on the Terra Lista di Spagne right on the Grand Canal. Apparently enjoying a holiday and picking up tourist girls. The Carabinieri are keeping a close eye on him."

"No! I don't want to spook him. Tell them to back off. Keep the stations and Marco Polo Airport covered, I want to know if he tries to leave but give him space. He'll spot surveillance a mile off and we may never get back on target." Smith glared at his colleague. "And this is strictly between us, yeah? I've already had a bollocking from DG and I don't want another. Let's get this right.

"DG wants Mason back to face the music but I'm wondering if he'll lead us to a more interesting catch. Let him loose for a day or two."

"Fine, Smith, but this is as far as my help goes. DG's put the word out that you're to have no special favours. You're in purgatory, my boy, and the magic circle is going to close ranks for now. You'll have to re-earn your spurs. And by the way, you are going to owe me for this. I'm sticking my neck way out."

"I won't forget it, Jimbo."

"Make sure you don't drop me in it with you. One mistake and the plug's pulled. Clear?"

"Okay, I know the score."

★ ★ ★

Smith walked to the south side of Lambeth Bridge. A chill wind was whipping off the Thames and he turned up his jacket collar. His Blackberry had internet connection and he sent his message. It wasn't long before a reply came back. '*£15,000 + exes*'.

Smith typed the word 'GO'.

★ ★ ★

Word had gone to Jeffreys that the Board had reached a decision. He allowed the public and press into the courtroom and called in the Board. One by one they filed in behind the president to sit at the high bench alongside Jeffreys. Not one looked at Ricky.

"You have reached a decision, Mr President?"

"We have, M'Lord. On the first count we have considered the matter as your Lordship suggested. It seemed apparent to us, in the light of the subsequent fire fight, that the traders were as much enemy as the al-Qaeda group, in fact they appeared to be allied to each other.

"In those circumstances the Board has decided that they were legitimate enemy combatants. We find the defendant not guilty of the first charge.

"We have considered closely the testimony of the prosecution's witnesses and decided we preferred the version offered by the defence. We feel that the main prosecution witness had ulterior motives and there, perhaps, should be an investigation to ascertain whether or not actual perjury has been committed in that his evidence would seem to be at odds with circumstances surrounding the case.

"As to the second charge, as opposed to your Lordship, we found it much more difficult to come to a decision. There is some wide degree of doubt and speculation as to whether the second man was armed or not armed. If it was the latter, and if it were proven conclusively that the man was unarmed, then we have no doubt that the defendant is guilty of the charge...

"However...it is far from clear that the man was unarmed and in the light of the fact that he did attack the defendant, albeit with a household implement, we find that the Defendant was within his rights to defend himself in whatever way he could.

"We find the defendant not guilty of the second charge."

★ ★ ★

Hathaway heard the news almost immediately. He had failed. The job he had been tasked with had ended up a high pile of reeking manure and it was about to descend on his head. He did not have to wait long. The clip-clipping of heels on lino announced the arrival of Gannon's secretary. She had an apologetic look on her face but her eyes belied the expression. He had trodden on her toes a few times in the past. What was it his old dad had said. *'Be nice to people on your way up cos you never knows who you'll meet on your way down.'* Wise old bugger was dad. Pity he'd forgotten that piece of good advice on his way up the greasy pole.

"Could you see Mr Gannon in his office please, Mr Hathaway."

Hathaway waved a hand. "I'll be there in a minute."

"He's on his way upstairs. I think he means now, Mr Hathaway."

Gannon was smacking the keys on his laptop as if the thing had done him a personal injury. He didn't turn. "Fucked up this time, Stan. Upstairs is orbiting Pluto right this minute and I'm about to get a rocket so far up my anus it'll come out of my right nostril. I don't like getting bollockings, especially when it's one of the minions who's dropped the bollock and not me. I told them you had this stitched up tight. Now they've got the remains of a couple of sunny-side-ups on their faces...and so have I."

"What d'you want me to do about it?"

"I think you've done enough. Or more correctly, failed to do enough. A right dereliction of duty, my old son. I'll play it down best I can. A backlash from being kidnapped and all that but they want your head on a plate with an apple in your mouth. 'Fraid it's curtains for you, old son."

"I know where the bodies are buried..."

Gannon stopped maniacally thumping his keyboard and turned to face Hathaway for the first time, a tight smile on his face. "Don't play that game with me, I've got gold medals in it and I'll make sure you won't get a job anywhere in this godforsaken country of ours. Not even cleaning the crappers in Waterloo station.

"Look. Shit happens, I know. You're finished here but I think I can fix you up with a nice little sinecure. I know an organisation that's looking for a deputy director of communications. Right up your street I'd have thought. I've rung the top man, he owes me a favour or three and he's looking forward to meeting you.

"We'll let the press know its all hunky dory and it's a job you've been salivating after for a while. What do you say? You gonna do this the easy way or do I have to cut you off at the knees?"

★   ★   ★

Pavlovich stepped off the British Airways flight at Marco Polo Airport and caught a water taxi straight to the Santa Lucia railway station in Venice which just happened to be at the end of the Terra Lista di Spagna. He knew Venice well and enjoyed the high-speed ride across the lagoon from the back of the speedboat. The price was extortionate but he could afford it and he gave the driver an extra twenty Euros. Not so much that the man might remember him, but enough that it did not cause resentment and a reason to think bad thoughts. Within an hour the man would have forgotten almost everything about him.

Venice was crowded which suited Pavlovich. He wore a light jacket over a sleeveless black shirt and a pair of Italian made slacks that were worth every penny he had paid for them. His loafers were Gucci and he wore no socks. His hair was slicked back and his naturally olive skin was already darkening in the strong sunlight. He might have been taken for a Venetian but his Italian was heavily accented. He would pass for French or Spanish.

He walked slowly past Mason's hotel, idly eyeing the cheap tourist souvenirs on the street stalls and in shop windows. It was a thorough close-target reconnaissance and when he had finished every doorway, pathway, alleyway and window was mapped in his mind. He also had a picture of Mason on his mobile. He would know him as soon as he saw him.

Alongside the hotel was a small piazza with two street stalls. The hotel on the opposite side to Mason's was undergoing renovation. Ramshackle scaffolding was surrounded by inadequate metal fencing and the floor was littered with discarded pieces of brick and timber. It abutted the Grand Canal so there was no through foot traffic just a lazy circling of pedestrians some of whom stopped to sit on the canal's bank to watch the constant water traffic. Everything in Venice was carried by boat. Even the rubbish collections were water borne.

Pavlovich sat at a small cafe opposite the piazza and ordered an aperitif. He blended in with the crowd around him. He would wait for Mason and an opportunity to present itself. He had already chosen a method. It would be another accident. Poor Mr. Mason would drown in the canal late at night so no one would witness his demise.

* ★ ★

Mason could not have made it easier if he tried. For the second night in a row he had seen his girlfriend to her hotel. On returning to his he bought a drink at the terrace bar and wandered onto the canal bank at the end of the piazza. There was no street lighting, it had been taken down for the hotel renovations and all Pavlovich could see was his outline silhouetted against lights on the far bank. Water traffic was still busy but the brightly lit interiors of the crowded water buses would not allow much to be seen through the salt-stained glass.

Foot traffic was negligible and the hotel windows that overlooked the piazza were darkened. He had sat and watched them come on and go out one by one as residents returned and went to bed. He checked his Breitling. Twelve minutes past one.

Mason was now sitting on the paving with his legs dangling over the edge. The tide was high; there would not be much of a splash when he went in, nothing to alert the tired waiters loitering on the terrace, wishing their last customers would go to bed.

Pavlovich had changed his slacks and Guccis for black jeans and trainers. He moved soundlessly towards Mason's back. He had already earmarked a short piece of scaffolding pole about five centimetres in diameter and made of heavy gauge steel. The builders had discarded it with other rubbish and it fitted his palm perfectly. One hard, sharp blow to the side of Mason's neck would stun him sufficiently so that he would not wake up before he drowned. There had to be water in the lungs. It needed to be carefully judged. One small miscalculation and the spinal cord would be severed and Mason killed instantly.

Just two metres to go. He placed his feet carefully, rolling his foot from the outside to the inside, just like a cat. Mason still stared across the canal, his now empty beer glass resting beside his right hand. Pavlovich pulled back his arm and swung.

★ ★ ★

Smith eyed the message, the paper sitting in perfect symmetry in the centre of his desk.

"Perhaps it's for the best. It'll save the government the cost of a trial," Jimbo said.

Smith did not take his eyes off the paper. It was a message from the British Consul in Rome sent to the Foreign Office and thence on to the Home Office and finally to 'A' Branch. "Are they sure it was an accident?"

"The Carabinieri couldn't find any signs of foul play. Mind you the body had been in the water for a while and had been chopped about by boat propellers and chewed on by god knows what. If it hadn't been for the passport in his pocket they might never have been able to identify him. The passport was all but illegible too. That bloody Venetian water would rot diamonds. They managed to lift the name with chemicals. It was Mason all right. The hotel reported him missing when he didn't turn up to pay his bill."

"So that's the end of it then. I expect DG will heave a sigh of relief as much of this bother died with Mason. Without him there's nothing they can make stick."

"What are you prattling on about, Smith? Is there something you're not telling me?"

Smith grinned, a tight little smile that barely creased his face. "Talking to myself. Nothing for you to worry about, Jimbo. It's need to know and it's covered."

Honi Soir Qui Mal y Pense
Evil be to him who evil thinks.

Note: 10 - Appended

And so it ends. The case is over and I have another notch on the butt of my legal reputation.

His Lordship, Judge Jeffreys, made much of showing his disagreement with the verdict, so much so that he went out of his way to state that he would view sympathetically any claim through the courts by the Pakistan trader, for compensation for the death of his two brothers, but he could do nothing other than release Ricky without a stain on his character. Jeffreys also effectively gagged the press which infuriated some of the reporters who had camped outside the courtroom for three days feeding off whatever crumbs they could glean. Many editors eyeing their scribes' expenses will no doubt rue the day for their return on investment will be negligible and unlikely to sell many newspapers.

The verdict was met with great relief by all concerned with the defence and the party in the mess afterwards was epic. It was there that Ricky and Gill announced both their engagement and their resignations from the army. Neither now has much faith in the Military Covenant.

Today I heard the news about Toff Mason. I had never met him but Gill kept me fully aware of the help she received from the man who risked his career (and possibly his life) to help us. They say it was an accident but if so it was a most convenient one. Gill, Ricky and Stu have all warned me to be vigilant and to be careful. I have moved home and I am in the process of starting my own chambers based in Farringdon. Away from the Inns of Court but in a renovated building which can be made much more secure. I have taken Stu's advice on security systems. He has taken sick leave and is now a constant companion. He says he likes to watch out for me and his presence is reassuring.

It is because of these worries that I am taking the precaution of putting this in writing and depositing it in the safest strong room I can find. Stu approves. So does Gill.

What Jeffreys did with my report into MI5 is an enigma. One assumes he passed it on but I have heard nothing. I hope that sleeping dog will lie. He has now announced his retirement from the bench and I for one will not miss appearing in front of him.

As I pen these final notes I cannot help but feel, for all the trouble this case has caused me personally, that I have come out from it a morally richer, more rounded, person. In a strange way I will miss the excitement and the aura of danger. I shall miss outwitting MI5's finest. It was an experience I shall never forget, with friendships made that will endure for a lifetime. However, my wish for a peaceful future lies in the hands of others.

My fervent hope also is that this will never see the light of day.

AFP,
Lincoln's Inn.

Epilogue

On the morning of July 2nd, Dr. Abib al Adine received a package by special courier at his office in Dollis Hill. The package was thick and padded. It did not have a return address on the outside. He was not expecting it. He laid it on his desk and wondered. Could it be that someone was taking a leaf out of the terrorist handbook. Live by the sword, die by the sword, had always been at the forefront of his mind ever since he had met bin Laden and become close to him. Was it a letter bomb designed to kill or maim him or was he being paranoid.

He was not a cowardly man and decided if god willed he would die if not he would survive and there was no point in worrying about it.

He slit the envelope open with an ornately carved dagger which did duty as a paper knife. Inside there was nothing but a flash drive for a computer. No note of explanation. He fitted the drive into a USB port on his computer and accessed the file. It was a schematic of a light aircraft, a Piper Seneca, with parts outlined in red and highlighted with pointers. On an accompanying Word file, in Arabic, was a location, a time and a date. In English were four names under four photographs. They were names he recognised.

Beneath the names again in Arabic were the words *'If God wills.'*

He looked at his watch. Time was short but time enough there was. He pulled on his robe and made for the mosque taking the drive with him.

★   ★   ★

The chairman of *Achilles Shield (Corporate and Personal Security) Limited* called an extraordinary board meeting for the morning of July 4th. It was Independence Day in the United States and many of their top commercial clients had the day off. Not that that was the reason Tim Bailey called the meeting.

"Ladies and Gentlemen, fellow directors. This is the end of our third financial year. I have to tell you that the accounts have been finalised, the audit has been completed and we are in profit..."

A small cheer went up and Bailey grinned. "...to the tune of... three...million...pounds."

"Whew! That was some year," Ricky said. "I thought we'd be lucky to break even."

"That's why you're the MD and Head of International Security and not the financial director," Stu chuckled.

"That's as maybe," Bailey said, "but we owe a debt to Gill who started the company with her own money when the banks wouldn't look at four ex-service people, starting a company from scratch to provide work for redundant SAS people, without a client, without offices and without a proper business plan. For that we have to thank Miss FitzPatrick who had the nous to plot our path through the legal and financial minefield."

"You're forgetting yourself, Tim," Gill said. "Without your contacts we'd have been struggling from day one."

"Well we can all pat ourselves on the back," Bailey said, "but that's not the main reason I've called you here. Gill, Ricky, Stu, Ann, stand up please. Tonka, Mo, you can bring it in now."

The double doors to the boardroom swung open and Tonka wheeled in a trolley loaded with champagne bottles and glasses, closely followed by Mo, still with her scarlet hair and two huge bouquets in her arms.

"Mrs Keane, Mrs Dalgleish; although I'm sure Ann won't break recent precedence and will call herself by her professional name of FitzPatrick, these flowers are my gift to you. I would like to propose a toast. Get that ruddy Champagne going, Tonka, before we all die of thirst."

"Right, Colonel." Tonka grinned and popped a cork with a bang.

"Angel's fart, Tonka, remember?" Mo scolded.

"Most of it's gone in the glass, babe and there's plenty of it."

"You just like a big bang," Mo said and laughed as Tonka unexpectedly blushed.

"Where was I," Bailey said, laughing too.

"A toast," Ann reminded him.

"Yes, of course. Tomorrow you four lovely people will be flying south for your belated honeymoons. Not only have we been exceedingly busy putting this company on the map but you've also had to wait while Ricky, our managing director, and your pilot, passed all his flying exams so that he was qualified to fly you in the first place. He now has sufficient experience and sufficient hours to do so safely and legally. He can do that super little plane of his justice."

"It was a wedding present from Gill," Ricky said. "How could I refuse? A Piper Seneca; it might be second-hand but it's a dream. I just had to qualify. It was good therapy too"

"It's not getting up there I'm worried about, it's coming down," Stu said. "Nobody ever crash landed at ten-thousand feet."

Ann nudged him. "Say thank you, Stuart. But for Ricky we would have to fly commercial all the way to Malaga. Now we can stop off with Gill's family in Bilbao then hire a car to drive all the way through Spain from top to bottom. Something I've always wanted to do."

"And it's cheaper," Stu said.

"I hope you're not so tight-fisted when you meet my parents," Ann said. "I want them to like you. Not sure why. Maybe it's because I want to re-build bridges and you can be the foundation."

"The toast!" Bailey interrupted. "Here's to you all. May your days together be long, and full of love and happiness."

"I'll drink to that," Tonka said. "And don't look at me like that woman, I'm too young to settle down." He winked at Mo and she pulled a face back.

"And not forgetting our two senior managers," Bailey laughed. "And Bill Cowley who's busy running ten security teams from the office in Baghdad and thoroughly enjoying it.

"As if we'd let you forget us," Mo said.

"Talent will out, Mo and you're damned good at your job. I think Stu's forgiven you by now," Ann said.

Gill squeezed Ricky's arm. "I'm sorry to break up the party before it's got going but I need to nip into London for a few final bits for the holiday." She hugged Bailey's neck. "Thanks for everything, Tim. You underplayed your part in pulling us all together. Without your leadership we'd have sunk at the start. And thanks for the party, it was a lovely thought.

"Mo, Tonka, I'll see you in three weeks. Ann, Stu, I'll see you tomorrow morning. And you, my darling husband, I'll see tonight. Don't be late and don't get drunk or you won't be able to fly." She kissed Ricky, waved her hand airily and left.

★   ★   ★

Blake stood on the Embankment with the Savoy Hotel behind him and stared across the Thames to the south bank.

"You watch too many spy movies," Gill said.

Blake smiled. "It has a certain fascination, this meeting in a public place, especially as the view is so captivating."

Gill had returned to her natural auburn hair and looked stunning. "You can turn off the charm, Blake. I'm immune."

"Of course. How is the new husband?'

"Everything I'd hoped for and more. He was worth all the chicanery."

"Does he know?"

"That I was working for you? No. I haven't told him. There's no need is there?"

"Not on my part. You did an excellent job. You helped put Five in their place. They were becoming an absolute pain and needed taking down a peg or two. Their new DG is now far more amenable. And of course you helped make the SAS beholden to us. There have been occasions when we needed a little skulduggery doing abroad, where the Regiment might normally and rightly turn us down. Instead they have been most helpful, especially in Iraq. The Americans are grateful. The SAS have been able to remove some of the most senior dissidents from the fray."

"This is the end of it, Blake. No more. I'm out now, I've paid my dues and I don't expect you to come knocking on my door in future; not ever."

Blake breathed a theatrical sigh. "You were so good too. The perfect spy. No one ever suspected someone as delicious as you."

"Apart from the man I killed in Ireland, you mean."

"Killick, yes, apart from him and I'm sorry for that."

"Me too."

"Don't punish yourself. Killer Killick was long overdue to meet the devil."

"I'm just sorry it had to be me that sent him on his way."

"Is that the real reason you want out?"

Gill looked sideways at him. The lights were coming on along the Embankment and Cleopatra's Needle was etched against the street lamps. Blake's face was half in shadow and she could not read his expression. "I want out for Ricky's sake. I did it all for him. I needed him to get off that trumped-up charge and I couldn't do it on my own. Now I've got what I most wanted and I don't need it spoilt by you or anyone else crawling back into my life. You made the deal, you keep to it."

"Very well, Mrs Keane. I'll miss you. The Service will miss you but I suppose we'll just have to shrug our shoulders and *crack on*."

Gill nodded. It had been easier cutting the tie than she'd imagined and she felt a small pang of doubt even as she thought it.

"Did you ever find al-Shamrani?"

Blake shook his head. "He disappeared like mist on a summer's morn. We thought we had him covered and for a few weeks we did. He led us to some contacts but they more-or-less turned into dead ends. Of not sufficient interest to warrant any more time being spent on surveillance."

"That's a pity. I felt sure he was up to something," Gill said. "But it's no longer my problem."

Blake held out his hand and Gill took it. He held it longer than was necessary. "I hope you have a good marriage, Gill. It cost you enough."

"She slid her fingers out of his. "Not as much as it cost Toff Mason."

"Talking of cost, did anyone ever discover it was you who paid that five-thousand pounds into Dalgleish's bank account?"

"One last thing Toff did for me. It was high risk but I had to take it. Ann was never going to use that file unless she was pushed into it. Everybody thought it was MI5 as the transfer was tracked back to Thames House. I had Dalgleish leave his bank details in his briefcase in my hotel room, after Colonel Bailey tipped me the wink, in the expectation that MI5 would come calling. Must have seemed like gold dust to them. That's the trouble when you deal in dirty tricks, everyone thinks you're guilty even when you're not. It's never been mentioned again and I've no reason to enlighten anyone."

"Nor about you impersonating an Israeli agent."

Gill had the grace to blush. "That was for Colonel Bailey. I needed to dig him out of the hole I'd put him in. I tried to illustrate how hard it would be for women working in the environments the SAS have to work in. It seems I was too successful. I'll have Oakley on my conscience now. If only he knew the difference between Hebrew and Basque he might still be alive."

"The way you controlled three interlinked operations at one time will go down in service history. Taking on MI5, organising the SAS's mutiny and delivering us what we needed. Pure magic!" Blake said.

"I had some help. Thanks for your people tracking down Abdullah; that was Stu's idea. And thanks for the two fake Special Branch men. They got Hathaway's attention at a crucial moment."

"Hathaway's ours now. There are rumours of communism raising its ugly head again inside various organisations and he's now ideally placed to keep an eye on it for us.

"It's been a pleasure doing business, Gill."

"Wish I could say the same. Goodbye forever, Blake." She turned to walk away and thought she heard Blake murmur, "*Nothing* lasts forever."

Addendum

El Mundo del Siglo Veintiuno, Bilbao Edición
July 7th

It has been reported that a light aicraft bound for Bilbao has disappeared over the Bay of Biscay. A Search and Rescue Operation has been mounted by 803 Squadron's CASA C-215 Search and Rescue aircraft and is being coordinated by the Madrid R.C.C. in co-operation with the British RAF which has sent a Nimrod MR2 SAR to quarter the area in which the aircraft was last reported prior to its disappearance.

The aircraft is a Piper Seneca, a twin-engine 5-6 seat plane that has a cruising altitude of between three and five-thousand, five hundred, metres and a range of around nine-hundred kilometres. The aircraft left Southampton, England, with a pilot and three passengers aboard and disappeared over open sea in an area out of range of both French and Spanish Air Traffic Control Radars.

The four are thought to be two married couples, all directors of the same company based in Camberley, England.

A spokesman for the company said *"All our people are capable and self-sufficient. We are not yet concerned for their welfare.*

"A fuller statement will be issued when the situation becomes clearer but for now the prayers and good wishes of all the staff for a safe return are with these popular founders of the company and their families."

The newspaper report did not make the British Press.

Author's Notes

The idea for this book was inspired by a newspaper report of an attack by the SAS in Afghanistan. The Ministry of Defence subsequently denied that the action ever took place.

What if it *had* happened? Might it have turned out like this story? It is fictitious, as are all the characters and some of the organisations portrayed, but it highlights the possible consequences these types of battles may have for our soldiers fighting on foreign soil, the dangers they face on a daily basis, and the basic lack of understanding of the difficulties they encounter. I hope this goes some way in redressing that lack of understanding.

It has been reported that in 2006 The Ministry of Defence quietly amended the Rules of Engagement for soldiers serving in Iraq and Afghanistan. Previously, unarmed dissidents were able to direct fire onto British positions secure in the knowledge that British soldiers would not be allowed to engage them. The rule changes reversed that decision and enemy dissidents could be engaged regardless of whether they visibly bore arms or not.

I am particularly proud to make a donation for every book sold to the wonderful charity **'Help for Heroes'** for those seriously wounded in action. For every one publicised there are hundreds more that need the support of all of us who care for the welfare of our courageous service people.

This book is a salute to their bravery and fortitude.

Ed Lane, Lincolnshire, 2010

Ed Lane

Whilst studying at the University of London Ed joined the Officer's Training Corps and was commissioned into the Royal Regiment of Fusiliers before eventually joining The Parachute Regiment TA.

He founded a graphic design company where he honed his writing skills on marketing campaigns for national and multi-national companies.

Ed has personal experience with many of the weapon systems he writes about. He is the holder of three gold medals gained in national Sport Rifle competitions and has represented Lincolnshire as a member of the County Lightweight Sport Rifle Team.

He has taken early-retirement which enables him to devote more time to writing and lives in the Lincolnshire Wolds with his wife Barb.

His novels are a personal salute to the courage, dedication and professionalism of Britain's armed forces.

Ed Lane

Full length Novels by Ed Lane:

Going dark Trilogy:
A Circling of Vultures
Soldier Girl★
The Lunatic Game★

Soldier Girl (★to come).

 How it all began. Gill Somers, Ricky Keane, Stu Dalgleish and Toff Mason battle ETA terrorists in the Basque region of Spain.

The Terrible Beauty is ETA's reign of terror. The Spanish are reeling from yet more huge explosions in their largest cities. The Policia Nacional is unable to cope and they ask the British for help.

Gill is half-Basque. MI6 need someone with her background and language skills to infiltrate a suspect ETA Cuadrilla.

Her lover is a Basque Terrorist. One tiny mistake could kill her. Sucked ever deeper into ETA's inner circle Gill walks a fine line of duplicity as she fights to maintain her cover, relay vital information to MI6...and stay alive.

The Lunatic Game. (*to come).

Even with the peace process in play dissident Republicans still plot mayhem. But it is the raising of funds through smuggling and drug dealing, bringing internecine conflict between the gangs, that most threatens the peace.

Whilst working for 14 Intelligence Company Gill Somers comes into contact with some of the most hardened terrorists. She is pitched into the battle between the groups. Her mission from MI6 is to identify and locate the IRA's most dangerous bomb maker before he can strike again. It means going deep into hostile territory where she comes face-to-face with Ireland's deadliest killer...and he knows her.

Glossary

A

AK47	Russian or Chinese made Kalashnikov short-7.62mm automatic rifle
AK74	Russian made Kalashnikov 5.56mm automatic rifle
AWACS	Airborne Warning and Control Systems aircraft

B

BG	Bodyguard
Box	MI5 (From postal address box number)
Browning High Power	Single-action 9mm self-loading pistol

C

C5	Canadian version of the M16 -203 with a 40mm grenade launcher under the barrel.
CP	Close Protection (by bodyguards)
CT	Counter-terrorist

Complete	In a vehicle
Cuadrilla	Loose association of friends usually with Basque separatist connections
C-130	Hercules Military Transport Aircraft

D

| The Det | 14 Intelligence Company or the Detachment based in Ulster. Sometimes known as Walts (short for Walter Mittys) |
| DZ | Drop Zone (for paratroops) |

E

| ETA | Eskardi ta Askatasuna (Basque Homeland and Freedom) Split into two factions, ETA Militar, the equivalent of the Provisional IRA and ETA Politico Militar, the equivalent of the Official IRA |

F

FEBA	Forward Edge of Battle Area
The Firm	MI6, aka the Secret Intelligence Service (SIS)
Foxtrot	On foot

G

GCHQ	Government Communication Headquarters
GIGN	Groupement d'Intervention de la Gendarmerie Nationale (French military police anti-terrorist unit)
Green Slime	Army Intelligence Officer

H

Halo	High altitude, low opening, parachute descent
Head Shed	Officer commanding SAS unit (or place where orders are issued)
Herc	Hercules C130 4-engine transport aircraft
Hexy burner	Hexamine solid-fuel cooker.

I

IA	Immediate action drill to clear weapon jams
ID	Identity
Intel	Intelligence

K

The Kremlin	SAS Intelligence Unit

L

Lalo	Low altitude, low opening, parachute descent
LZ	Landing Zone (for helicopters)

M

Mike	On the move in a vehicle
MI5	British Security Service (aka Box)
M16	American made 5.56mm automatic rifle
Minimi	Belgian made 5.56mm light machine gun
Mobile	Motorised unit
MoD	Ministry of Defence
The Mossad	Israeli Secret Intelligence Service
(HK) MP5	Heckler and Koch 9mm machine pistol favoured by many police and anti-terrorist units

| (HK) MP5SP | As above with attached muffler for clandestine operations |

N

| NVGs, | Night Vision Goggles |
| PNVGs | Passive Night Vision Goggles |

O

| OBE | Order of the British Empire decoration |

P

| Predator | Unmanned Aerial Vehicle. A spy plane operated by remote control from distant bases and armed with Hellfire missiles |

R

Riverside	MI6 London Headquarters (also known as Vauxhall Cross)
RTI	Resistance to Interrogation
RTU	Return to Parent Unit
Rupert	Army officer (usually derogatory)

S

SAS	Special Air Service Regiment (usually known as the Regiment or Reg)
Scaley	Signaller
SIS	Secret Intelligence Service (aka MI6 or The Firm)
Sixty-six (66)	Single use 66mm Light Anti-tank Weapon (LAW). Sometimes known as a Laws Rocket
SOP	Standard Operating Procedure

W

Walts

14 Intelligence Company Operatives. From the delusional character Walter Mitty created by James Thurber.